CW01512249

Ebook ISBN: 978-1-956335-18-7

Paperback ISBN: 978-1-956335-23-1

Audiobook ISBN: 978-1-956335-24-8

Ebook and paperback cover design by Molly Burton at Cozy Cover Designs.

Chapter header and scene break drawings by Etheric Tales.

Axia map designed by Sarah Waites at The Illustrated Page Design.

First published in 2024 by Ringtail Press.

www.melissajacksonbooks.com

 Created with Vellum

A Mythical Case of Murder

A MYTHICAL PET SITTING MYSTERY

MELISSA ERIN JACKSON

Ringtail PRESS

SUMMARY

Job hunting is a deadly sport.

Deandra "Dee" Hendricks is settling into her new life in Axia. She's got her trusty baby dragon, Havoc, by her side; is sharing an apartment with her best friend and roommate, Wendy; and even has her first pet-sitting client. Things are looking up!

Shortly after launching her new website, Dee receives an invitation to a pet-sitter happy hour where she meets Sarah, the owner of Axia's largest pet-sitting operation. Other attendees include sole proprietors, like Dee, and a few of Sarah's employees. Everyone is welcoming and willing to share advice—mainly to steer clear of their notorious fellow sitter, Lydia Monroe.

They accuse Lydia of everything—from magically manipulating her animal charges and poaching clients from Sarah to making false claims about possessing "zoolingual" abilities. The sticking point is Lydia's questionable acquisition of a lucrative gig offered by Oleander Basnet, a yeti whose son needs one-on-one care. Sarah's company fought hard for the opportunity, only to have yet another job snatched away by Lydia.

The peaceful get-together is interrupted when a late arrival informs the group that Lydia has been found murdered. Worse still, the time of death doesn't exonerate anyone at the event. Dee fears she's just shared discounted appetizers with a murderer.

Later that night, a job offer from Oleander hits Dee's inbox. Dee's wallet desperately wants her to take the job, but could there be someone in town so desperate to beat the competition that they murdered Lydia? And could Dee be next?

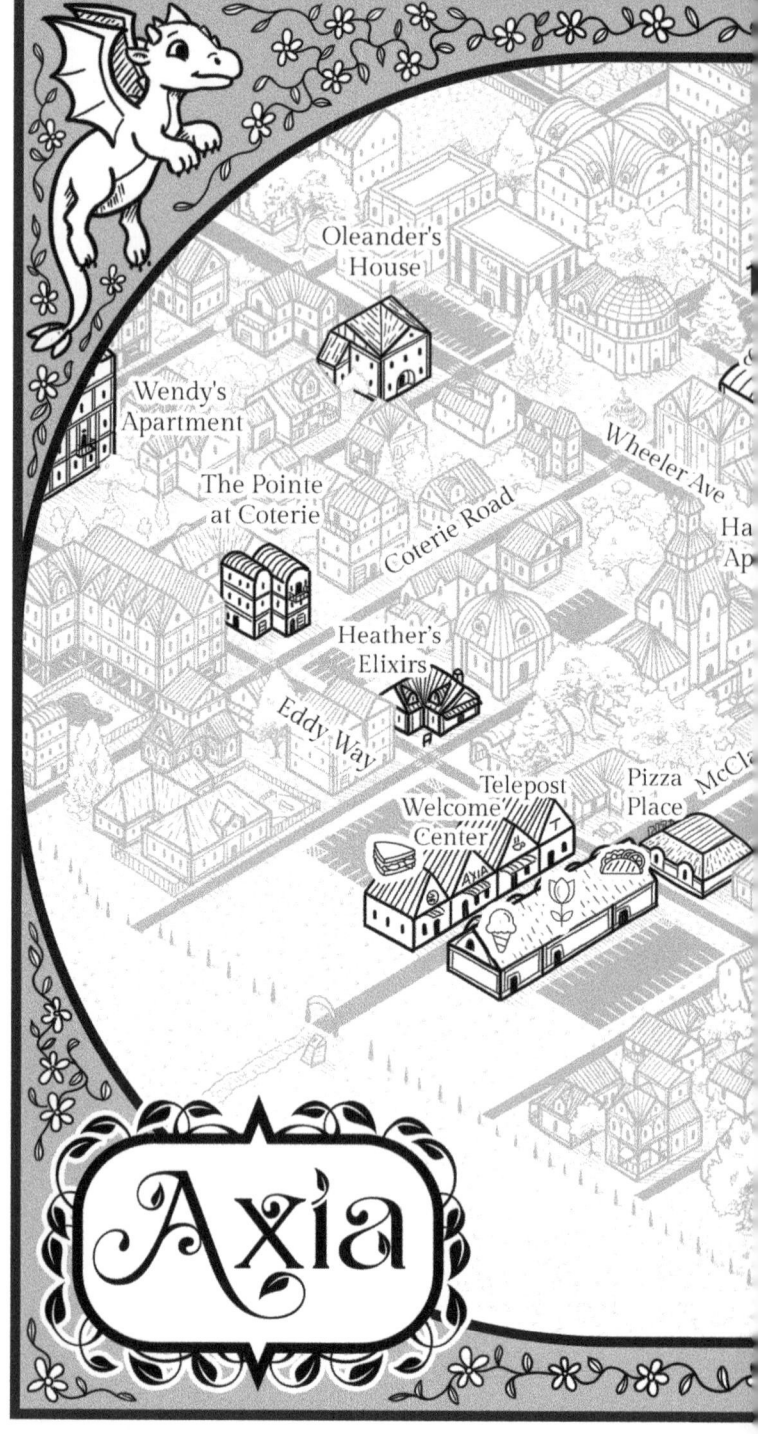

Mythic Pet
Kitchen

del's
e

Purl Way

Art
Gallery

Drug
Store

Burned
Building

Cottage

Gorgon's
Alley

Hogarth's
Hoagies

Zombie
Cactus

Telepad
Station

Police
Station

ensory
try

Oracle
Park

Sarah's
House

Grandparents'
House

CHAPTER ONE

The screech that echoed from down the hallway made the hairs on Deandra's arms stand on end. She told herself it was an excited screech and not a battle cry that preceded an attack to the jugular.

She'd had to tell herself this a lot over the past two weeks. If only she had Havoc, her dragon, with her. But it didn't seem right to bring another animal into this house yet. When she'd left Wendy's apartment this afternoon, Havoc was curled up on the couch watching a Bugs Bunny cartoon with great interest.

Another screech rent the air, and Deandra halted in the middle of the hallway, once again questioning her life choices.

After she'd met Angela Gunderson at Oracle Park nearly two

months ago, Deandra really should have done more research on "frilled dendrunes." She had to assume that most people venturing into entrepreneurship at least asked basic questions.

Deandra had been distracted by the newness of living in Axia, being the owner of a precocious baby dragon, and hanging out with her best friend and cousin, Wendy, every day, just like they had when they were kids. Basking carefree in all the life changes only lasted for about a week, though, before the guilt of not financially pulling her weight started to gnaw at her.

Wendy hadn't applied even an ounce of that weight, but Deandra had succumbed to the self-induced pressure all the same. It had been in a moment of weakness—triggered by a quick scan of the Help Wanted section of a newspaper Wendy had left on the kitchen table—that Deandra had texted Angela, telling her that, if she still needed a pet sitter, Deandra would be happy to meet with her.

Deandra couldn't imagine how unprofessional she'd seemed —with no website, no business cards, and no clue what to charge this new client with a pet of an unknown species. But Angela had been so desperate for help with Barnaby, she either didn't notice or didn't care that Deandra had no clue what she was doing.

She supposed Angela's observation of Deandra's training sessions in the park with Havoc, and even the brief one with Sunshine the Homicidal Fire Newt, had been all the convincing Angela needed. Angela had been so impressed with Deandra's supposed skill with animals that she'd been ready to hire Deandra on the spot. Perhaps Angela had figured that professionalism didn't matter when Deandra had such an aptitude for training difficult animals.

But the fact that Angela's frilled dendrune *needed* training should have been red flag number one.

Angela's confession during their first meeting at her house that Barnaby had gone through eight pet sitters in five months should have been red flags two, three, and four.

But Barnaby, a two-foot-tall lizard creature with chicken-like legs, had stood calmly by Angela's ankle during that meeting and made nary a sound. His short alligator snout didn't snap menacingly. His long scaly neck didn't undulate like a snake. If it weren't for his occasionally blinking yellow eyes, he would have looked like a quirky bit of yard art made from recycled materials and purchased cheap at a flea market.

Deandra hadn't known then if Barnaby had tiny arms like a T-rex that he kept out of sight, or maybe even a pair of wings tucked close to his back like Havoc's. There hadn't been a scary, calculating intelligence behind Barnaby's beady eyes like there was with Sunshine. If anything, Deandra got the impression that the poor thing only had two brain cells rattling around in that little skull of his—and both had been asleep.

The only times Barnaby had reacted were when he'd heard his name, his head sharply whipping to the side and his eyes widening as if he'd just seen a ghost, and the time he'd spotted a spider scuttling across the floor. He'd ducked his head, scratched at the hardwood like a bull gearing up for a charge, and taken off after the arachnid.

Barnaby wasn't built for tracking prey, however. The spider escaped to safety through an unseen crack in the baseboard, and Barnaby had crashed headlong into the wall with so much force that it was a wonder his skull hadn't split open like an overripe melon.

He'd knocked himself clean out.

It was then, as Barnaby lay flat on his back with his chicken legs pointed toward the ceiling, that Deandra first saw the T-rex arms. They'd flopped to either side of Barnaby's supine body.

Angela hadn't even flinched when Barnaby slammed into the wall.

Which had been red flag number five.

But Angela had offered double the rate Deandra had originally proposed, so Deandra had quickly agreed.

The first week had been easy, if only because Barnaby had been so scared of her that he'd squished himself into a corner of his large rabbit hutch and quaked like a leaf in a hurricane. Deandra was able to refill his food and water dishes and clean his tray of litter made of shredded newspaper without needing to interact with the dendrune.

Angela eventually wanted Barnaby to be walked, but whenever Deandra texted Angela her daily update, Angela remained unfazed by Deandra's lack of progress. Angela had said more than once, "Once he warms up to you, he's as friendly and playful as a golden retriever!"

The hair-raising screech came again, and Deandra reluctantly moved farther down the hallway.

Last week, Barnaby had been terrified. This week had been another matter entirely. On Monday, the moment Deandra had opened one of the doors of the hutch, Barnaby had hissed like a ticked-off tiger and come charging at her. She'd been so startled, she'd fallen onto her backside. Barnaby shot out of the open door like a scaly torpedo, landed on Deandra's stomach, and then launched off it a breath later as if he'd bounced on a trampoline. He'd screeched and taken off down the hallway.

After assuring herself that she had not, in fact, suffered from heart failure, she'd crept after him. She'd eventually found him under the bed, panting hard with his little pink tongue lolling out the side of its alligator snout. His teeth were roughly the size of grains of rice, but there were a *lot* of them.

Every day this week had been the same: No matter what Deandra tried, nothing worked to keep the mischievous, mentally impaired, miniature T-rex in his hutch.

Deandra crept into the bedroom. "Hey, Barnaby," she said slowly. "We gotta stop doing this."

Barnaby screech-hissed.

Deandra would have closed the bedroom door before opening Barnaby's hutch, but Angela didn't "believe in traditional doors" on any room except the bathroom. All rooms either had an open doorway or a beaded curtain, like something out of a seventies love den.

Really, the door thing should have been more of a red flag than anything else.

Deandra slowly lowered herself to her belly so she could get eyes on Barnaby. He was hunkered low to the floor, reminiscent of a bird squatting atop a nest. He had his head turned to the side so he could watch her better. As he panted heavily, his tiny arms quivering, her instincts to flee were going haywire. The little beast looked a touch mad, and despite knowing the strange lizard wasn't smarter than a sack of pebbles, Deandra wanted to quit, just like the eight sitters had before her.

Over texts yesterday, Angela had gushed about how happy she was that Barnaby liked Deandra enough that he was playing his favorite game of keep-away. However, the text that came next had given Deandra pause.

ANGELA

> Sometimes he bites when he's overstimulated. If he breaks the flesh and holds on for longer than thirty seconds, you might need a distemper shot. That hasn't happened to me in at least a month, though!

Deandra had already planned to call Dr. Cruz Caddel this week to ask what kind of vaccines she might need to consider when working with exotic animals—especially when several of those animals had originated from another realm. Angela's casual mention of distemper—which Deandra had thought only afflicted mundane cats and dogs—had moved that call to the top of Deandra's priority list. She'd had plenty of odd jobs in her life, but this one definitely took the cake.

"Hi, buddy," she said calmly to Barnaby now. "Don't you want to go for a walk? You could sniff some grass. Maybe catch a bug or two? Get some of that really unsettling energy out, hmm?"

This pep talk hadn't worked at all week, so Deandra wasn't sure why she thought it would now. The visit usually involved Deandra chasing Barnaby all over the house until he tuckered himself out and flopped face-first on the floor, allowing her to then carry his clammy, deadweight body back to his hutch. Or, as she'd discovered two days ago, if Deandra tossed a treat from the bag of O'MALLEY'S GIGANTINE FROZEN COCKROACHES™ into Barnaby's cage before he exhausted himself, he'd launch into the hutch on his own. Barnaby loved cockroaches the way Havoc loved mealworms. Deandra still didn't enjoy handling insects, but her tolerance for it grew by leaps and bounds every day.

Cockroaches were the only surefire way to get Barnaby back into his hutch, and once she'd resorted to pulling the bribe from the freezer, it meant the visit was over.

Barnaby started bouncing up and down on his chicken legs like he was doing rapid-fire squats.

"Oh no," Deandra muttered to herself. "What the heck are you doing now?"

He snapped his alligator-like mouth shut, widened his eyes, and started bouncing even faster. Deandra skittered backward on her stomach, just in case Barnaby was planning to detonate.

Barnaby opened his mouth so wide, it was a wonder his jaw didn't dislocate. He unleashed a hiss that made Deandra's heart stop beating for two long seconds.

And then she discovered where the "frilled" part of Barnaby's species name came from. The tiny demon came barreling toward her like something out of *Jurassic Park*. The moment he cleared the bottom of the bed, he stood straighter, and without breaking stride, he flared a flap of skin reminiscent of the underside of an umbrella around his head. It was an alarming shade of red.

Deandra scrambled onto her backside and scuttled backward until her back hit the wall. She yelped in surprise and wrapped her arms around her knees as if she were a little kid again, hiding in the closet, hoping the small dark space would save her from the raging thunderstorm outside.

Barnaby slid to a stop an inch from Deandra's shoes, shook his frilled neck flap at her, and then darted out of the room, screeching the whole way.

Once she was sure Barnaby wasn't going to murder her—at least not yet; for all she knew, he'd run off to the kitchen to fetch a butcher knife—Deandra sagged, loosening her grip on her knees. Her legs flopped out in front of her. She raised an arm and held it in front of her, parallel to the floor, watching her hand shake.

As she let her palm flop to her thigh, she considered the windows in the bedroom and whether she could shinny out one of them to safety. While Angela didn't believe in doors, she *did* believe in steel bar–reinforced windows. There were no bars on the windows that faced the street. Why on earth were there ones on the bedroom windows?

Perhaps the previous eight sitters *hadn't* quit. Perhaps Angela and Barnaby had planned and executed their deaths. Deandra had perused Angela's freezer many a time in search of cockroaches. But that didn't mean there wasn't an industrial freezer in the garage, full of pet-sitter body parts.

The pitter-clatter of little clawed feet sounded in the hallway, accompanied by a scraping metallic noise.

"*Oh no*," Deandra whispered to herself, horror-stricken.

Who would have thought her life would be in jeopardy—not from a fire-breathing dragon, but from a lizard demon the height of a small toddler? Her family would be heartbroken about Deandra's gruesome demise, but she figured Wendy would still get a kick out of writing the obituary.

Beloved Daughter, Dragon Mom, Cousin, and Friend—Mauled to Death by Miniature Reptilian Serial Killer.

(CLOSED CASKET. TRUST US. THE MORTICIAN RETCHED INTO A TRASH CAN.)

The serial killer in question slid and clacked into the bedroom. Something *thunk*ed into the toe of her tennis shoe, but she didn't know what; she'd already squeezed her eyes shut by then. If her death were imminent, she didn't want to see it coming.

Clack, clack, clack.

That had come from directly in front of her.

Clack. Muted hiss.

Deandra cracked open an eye. Then her mouth dropped open.

From Barnaby's snout hung his harness, the leash already affixed. A metallic poop-bag holder hung near the leash loop—that was what had been making the scraping sound.

"You—" Deandra coughed and cleared her throat. "You want to go for a walk?"

Barnaby spit out the harness so he could, once again, flare his bright-red neck fringe. He shook it at her like someone trying to knock excess water off an umbrella. She flinched hard—and might have soiled herself.

He flailed his T-rex arms in delight before pulling the fringe back against his neck as if it had never existed. Bending forward, he nudged the harness and leash closer to her with his snout.

How was he both utterly terrifying and also kind of cute?

It took an inordinate amount of time to get Barnaby into his harness. Thankfully, since he'd decided he liked her, he didn't get annoyed by her ineptitude and sink his distemper-laced teeth into her flesh. Deandra was a sweaty mess by the time they finally made it out of the house, but Barnaby was pleasantly well behaved on-leash.

Well, mostly.

He and the squirrel population at large harbored a hatred for each other that rivaled that of the Hatfields and McCoys. If Deandra kept up a running commentary with him, doing her best to drown out the aggressive chittering coming from the branches, it usually kept him from slipping into a literal hissy fit.

Angela lived in a peaceful neighborhood that boasted one- and two-story homes with well-tended lawns and gardens. It was still summer, so the occasional gaggle of kids went by on bikes or scooters, even though it was the middle of the afternoon. Barnaby was oblivious to most things, so the "what the heck is *that* thing?" rhetorically shouted in dismay by a young boy on a skateboard didn't bruise Barnaby's ego.

Deandra halted at a stop sign, intending to cross the street, but she let the one idling car go first, as Barnaby was busily scratching at a patch of dirt searching for a snack. When the intersection was clear, she tugged at Barnaby's leash, but he dug his heels in. He cocked a beady little eye at her.

"Don't look at me like that!" she said. "You have cockroaches at home. You don't need dirty street worms."

She winced at her own illogical argument.

Barnaby offered a noise that sounded suspiciously like a derisive snort, then resumed scratching.

"*Hi, Barnaby,*" someone sing-songed from behind Deandra. She whirled to find a young woman around her age walking toward her.

The sound of his name still made Barnaby startle as if he'd seen a specter, and he whirled around, too. A long brown earthworm flaked with dirt hung from his mouth. He threw his head back to quickly gobble down the worm, then angled an eye—not at the exuberant Pomeranian in the yellow polka-dot dress who accompanied the woman, but at the woman herself. He stared at her for a long beat, then violently hissed before darting behind Deandra's legs.

It took everything in Deandra's power not to react to one of his little T-rex arms brushing against the back of her calf. It was cold and scaly, like a tiny snake.

"*Ooh, Barney-Bee,*" the woman said in an overly affected baby voice, placing her hands on her knees. She angled her head from side to side to get a better look at him.

Deandra noted that every time the woman looked left, Barnaby shifted to the right. He quaked harder.

"Uh, hi," Deandra said, trying not to be annoyed that the woman hadn't even acknowledged her existence. "I'm Dee."

The woman finally gave up on Barnaby and eyed Deandra, her mask of friendliness instantly replaced by one of mild disinterest. "Lydia."

"And who's this?" Deandra asked, gesturing to the Pomeranian who was lying down on the sidewalk beside Lydia's feet—not because she'd grown tired, but because she was clearly enamored of Barnaby, who still shivered behind Deandra. The pup had her head between her paws, and her fluffy tail wagged so hard, it practically vibrated.

"This is Goldie," Lydia said flatly.

Goldie popped to her feet at the sound of her name and barked once. She stood on her hind legs and waved her forelegs in unison, gazing up at Lydia all the while.

Deandra grinned. "Oh my gosh, she's adorable."

"Stop begging for treats, Goldie! I ran out. I told you that already."

Goldie immediately dropped back to her stomach with her head between her paws once more. She rolled her eyes up at Lydia periodically. Her tail lay listlessly on the ground.

Deandra coughed awkwardly. "Are you, uh, one of Barnaby's neighbors?"

Lydia tore her gaze from her treat-loving dog to level a flat look at Deandra. "No, I don't live around here. I'm one of Barnaby's *former* caretakers. That is until hateful Angela fired me for no reason, just like she fired everyone before me. I told her she wasn't going to find a sitter better than me unless she lowered her standards." She sniffed, scanning Deandra from head to toe. "You a relative of hers or something? Or did she finally make good on her threat to hire someone from another hub?"

Deandra figured decking a total stranger while walking Barnaby would be a perfectly good reason for Angela to fire Deandra. But if Angela had fired this woman for being an awful human, maybe Angela would give Deandra a raise for clocking Lydia in the nose.

Normally, when confronted with rude people, Deandra's brain glitched. But this woman had the same pretentious attitude as so many of her former customers from Urbean Edge that she felt her barista persona slip into place. No one tells you that working in the service industry in Los Angeles gifts you with the ability to deal with asshats while keeping a smile on your face. In her overly friendly barista voice, Deandra said, "Angela told me she needed to find a sitter who could *actually* handle exotics. She said her last sitter didn't have the necessary … qualifications. She didn't divulge names, though. Did you say *you* were her last sitter?"

Lydia's nostrils flared. "I've been a pet sitter in Axia for years and worked for an agency in Pinebough before that. What Angela *needs* is experience. But she's not willing to pay for it. It's a shame, too, because Barnaby would have thrived with me." She hinged at the waist. *"Isn't that right, Barney-Bee?"*

Barnaby ineffectually hugged the back of Deandra's calf with his tiny, scaly arms. Deandra inwardly shuddered.

"Good luck meeting all of Angela's demands," Lydia said. "I've been in this industry too long to put up with ridiculous clients. C'mon, Goldie." She yanked hard on the Pomeranian's leash, and the yellow-dress-bedecked dog reluctantly lurched to her feet to trot after her grumpy sitter. They passed Deandra and headed through the intersection.

Goldie cast a longing look at Barnaby, which earned her a sharp rebuke from Lydia. It wasn't until the pair had disappeared around a hedge-lined corner that Barnaby came out of hiding.

Deandra stared down at him, hands on hips. "Please tell me you bit her."

Barnaby hopped three times in quick succession. Deandra took that as a yes.

"I think we'll get along just fine," she told him.

CHAPTER TWO

Deandra felt considerably lighter about her new gig after her interaction with Lydia. Gaining the favor of a psychotic alligator-chicken when an experienced, albeit cranky, rival sitter couldn't wasn't anything to write home about, but Deandra would take her wins where she could find them.

Since Angela was Deandra's only client, and Bugs Bunny was keeping Havoc company, Deandra wasn't in an immediate rush to get back. So when Barnaby started scratching at the ground again, she merely waited for him to finish.

"I'm very impressed!"

"Nuaugh!" Deandra said eloquently, quickly scanning the

surrounding area for the owner of the voice. She clapped a hand over her racing heart.

"Over here!" the small voice added unhelpfully.

Deandra eventually found the person—uhh, gnome—peeking from behind one of the redwood trees that dotted a grassy swatch of land stretching before the black metal fence of an apartment complex. The pointy hat sitting on the gnome's head was orange, and what looked like an appliqué had been affixed to the bottom. As the gnome emerged from her hiding place, Deandra noted that the appliqué was of a black cat's face from the nose up, so it looked as if the cat were peeking at Deandra from the brim.

The gnome had rosy apple cheeks; a black braid hung over either shoulder, each dotted with small pink flowers; and she was dressed in a rose-patterned dress. Even her shiny black shoes had flowers adorning the buckles. She was so cute, like a doll come to life, that Deandra could hardly stand to look at her.

"I was saying that was really &$!#% impressive how you gave Lydia a taste of her own &$!#% medicine! That &$!#% is &$!#% awful."

Deandra's mouth dropped open after the first expletive. Not because she was offended by such language, but because the words were literally replaced by bleeps. "Uhhh …"

The gnome stood a few feet away, casting wary glances at Barnaby. They were, after all, about the same size. But Barnaby only cared about finding fresh grubs.

"Not too &$!#% bright are you?"

"Hey!" Deandra finally said. "No need to be rude. I just haven't seen a—"

"A what? A &$!#% gnome?"

"A spell that bleeps curse words," Deandra said, wondering if all her interactions with Axian residents were going to be hostile today. "It *is* a spell, right?"

"Oh! So you can't hear me when I say—"

There was a long string of bleeps, broken occasionally by short inoffensive words like "the" and "and" before the flurry of bleeps started up again. It was honestly impressive her vocabulary was that filthy.

"Uhh, nope," Deandra said once the bleeping had stopped. The absence of it left her ears ringing. Though she supposed if she'd heard what the gnome had actually said, her ears might be *bleeding*.

"&¢$!#%," the gnome said. "It's a tonic my parents slip into my food sometimes. I've got an interview later for a job at a preschool, and they think my &$!#% vocabulary will somehow affect my &$!#% ability to get a &$!#% job."

Deandra stared at her. She honestly wasn't sure if hearing the actual curse words would be worse than the bleeping. It was like flashing a neon sign that pointed to her foul mouth, rather than masking the problem. Deandra thought of movies where replacement words were dubbed over the bad ones, the sound quality of the replacements always a bit off.

Her favorite was, *"Get out of my face, you ninny, or I'll kick you in the kazoo!"*

"What you &$!#% smiling at? You don't think I'll get the &$!#% job either?"

Deandra held up a hand in placation, tamping down her amusement at the memory. "Sorry. It wasn't about you. I think if you manage to not trigger the cursing alarm, you'll probably do fine."

"I can stop cursing whenever I want," the gnome said. "It just &$!#% me off when people &$!#% doubt me."

"I bet you can get through the rest of this conversation without triggering it," Deandra said, hoping reverse psychology would work on the irate, cherub-faced gnome. "You said something I did earlier was impressive?"

"Oooh, I see. You're just—" The gnome cleared her throat. "You're just fishing for compliments."

"Since you insulted me at least once that I'm aware of, I think a compliment isn't too much to ask for," Deandra said, shrugging.

The gnome grinned. "My first assessment was right: you've

gotta be pretty fu—uhh … pretty stinkin' great if you could manage to ruffle Lydia Monroe's feathers." She took a few steps forward and held up a tiny hand. "I'm Harmony, by the way."

Deandra bent to shake her hand, but it turned into Harmony giving Deandra's pointer finger a hearty pump in greeting. "Dee. And this is Barnaby."

The lizard creature's head shot up, and his body stilled completely. He cocked a wide eye up at her.

"Everything's fine," Deandra told him. "Just doing some introductions. This is Harmony."

Barnaby turned his focus toward the gnome and hopped a foot in the air as if he'd only just noticed her. One beat, two—*hiss*. He flared his neck fringe at Harmony, who cursed a blue streak that sounded as if someone's life support screen had just registered a flatline, and then Harmony fell hard on her back. Barnaby calmly tucked away his fringe and resumed his search for worms.

Deandra's hand was clapped over her heart again. "Sorry! He's, uhh, excitable." The gnome didn't move. "Umm … Harmony?"

The gnome had gone rigid. Deandra took a few cautious steps forward, noting that the gnome's skin had taken on an unhealthy sheen. What if she'd had a heart attack? Had Barnaby literally scared her to death?

The longer Deandra stared at her, the more she was convinced Harmony had spontaneously petrified—as if she'd turned into a literal garden gnome one could buy from a home goods store. Tentatively, she gave Harmony's shiny black shoe a soft kick with her own tennis shoe. It sounded hollow. The second kick did not.

"Ow!"

Now it was Deandra's turn to curse voluminously and colorfully. "Oh my God, I thought you were dead!"

Harmony got back to her feet, cursing wildly all the while. She readjusted her pointed hat, which amazingly hadn't been knocked off during her fall. "It takes more effort than that to take down a gnome. We're hearty as &$!#%. Going full rigor is a defense mechanism when we're in danger or we get scared. Kind of embarrassing. Not as embarrassing as it is for my Uncle Wendel, though. That poor &$!#% is scared of his own shadow—literally!"

Deandra was just so relieved she wouldn't have to tell Angela that Barnaby might be investigated for homicide.

When Harmony shot a death glare at Barnaby, Deandra figured it would be best to distract her. "Did you hire Lydia as a pet sitter?" Deandra asked, hoping her heart rate would slow down soon. Deandra eyed the black cat featured on Harmony's hat, wondering if the gnome was a cat owner or if she just liked the design. Deandra got lost in the image of Harmony riding a giant Maine coon like a horse.

"Yeah," Harmony said, her lip curled. "A lot of people in this neighborhood have hired her. She's … a pill, though. She's got terrible communication skills, she's been caught yelling at her charges a lot, and she allegedly poached clients from a sitter who hired her when Lydia first moved to Axia from Pinebough.

"Lydia was new here, so even though she had the experience of being a sitter somewhere else, she had to start over in terms of building her client base. Sarah over at Pawsome Pals—that's who I use now—hired Lydia when she first got to town. After about a year, Lydia branched out on her own. She started offering her regulars cheaper rates. Sarah thought those clients had just stopped booking with her. Sarah's got a deep client base and a team of six sitters, so that's why it took her months to figure out Lydia had stolen at least ten clients. A nasty online fight broke out in the comments section of a review app. It was all very messy."

"Guess there's drama in every industry," Deandra muttered.

"Most people are scared to confront Lydia, though, since she's supposedly a fire elemental," Harmony said.

Deandra's eyes doubled in diameter.

Harmony laughed. "Guessing you didn't know that part? She doesn't have strong magic, from what I hear, but it *does* mean she's got a raging temper. The littlest thing sets her off." She jutted her chin at Barnaby. "Lydia also claims she's an animal empathslash-medium—not a powerful zoolinguist like Dr. Caddel or anything; she's not stupid enough to make a claim *that* bold. She says she can feel what her animal clients feel and that she sometimes gets messages from beyond the rainbow bridge. She uses that claim in all her advertising. Gullible people hire her, hoping they can get messages from their pets—both living and dead."

"You think it's a false claim?" Deandra asked.

"Oh yeah," Harmony said, nodding. "Total &$!#%"

It was the first time Harmony had slipped in a while—getting knocked unceremoniously on her keister by Barnaby notwithstanding—so Deandra decided to ignore it.

Deandra asked, "How can you tell if she's the real deal or not? Animals can't talk to confirm or deny her claims. Wait. I'm new to the hub system. Animals *can't* talk, right?"

Harmony giggled—a high and girlish sound. "No, thank &$!#%! Not in the way you're asking, anyway."

Deandra wasn't sure what the heck *that* meant. "It's the perfect scam if Lydia really is lying about her skills, then. No one can prove or disprove what she says."

Harmony tipped a small hand from side to side. "I adopted my cat, Marshall, from a shelter. He was a year-old stray who was brought in by a man who'd witnessed Marshall get clipped by a car. Marshall somehow only sustained a broken leg and tail. His back leg healed fine, but his tail bends at a funny angle, even three years later.

"When I first met Lydia, she asked me if I'd had Marshall since he was a kitten. I said no, that I'd adopted him when he was one, and that I didn't know his history. Before I could even mention the accident, Lydia let out this very dramatic groan, pressed her fingers to her temples, and said, 'Marshall wants me to tell you how he sustained that injury to his tail. He was attacked by a male cat who wanted to stake a claim on his mother, and to do so, the male had to eliminate the litter of the previous male. The cat successfully dispatched Marshall's littermates. Yet Marshall, at only three months old, fended off a full-grown cat and escaped with his life. Marshall almost lost his tail in that fight. Your boy is a fighter.'"

Deandra knew that male cats—both the wild and domesticated kind—were known to take out the litter of a rival male, so it was a decent enough story concocted by Lydia. Just so happened that, in this case, Harmony could catch the so-called animal empath in a lie.

"Did you call her out on it?" Deandra asked.

Harmony wrinkled her little nose. "I probably should have, but we'd had a family emergency, and Lydia was helping us out a lot by agreeing to sit for Marshall on short notice. Didn't seem like a good idea to &$!#% her off. Plus, for all I knew, that story *was* true, and Marshall's tail had been broken *before* the accident."

"Fair point," Deandra said.

"But over the years, after talking to other people who hired her, it was pretty clear that a lot of Lydia's stories didn't add up—pair that with everything else, and it doesn't paint her in the best light."

"She was certainly rude to me right off the bat," Deandra said. "And Barnaby was terrified of her. If she's able to read animals' emotions, you'd think she would have backed off when she realized her behavior only scared him more."

Harmony nodded. "Exactly that." She gestured at Barnaby, who was apparently glutted on grubs because he was on his back now, feet in the air. One foot twitched, and he chirped a few times, suggesting he was fast asleep and not that he'd shuffled off this mortal coil. "I don't know Angela well, but Barnaby is a unique animal, so most people in this neighborhood recognize him. I've talked to her enough times to know she's never been able to find someone who can walk him. He's honestly even better behaved with you than he is with Angela. Lydia can make all the claims she wants, but if one of you has a special skill with animals, I'm betting on you."

Deandra smiled. "*There's* the compliment I've been waiting for. Took us a while, but we got there."

Harmony giggled again. It was a sweet sound that matched her cutesy exterior. "Hey, do you happen to have a business card on you?"

Deandra really needed to get some of those made. And design a website. And decide on a business name. And get vaccinated for reptilian distemper. She made a show of patting her pockets, then winced. "Not on me. But I can give you my number."

Harmony produced a tiny cell phone from the pocket of her dress. She tapped in Deandra's name and number as Deandra rattled them off. "Sarah's often booked months out, so it would be nice to have a back-up sitter. I'll also let all my friends with exotic pets know there's a new sitter in town—and that Lydia already hates her. I swear, you taming Barnaby *and* ticking off Lydia &$!#% Monroe should be enough to instantly land you five new clients."

Deandra laughed. "I appreciate the referrals. Starting from scratch is daunting."

"No doubt." Harmony must have seen the time on her phone because she cursed vociferously in response. "I gotta get ready for this &$!#% interview, but it was nice to meet you."

"You too," Deandra said as she scooped Barnaby's deadweight body off the ground. He flopped in her grip as if his bones had gone liquid. She hung his head over her shoulder and held his scaly body to her chest. She just hoped he didn't wake with a start and attack her out of confusion. "And good luck with the interview. Just think of what Lydia bleeping Monroe would do, and then do the opposite."

Harmony pointed a tiny finger at her. "That's solid &$!#% advice." She scampered toward the gate of the apartment complex.

"And stop cursing!"

"I &$!#% will!"

Deandra sighed, then started the trek back to Barnaby's house, brainstorming business names as she went.

CHAPTER THREE

I t took the better part of a week for Deandra to get her entrepreneurial affairs in order, which included creating an account on Forage—the hub system's internet provider—deciding on a business name, *registering* the name, starting a business banking account, launching a website, and getting business cards printed. A local place printed the cards. Along with the reasonable price, the shop owners presented her with a surprising offer: For no extra cost, she could pick the cards up within twenty-four hours of placing the order. The couple who owned the shop were witches—one with an earth affinity and one with water—and between the two of them, they could perform literal magic with ink.

Deandra currently sat at Wendy's dining room table after a successful afternoon of walking Barnaby and completing her latest round of errands, including picking up her new cards. They were even prettier than she'd imagined.

She stared at the words "Dee's Mythical Pet Sitting" and smiled to herself. As impulsive as it had felt to drop everything and move to Axia, sitting here now with one of her cards in her hand and Havoc lying beneath the table, quietly gnawing on a bone the size of her leg, everything felt like it was coming together.

The owners of InkCraft had turned her business name into a unique logo. In addition to her name and phone number, her cards featured three animals: a Bengal cat snoozed in the open space of the D in her name; a beautifully rendered purple dragon lounged atop the "M" in "Mythical," while its tail made up the length of the "y"; and a monkey-like creature covered in colorful feathers instead of fur hung from the top of the "S" in "Sitting" by one hand.

But even more impressive than that was the bespelled ink and paper. Bright blinking eyes materialized in the O's, then disappeared, only to have one of the A's sprout wings and fly away. S's became slithering snakes. The dots of the I's grew legs and feet and scampered away. The movement on the cards cycled every sixty seconds, and only a few things changed at a time, so the magic wasn't distracting or busy. The ink, according to the InkCraft couple, would hold its magic for upward of a year, assuming nothing catastrophic happened to the card itself. Deandra almost didn't want to give any of them away.

A notification popped up on her phone then, snapping her out of staring at the card as if it were a television.

AXIA'S EXOTIC VETERINARY CLINIC

Havoc's appt is today at 3:30 PM. If you have
any questions, please give us a call

Deandra had almost forgotten her last errand of the day. Even though Havoc's cold had long since cleared up, and he didn't seem to be experiencing any lasting ill effects from the Quowlaxliquin that had been pumped into him prior to winding up in the dumpster, Dr. Caddel still had wanted to do a follow-up a month later.

Deandra took a quick shower, then spent entirely too long trying to decide between wearing a sundress or a tank top and shorts. Dr. Caddel—*Cruz*—had told her she could pay him back with lunch for all his extra help with Havoc after her dragon had been whisked off to animal jail by the hateful Ranger Vicks. Deandra didn't have any idea how serious Cruz had been about that—and if he *had* been serious, was it a platonic suggestion, or had he been hinting at a date?

On the evening that Cruz had reunited Deandra and Havoc— and Rae Corly had been arrested—Cruz had dropped the cousins off at Wendy's apartment with a promise to check on them in the morning. He'd shown up early, on his way to work, with coffees and pastries. He hadn't stayed long, but after he left, Wendy couldn't stop nudging Deandra in the side with her elbow like someone out of an old vaudeville act while uttering variations of "*Oooh*, that doctor has a *crush* on you."

Yet she hadn't heard from him during the two weeks she was in Los Angeles, even though he'd been sharing dragon-sitting duties with Wendy. He also hadn't contacted her during the two weeks since she'd officially moved into Wendy's apartment. Even the check-in call about Havoc's cold and the reminder about the dragon's upcoming follow-up visit had come from one of his techs.

But he *had* said that she owed him lunch—so did that mean the ball was in her court, and he was waiting on *her*? He was handsome, loved animals, had a stable job, and was considerate. All good qualities. All good reasons she should text him. But she wasn't sure if she even *wanted* to date right now.

Deandra realized then that part of the problem was that she'd grown a little desperate for friends. Cruz seemed like the kind of person she'd want to be friends with. Dating would complicate that, if not ruin it entirely. What if he was exceedingly rude to waitstaff, was a litterbug, or didn't return shopping carts to their designated areas? Little annoyances could strain a friendship— while being deal-breakers for relationships.

As much as Deandra loved hanging out with Wendy, her cousin had recently started dating Nathan, the guy she'd met while she and Deandra were poking around town searching for an arsonist. Nathan lived in a hub in Michigan—Wendy had been unsure a month ago if he'd been from Massachusetts or Maine; she'd ben wrong twice—but he returned to Axia often to help his parents with their pharmacy. Last weekend, he'd come to Axia to see Wendy. This past weekend, however, Wendy had gone there. Deandra had spent most of the weekend on the couch with Havoc, watching an obscene amount of TV—which had been great, honestly—but if Deandra wanted this fresh start to actually *feel* fresh, she knew she couldn't turn into a homebody who had only animals for companionship.

Especially when one of those animals was Barnaby.

Deciding on the tank top and shorts, she pulled her hair into a ponytail, swiped on some lip gloss, and called it good. After putting on her tennis shoes—one of which she found in Havoc's bed—she leashed up her dragon and took him for a quick walk before piling him and herself into the car.

Dr. Caddel's office was in the middle of town; otherwise, she would have walked. She had yet to try a telepad. The "your limbs and/or organs might be rearranged and/or lost" warning kind of turned her off the whole thing. Plus, she wasn't sure how much it cost. Teleporting around the town probably wouldn't cost as much as an airplane ticket or anything, but it wouldn't be free, either.

Most animals weren't allowed in the teleportation tubes, anyway.

Deandra made it to the office with fifteen minutes to spare. The same two techs Deandra had interacted with the last time she was here were in position behind the reception counter. The nice one was on the phone, so the grouchy one waved Deandra over.

"Hi," Deandra said. "I'm here with—"

"Havoc," the woman said, eyeing the dragon warily as she noisily clacked away at her keyboard without looking at the screen.

Deandra glanced over her shoulder when the grouchy tech's lip curled in mild disgust at whatever Havoc was doing. The menacing beast had the loop of his leash in his mouth and was marching around the lobby like a dressage horse. Deandra didn't know what exactly the tech was seeing, as the world at large saw his glamoured form—a shaggy dire wolf puppy. Even still, Deandra figured whatever the tech had seen still had to be pretty cute.

Havoc got tangled up in the leash, stumbled, and face-planted. He chirped a moment later as if to say, "I'm okay!" and resumed prancing.

When Deandra turned back to the tech, it was evident she hadn't been swayed an iota by Havoc's natural charms. The tech was made of stronger stuff than Deandra, that much was clear.

After consulting her screen a few times and asking Deandra a few questions, the tech flatly said, "You're all checked in. You can have a seat."

"Thanks!" Deandra said cheerfully, hoping she could wear the woman down with kindness.

That didn't work either.

Deandra sat on one of the bench seats and watched Havoc as he army-crawled after a fly, his leash trailing behind him. When the lobby door opened and a woman came in with her

Chihuahua, Deandra called Havoc back to her. Thankfully, his recall was stronger than his desire to catch flies. The Chihuahua shook violently in the doorway of the office, gaze glued to Havoc. Her owner had to pick up the small dog just to get inside.

When the owner put the shivering pup on the scale, the dog trembled on her spindly legs, staring at Havoc like he was one of the four horsemen of the apocalypse.

Then her bladder gave out.

"Oh, my heavens! Mitzy!" the owner exclaimed. Then she whirled toward Deandra. "Control your dog!"

"He didn't do anything," Deandra said, pointing at Havoc, who was lying on his belly with his head between his paws. To Deandra, he was still a good four feet away from Mitzy the Chihuahua, but maybe he was closer as a dire wolf. "Up, Havoc."

The dragon scrambled into a sitting position, then tipped his head back to grin at her. She gave him a scratch under his scaly chin.

"Mitzy!"

Deandra and Havoc returned their attention to the scale. Mitzy had also defecated.

There was a flurry of activity as the techs scrambled to clean up the mess and wipe down Mitzy. A third tech, this one male, who Deandra hadn't seen before swept into the lobby to bring Deandra into an exam room early, in large part to give Mitzy a breather.

"Don't feel bad," the tech said from the doorway once Deandra and Havoc were inside. "Mitzy is terrified of the vet's office—well, life scares her, period. Dr. Caddel says reading her leaves him so stressed out after a visit, he feels like *he* needs Prozac. She also usually pees on him, so a big thank you to Havoc for making her empty her bladder early."

Havoc chirped, clearly pleased with himself.

The vet tech laughed. "Dr. Caddel will be with you two shortly," he said, then closed the door.

It took twenty minutes for Dr. Caddel to enter the exam room, and while he still maintained his professional air, he was clearly a bit flustered. Even more so than the first time she'd met him; that day, he'd immediately apologized for his tardiness, caused by a misbehaving pegasus.

"Hi," he said with a sigh, a file folder tucked under one arm of his blue scrubs. "Sorry for the wait."

Havoc had been practicing his dressage routine again, but he abruptly spun around at the sound of the vet's voice. Havoc peeped and bounded over to Dr. Caddel, then flopped over onto his back across the vet's shoes.

Dr. Caddel grinned. "Hi, buddy. You're clearly feeling better." He bent to give Havoc's belly a scratch. It was odd that people could see *and* touch the glamour. Instead of feeling smooth scales, Dr. Caddel would believe he was petting shaggy fur.

Magic was weird.

"Havoc, let the poor guy fully walk into the room before you love-bomb him," Deandra said, laughing.

Havoc immediately scrambled to his feet and charged over to her. He was moving too fast, so his muzzle bounced off her shin before he could properly put on the brakes. He gave his head a shake, then plopped onto his haunches, his face between her knees. He offered a dog-like smile, his tongue hanging out the side of his mouth.

She grabbed either side of his face and gently squeezed. "You're lucky you're so dang cute," she said, then kissed him on the muzzle.

He chirped before swiping his tongue up the entire length of her face. Deandra squawked in disgust, eyes squeezed shut as she laughed and wiped her face with the back of her hand. "I am full of regret."

Dr. Caddel's laugh sounded from nearby. When Deandra opened her eyes, she found him standing in front of her, tissue held out. She gratefully took it and dabbed her face, glad she hadn't bothered with makeup today.

All business, Dr. Caddel asked her a few questions as he

headed to the center island where he deposited the file folder. He flipped through a few pages and started making notes based on Deandra's answers.

In the space between the bench seat Deandra was perched on and Dr. Caddel's position at the island, Havoc was caught in the eternal war between him and his tail. He spun so fast, snapping ineffectually at the spade at the end, it was making *Deandra* dizzy.

Dr. Caddel peered over the island. "Oh, you didn't have to take off his collar for this appointment, Deandra. Dee." He paused thoughtfully. "Can I call you Dee?"

"Dee is fine," Deandra said slowly. "But what are you talking about? I didn't take off his collar."

"The magic in the runes on his collar will fade over time much quicker if the collar's removed too many times. It …" He trailed off, finally registering what she'd said. "You *didn't* take it off?"

"Nope," Deandra said, tamping down a smile. "Havoc. *Havoc!*"

The dragon stopped spinning, listed sideways, and bumped into the side of the island. He shook his head, then he staggered toward her, looking a little green.

"If you throw up on my shoes, we're going to have words, sir," she told him.

He peeped once, as if assuring her once again that he was okay.

"Hey, Havoc?" Dr. Caddel said, slowly stepping around the island. The direction of his eyeline *would* suggest he was actually seeing the dragon right now, and not a dire wolf.

The dragon turned toward Dr. Caddel, sat on his haunches, and gazed up at the vet.

"Wow," Dr. Caddel breathed, all but confirming that, even if Havoc had been a dire wolf when Dr. Caddel had walked into this exam room, he was in his true form now. The vet lowered himself to the floor to sit cross-legged in front of the dragon. He listened to Havoc's heartbeat, peered into his ears, eyes, and mouth, and palpated his belly. The only commentary Havoc offered was to lick Dr. Caddel's chin at the end of the exam.

The doctor's wide brown eyes finally angled up toward Deandra. "Has the glamour dropped for anyone else?"

"Not that I know of," she said.

The fond smile Dr. Caddel aimed at Havoc made Deandra's heart ache a little. "Thanks for trusting me, buddy. Can't say I usually gain the trust of patients this quickly."

"He's a trusting guy."

Dr. Caddel frowned down at Havoc. "I say this as a friend: I'm deeply honored to be included in your pod, but you have to be *very* careful about whom you trust. Some people might act trustworthy only because they want something from you. You just need to be sure in your gut that you're trusting the right people."

The dragon cocked his head curiously at Dr. Caddel for a long moment. Then the vet yelped, startled, and scooted away on his backside. Dr. Caddel's head was slightly angled back now to better watch Havoc, no longer looking down. Havoc was back in dire wolf form for him.

The flash of crestfallen disappointment that swept over Dr. Caddel's face was so sharp that she had to resist the urge to hug him.

Havoc glanced over at Deandra then, and as much as Havoc was clearly an animal, there was something almost human in his expression. The corners of his eyes and mouth drooped. Somehow she knew that Havoc had believed looping Dr. Caddel into his trust circle was a good idea, and now he was no longer sure. He wanted her to weigh in.

Though Deandra had initially harbored concerns that Dr. Caddel was going to try to take Havoc from her, he'd never once done anything that wasn't in Havoc's best interests. If anything, he'd gone out of his way to help make sure Havoc was safe. "You can trust him."

Havoc peeped happily, then launched himself at Dr. Caddel.

The vet was flat on his back and being licked half to death by a wiggly dragon before he could react. He was laughing, though.

Eventually tiring of harassing Dr. Caddel, Havoc hopped off his chest and went wandering off to give the rest of the exam room a thorough sniff.

Dr. Caddel levered himself into a sitting position. His hair wasn't that long, but it was still in disarray. A few splatters of dragon slobber decorated his scrubs. Deandra figured that was still better than getting peed on by Mitzy.

"Welcome to the pod," Deandra said, grinning.

"Thanks for vouching for me."

Deandra tried to work out what had happened. "So Havoc can't alter the spell written on his collar," she said slowly, "but his granting you entrance into the pod overwrites the glamour magic. Do I have that right?"

Dr. Caddel got to his feet and then moved to lean against the center island, facing her. "That's my guess. Then, when he took that trust back, the glamour magic took over, shutting me out."

Deandra thought it was sweet that Dr. Caddel had been that visibly upset about Havoc clawing his trust back. Granted, if the same thing ever happened to her, she'd be inconsolable.

She hoped Havoc really *did* understand Dr. Caddel's warning, though, and that he wouldn't throw his trust at just anyone who was nice to him. Havoc had spent far more time with Wendy than with Dr. Caddel, yet Wendy still saw Havoc's dire wolf form.

Something she'd heard about Dr. Caddel twice now niggled at her. She wondered if it played a role in Havoc's deciding to trust him. "Hey, Dr. Caddel, can—"

"Cruz," he interrupted. "Secret club, remember?"

She laughed. "What exactly *is* a zoolinguist? If it means what I assume it does, I'd think being able to talk to your patients would mean most of them would trust you more than they'd trust a non-zoolingual vet." She was pretty sure she'd just made up a new word.

"The ability to talk to animals is the most simplified definition, yes," Cruz said. "But most can't speak the way you and I can, so they don't speak to me telepathically in words or anything."

"*Most?* Some animals *do* speak to you telepathically?" she asked.

"I'm sure you've heard the whole sentient-versus-sapient argument by now. No doubt Ranger Vicks trotted that one out while he was accusing Havoc of arson," Cruz said.

Havoc issued something like a hiss from the other side of the center island, but Deandra couldn't see him. Hopefully, he wasn't pawing around in cabinets. Last week he was investigating Wendy's bathroom and got his head stuck in the trash can. He'd come sprinting out, crashing into everything possible for ten full seconds of absolute mayhem before Deandra could get him unstuck.

"Yeah, Vicks said Havoc was considered a sapient animal because of the level of magic and intelligence dire wolves obtain by adulthood," Deandra said.

"Right," Cruz said, nodding. "The distinction really only matters in legal cases. Take shifters for example. If they commit a crime while they're in bear form, should they be tried as a human or a sapient animal? Drugs, alcohol, and even some common illnesses can affect a shifter's ability to control their animal form. If a solicitor ignores a bear shifter's 'No Solicitors' sign and knocks on the bear's door while the bear is suffering from a fever, and the solicitor then gets mauled, do you try the fever-addled bear who can't control his temper when he's sick? Or do you try him as a man who should have taken more precautions when he first showed signs of illness?"

Deandra blinked several times. She didn't have an answer. And now she was worried about ever running into a bear shifter with the sniffles.

"Then there are beings like yetis—they're very clearly more animal than human in appearance. Yet they can hold a conversation just like we are now, they have an intelligence that rivals—and often exceeds—a human's, and they're able to integrate into society. Despite all that, they usually fall into the sapient animal category," Cruz said. "Much to their chagrin."

Deandra thought of the Clarion family of pixies she'd met. Even though the creatures were tiny, they were humanoid, intelligent, and used spoken language to communicate. According to the pixies, however, their grievances had to go through Parks Management because they were too small to be considered "people"—which didn't seem to be an accurate term anyway, given how many species lived in Axia. Deandra hoped the pixies at least were classified as sapient.

"Can you speak telepathically to shifters in their animal form?" she asked.

He nodded. "Yep. And that's something that doesn't even happen between shifters. It's a very odd quirk of my ability, but it's proven helpful when a shifter is very ill or injured and is stuck in their animal form. It's better for them to come to someone like me, rather than go to the hospital, because the shifters can speak to me."

And here Deandra was, thinking Cruz only dealt with smaller animals. She eyed the center island he rested against and tried to picture a bleeding grizzly bear lying atop it.

Cruz must have sensed where her brain had gone, because he said, "There's a larger facility behind this one that caters to the ... uhh, bigger patients."

"I can't imagine Mitzy's little heart would hold out if a bear came stumbling into the lobby," Deandra said.

Cruz laughed. "Exactly." He looked down at Havoc, who now lay on his belly in the space between them, his limbs splayed in four directions. He was fast asleep. His ability to go from a hundred miles an hour to conked out still amazed her. "Sapient animals like Havoc are a curious case. Shifters are humans first but can shift seamlessly into animals. While there is a precedent for dragons being able to shift forms, they're dragons first. The ability to change forms—not always to a human form, either—depends on the dragon's lineage. Seeing as I've never met a dragon before Havoc, I don't know how my ability is going to manifest with him. I'll tell you now that, despite being a member of his pod, we're unable to speak telepathically. I've tried quite a few times already. But that may change as he ages."

Somehow, it felt as if Deandra and Cruz had just gotten thrown into a joint custody agreement for a child that had adopted *them*.

She remembered all over again that Havoc's original owner was still out there and might come back for him. She knew Cruz had put out feelers online, asking if anyone was missing a dire wolf, but the last she'd heard, there'd been no bites. She figured he'd tell her if anyone had made inquiries, but she was also actively *not* asking.

One didn't get answers one didn't want if one didn't ask the questions in the first place.

Was that healthy? No.

She still wasn't going to ask.

"Does Havoc 'talk' to you in nonverbal ways, like the way your patients do?" Deandra asked, trying to distract herself from the image of a stranger showing up to take her dragon away.

"No," Cruz said, still staring down at the dozing dragon. "I thought my ability might kick in with the whole inclusion-into-the-pod thing, but still nothing. Sentient animals—the vast majority of my clients—speak to me through pictures and feelings. It's not a perfect form of communication, and without a ton of practice, there's room for a lot of error. Heck, there's room for error even *with* practice. And just like people, every animal is different. It takes a lot of patience and listening."

"No pictures or feelings *at all* from Havoc?" Deandra asked, hoping there wasn't something defective in the dragon, something that Cruz hadn't found yet. Maybe the Quowlaxliquin had lasting effects after all.

"Nope," Cruz said, though he sounded more intrigued than concerned. "But dragons are new for me. Something new to research," he added cheerfully.

A knock sounded on the door, and Cruz stood straight, checking his watch. "Mm. I think we're still okay on time. One second …"

The moment Cruz pulled open the door, a small, croaky howl sounded in the distance. Havoc woke with a start but otherwise didn't move.

"Mitzy's appointment still isn't for another twenty minutes, but I just needed to warn you," one of the techs said from the other side of the door. If Deandra concentrated really hard, she could hear everything the tech was saying, even with the howling and general commotion from the lobby. "Mr. Pinyon's hedgehog got loose again, somehow got into the lobby, and snuck up next to Mitzy. Mitzy got so scared, she almost expired on the spot. Mitzy's mom is scared of rodents, so she's currently standing *on* the counter. She abandoned Mitzy on the bench seat, which is too high for Mitzy to jump off … hence, the howling."

Deandra winced.

"Oh boy," Cruz said. "Put Mitzy in Exam 4. I was trying to keep that one open, since Mrs. Tawny's calves are due soon. Did you catch Needles? I don't understand how a hedgehog with a foot in a cast keeps getting out of her cage."

"Yeah, Needles is locked up again. I put her in the magic-dampening cage, just in case. I know the owner thinks Needles is mundane, but I'd bet money the ghost of Houdini is trapped in that little body."

"All right," Cruz said. "Thanks, Elise. I'll be out soon."

"Sorry for the interruption, Miss Hendricks and Havoc!" the tech called out.

"No problem!" Deandra called back.

Havoc chirped his agreement.

Cruz closed the door and sagged against it. "Sorry about that. It's been wild in here. One of the other doctors gets back from vacation today, but she's over an hour late, so I'm pulling double duty." He rubbed the spot between his eyes. "Sorry. Too much information. Was there, uh, anything else you wanted to ask me?"

She suddenly wanted to ask him if he wanted to grab dinner or go bowling or something later, because he looked stressed. She still wasn't sure if she'd mean that platonically or as a date—he really *was* handsome—so she just stared at him dumbly for entirely too long before blurting, "Do I need a distemper shot?"

He blinked several times. "Excuse me, what?"

She did her best to succinctly explain her new gig pet sitting for Barnaby the frilled dendrune.

"First of all, I'm genuinely impressed you're able to walk him," Cruz said. "His thoughts are … somehow both chaotic and simple."

"That tracks," Deandra muttered.

"Second," he said, smiling, "I don't know how many times I've told Angela this, but Barnaby can't get distemper. *Humans* can't get distemper. The worst threat Barnaby poses to you is probably salmonellosis—and as long as you wash your hands after handling him or anything in his cage, you'll be fine."

"Even if he bites me?"

"*Has* he bitten you?" Cruz asked, brows hiking in concern.

"No. He's never even gotten close, but Angela made it sound like he'd bitten her recently," Deandra said.

"Her husband inherited the dendrune through a family friend who passed away. They quickly realized they didn't know what they were in for when they got Barnaby," Cruz said. "Angela was doing some research and found a *single* article from years ago that detailed someone who was bitten by a dendrune, contracted botulism, and then perished in a rather excruciating manner. Angela's been terrified of the possibility ever since. Sounds like her new fixation is distemper, which doesn't even affect reptiles."

Deandra heaved a breath. "Well, that's a relief. Now I have botulism to be scared of, though, so thanks for that."

He grinned. "Between taming a frilled dendrune and being added to a dragon's pod, I have to say I'm more than willing to recommend you to clients if you're serious about starting up this pet-sitting business."

"Oh! Really?" Deandra dug around in her purse sitting on the bench seat beside her. She pulled one of her new business cards from her wallet. "I just got these made."

He took the card and stared at it, smiling softly. "These are great. And yes, I'm happy to recommend you if the topic of needing a sitter comes up. You vouched for *me*, after all," he said, gesturing to Havoc, who had conked out again.

"Well, thank you," Deandra said. "I should probably let you get back to work instead of answering my endless questions, though. Mitzy awaits."

He sighed. "That she does." He headed for the door and pulled it open. "Havoc has an official all-clear from me. The techs will be in touch in a few months for a routine checkup."

Deandra slung her purse over her shoulder and grabbed Havoc's leash. With a gentle tug, he was wide awake and trotting for the door.

Cruz squatted to give Havoc a scratch under his chin. "Thanks again, buddy," he whispered. "I'm truly honored."

Havoc licked his chin.

Cruz stood and stepped out of the way to let Deandra pass. "Good to see you again, Dee."

"You too," she said, again considered asking if he wanted to hang out sometime, couldn't figure out how to word it, felt her face flame hotter than a thousand suns, and decided against saying anything. She scuttled past him and down the hall. She'd almost reached the door that led into the lobby when Cruz called her name.

When she turned around, he was leaning against the doorway of the exam room. "You *do* remember you owe me lunch, right?"

She tried very hard to tamp down a smile and failed miserably. "I'm still getting my business off the ground, so the only thing I can afford is a picnic in the park. And by picnic, I mean a bag of chips and a soda from a vending machine."

He shrugged. "Don't threaten me with a good time. Tell me the time and vending machine, and I'll be there."

"I'll text you."

"Sounds good."

Not even the sound of Mitzy howling plaintively from down the hall dampened Deandra's mood as she and Havoc left the office.

CHAPTER FOUR

Wendy was home by the time Deandra and Havoc returned, padding down the hallway with her damp hair hanging around her shoulders. It was only a little before five o'clock, but Wendy looked exhausted already. She'd gotten back into town late the night before, then had to be up for a full day of work today. She'd picked up sandwiches on her way home, if the plastic bag sitting on the dining room table was any indication.

After filling Havoc's bowl with raw ground beef, broccoli, and two tomatoes sliced into wedges, Deandra left her dragon to eat in the kitchen before joining Wendy at the table.

"I thought it was my night to cook dinner," Deandra said, unwrapping her turkey sandwich.

"I'll probably be asleep in an hour, so I didn't want you to waste the effort," Wendy said, practically shoving an entire fistful of chips into her mouth.

Deandra eyed her warily. "Rough day at work?"

A haunted look flitted across her cousin's face. "We hosted another potion-making class today. Long story short, I was turned into a rabbit for two hours."

Deandra choked on a bite of her sandwich. She coughed and pounded on her own chest. "Come again?"

Wendy's distant gaze sharpened suddenly, and she stared Deandra dead in the eye. "It was the scariest two hours of my life. I don't understand how rabbits live like that! I was scared of literally everything for two hours—but in rabbit years, that was essentially a decade. It shaved years off my life."

Deandra tried hard not to laugh. "Did you, uh, get turned back magically, or did the magic just wear off?"

"It wore off," Wendy said as she stared into the middle distance again, her eyes comically large. "The witch kids' moms put together a potluck lunch—partly as a thank you to Heather for offering to host the event once a month. It's also Heather's birthday next week. I was *inside* a Jell-O bowl when the spell wore off. Do rabbits even *like* Jell-O? I don't like Jell-O as a human!"

Deandra tucked her lips between her teeth.

"Hence the shower," Wendy said, pulling on a chunk of her still-damp hair. "One of the moms was in the break room getting something out of the fridge. She hadn't realized a rabbit was going to town on the Jell-O until I suddenly materialized as a full sized human. She screamed. I screamed. The table beneath me collapsed, and all the food and I hit the floor."

A snort escaped. "I'm sorry." Deandra coughed. "Are you okay?"

"My tailbone hurts, but otherwise okay. Other than, you know, my pride and dignity," Wendy said.

Deandra waved a dismissive hand. "Pah! Who needs that stuff anyway?"

"I also can't stop thinking about carrots."

Deandra lost it. Wendy cracked a smile, which turned into a light chuckle, then morphed into a hysterical cackle. That set Deandra off even more, and eventually they were both scream-laughing.

"Deandra!" Wendy wheezed, holding her side. "I bit a child on the ankle!"

Deandra nearly fell out of her chair.

Havoc, clearly concerned about the racket, stumble-hopped into the chair next to Deandra, his gaze swiveling back and forth between her and Wendy. He was grinning at them, seemingly happy to be involved, even if he had no idea what was going on.

When they had finally calmed down, Deandra said, "I *am* sorry it was a stressful day."

Wendy wiped at her eyes with a napkin. "Thanks. I do feel better, though. Maybe now there won't be any lagomorph night-mares tonight." When Deandra cocked a brow, Wendy added, "I spent a lot of time looking up rabbit-related terminology to broaden my vocabulary in case I develop a debilitating phobia."

"A totally logical use of your time," Deandra said, laughing.

"Ut!" Wendy said sharply, making Deandra jump. She followed the trajectory of Wendy's pointed finger and found Havoc's front paws on the table and his mouth dangerously close to Deandra's dinner.

He'd frozen mid sandwich heist and rolled his eyes toward Deandra.

Deandra shook her head. Havoc harrumphed and sat back, dejected.

"You know dog—*dragon*—feet aren't allowed on the table," Wendy admonished, her eyeline hovering a good foot above Havoc's head.

"I think Dr. Caddel asked me out," Deandra said suddenly, remembering then that Havoc had looped the vet into the pod. Deandra left that part out though, not wanting Wendy to feel bad that she apparently hadn't earned Havoc's trust yet.

Wendy's eyes went comically large again. "Give me every detail from the beginning."

When Deandra finished her tale, Wendy was beaming. "Maybe your mom will be less freaked out about you moving to Axia if you bag a doctor."

They both knew that wasn't the kind of thing that mattered in the slightest to Tempest Hendricks, but if Deandra started dating someone, it *might* be enough to finally get her mother to set foot back in a hub.

Deandra's phone chimed the tone she'd assigned to her new business email, and she rushed to pick it up. The last three emails she'd gotten were spam messages—one from a telephone company hoping to be her choice for her nonexistent call center, one offering a discount on office supplies, and one from a scheduling app company that specialized in pet-sitting businesses. Obviously, when she'd registered her new business name, several other businesses had been notified that there was fresh chum in the water. She wasn't sure if it was comforting or not that the same predatory business practices that plagued the mundane world existed within the hub system, too.

This new email wasn't spam, though.

Hello from a fellow Axian Pet Sitter!

Hi, Dee. My name is Sarah. I'm the owner of Pawsome Pals! I just happened across your website (I have web alerts set up to notify me of everything and anything pet-sitting related in Axia!), and I wanted to welcome you to the fold!

This is short notice, but every Monday (today!) a group of local pet sitters, their partners (business, platonic, and/or romantic!), and their pets meet for happy hour from 6 to 7pm at Gorgon's Alley. Don't worry. The only gorgons are the ones in the decor. It's a bowling alley connected to a bar with outdoor seating. It's a lot of fun. Please join us if you can! We'd love to meet you!

Best,
Sarah

Deandra stared at the message, not sure how to feel. Sarah was either exceedingly friendly—as all the exclamations points would imply—or she was a bit of a stalker.

Maybe she was just nice.

Or maybe she was trying to size up the competition.

Foul-mouthed Harmony the gnome had both sung Sarah's praises and besmirched grouchy Lydia's name, which tracked with Deandra's albeit limited information. All current evidence pointed to Sarah being nice. Maybe Sarah wanted to get to Deandra before Sarah's nemesis Lydia did.

"You gonna share with the class?"

Deandra snapped out of her musings to find both Havoc and Wendy staring at her. "I know you're tired, but do you want to go to happy hour at Gorgon's Alley?"

Wendy cocked her head. "Was that an invite from Dr. Cruz and you're too scared to go alone so you want to bring me along as a buffer? If so, the answer is no. If it's from literally *anyone* else, I'm in."

"Someone else."

Wendy pushed away her chair and stood in one fluid motion. Her sandwich was already gone. Deandra had barely gotten through half of hers. "How long do I have?"

Deandra checked the time on her phone. It was just after five thirty. "I don't know where Gorgon's Alley is, but happy hour starts at six. Is half an hour enough time?"

"I'll be ready in ten," Wendy said definitively, then scurried down the hallway.

"Hurry! I need to shower."

"You can't rush perfection!"

"Perfection only needs ten minutes?"

Wendy gasped in mock horror from clear down the hall. "Don't question my abilities!"

Deandra ravenously attacked her sandwich. Out of the corner of her eye, she was aware that Havoc was in his dejected Eeyore pose beside her, but she wasn't sure if it was because she hadn't shared her now-soggy sandwich with him or because he thought he was going to be abandoned in the apartment alone. She'd scarfed her sandwich down so fast that she'd practically inhaled it.

Turning in her seat, she stared down at her sad dragon, who gazed forlornly at the table. "You're invited, too."

Havoc's head shot up. He stared at her a beat, then quick as a snake, wrapped his forelegs around her neck and licked her ear. She laughed and gently shoved him away.

"Now I *really* need a shower!" Deandra said, as she quickly cleared the table of trash and food scraps, then joined Wendy in the delicate dance of two ladies scrambling to get ready in a small apartment with only one bathroom.

The trio was out the door in fifteen minutes. Havoc hung his head out the back window of Wendy's car, snapping at the air as it wafted over his face.

As Wendy drove, Deandra explained who they were meeting at Gorgon's Alley and what Harmony the gnome had told Deandra about the tumultuous past between the two rival pet sitters, Sarah and Lydia. She also mentioned the odd detail that, though Lydia claimed to be an animal empath, she might be a fraud.

"Weird flex," Wendy said. "Claiming a skill no one can confirm."

"I wonder if there *is* a way, though," Deandra said, thinking about what Cruz had told her about his own zoolinguistic ability. "I don't know if there's some kind of special magical certification

Cruz had to get to officially be labeled as a zoolinguist, but he doesn't really strike me as a guy who's BS-ing the whole town."

"Well, of course *you* think he's trustworthy," Wendy said, offering Deandra a wide grin and dramatically waggling eyebrows.

"Pay attention to the road so we don't end up in a ditch," Deandra muttered irritably, as if she and Wendy were teenagers again, teasing each other about their crushes.

Her childish reply was made even more ridiculous by the fact that they were idling behind a station wagon waiting at a red light. They hadn't moved in a full minute.

"Yes, *Mom*," Wendy sing-songed. "But you're right. Dr. Caddel is well respected in town. So is the other main vet there—I don't know her name, though. The friend I mentioned a while back who has the pygmy phoenix? She swears by Dr. Caddel. The phoenix had a cough, and my friend took it to a non-zoolingual vet in town first. The meds didn't totally clear the cough, so a few weeks later, she took Sparky to Dr. Caddel for a second opinion. She said it was like watching him have a one-sided conversation, but she could also tell they were *actually* communicating. Dr. Caddel found some kind of rare bacterial infection. Apparently, if it hadn't been treated when it was, Sparky wouldn't have lasted more than a few months."

"Seems risky of Lydia to claim she can communicate with animals in cases where their lives might be in danger," Deandra said.

"Sounds like Lydia has questionable morals anyway, if Harmony is right, and Lydia stole clients from Sarah," Wendy said. "Claiming to be an animal medium is probably an easy way to make good money if you can get past the whole swindling-the-bereaved thing."

Deandra laughed. "I guess so. It would be hard to prove whether or not someone is talking to animals, but it would be even harder to prove in the case of *ghost* animals." She wrinkled her nose. "It's a really crappy thing to do."

Havoc peeped from the back seat. Deandra wondered if he'd been hanging on to their every word and was now offering his agreement with Deandra's most astute observations. But when she glanced into the back, she found him furiously flicking his tongue in and out of his mouth. Then he gagged, his whole body convulsing as he made the sound all pet owners recognize instantly.

"Don't you dare vomit in my car, Havoc!" Wendy said, gaze flicking to the rearview mirror several times. "Do I pull over?"

"I don't—" Deandra started to say.

Hork!

Havoc threw up a mangled grasshopper onto the upholstery.

"Havoc!" Wendy said. "Rule number one is no paws on the table. Rule number two is no barfing in my car."

Havoc belched.

Wendy moaned pitifully.

Though Deandra's face contorted in disgust at the mess on the seat, Havoc must have mistaken her wide-eyed stare because he quickly gobbled the grasshopper back down as if was worried she was going to snatch up the insect for herself. He grinned at her, then stuck his head back out the window, mouth agape, apparently hoping to find another tasty treat—even though he'd nearly choked on the last one.

How Ranger Vicks had ever thought Havoc was capable of masterminding a complicated arson plot was beyond her.

CHAPTER FIVE

G orgon's Alley sat at the back of a shopping center, the view of its front blocked by innocuous businesses, including a dry cleaner and a hoof, claw, and nail salon—which was probably wise, as the entrance to the place was terrifying. The building itself was constructed of dark, smooth, unadorned cement, though there was a sheen to it that reminded Deandra of damp river rocks. The building was rectangular, and the literal mouth of the entrance sat directly in the middle.

Two glass doors filled the open maw of a roaring stone gorgon head. A pair of massive stone bowling pins bracketed the head, serving as pillars. Half a dozen snakes jutted out around the opening—one twisting around a bowling pin. The snakes and the gorgon herself all sported shiny black eyes made of ebony, and the closer Deandra got, the more she suspected that at least a few of the eye sockets held cleverly disguised security cameras.

Even Havoc seemed disconcerted by the façade, pressing himself against Deandra's leg as they walked into the shadow cast by the gorgon's snakes. One such snake hovered directly above the walkway, its head turned just slightly so its eye—roughly the size of Deandra's fist—could watch as people entered the building. The promised outdoor seating area wasn't immediately visible.

Wendy strolled in first but had to double back to hold the door open for Deandra, because as soon as Havoc heard the first crash of ball against pins, he'd gone as still as one of the gorgon's snakes. After lots of shoving to no avail, Deandra hoisted the big baby off the ground to carry him in. He wrapped his forelegs around her neck—though they didn't make it all the way around —and pressed both back legs into her sides. She could only imagine what she looked like to the patrons, walking in with a dire wolf puppy clinging to her like a koala.

Deandra couldn't take in much of the decor, what with a good chunk of her vision being blocked by a shivering dragon, but the place smelled like disinfectant spray, oil, and stale fries, just as any good bowling alley should, mundane or not. The threadbare carpet was patterned with a busy repeating design of owls, fists holding thunderbolts, and winged shoes, so she figured the place heavily leaned into its Greek god theme.

Wendy asked the teenage boy eyeing Havoc warily from behind the shoe rental counter for directions, and then she led Deandra and her scaredy-cat dragon through a set of heavily tinted glass doors near a small arcade packed with screaming and laughing kids.

Once safely outside on the covered patio, Deandra got Havoc back on the floor, though Wendy had to help peel the little guy off Deandra's front. Spade-tipped tail tucked between his legs, Havoc melted to the floor as if he'd turned into a puddle.

Deandra huffed a laugh and squatted in front of him. "I'm sorry, boy. I didn't even think about how loud a bowling alley would be. You're always so fearless. I can take you back home and you can watch cartoons, okay? No more scary adventures for you. I was going to get you a hot dog as a thank you for hanging out with me and helping keep me calm while I'm meeting new people, which is even scarier to me than bowling alleys are to you. But if you'd be happier at home, I can drop you off."

Wendy squatted beside Deandra, both of them facing the tinted doors that led back to the bowling alley. Wendy had apparently picked up on Deandra's strategy. "And *I* was going to get you a bacon cheeseburger. Plus, who knows how much stuff gets dropped on the ground here that someone like you could find? You think grasshoppers are good? You haven't tried nachos, my friend. I'm talking cheese sauce."

Cheese had recently been added to Havoc's extensive and quickly expanding list of favorite foods. He seemed to have an iron stomach, limited only by his own preferences.

Havoc's head popped up, and he discreetly licked his lips. He peeped softly. Deandra wasn't sure what the peep meant, but she got the impression he needed more reassurance. Though the thunderous crash of bowling ball against pins was muffled almost entirely for her out here, she figured his superior animal hearing could still detect it.

Something suddenly occurred to her.

"Aw, buddy," she said, petting the top of his head. "Does the sound remind you of being trapped in that dumpster?"

He issued a soft, pitiful howl, then turned his sad puppy dog eyes on full blast. Deandra almost scooped him up and ran home with him right then and there.

"You know you're family, right?" Wendy asked him. "We won't let anything happen to you."

Havoc considered that, then slowly rose into a sitting position. He chirped. A moment later, he sharply craned his neck to peer around Deandra.

Deandra and Wendy glanced over their shoulders in unison. The young woman who was quietly walking their way halted on her ... hooves.

"*She's a faun,*" Wendy whispered to Deandra.

A pair of four-inch-long curving black horns sprouted from the sides of the faun's head of shoulder-length curly light-brown hair. Her ears angled up and out, reminding Deandra of a bunny, though they were only a few inches long. Her facial features came to a point at her small button nose in a more pronounced way than on a human, yet not quite so pronounced that it made her resemble a goat or fox. She was somewhere in between human and animal, making her disconcertingly adorable rather than off-putting.

From the waist down, however, the woman was a goat. Both legs were fully covered in thick light-gray fur and ended in black hooves. She wore a cap-sleeved forest-green dress that hit her knees.

"Hi there," the faun said in a light, pleasant voice. "I'm Sarah. Are you Deandra? I was tipped off by the dire wolf."

Wendy quickly stood, yanking a gaping Deandra up with her. Deandra could hardly process that this whimsical being not only existed but *wasn't* someone in elaborate cosplay at a nerd convention. This was a flesh-and-blood person—who apparently owned and operated a miniature pet-sitting empire in Axia. Wendy elbowed Deandra lightly in the side.

"Ooh, hello!" Deandra blurted, resisting the urge to stomp on Wendy's toes in retaliation. "Sorry. I had to give the pup a little pep talk. The sound of the bowling alley freaked him out."

Sarah thunked herself in the forehead. She had perfectly manicured French-tipped nails. "I was in such a rush to email you that I forgot to tell you that you can come in through the back patio entrance. Most of the pet-guests don't like the bustle of the bowling alley either." She smiled brightly. "Everyone else is here. Want to join us?"

"Sure," Deandra said after a beat of hesitation, reminding

herself that she'd been wishing for more friends earlier today. Making friends as an adult shouldn't be this stressful. Wendy had always been the more extroverted one in high school, pulling Deandra along with her, but Deandra couldn't revert to her teenage tendencies here in Axia. "Thanks for inviting us."

"You bet!" Sarah said. "We're over in the corner."

When Sarah's back was turned, Wendy offered Deandra a dramatic thumbs-up and whispered, "You're doing great!"

Deandra chuckled nervously, some of the tension in her shoulders easing.

Havoc trotted along beside Deandra with no problem, though he stuck close to her side, his tail still tucked underneath him. His tension seemed to ease the farther into the covered patio area they went, distancing themselves from the bowling alley.

A table that ran parallel to one of the long sides of the rectangular patio was ringed by ten chairs. Five of them were occupied. A few feet from the head of the table stood a gate with the word EXIT printed in bright red above it. Deandra gestured at it and glanced down at Havoc. "We'll go out that way when it's time to leave."

He licked the back of her calf in thanks.

A low, freestanding accordion gate blocked off the occupied table and a smaller round one from the rest of the patio. On the other side of the gate, half a dozen animals milled about. The smaller table was piled with harnesses, leashes, and a wide variety of treat bags.

Sarah stopped at the gate and turned around. "We're such regulars here, the staff blocks this area off for us every Monday. They even bought the gate for us! We're the only ones with access to the gate code for the exit, so we don't have to worry about a random person coming by and accidentally setting the animals loose."

With that, Sarah opened a latch in the middle of the accordion gate and stepped through. Deandra, Wendy, and Havoc followed, quickly getting the gate closed again before a pushy potbellied pig could make its escape.

Deandra unhooked Havoc's leash from his harness and then braced herself. She was worried that the other animals would be intimidated by Havoc's glamoured size. After a moment of silence, where the established animals stood in a pack on one side of an invisible line and Havoc on the other, an all-black German shepherd crept forward. Havoc stood stock-still. When the shepherd's nose was an inch from Havoc's glamoured one, a pink tongue shot out and booped Havoc over the nose. Somehow Havoc felt it, even though his actual nose was several inches lower.

And that was it.

Initiation complete.

Havoc dropped into play stance. The shepherd mimicked him. A raven croaked from the back of a nearby chair, and, like a checkered flag was waved at a car race, the two "dogs" were on each other—albeit very playfully. The rest of the animals resumed their previous activities as if Havoc had always been part of the group. Deandra heaved a breath of relief. Her dragon had made friends; now it was her turn.

Deandra wasn't sure if she was imagining it, but the smell of pine wafted past her. It was a crisp, comforting scent, instantly making her think of Christmas morning with her parents. When Deandra glanced around the assembled group—animals included—everyone had their attention focused on Sarah.

Curious.

"Sorry to interrupt, everybody," Sarah said, casting her smile around like the sweep of a flashlight beam chasing away shadows. "But I want to introduce the newcomers. We have Deandra Hendricks, Axia's newest pet sitter ..."

The group of people sitting at the table waved. Deandra angled a gentle elbow into her cousin's side, knowing without looking at her that Wendy was about to chant, "*Speech! Speech!*"

Wendy's muffled "Oof!" was drowned out by Deandra saying,

"Hi, everyone. Please call me Dee. This is my cousin Wendy. The dire wolf is Havoc."

Havoc chirped in greeting. Several people flinched at his apparently loud bark.

"Come, come, have a seat," Sarah said, gesturing to the table. "We already ordered a bunch of apps, but someone will be by to grab drink orders soon."

There was a flurry of chairs scraping on cement as people shuffled around—moving bags off empty chairs and making room for the new arrivals. Deandra ended up sitting along the side closest to the patio's wall, between Wendy and a middle-aged man who at first glance looked as human as herself. But after Harmony's revelation that Lydia Monroe was a fire elemental, Deandra knew better than ever that appearances could be deceiving in Axia.

Aside from herself, Wendy, and Sarah, there were five others in attendance. They went around the table introducing themselves. Three were sitters under Sarah's employ at Pawsome Pals, and the other two were free agents, like Deandra. After the introductions were over—and Deandra had promptly lost her already tenuous hold on everyone's names—Sarah aimed a beaming smile at Deandra. The faun sat directly across from her and had her folded hands propped under her delicate chin as she sized Deandra up.

"So, Dee! Tell us *all* about you," Sarah said. "Where do you hail from? Any special abilities? What are your plans for the future? Do you—"

The guy next to Deandra chuckled. He was fair skinned, had short graying brown hair, and a dusting of day-old stubble marked the start of a beard. "Let her get settled before you give her the third degree, Sarah." He slightly leaned toward Deandra. "Trust me, I know what this is like. I was the new guy only a year ago. Happy I get to pass the mantle to someone else."

Color flooded up Sarah's neck, across her face, and bloomed along her rabbit-like ears. She winced. "I'm so sorry, Dee. I swear this is me trying to be friendly."

The guy stage-whispered, "Sarah's got a nurturing ability. Part of the whole faun thing. It's tied to fauns needing to tame wildlife back in the fae realm or some such. Fauns were often shepherds and farmers. Anyway, when Sarah's anxious—which is a *lot* lately—the nurturing ability goes on the fritz and turns her into something more like a nitpicky, borderline judgmental, helicopter mom."

Sarah scoffed good-naturedly. "I'm not *that* bad."

Two of the women at the table visibly winced, while another grabbed a glass of water to *hide* her wince. Sarah sat back hard in her chair, arms crossed, though she still looked more amused than upset.

Deandra cleared her throat. "I have a question for *you*, actually."

Sarah perked up. "Shoot."

"So, uh, Axia's not that big, all things considered," Deandra said, wilting a little under all the sudden attention angled at her from strangers. "Is there room here for a team as big as yours *and* individuals trying to forge their own paths?"

It wasn't until the question was out of her mouth that she realized it might have been a rude thing to ask, indirectly implying that the "free agents" at the table were doomed to fail because Sarah had created a pet-sitting monopoly.

Instead of uncomfortable looks, several of the attendees nodded or smiled knowingly.

"Totally valid question," Sarah said. "It's a big part of why I set up this weekly happy hour in the first place. Not everyone is coming into the business for the same reason—some are retired and are just looking for an excuse to get out of the house, some need supplemental income, and others want full-time work. It felt important to have a group where we could share what we're all looking for, and then we could pass jobs along to others if we believe someone else would be a better fit. I've been in business for ten years, and I've made full-time income for nine of them.

Some of my employees are full time, some part time, and I *still* pass on business to other sitters all the time."

"For better or worse," the guy next to her muttered under his breath, but Sarah either didn't hear him or chose to ignore the comment. Deandra was almost positive his name was Keith.

"The hub system helps a lot, too," a woman a few chairs down said. She was around Deandra and Wendy's age, and other than the lavender hue of her skin and her vibrant green catlike eyes, she looked human. "I was born and raised in Axia, but I wanted to work in a different hub, just to mix things up a bit. Sarah helped me get a client base going in Kensey, which is five times the size of Axia. Almost all my clients are over there, and even though it's in a totally different state, I can commute from California to Washington in twenty minutes, assuming the lines in the telepad station aren't too long."

"Fialova was overwhelmed by the business side of everything," Sarah said, gesturing to the lavender-skinned woman. "So I set up an arm of Pawsome Pals in Kensey, and Fialova got so busy there, we hired an additional Kensey-based sitter just last month to help out."

"I *tried* to recruit Keith to work with me out there, but Axia got her claws into another one," Fialova said, grinning at Keith.

"His entrepreneurial spirit was just too strong," Sarah said wistfully.

"Eh, don't give me that much credit," Keith said, waving a dismissive hand. "I just didn't want you taking a cut."

"Oh, don't listen to him. Working for Sarah is *so* worth it," Fialova said, addressing Deandra. "I don't have to deal with most of the admin stuff. She does scheduling, billing, *taxes*—all of it. I just show up and take care of the pets. It's ideal for me."

Sarah beamed an almost motherly smile at Fialova. There was a definite nurturing air to the faun, and even if there was magic at work under the surface, it seemed genuine.

Wendy rested her forearms on the table, having been uncharacteristically quiet for a while. "Can I ask a potentially super-nosy question?"

"Absolutely!" a woman at the end of the table said. The raven was apparently hers, as it was sitting directly on top of the woman's head, preening its feathers. She was in her sixties, Deandra guessed, and the bird had made an absolute mess of the woman's heavily gray-streaked black hair. Twigs, dried leaves, a few feathers, and something small and shiny stuck out of the ... well, nest. Deandra wondered if that was where the bird lived. "Sarah says this group is all about transparency and sharing trade secrets, blah, blah. And it is! But would this group be worth *anything* if there wasn't a healthy amount of gossip?"

"And griping!" Keith said from beside Deandra. "Griping openly and without remorse with colleagues keeps you from sending obscenity-laced, passive-aggressive text messages to rude clients. Isn't that right, Tansy?"

Tansy the bird lady wrinkled her nose, then shot a pointed look at Deandra and Wendy. "It's the kind of mistake you only make once."

"*Twice*," Fialova coughed, then hastily picked up her water glass and pretended to sip. Plain silver bands ringed nearly every one of her lavender fingers, and her nails were painted dark purple.

Sarah laughed. "What's the question, Wendy?"

"We heard that there's another sitter in town—Lydia Monroe? There was something about a falling-out? Is that true? Does she come to these happy hours, too?"

That sucked the mirth out of the group in an instant.

Tansy articulated her opinion about Lydia using so many curse words, Harmony the gnome would have high-fived her. Fialova must have flushed hot because her cheeks went almost as dark as her nail polish. Keith harrumphed and muttered something that sounded like "backstabbing liar." The other two women stared into the middle distance as if lost in their own memories of Lydia.

It was Sarah who finally answered the question. "She's got an open invitation to join us whenever she wants, but we haven't seen her here in ages. One of my other sitters who isn't here yet is still friends with her. They both moved to Axia from other hubs around the same time and bonded over being the new girls in town. I hired them both on the same day. Even though Mavis still works for me and is a very loyal employee, she and Lydia are like sisters. That falling-out, as you say, is still a bone of contention between the three of us, but we're making it work. I like to think so, anyway."

"That's because you're entirely too nice," Tansy said. "Or that nurture faun magic of yours blinds you, I don't know. Lydia doesn't show up here because she knows we'd kick her butt into the next century if she did. No one messes with Sarah."

A heavy quiet fell over the group.

Keith cleared his throat. "I, uh, heard she landed the Basnet gig."

Sarah's head jerked back as if she'd been slapped. That comforting scent of pine drifted past Deandra again, only this time the smell soured and went acrid as if the pine forest was now on fire. The raven croaked loudly and abruptly launched off Tansy's head. One of the milling dogs issued a low howl. The potbellied pig snorted in agitation.

Deandra peered under the table to find Havoc tucked between her feet. Maybe he could also smell the forest fire smell Sarah was apparently giving off. His big doe eyes pleaded for an explanation she couldn't give him.

Fialova placed a gentle hand on Sarah's arm. "Sorry, girl. I know you fought hard for that job."

That seemed to snap Sarah out of her silent—though pungent—rage. She gave her head of perfect ringlets a shake. Deandra idly wondered if the horns on her head were heavy. Deandra's neck ached just looking at them.

"Wonder what lies she told Mrs. Basnet," Tansy muttered. "Probably preyed on the poor woman's emotions."

"And claimed to have skills she doesn't actually possess," Keith added.

Fialova said, "She can barely handle Goldie's antics. Does she really think she can handle a baby yeti who's so wild, he was kicked out of daycare?"

The group at large chuckled.

Recalling her one and only interaction with the apparently infamous Lydia Monroe, Deandra asked, "Have any of you worked with Barnaby the dendrune?"

Now the group collectively groaned. Keith, Tansy, Fialova, and Sarah all raised their hands.

"Did Angela really fire *all* of you?" Deandra asked, surprised.

"Fire us? No," Sarah said, brow creased. "I think she contacted Keith first. After a month of not being able to get Barnaby out of his cage, he suggested Angela contact Tansy to see if she'd have better luck."

"When *I* failed," Tansy said, "I passed Angela on to Sarah's team."

"I ran *all* of my employees through in three-week spans each," Sarah said. "No one could get Barnaby out. He bit all of us. He was so scared of me, he fainted at least twice."

"I got him out once," Tansy said, her tone a touch haunted. "He projectile-vomited all over me and *then* fainted."

"Sounds like Lydia had just as much trouble," Deandra said. "I was out walking him when I met Lydia. She told me Angela had fired her and every sitter before her because Angela was both too picky and unwilling to pay a reasonable wage."

"Definitely sounds like something that … *woman* would say," Keith muttered. "She just didn't want to admit that she'd failed. So *you're* the one who finally tamed that little dinosaur?"

Deandra nodded, feeling a bit embarrassed for some reason. All these people had far more experience than she did; Deandra had just gotten lucky—if one could call it that—that Barnaby liked her.

"You must have the magic touch." Then Tansy gasped and

leaned forward. "*Do* you have a magical touch with animals? Are you a zoolinguist?"

Deandra laughed, holding up her hands. "Mundane through and through."

A harried waitress all but crashed to a stop outside the accordion gate. "Whew! I'm *so* sorry it's been so long. Dual birthday parties are happening right now, and the mothers of each of the birthday boys hate each other. We had to beg a practicing bowling league to move over several lanes so they'd be a buffer between the two parties. Everyone in there is peeved. I swear your food is coming up soon. Can I get drink orders? First round is on the house!"

Everyone quickly pored over the drink menus. All the names were a nod either to the Greek god theme of the place, the bowling alley, or both. Dionysus's Poison Ivy, The 7-10 Split, Stone Strike, Artemis's Sizzling Turkey.

Deandra settled on the Sour Apple Split, and Wendy took one for the team and got a soda since she was the night's designated driver.

A waiter hustled out onto the patio within a few minutes, carrying a massive tray piled with sliders, nachos, chicken wings, and beer-battered vegetables.

Everyone had tucked into their appetizers and drinks, and they were chatting amiably when another woman came running up to the accordion gate with such speed, she almost pitched over it. Deandra expected it to be another waitress, but the outfit was all wrong.

The raven croaked loudly and landed in Tansy's hair once more. Havoc and the other animals stood at the gate, gazing up at the heaving woman.

Sarah's hooves clomped sharply on the cement as she hurried to the woman and grabbed her hands. "Mavis, what the heck is the matter?"

Mavis's gaze frantically searched Sarah's face, scanned the

happy-hour group, and then settled on Sarah again. "You ... you really haven't heard?"

The fresh scent of pine swept through the patio area. Deandra could almost see some of the tension leach from Mavis's shoulders.

"Heard what?" Sarah asked, giving Mavis's hands a gentle shake.

Mavis let out a shuddering breath. "Lydia's dead."

CHAPTER SIX

S arah wavered on her hooves. "Mavis, what do you mean
she's dead?"

That inexplicable scent of pine swept past Deandra again.
Mavis took several steps back as Sarah let herself through the
accordion gate. She walked farther into the patio area—back
toward the entrance to the bowling alley—with Mavis hot on her
hooves.

Deandra wasn't sure what to do. Were they just supposed to
wait to see if they'd get more information from Sarah or Mavis?
Would leaving—sprinting away at a high rate of speed—be
considered rude? Everyone at the table seemed stuck in a state of
quiet shock.

"This is so *awkward*," Wendy hissed in Deandra's ear. She sat back and literally twiddled her thumbs, whimpered softly to herself, then sat forward again. In a normal volume she asked, "Does anyone else keep smelling vanilla cupcakes?"

Keith, on Deandra's other side, leaned forward to address Wendy. "That's Sarah's nurture magic again. In situations where tensions are high, her magic gives off a scent that's tied to a comforting memory for whoever is in the vicinity. It's different for everyone. For me, lately, it's the scent of my late wife's favorite perfume."

Deandra was a little relieved to have a distraction by way of idle chitchat, even if Keith's conversation topic wasn't any cheerier than the news of Lydia's sudden death. "I'm glad that's a comfort, and that it doesn't trigger sad memories."

Keith heaved a deep sigh that rounded his shoulders. "Honestly, the first time it happened, the scent was so strong—and eerily accurate—that I went running to the front door, thinking Nancy had somehow come back. It didn't make sense, though, for any number of reasons—Nancy had never been to Axia, let alone to Sarah's house. We'd all gotten together for dinner at Sarah's that night.

"Then I thought maybe Nancy had returned as a ghost, so I ran around the house looking for her specter." His smile was sad. "I'd been coming to these happy hours for at least six months before then, and the scent from Sarah's magic had always been baking bread for me. I remember that dinner so well because Mavis had tricked Lydia into coming: Mavis told Lydia that Sarah wanted to apologize, and she Sarah that *Lydia* was going to apologize. Poor Mavis somehow thought just getting everyone in the same room would force the ladies to resolve their issues.

"I hadn't even met Lydia before then, only heard about her. In all honesty, I thought everything I'd heard had been an exaggeration. Let me tell you, it was all accurate. I felt bad for Mavis. She tried so hard to help Lydia that night; I think Mavis worried about her being too isolated. The confrontation, as you can imagine, didn't go well. Maybe the heightened emotions of that night are what changed the scent of Sarah's magic for me. That's the only explanation I have for why it changed from baking bread to Nancy's perfume. Maybe the magic figured if I could survive a blowout fight between Sarah, Lydia, and Mavis, I could handle anything."

"Even thinking you were being haunted," Deandra said, then mentally winced, worried it had been a tasteless quip.

Luckily, Keith laughed. "Once Sarah realized what had happened, she apologized and explained that she has no control over what scents her magic gives off. She hugged me. I sobbed in her arms like a baby."

"Oh no," Wendy and Deandra said in unison, both laughing awkwardly.

Keith waved this away. "It was cathartic. I cried even harder that day than when I'd learned Nancy died. Which is to say I made an absolute fool of myself in front of everyone—especially Sarah. But I purged something that day. Smelling the perfume makes me smile now. It's like getting a little unexpected visit from her."

What a lovely, odd side effect of Sarah's magic.

Deandra glanced across the patio then, wondering what wonders Sarah's magic was working on Mavis. Because, like Keith had, Mavis was currently sobbing on Sarah's shoulder.

The group at the table quietly picked at their food and made idle, strained chitchat while they waited. Keith and Fialova seemed to have the best rapport.

Sarah appeared to be the glue that held this group together.

Deandra had just "accidentally" dropped a cheese sauce–laden chip on the floor for Havoc when the sound of slow clomping hooves redirected her attention.

Sarah, with her arm around a red-eyed Mavis's shoulder, was headed back toward the table. After the pair was through the gate—once again narrowly preventing the escape of the potbellied pig—Sarah guided the crestfallen young woman to an open seat, putting her next to herself and directly across from Wendy.

Silence descended.

Guilty gazes flicked to Mavis, then away. After all, they'd been lambasting her best friend only minutes before.

It was Tansy who finally broke the ice. "What, uh, what happened? Lydia wasn't sick or anything, was she?"

Deandra's first thought was that it had been a pedestrian accident—surely dog walkers were under constant threat of being hit by cars. Axia was largely a walking town, but cars were used often enough. Someone getting hit because they stepped off the curb in front of a distracted driver surely must happen everywhere.

"She, uh ..." Mavis tried, but her chin wobbled, and she clamped her mouth shut again.

Deandra guessed the young woman was in her mid to late twenties. She was petite, fair skinned, and her straight brown hair fell around her slight shoulders in a shiny sheet. She was dressed in paint-flecked overalls with a white tank top underneath. The casual attire would suggest she hadn't planned to be here for happy hour. Deandra wondered why she'd rushed over to Gorgon's Alley to tell the happy-hour group in person rather than calling Sarah—especially if the relationship between the group and Lydia had been fraught.

"I meant what I told you, Mav," Sarah said in her soothing tone, punctuated by a fresh wave of pine. She had her arm around the small woman's shoulders again and was doing her best to get Mavis to look at her, though Mavis only had eyes for her own lap. "You don't have to talk about this if you don't want to. You don't owe any of us details. I'd be more than happy to drive you home if this is too much."

Owe any of us details seemed to imply that, despite their private chat, Sarah didn't know what had happened to Lydia either.

Mavis shook her head. Her hair was so sleek and shiny, it reminded Deandra of a cascading waterfall when it moved. "No," she said, sniffing and running a hand under her nose. She glanced up and made brief eye contact with everyone. "I can talk about it."

Sarah gave Mavis's shoulder a slight squeeze, then let go.

With one final sniff, Mavis rolled her shoulders back. The look in her red-rimmed eyes was one of determination or resolve now, rather than pure grief. "I wanted to talk to you all in particular because I want to know which one of you killed her."

Deandra's dumbstruck fog cleared a few moments before it did for everyone else. "Wait. Wait, wait. Lydia was *murdered,* and you think someone here was responsible?"

She knew this was an exceedingly serious situation—a *tragic* one—but she couldn't keep incredulity from screwing up her face.

The expression didn't sit well with Mavis, whose nonlinear trip through the five stages of grief had swung back toward anger. "I don't even know who *you* are."

"I'm Deandra … a new pet sitter in town."

"How *convenient* for you that there's now a vacancy in the industry for you to fill," Mavis snapped.

In her previous job, Deandra had dealt with countless people who got furious with her over ludicrous things. It was easier to unleash frustrations on a stranger than on a coworker, boss, partner, friend, or the world. Deandra wasn't put off by Mavis's outburst and instead saw her as if she were a customer who was ticked off that their iced coffee had two pumps of vanilla creamer instead of two and a half.

The fact that Deandra had only met Lydia once, and for only a few minutes, should immediately take Deandra off the suspect list, assuming Axian authorities would even put her on one to begin with. Deep down, Mavis had to know that, aside from Wendy, Deandra was the least likely person there to have anything to do with Lydia's demise. Therefore, Deandra was the easiest person for Mavis to lash out at. So, just as she'd learned to do with grouchy customers, Deandra merely stared at Mavis impassively and let her stew in her tantrum.

Deandra's lack of reaction made Mavis wilt a little.

"You're just hurt," Sarah said soothingly, placing a hand on Mavis's arm.

That was enough to reignite Mavis's fury, and she snatched her arm away from the faun. Turning in her seat, Mavis glared at Sarah. "Was it you? Or did you send one of your *loyal* employees after her because she stole the Basnet job out from under you?"

Using the word "stole" didn't exactly speak highly of Lydia's character, but Deandra knew better than to point that out.

Unlike Deandra, Sarah *did* take offense at Mavis's accusation. "How can you even ask me that? Or accuse my employees? *You're* one of my employees, for Goddess's sake, Mav."

The comforting pine scent that wafted past Deandra morphed into the smell of a raging forest fire again. Deandra's lungs seemed to fill with toxic black smoke she couldn't actually see.

A few of the people at the table coughed. The raven croaked. Havoc howled plaintively from under the table.

The sound of a howling dire wolf was enough to snap Sarah out of her mounting irritation. The acrid, invisible smoke was instantly swept away by a cool breeze.

"What the heck was *that*?" Mavis asked, quickly scooting her chair back so she could poke her head under the table. Havoc peeped a greeting, but the flinch from everyone at the table suggested it had come out as a concussive bark. The sound startled Mavis so badly, she whacked the back of her head on the underside of the table. She sat up, wincing, and glared at Deandra, as if somehow all of this was *her* fault.

Keith spoke up. "What exactly happened, Mav? Look, it's no secret that there was bad blood between us and her, but I'm willing to speak for everyone here when I say none of us would wish for her death."

Several people murmured their agreement.

Mavis sharply leaned forward, the edge of the table pressing into her chest as she looked down the table at Tansy. As vocal and animated as Tansy had been earlier, she'd hardly said a word since Mavis's arrival. "That true of you, too, Tansy? Guess you can stop leaving threatening messages on Lydia's phone now, like the total psycho you are. Unless *you're* the one who pushed her down the stairs; then you're even more of a psycho than I thought."

Sarah's shoulders slumped as she swiveled her focus to the older woman at the foot of the table. The raven croaked irritably from its perch on Tansy's head.

"I thought you said you'd stopped harassing Lydia," Sarah said, sounding much like a disappointed parent.

Tansy's lips pursed, and color rose high in her cheeks. "I haven't called her in a while. And I only ever did when she harassed me first!"

It sounded like an argument a teenager would make, not a grown woman.

Mavis said, "She wasn't harassing you! You really think she had nothing else better to do than waste her time pestering you?"

Tansy folded her arms heavily on the table. In a much calmer tone, she said, "I don't need to prove anything to you, little girl." When she cut a glance toward Sarah, though, her brows furrowed.

"Can you tell us what happened?" Sarah asked.

Tansy seemed like a bit of a wild card. She was fiercely protective of Sarah, but was she *so* loyal, as Mavis implied, that she'd take Lydia out after one offense too many?

Addressing the group, Tansy said, "I don't know what the nature of Lydia's animal empathy really was, but she *could* influence animals. There was a day about a month ago when we bumped into each other at the Mythic Pet Kitchen. She was acting civil enough while we were talking, but it turned out that was subtly using her ability on Rufus at the same time. Rufus all of a sudden launched out of his nest and attacked a man in the next aisle. He dive-bombed his head, was croaking up a storm, and pecked at the man's dog a few times. The dog yelped and ran through the store. Rufus dive-bombed the dog, chasing him up and down the aisles. I was yelling at Rufus to come back. The man was yelling at *me*. That poor dog was yipping, clearly terrified.

Rufus had never done anything like that before. The only time he'd ever acted aggressively was the night some teenage boy tried to steal my purse. Rufus chased him off but never hurt the boy. This … this was as if Rufus was a totally different bird."

Deandra's gaze flicked up to the raven sitting atop Tansy's head. She swallowed nervously.

"The store manager had to come help me catch Rufus with a net. Rufus has excellent recall; a net shouldn't have been necessary. The store manager could have called Parks Management—it was within his right to do so. Goddess knows what might have happened to Rufus then," Tansy said, tears welling in her eyes as she reached up to pet Rufus. The bird closed its eyes and nuzzled affectionately against Tansy's hand. "The manager said he wouldn't call Parks Management if I agreed never to bring Rufus back. He said he was a danger to customers." Tansy lowered her hand and sat back in her chair, arms crossed. "As I was walking out of the store, humiliated, and with Rufus tucked under my arm, Lydia was standing near the front door pretending to be looking in the clearance bin. When no one was in earshot, she said, 'Slander my name again, and I'll make Rufus go after *you* next.' She then offered some very gruesome details about what those injuries would entail."

Jeez.

"You slandered her name?" Sarah asked cautiously. "Did you two get into an online fight again?"

Tansy pursed her lips. "A couple of weeks before that, she left a comment on one of your ads online. She said all kinds of nasty things about you, Sarah. I couldn't let them go unchecked. So I told everyone not to listen to Lydia because she was so bitter and grouchy that she had to poach clients from people with *actual* social skills."

Deandra winced internally.

"She had social skills!" Mavis snapped, though she just sounded petulant.

Staring at Mavis, Tansy said, "So, yeah, a few days after the confrontation in the Pet Kitchen, I called Lydia and left a voice-mail telling her that if she *ever* targeted me, Rufus, or any of my clients again, she'd regret it. It was an empty threat. And it was made in poor taste after I'd had a bit too much wine with dinner."

Fialova said, "I've told you a million times: If you're going to be drinking, you need to put that phone of yours in the freezer."

She'd said it good-naturedly, but a look of concern passed over the woman's lavender-tinted features. Deandra wasn't sure if Fialova was more worried about her friend's penchant for wine or the "empty threat" made against a woman who was now dead under apparently suspicious circumstances.

"How do you know it was murder and not an accident?" Wendy asked. "I mean, people must trip and fall down the stairs all the time. Bathrooms are the most common place people suffer from accidental deaths in their homes. Staircases have to be a close second ..."

Mavis's gaze went a bit distant, her mind traveling back in time as her brown eyes limned with silver. Her bottom lip shook again. "In her townhouse, there's a winder staircase—a set of stairs that leads to a small landing, then the staircase continues to the ground floor. Sort of L-shaped, I guess? Anyway, she ... umm ... she went down that first set of stairs so hard, there's a huge divot in the wall—like a wrecking ball hit it. She couldn't have hit the wall that hard if she accidentally tripped. There were bits of plaster *embedded* in the back of her shirt. They think whoever it was threw her down the first set of steps, picked her up from the first landing, and then tossed her down the second set of stairs to the ground floor. She was found in front of the door." A tear slipped down Mavis's face. "They said the impact with the wall killed her instantly. That's how hard she hit it."

Deandra's throat tightened. Her first impression of Lydia Monroe hadn't been favorable, but no one deserved that kind of treatment. "Were ... were you the one who found her?"

Twin tracks of tears ran down Mavis's face now as she nodded. "I'm her emergency backup for her clients if something happens and she can't make it. She was scheduled to walk Goldie this afternoon. Lydia has been walking Goldie for three years, and she's *always* punctual. Say what you want about her, but she always showed up to her gigs on time.

"Goldie's owner has a camera that faces the front door, so when she didn't get an alert about Lydia's arrival for over two hours after her scheduled time, the owner called me. I said I hadn't heard from her either, so I rushed over to walk Goldie, and then I went to Lydia's place to check on her. I ..." Mavis swallowed. "I have a key, so I let myself in. She ... she was ... I found her at the base of the stairs just inside the front entryway. I could tell immediately that she hadn't survived the fall. I searched for a pulse anyway and her skin was ... already ice cold. Her body was stiff.

"That's when I called the werecats. When they arrived, they had a death witch with them. He said it had been too long since the time of death for him to see all the details, but he saw that the cause of death was from the hard impact with the wall, not the fall. The witch said he wasn't sure Lydia's body had ever touched that first set of stairs at all—as if someone had thrown her. He couldn't tell if it was by strength or magic. He said he could tell the attack had surprised Lydia, and that shortly after that moment of surprise, she was gone. She didn't suffer; it all happened too fast for that."

"I'm surprised they gave you so much information," Wendy said. "Cops usually aren't that forthcoming."

Deandra added, "Officer Sutter *definitely* doesn't give that many details about an on-going case."

Mavis glared daggers at Wendy and Deandra both. She faltered for a moment before saying, "Sounds like a *you* problem."

Scents of pine, hot chocolate, and freshly made pancakes topped with a dusting of powdered sugar swept past Deandra in a decadent wave.

Mavis shot a glare at Sarah now. "That's not going to fix anything."

The faun frowned. "You know I can't control it. My magic wants to soothe anyone who might need it."

"What I *need* is my friend back," Mavis said, her voice breaking on the last word. "Or to know who did this to her." As she angrily wiped away tears, she said, "The death witch put her death somewhere between noon and one I found her just after four thirty."

"Her body was already that cold after only four hours?" Wendy asked.

Several sets of shocked expressions were angled her way.

"Oh my Goddess! I said that out loud. Sorry. I … I watch a lot of true crime."

Keith leaned forward to smile awkwardly at Wendy. "For what it's worth, so do I, and I was thinking the same thing."

"The old lady next door to Lydia kept trying to say she'd heard a commotion around midnight the night before," Mavis said, sniffing. "But that lady can't keep details straight to save her life. She calls the cops on everyone for every little thing. She's called them on Lydia for playing her music too loud in the middle of the afternoon on the weekend. She claims she's got sensitive hearing, which might be true, but she's definitely blind as a bat." She huffed. "Anyway. I'm going to believe professionals over old busybodies and people who *think* they're experts just because they've watched every episode of *Dateline*."

Wendy and Keith kept quiet.

Mavis soldiered on. "I went in to the station to give an official statement after they took her body away. I came straight here afterward." She rolled her shoulders back once more, trying to put on an air of confidence, when she was obviously a wreck. "I gave the police all of your names and phone numbers." Her gaze cut to Deandra and Wendy. "Well, not you two, but I'll tell them about you when I leave."

Mavis abruptly pushed her chair away from the table. After swiping angrily at her face again, brushing away the tears that continued to fall, she said, "I don't want to believe any of you could have done this, but you're the only ones in this whole *stupid* town who hated her. She was my best friend—like a sister—and it makes me sick to think any of you would do something to her. But so help me, I'll do whatever it takes to make sure you go down for this."

Deandra barely knew any of these people, but the idea that any of them despised Lydia enough that they'd kill her was hard to fathom. From what Keith had implied, Lydia had made plenty of enemies over the years. Mavis had gone out of her way six months ago to try to force Sarah and Lydia together in the hope that the ladies could forgive each other. Had Mavis come here, of all places, because, despite disliking Lydia, the group was the closest thing Lydia had to friends?

With one final parting sob, Mavis let herself out of the gate and stalked back across the patio, her shoulders quaking as she walked.

The potbellied pig, sensing that the gate hadn't been properly closed, nosed it open and went galloping into the open area of the patio, squealing in delight at its newfound freedom. A few patrons at the far end of the patio yelped when the pig dove under their table, presumably in pursuit of crumbs.

Deandra cast a wary glance around, eyeing this group she'd only just met, fearing one of them might be a murderer.

CHAPTER SEVEN

Deandra and Wendy sat at Wendy's dining room table in shell-shocked silence. Havoc, apparently wiped out after the excitement of the evening, had fallen asleep in the car. He hadn't stirred when they'd arrived home, so Deandra had to carry him up the stairs. He was currently flat on his back on the dog bed in the living room, snoring softly.

"Well, that was … a lot," Wendy finally said. "That was not at all what I was expecting from a pet-sitter get-together."

There hadn't been much discussion after Mavis's dramatic departure. The waitress had arrived with their drinks shortly afterward. A pointed "we need to get the heck out of here" look from Wendy made Deandra tank her Sour Apple Split, and then the two cousins had issued polite goodbyes before grabbing Havoc and booking it out the patio exit.

Deandra asked, "Do we really think that someone we just spent hours with threw Lydia down the stairs to her death? Because if so, I think that needs to be my last happy hour."

Wendy huffed a laugh. "Yeah, no kidding." After a few moments of thoughtful silence, she added, "My bets are on Tansy. I honestly don't know if she's got some kind of animal-related ability or if she's just a mundane hippie who lets a bird live in her hair, but she seems a little unstable."

"Weird or not," Deandra said, "it doesn't mean she's, A) capable of murder, or B) possesses the strength or magic needed to throw a person into a wall so hard that it can crater it."

"Maybe one of her animal clients is a miniature rhinoceros who obeys her every whim—even murderous ones," Wendy said.

"I'm undecided if you'd be this same level of ridiculous had you not been turned into a rabbit this afternoon."

Wendy shuddered violently.

"Hey, there's *your* alibi, though! You couldn't have hurt Lydia, because the only crime you were committing was against Jell-O."

Wendy gagged and pressed a fist to her mouth. "House rule number three after no paws on the table and no vomiting in my car is that the J-word is banned indefinitely."

While Deandra was feverishly working on a truly terrible pun, she was distracted out of her brilliance by her phone. It was issuing that same business-email chime that had resulted in her and Wendy attending the surprisingly eventful happy hour. She scooped up her phone, hoping there was another email from Sarah full of sordid details.

It wasn't from Sarah, though. Nor was it another spam email.

"Why are you making that face?" Wendy asked.

"Uhh … I'll just read it," Deandra said. "The subject line is 'In need of a new sitter ASAP.' *Hello, Deandra. Though news travels fast in Axia, you may not have heard that your fellow pet sitter, Lydia Monroe, has passed away. I do hope it's not in bad taste that I'm seeking a replacement so soon, but Lydia was due to start services on Wednesday, and I am now in the lurch.*

"*My son, Kiwi, has become too much of a handful for Axian daycare centers. Travel by telepad is still too dangerous for a child his age, so I am unable to take him to a center in Kensey, where I work, that has better resources for a boy like him. He'll be of age for telepad travel in about four months, so this won't be a long-term assignment. I'm impressed that I've already heard of your skills with both a dendrune and a dire wolf, despite your not being in Axia that long. And being a mundane, no less! I hope you're the solution to my problem.*

"*I'm happy to pay the same rate I would pay the daycare center if you're able to care for him from 9 am to 2 pm, five days a week. My husband is home by 2 and can take the little bugger off your hands.*

"*If you're interested, I would love to meet with you tomorrow any time before 6 pm so you can meet me and Kiwi and get a rundown on his care. Please find basic instructions and a payment breakdown attached. Sincerely, Oleander Basnet.*"

Deandra looked up to find Wendy's mouth hanging open.

"Isn't Basnet the name of the client Sarah was trying to get hired by, and then Lydia 'stole' the job from her?" Wendy asked.

Deandra nodded as she clicked on the attachments. She goggled at the rate Oleander Basnet was offering. Blinking rapidly, Deandra placed her phone on the table in front of Wendy. She mostly just needed confirmation from her cousin that her own eyes weren't rearranging decimal places.

Wendy whistled. "Dang. I knew daycare rates were wild, but fifteen hundred bucks a week is crazy."

Okay, so that *was* the number she'd seen.

"Both Fialova and now Oleander have mentioned Kiwi's

trouble at daycare, though," Deandra said. "Oleander said 'too much of a handful,' but Fialova straight up said Kiwi was *kicked out*. Maybe the fifteen hundred is hazard pay."

Wendy laughed.

"Oh gosh! I'm pretty sure Fialova said 'baby yeti.' A baby *yeti*, Wendy? I don't know anything about yetis!"

"You didn't know anything about dragons either, but you're doing great with Havoc."

Deandra chewed on her bottom lip as she read the email again. "I'd have to figure out the logistics of being able to check on Barnaby, too. I'm not going to bail on Angela just because a higher-paying gig came up. Especially when this one is temporary."

When Wendy was quiet for longer than usual, Deandra glanced up, half expecting her cousin to be passed out face down on the table. Instead, she looked deeply concerned.

Deandra put her phone down. "Hey, what's up? Are you reliving a lagomorph memory?"

The fact that Wendy didn't even crack a smile said a lot. "I know we just met all those people, but I liked Sarah a lot—and not just because her magic kept sending me scents of warm vanilla cupcakes. The others were really nice and friendly, too. Even Tansy was kind of cool, in a weird way. Thinking any of them are capable of murder is ludicrous. But, also, Sarah seemed *really* bothered when she heard Lydia had gotten the Basnet job. I don't know what you smelled, but for me, it was like a cupcake shop got doused in gasoline and then set on fire. And, yeah, Sarah is running a little pet-sitting empire, so she's probably doing well financially, but fifteen hundred a week is still a lot of money— who knows what kind of expenses she has if she's also running an operation in Kensey, you know?"

"All this rambling have a direction?" Deandra asked, knowing her cousin was stalling more than anything.

"What if Sarah already knew Lydia had gotten the Basnet job, and she was so mad about it that that was the final straw? Maybe she confronted Lydia about it and pleaded her case for why Sarah should get it instead."

"And what?" Deandra asked. "When Lydia refused, Sarah got so mad she threw her down the stairs?"

Wendy shrugged. "Love, revenge, and money are the main reasons people resort to murder. The last two would apply to Sarah. People have killed for a lot less."

Deandra frowned. Wendy had always been more of a true-crime buff than Deandra. "So you're saying I *shouldn't* take the Basnet job ... in case Sarah comes after me next?"

"I'm just saying be careful is all."

That night, Deandra's dreams were plagued by a giant stone snake who relentlessly chased her through Axia. It eventually caught her in its stone jaws and bodily threw her down an impossibly long staircase. As she lay crumpled on the floor, her vision slowly going dark, the sound of hooves echoed in the distance.

Deandra woke with a start, the fading sound of maniacal laughter ringing in her ears and the faint scent of pine tickling her nose.

BY NOON THE NEXT DAY, DEANDRA HAD CONVERSED WITH OLEANDER Basnet via email a few times, and the two planned to meet at Oracle Park at one thirty. Deandra walked Barnaby, then looped back to the apartment to grab Havoc, figuring it would be good to know if the dragon and yeti were going to get along. If they did, perhaps her dragon could help keep baby Kiwi entertained.

Deandra took Havoc on a long walk around the park before the meeting, knowing it wouldn't tucker the dragon out entirely, but it would at least take the edge off his exuberance. On her walk, she texted Angela.

DEANDRA

Hi, Angela! I wanted to run something by you

ANGELA

OMG, you're not quitting are you? Barnaby loves you!

DEANDRA

No, nothing like that.

ANGELA

Goddess above! Thank you!

Oof.

DEANDRA

I picked up a new client recently, and they need me for 6-hour blocks. Is it okay if I bring my new charge with me when I check on Barnaby? If it's *not* okay, I'll turn this new job down.

ANGELA

😭 😭 😭

Deandra didn't know what the reply meant. She decided to wait Angela out.

ANGELA

You're the sweetest. Of course you can bring the new client to the house! Barnaby needs more socialization anyway. Feel free to bring your puppy anytime, too!

DEANDRA

Thank you!

Deandra shrugged and pocketed her phone. Angela was a bit of a high-strung mess, but she was surprisingly easy to work with.

A few minutes before one thirty, Deandra came around a bend in the walking path that circled the pond. She stopped dead in her tracks. On a bench beneath the lush canopy of an oak sat an absolutely massive white-furred creature. Deandra wasn't sure what was the most shocking sight: that the creature must be at least seven feet tall; that over her long, sleek fur—like that of an Afghan hound's—was an exquisitely tailored business suit; or that she held a squirming, colorful, beach ball–sized creature in her lap. The ball of fluff was mostly blue, with short pink arms, and a ruffled mane that was some combination of blue and green. Its face was mostly white, and the tips of its rounded ears were pink. It was currently trying desperately to break free of its mother's arms and had resorted to gnawing on her jacketed arm. The woman either couldn't feel it or she was so used to being chewed on by the rabid multicolored cotton ball that she was immune.

The yeti woman's fur had initially looked snow-white, but as a light breeze blew and shifted the sunlight filtering through the oak's canopy, Deandra thought it might have been closer to a soft gray. Her fur was probably made up of a combination of hues. Maybe Kiwi would lose some of his fur's coloring as he aged. Unless his father was blue and pink, of course.

Havoc, who had grown bored—since Deandra was just standing in the middle of the path gaping—issued a friendly chirp of greeting.

Oleander Basnet snapped out of her staring contest with the pond and glanced over. Despite looking like a relative of Bigfoot, there was something elegant about the yeti. Her face was completely covered in fur, yet she had defined feminine features. She smiled warmly and waved.

Deandra finally got her legs moving and closed the distance between herself and Oleander.

"I apologize for not getting up," Oleander said, her voice deep and a bit husky. "Kiwi just woke from his nap about an hour ago and he's ... energetic. As soon as I stand up, he'll get even more riled."

Kiwi had a perfect oval of pink fur circling each of his big black eyes, sort of making him look like a psychedelic raccoon. He was watching Deandra intently, but he had yet to stop chewing on the sleeve of his mother's jacket.

Havoc sat dutifully by Deandra's feet, but his focus was

squarely on Kiwi. He was practically vibrating, though Deandra was unsure if that was excitement or fear. A little yip burst out of her dragon, as if he couldn't help himself. Kiwi glanced down, finally spotted Havoc, and spit out his mouthful of gray pinstripe fabric.

Kiwi blinked once, twice, then screeched. Tiny pink arms flailed as he bucked and thrashed to get out of his mother's grasp.

"Kiwi!" Oleander yelped, struggling to keep her son contained.

Havoc darted behind Deandra and peeked around the side of her calf.

"He's not a pony, Kiwi! You can't ride him," Oleander said. "No, he's not from the petting zoo!" She shot a vaguely embarrassed look at Deandra, still struggling to keep her hold on Kiwi. "Sorry. We went to a petting zoo over the weekend, and he got to ride a pegasus, which was apparently the highlight of his young life. He won't talk about much else." She yelped when Kiwi clamped down on her hand. "Chanting demands is not the way to get what you want!"

Deandra was ninety-nine percent sure that fifteen hundred a week wasn't enough. She took an involuntary step back, only to be halted by Havoc, who still huddled behind her. "He, uh, talks?"

Oleander shot an annoyed glare at Deandra. "Of course he does. He's not a pet."

Deandra winced. "I'm sorry. That's not what I meant. I just meant that it seems like you're reacting to things he's saying that I can't hear."

Tears inexplicably filled the yeti woman's eyes, and her shoulders sagged. "Oh, Goddess. I'm sorry."

"It's okay," Deandra said, almost instinctively.

Oleander gusted a sigh. "I'm just so tired. Work has been stressful. Finding a sitter has been a nightmare. Kiwi can be ... he's a lot."

Kiwi was still screeching like a miniature banshee.

Deandra turned to Havoc and squatted before him so her back was to the Basnets. "Do you think you could play with Kiwi for a while? He might even like a ride on your back. Can you do that for long enough that his mom and I can talk for a little bit?"

Havoc looked up at her, peered around her at the presumably still-thrashing Kiwi, up at the frazzled Oleander, and then back to Deandra. He peeped, though he sounded reluctant.

"I'll buy you an entire block of provolone. You haven't tried that kind yet."

His follow-up peep was much happier.

"I'm gonna pick you up now, okay?" she asked him. "Just follow my lead."

Havoc licked her chin.

Deandra scooped him up and propped him up on her hip, using one hand to hold his back feet and placing her other hand flat on his chest. With Havoc positioned face first, Deandra stopped before the Basnets.

Kiwi instantly stopped thrashing as he gaped up at Havoc. Oleander appeared a bit shocked, too, but mostly because, to her, it looked like Deandra was easily carting around an eighty-pound puppy.

"Kiwi," Deandra said.

One of Kiwi's rounded pink ears swiveled in Deandra's direction, but otherwise he gave no indication that he'd heard her.

"This is Havoc," Deandra said. "He'd like to play with you."

Kiwi finally looked at Deandra, his eyes wide.

"You have to play nice, though. If Havoc thinks you're playing too rough, then he'll stop playing with you, and I'll take him home, okay?"

Kiwi vibrated with excitement, much like Havoc had earlier. His mane quivered so fast, it was as if it were made of static. "Okay!"

Deandra looked up at Oleander, brows lifted in question. The yeti woman hesitated a moment, then nodded.

Slowly, as Deandra lowered Havoc to the grass, Oleander

lowered her son toward the ground, too. The two babies stared at each other, dragon and yeti, before they both shrieked in delight and raced toward each other. They slammed together and went tumbling toward the pond in a tight ball of scales and fur, broke apart at the water's edge, frolicked down the path, and then raced back the other way, never too far that Deandra couldn't see them.

Both women gusted relieved sighs at the same time, shot each other a look, and then laughed.

Deandra took a seat beside the woman, the two sitting quietly as they watched the dragon and yeti romp around in the grass.

"I'm sorry again if I implied—" Deandra started.

Oleander waved a large, furry hand. "No, I apologize. I had a rough day at the office, then had to come home early to relieve my husband, who had to take a partial day off to look after Kiwi since our childcare situation has been … a challenge." She sighed so deeply that Deandra could feel the vibration of it through the bench. "I'm not sure if I mentioned it, but I'm a lawyer in Kensey. My focus is sapient animal law. I got into it because I know what it's like for beings like me to slip through the cracks in a legal system that doesn't know how to classify us. We often get poor treatment from multiple sources. So even though your question was innocent, I instantly went on the defensive, and I apologize for that."

Deandra wasn't sure what to say. The woman, from her posture to the tone of her voice, suggested she was burned out. "Can I ask you a question?"

The yeti glanced down at her, a soft smile pulling up the corners of her thin pink lips. "I should hope you have more than one."

"I guess it's a two-parter: What was it about Lydia that made you choose her for the job, and now that she's … now that she can't do it, why me? There are many other more experienced sitters in town."

"Would you like me to hire someone else?" she asked in what Deandra figured was her inquisitive lawyer tone, as opposed to panicking that Deandra had shown up today only to turn down the offer.

Deandra got the impression that the yeti preferred honesty, so Deandra gave her a truthful answer. "I just want you to be one hundred percent certain that you'd prefer a mundane like myself over someone like Sarah at Pawsome Pals or one of her employees. Even Lydia wasn't a mundane. If they all have skill sets I don't have, *and* you're currently biding your time until Kiwi is old enough to travel to Kensey with you because you believe a bigger city will have the resources necessary for him, I'm genuinely not sure why *I* was chosen, let alone why I was in the running at all."

Another small smile graced the woman's face, though her focus was on her son. A peal of laughter drew Deandra's gaze in the direction of the pond. Kiwi was on Havoc's back, and the goofy dragon was trotting around like a dressage horse again. The bouncy gait meant Kiwi was getting tossed about on the dragon's back, which the yeti found especially hilarious. Deandra laughed, shaking her head.

"Honestly, that alone is a pretty solid reason," Oleander said, still watching Kiwi and Havoc. "You may not have any magical ability, but you're adaptable. You see a scenario and puzzle out the best solution. You defused your dire wolf's fear, redirected Kiwi's focus, and got him to listen to you *and* give you a verbal confirmation that he understood the rules as you laid them out. The parental bond among yetis means my husband and I can speak with Kiwi telepathically, in a way. Kiwi is still young enough that most of his communication is in pictures or feelings, rather than words."

"Oh! Like Cruz, uh, Dr. Caddel and the zoolingual ability he uses with his clients," Deandra said, then immediately worried she'd put her foot in her mouth again. If yetis were one of the beings who fell in that murky space between person and animal—which they found offensive—maybe it was rude to bring veterinarians into the conversation.

Oleander stiffened for a moment beside Deandra, then relaxed.

"Similar to that, yes. The telepathic link dissolves around their third birthday, which is usually the time they've mastered spoken language. Kiwi has quite a few words he uses now, but he rarely uses them with anyone but my husband, me, and a few friends. He never used them at the daycare, often just throwing epic tantrums when he didn't get his way. He's already used one with you. That might not seem like a big deal to you, but it is to me." She smiled down at Deandra then. "Incidentally, Kiwi also used a word with Lydia Monroe, which he'd never done with anyone else we interviewed."

Deandra wondered again about Lydia's supposed ability to communicate with animals—both living and dead—as well as Harmony's claim that Lydia had been bluffing about the extent of that skill. Tansy's story, however, suggested that Lydia had been able to manipulate Rufus the raven to the point that the bird turned aggressive against its will.

"What word did Kiwi use with Lydia? The same one: 'Okay'?" Deandra asked.

Oleander gusted another full-body sigh. "I don't wish to speak ill of the dead … but the last interaction I had with Lydia—the day I decided to hire her—haunted me to the point that I wasn't sure if I'd made the right decision."

"What do you mean?" Deandra asked, unable to help herself. She didn't *mean* to be a gossip, but … well, maybe Wendy's love of mysteries was starting to rub off on her.

Plus, Oleander seemed like she *wanted* to talk about this. This was a way to show the woman Deandra was compassionate, right? Yeah, she was going to go with that.

"I met with her … when was it? Two days ago? On Sunday," Oleander said slowly. "Even if Lydia herself was a bit brash, I've dealt with way worse in my line of work, so her abrasive personality didn't put me off as much as it might others. It was the third time I'd met with her, first to get to know her one on one, and then a couple of times to make sure Kiwi took to her. He was mostly indifferent to her during the first visit at our house. After the initial greeting, Kiwi took one of his toys and sat down in a far corner of the living room to play by himself. I figured indifference was better than a tantrum like the ones he threw at daycare. On Sunday, almost the exact same thing happened: He greeted Lydia with mild disinterest, and when she and I sat on the couch, Kiwi took one of his toys and started to walk away.

"Lydia called his name in this very decisive way. Kiwi stopped in his tracks, turned around, and stared at Lydia with an intensity I hadn't seen from him before. In a controlled tone she said, 'Don't be rude. Let's show your mom how much fun we can have.' He stood there for a long while, staring at Lydia. Then he finally joined us—though he hopped onto an ottoman instead of sitting on the couch as he usually does.

"Lydia reached out for the toy in his hand. Kiwi clutched it to his chest and said, 'No.' I told him that wasn't very nice. When he looked at me, he sent me a picture-thought of what I took to mean 'She's being pushy.' He sent images of two kids pushing each other on the playground and of someone running up behind someone else and shoving them in the back so that they fell to the ground."

Deandra's brows bunched up. Was it a coincidence that *pushing* was potentially how Lydia was killed?

"While I was sending a picture-thought back, trying to encourage him to be nice to Lydia and to share his toy, all resistance from him suddenly vanished, and he rushed to her, handed her his toy, and then sat in her lap. Lydia laughed and said something like, 'See! I knew he'd come around.' Lydia wrapped her arms around him and hugged him. I just remember him looking at me with this ... expression of fear on his little face. He sent me a picture-thought of himself in a small cage, hands grabbing the bars, at the same time that he verbally said, 'Like Lydia. Lydia friend.'"

"How weird," Deandra said. "Do you think she was somehow *forcing* him to comply?"

"At the time, I chalked it up to Kiwi just being difficult and combative on purpose. He's such a willful boy, and he can be a bit manipulative. Nothing malicious—it usually involves small lies told to get one of us to give him an extra cookie after dinner."

Deandra laughed. "That sounds normal enough."

"I think deep down I knew the daycare situation wasn't ideal for him, but my desperation clouded my judgment. I needed a solution because my workload has increased exponentially recently. So we kept forcing Kiwi to go to this daycare, even though we knew it wasn't the right fit. Nothing against the daycare center. He just needs something other than what their program allows. I took a few days off work this week to resolve the sitter issue, and my work is piling up." Oleander sighed. "Being a working parent is harder than I expected, honestly."

Deandra could hear the guilt in her tone. The woman clearly worried that the choices she'd made based on her career needs might have irreparably harmed her son. And now, in hindsight, she had concerns that the woman she'd intended to hire had been magically manipulating her child.

"So," Deandra said, the reason for this meeting becoming clearer, "when you heard rumors about this newly arrived mundane who had an uncanny knack for connecting with difficult animals, you thought I could be a good fit as Kiwi's caregiver, while also giving you the peace of mind that I couldn't use magic on him in a negative way even if I wanted to."

Oleander shrugged helplessly. "I don't think I'd even pieced all that together until just now. My gut told me something about Lydia was … off. And that she wasn't a good fit for him, just like the daycare wasn't. I didn't sleep at all Sunday night, tossing and turning because I was worried sick I'd made another mistake— made a choice that benefited *me* and not Kiwi." She turned abruptly on the bench, making the wood creak. Deandra scooted back a couple of inches. "I, of course, didn't want Lydia out of the picture *this* way. Now I feel even worse, like I put it out into the universe that I needed a sign I'd made the right call, and then the object of my anxiety winds up *dead*!" She hissed the last word.

Deandra cowered a little under the looming gaze of the woman whose expression seemed to be pleading with Deandra to tell her that Lydia's untimely demise wasn't her fault.

Oleander shook her shaggy head. "Death by tumbling down stairs. What a tragic accident ..."

Hm. So the suspicion that it had actually been murder hadn't made its way to the public. After all, if Mavis hadn't come to Gorgon's Alley right after being interrogated at the police station —*and* having witnessed the crime scene firsthand—the details of Lydia's death might not have reached the pet-sitting happy-hour group yet either.

"What I think you need more than anything is a good night's sleep," Deandra said. "What if we say that I'll look after Kiwi Wednesday through Friday this week, you can talk to Kiwi each night and make sure he feels comfortable with me, and then we'll go from there. If Kiwi decides I'm the worst, I'll stick with him until you can find a replacement. No hard feelings, okay?"

Oleander's blue eyes welled with tears again. "You're very kind."

For the next several minutes, they talked logistics. Oleander said Deandra was free to spend the whole six hours at her house, was fine with Deandra bringing Kiwi with her to look after Barnaby, and that Havoc was welcome in all circumstances. Kiwi apparently took an hour-long nap around noon most days, especially if he was given his favorite treat of dry-ice chips a half hour before. He loved crafts, baking, and cartoons. If Deandra ever needed to calm him down, strapping him into his baby carrier and taking him for a walk was sure to knock him out.

It was a lot of information, and Deandra was terrified she'd screw it up somehow, but she desperately wanted to help Oleander, even if it was only for a few days until Oleander found a better fit.

After Deandra officially accepted the job and the two women shook on it, Oleander said, "I should be getting home. My husband will be back soon."

They both stood.

Havoc and Kiwi were still roughhousing, but they both looked like they were running on fumes.

"Havoc!" Deandra called.

The dragon halted, glanced over his shoulder, then galloped toward her. Though Kiwi had been running on all fours earlier, he was on two legs now and waddled at half speed. Havoc reached them before Kiwi even made it halfway back.

Oleander laughed and gently patted Havoc on the head. "Thank you for tiring him out."

Moments later, Kiwi issued a pathetic wail and flopped onto his back. "Mama! Mama! Maaaamaaaaa!"

"That's definitely my cue," Oleander said. "I'll email you the list of his favorite foods. I'll leave a copy of it on the counter, too. Thank you again. You don't understand how much of a relief this is." She headed off after her boy, who was still flailing around in the grass. Oleander scooped him up and held him to her chest.

His little face peeked over his mom's shoulder, and he waved as they walked away. "Bye, horsey!"

Havoc chirped his farewell.

When they were alone, Havoc looked at Deandra and cocked his head.

"I don't like that calculating look in your eye ..." Deandra said.

Havoc stood on two feet, wavered a bit, and then suddenly tipped onto his back, as if he were doing a trust fall with a ghost. Once on his back, he kicked his feet in the air, like he was riding a bicycle. He peeped and chirped and carried on until she figured out what he was doing. Deandra, hands on knees, hovered over him. "I'm not carrying you all the way back to the car."

He peeped sadly, letting his limbs all flop to the ground as he did a very impressive imitation of a starfish.

"Well, I *could* carry you ..." Deandra said.

Havoc lifted his head.

"But if I do, I'll be too tired to go cheese shopping."

It only took him a moment to make his decision. He scrambled to his feet, grabbed his leash off the bench with his mouth, and shook it violently, the way he sometimes shook his toys. Laughing, she took the slightly damp leash, hooked it to his harness, and let him lead the way to the grocery store.

Though she felt confident in her decision to accept the caretaking job, a quiet, dark thought kept lurking in the back of her mind. Was Oleander exhausted because her job and home life were draining, or had she lost sleep Sunday night because she'd suspected that, not only had Lydia Monroe forced Oleander into hiring her under false pretenses, but she'd also harmed her child? Had the sleep-deprived woman been so distraught about her decision that she'd violently confronted Lydia the following afternoon?

Deandra remembered Cruz telling her that a hospital had needed *three* bottles of Quowlaxliquin—a controlled substance— to knock out a yeti before surgery. According to Mavis, either magic or strength had been used to hurl Lydia to her death. Would a yeti—especially one who had hit her limit when one person too many mistreated her son—be strong enough to cause the crater in Lydia's wall?

Wendy had been concerned that "stealing" the job from Sarah could be a dangerous decision, one that could further upset the faun if she had truly retaliated against Lydia for once again poaching clients.

But now Deandra wondered if accepting the job from an emotionally spent Oleander Basnet was an even *more* dangerous proposition.

CHAPTER EIGHT

Deandra was on her own for dinner, as Nathan had hopped in a telepad to take Wendy out. Deandra knew if she'd told Wendy the full extent of her meeting with Oleander Basnet—and not just the part about Deandra getting the job—Wendy would have called off her date so they could hash out the details. But Deandra wanted her cousin to have a good time without worrying about her.

Wendy and Nathan were going to the fancy Axian Delights

that Deandra only knew of thanks to her welcome booklet. As Deandra's gift to her cousin, Deandra had torn out the coupon from the back of the booklet and told Wendy that one starter was on her.

With Havoc sprawled on his belly on the floor—a belly that now contained an entire block of provolone cheese—and sleeping deeply, Deandra curled up on the couch, intending to catch up on a TV show for a while before deciding which restaurant to order take-out from.

She draped a blanket over her legs, grabbed the remote, and ... just sat there. She was desperately curious to find out what happened next in *Faet of the Heart*, a long-running soap opera–like show that only existed within the hub system. And yet she couldn't make herself hit play.

She didn't feel lonely so much as restless. Maybe it was anxiety from starting the Basnet job tomorrow. Or that she'd possibly been sharing discounted apps with a murderer last night. It felt wrong somehow to casually sit here on the couch without a care in the world when there might be a killer loose in town. She didn't think it was anything as dramatic as someone picking off pet sitters, but it was unsettling all the same.

She had so many unanswered questions floating around in her head—how could she possibly concentrate on a show?

She cut a glance toward her phone where it lay on the arm of Wendy's plush teal couch.

Before she could convince herself not to, she snatched it up. She pulled up a text thread, selected her contact of choice, and then carefully typed out a message, taking care with each word before—stomach in knots—she hit send.

DEANDRA

Hey

When a reply didn't materialize after ten seconds, she softly squeaked in horror at her sheer stupidity and tossed the phone toward the other side of the couch as if the device had scalded her.

Another ten seconds passed in silence.

It wasn't too late to move back to Los Angeles, right?

Heck, she could just move back to Denver, get a job in her parents' restaurant, and live in their—

Ding!

She flung herself across the couch to pick her phone back up.

CRUZ

Hey

She grinned like a dang fool and she wasn't even sure why. And then she panicked a little again because offering a noncommittal greeting had been the entirety of her impulsive plan.

She worried at her bottom lip, hoping something brilliant and witty would strike her like lightning.

Havoc whimpered, then chirped. He still lay flat on his belly, all four limbs gently flicking and his eyelids twitching. She wondered if he was chasing Kiwi in his dreams. Or perhaps it was Havoc's uncatchable nemesis: the butterfly.

She carefully climbed off the couch to take a short video of the dreaming dragon, then sent it to Cruz. She'd been wondering if the magic in Havoc's collar would override technology, now that Cruz was in the pod. If she sent the same video to Wendy, would she see something different? Or would anyone Deandra sent it to see a dragon, since *she* was the one who took the video?

CRUZ

Did our charge have a particularly eventful day today, or is this typical for a Tuesday night?

DEANDRA

Both. Do I have *you* to thank for putting me on Oleander Basnet's radar?

90

CRUZ

Wasn't me. Have you managed to charm
Kiwi, too?

DEANDRA

That was all Havoc

CRUZ

I heard Kiwi got booted from daycare. Again. I
only know because Angela Gunderson heard
about the latest incident and called me in a
panic, worrying what steps she might need to
take if she were ever bitten by a rabid yeti.

DEANDRA

Deandra wondered if she should inform Angela that her new
charge was none other than Oleander Basnet's son, the possible
carrier of yeti rabies. She wrinkled her nose.

DEANDRA

I have some juicy pet sitter gossip that Angela
might be able to shed some light on, but given
how high-strung she seems to be, that might be
a bad idea

She startled and fumbled her phone like a hot potato when all
of a sudden it started ringing. Who used phones to actually *call*
people?! Yes, she'd talked to Cruz on the phone several times, but
that had always been for professional reasons. This would be a
personal call, right?

He'd asked her out, after all. Kind of.

No, he had.

She smacked herself in the forehead with the heel of her free
hand. How had she grown this rusty already? Did she even
remember *how* to flirt? Because she *wanted* to flirt, right?

She swallowed hard and hit accept.

"Hi," he said.

Her foolish grin returned. "Hi."

"So there's something you need to know about me ..."

His tone was so serious that her palms started to sweat. Had she said something offensive in her last message somehow—and he'd called her to voice his disappointment?

"What's that?" she asked, leery.

"I'm incredibly nosy."

She laughed.

"You can't tell me you have gossip and not expect a phone call," he said. "I can put a spin on it and claim that *of course* I'm inquisitive. It's my love of learning and natural curiosity that led me to my profession, right? But I'd be lying to us both if I said nosiness wasn't a factor."

"And here I thought you just wanted an excuse to call me ..."

She *did* remember how to flirt. Go her!

The smile was evident in his voice. "Oh, that was definitely part of it, but it's a sixty-forty split."

Deandra offered a mock gasp. "Am I the sixty or the forty?"

"Depends on how good this gossip is."

She laughed again.

"Your laugh tips it to seventy-thirty—in your favor," he said. "Now, supply me with my fix."

She settled more comfortably onto the couch, head resting on the back cushion, as she told him about meeting Lydia Monroe, then attending the pet-sitter happy hour, followed by the arrival of Mavis with news of Lydia's death, and ending with Deandra being hired by Oleander. She left out the rumors Harmony the gnome had told her—about Lydia's supposed ability to not only communicate with animals but with their spirits. She didn't mention Tansy's suspicion that Lydia had manipulated Rufus the raven into acting aggressively against his will, either.

Those parts of Lydia's story felt more like hearsay, and Deandra felt bad about spreading rumors about a woman who could no longer defend herself.

Then there was the smaller, darker worry that, if Lydia *had* been a zoolinguist, it meant that someone like Cruz could have a malicious side to his magic, too. The same magic that was now hitched to her innocent dragon.

Her gut told her she could trust Cruz, just as Havoc did, but she didn't think it was a bad thing to hold onto a bit of skepticism. She hadn't known Cruz for that long, after all, and Deandra had only just scratched the surface of what delights and horrors alike lurked within the hub system—the same hub system that had been so overwhelming to her mother and aunts that they'd all fled at the first opportunity and hadn't looked back.

Cruz had quietly listened to her ramble, offering only occasional comments or asking a clarifying question. He was silent for several long seconds once she'd finished talking, though. "I might have to change my answer to a fifty-fifty split because that was some high-quality gossip."

With a laugh, she said, "I had no idea being a pet sitter here would be this … eventful. Wendy seems to think someone in town might take offense to me getting the Basnet job over Sarah. She didn't tell me to watch my back, but she came close."

"Can I play devil's advocate?" he asked.

"Please do."

"If Sarah has enough business that she's happy to pass clients along to others *and* has started up an arm of the business in another hub, why would she risk all of that over *one* gig?" he asked. "Plus, to me, it says a lot that she has relationships that strong with people who are, essentially, her competition. There's probably a reason why people have lots of nice things to say about Sarah and very few about Lydia—Goddess rest her soul."

It was a fair point. Deandra thought of how many scandals and rumors cropped up around celebrities and politicians that usually wound up being true. It was easier to unearth dirty laundry when there was dirty laundry to find. It didn't mean that plenty of people who appeared one way didn't act another behind closed doors, or had closets stuffed to overflowing with skeletons, but Occam's razor probably applied more often than not. The simplest answer was probably the one closest to the truth: Sarah had too much to lose by attacking Lydia; therefore, it was more likely that someone *else* had killed her.

Deandra said, "I'm not sure I buy the 'you stole my job so now you must die' motive anyway."

"Oh?"

"I'll preface this with the fact that if my financial situation were more dire, I'd have a totally different perspective on this, but even *I* keep wondering if taking on the Basnet job is a good idea, despite the paycheck," Deandra said. "That kid is going to be a challenge."

Cruz chuckled. "Baby yetis are ... how can I put this delicately? Unhinged. But Kiwi is even wilder than average, at least from what I've seen. Oleander seems to alternate between using pediatricians and me, trying to find someone who can offer Kiwi the best care. I can't tell if Oleander is offended or embarrassed when she brings Kiwi in for a checkup."

Deandra nodded, even though Cruz couldn't see her. "It must be very hard to feel like you don't belong in either system. But at least she found a way to channel her frustrations into a career."

"True," he said. "Want a bit of gossip from *me*?"

"Obviously."

"Remember that scenario I gave you about the bear shifter who mauled a salesman?" Cruz asked. "That was one of Oleander's cases, and the bear shifter was one of my patients. I got called in as an expert witness on the case a few years ago."

"No way!" Deandra said. "Who won?"

"The salesman. In this case, it was a newspaper salesman. His injuries were ... severe. The jury, I think—which happens in a lot of these cases—let their fear influence their ruling. They put themselves in the position of being in the wrong place at the wrong time. The very convincing closing argument from the prosecution included the question, 'What if my client had been a Girl Scout selling cookies?'"

Deandra winced. "Not going to lie, that probably would have swayed me, too."

"Yeah," Cruz said, sighing. "I only knew him in a patient-client capacity, but I liked him. He seemed like a good guy. Had a wife and kids—cubs, I should say. He's serving a fifteen-year sentence for the mauling. His wife made sure to tell me, in no uncertain terms, that I should be ashamed of myself for my testimony."

"And what *was* your expert opinion?"

"That since Fredrick had been ill enough that he needed to seek medical assistance, he should have taken extra precautions to ensure nothing triggered his innate rage response. Fredrick's doctor's note said the same thing; in addition to prescribing medication and bed rest, his human physician advised him to stay away from anyone except his family until the illness subsided. Fredrick hadn't sought additional care from me; otherwise, I would have told him the same thing."

"Must have been hard to be honest in that situation since you knew the guy," Deandra said. "What exactly happened? The salesman rang the doorbell, and Fredrick came out swinging his claws?"

"Depends on who you ask. According to Fredrick, he was down for the count with a potent strain of the flu. On the day in question, his wife was out shopping, and he was home with the cubs. He'd gone into the kitchen to get a glass of water when a solicitor selling subscriptions to the *Axian Gazette* came to the door. Fredrick's youngest cub was napping, so he opened the door intending only to get the guy to go away and not wake up his son. Fredrick claims the salesman kept pestering him no matter what he said to him. The salesman asked if he could show the *Gazette*'s new kids section to Fredrick's cubs, since it was going to be rolling out in earnest soon, and they needed more feedback from a younger audience. Fredrick told him to come back later when his wife was home. The salesman was persistent, so Fredrick eventually slammed the door in his face. The sound woke his sleeping son, so then he had to get him back to sleep, which only aggravated Fredrick further.

"After his son was asleep again, Fredrick went back into the kitchen to get that glass of water. While he was standing at the kitchen sink filling his glass, he looked out the window and saw the newspaper salesman talking to Fredrick's daughter, clearly trying to win her over with the newspaper's coloring pages and puzzles. Fredrick snapped and ... well, like I said, the injuries were severe. If he hadn't been sick, things wouldn't have escalated as they did."

"But they also wouldn't have escalated," Deandra said, "had the salesman gotten the hint the first time the shifter said he wasn't interested. Which I'm sure only got worse when the salesman approached Fredrick's daughter without permission."

"Right." Cruz sighed. "The family relocated to another hub not long after the trial. The cubs were bullied in school. The wife owned a florist shop, and not only did business almost stop entirely, but her shop was vandalized more than once."

Deandra frowned. "That's awful. How long ago was this?"

"Hmm. Maybe five years now? It was shortly after I'd finished my residency. I'd only been working full time at the clinic here for about a year. Let's just say I hope never to be an expert witness again," he said. "I'm thirty-six, by the way, in case you were trying to do math."

"I was, which was very hard since I didn't know how long your schooling or residency lasted, so I was not only doing mental math, I was doing it with made-up numbers," she said. "I'm thirty, just because we're sharing."

Deandra started to say something, then hesitated, not sure how to ask her next question. It was something she'd been wondering about for a while.

"Out with it," he said, chuckling softly. "You sound like a beached fish."

Her cheeks flushed. "Is there some kind of formal test you take to become a certified zoolinguist? I ... this might be rude ... but, like, how can you prove you can *actually* communicate with animals?"

He gasped. "Are you calling me a liar, Miss Hendricks?"

She tamped down another smile. "I conduct thorough interviews with *all* new members of the pod. Standard procedure."

"Ah," he said sagely. "That makes sense. So, actually, there *is* a test. I majored in zoolinguistics—don't laugh; that's an actual thing. During the final exam, heavily vetted shifters of all types were brought in to run various tests. Since shifters can flip back and forth between their two forms, they can easily report whether the zoolinguist in question was actually able to communicate with the shifter's animal form."

"And you passed with flying colors?"

"Top of my class," he said smugly. "But by the time I reached my final exam, the class size had been reduced to twenty, so it's not *that* impressive."

"What was the class size when you started? Why were so few left?" She dramatically sucked in a breath. "Did you have to fight to the death in intense strength trials every year? How many brilliant minds did you snuff out in the pursuit of excellence, Dr. Caddel?"

"Nineteen," he said, deadpan. He only let the silence linger for a moment before he snorted a laugh. "Zoolinguistics has ... specialties, for lack of a better term. My personal ability covers the full spectrum—emotions, thoughts, and spoken language shared between me and animals. As students pass or fail certain tests during schooling, they're slotted into classes based on their specialty. Once you plateau as far as test results go, you graduate at your current level. The twenty of us were the only ones who tested into the end of the program."

"I *am* pretty impressed, for what it's worth," she said.

"Says the woman imprinted upon by a thought-to-be-extinct dragon," he said with no small amount of reverence.

She eyed the dragon in question. A small puddle of drool had formed under his chin. He'd stopped twitching in his sleep, at least. She wondered what he'd been dreaming about, if his thoughts were in picture form, and whether those images were in black and white or full technicolor.

Thoughts straying to Lydia Monroe's supposed ability, Deandra asked, "Are animal empaths the most common, as far as zoolinguists go?"

"Yep. And there are levels within that, too—some can read only really strong emotions, or only the emotions of certain types of animals. The guy who graduated first in our freshman year was someone who could only pick up on fear ... and exclusively from gray squirrels."

Deandra kind of liked that it was called "graduating first" and not "flunked out."

She asked, "Are animal empaths also often animal mediums?"

"Uhh ... not that I know of. Mediums are a brand all their own," he said slowly. "What an oddly specific question ..."

"I'm only telling you this next part because I want your expert opinion," Deandra hedged. "I feel sort of guilty talking about Lydia."

"I'm a horrible person because the ratio just shifted to forty-sixty with this promise of new information."

Smiling to herself, she really, *really* hoped her gut instincts—and Havoc's instincts—were right about Dr. Cruz Caddel.

Taking a deep breath, she told him the breadth of Lydia's supposed zoolingual claims.

"Wow. Now that I'm hearing all this, something about her sounds vaguely familiar," he said. "I have a memory—from at least four or five years ago—of the staff telling me about a pet sitter who kept coming in asking if we could display her business cards on the counter. She was really pushy about it. One of the newer techs eventually caved and said it was fine.

"Our other doctor—Paula Jasper—just so happened to come into the reception area within seconds of the sitter leaving to ask one of the techs a question. She noted that the cards stated the sitter was both an animal empath and a medium.

"Dr. Jasper chased the sitter down in the parking lot and asked for her license number to prove she was a certified medium. She also asked who the sitter studied under during her zoolinguistics schooling. The sitter was deeply offended that her honor was being questioned, then more or less melted down before taking off." He slipped into thoughtful silence. "Yeah, it's clicking now. I never met the sitter myself—only heard about the incident from the techs and Dr. Jasper. I'd been out of the office for a full week because of that trial, actually."

Deandra wondered—if this sitter and Lydia were one and the same—if Lydia had chosen that week to harass the staff specifically *because* Cruz was otherwise engaged. "Is Dr. Jasper a zoolinguist, too?"

"Yes. She's a very powerful animal empath, but she can only read the emotions of non-shifter animals. Her skill is so focused, she can pinpoint specific places where an animal's pain originates." He chuckled. "One of her biggest bugbears is when people pretend to have an ability she personally spent years honing and perfecting. I'm sure she tore Lydia—if that was truly her—a new one for potentially making a false claim."

"It's such an odd thing to do—claiming you have a magical ability when you don't," Deandra said, though she supposed the mundane world had its own fair share of sham psychics, mediums, and empaths. Lydia might have found more success *outside* the hub system.

"It happens more often than you think," he said. "Not having a connection to magic while living in a town full of unique people can do a number on some people's egos."

Or have the opposite effect, as it had in the case of Deandra's mom and aunts. Rather than trying to force a mundane peg into a magical hole, the mundane pegs had fled into the "normal" world full of appropriately magic-less holes. She wrinkled her nose at herself. Her analogy might have gotten away from her. At least she hasn't said it out loud.

"Penny for your thoughts?" Cruz asked. "You sound like you're doing some deep thinking over there."

"These thoughts are no deeper than a puddle."

She could hear the smile in his voice when he asked, "Nervous about your first day with Kiwi tomorrow?"

"You have no idea. Any advice?"

"Frankly, not really," he said. "He thinks in pictures for the most part, but he can block me from reading them. He gets frustrated very easily, so if you can't figure out what it is that's bothering him, he's likely to have an epic tantrum. Sometimes, when he's having a conniption, his defenses are down, and that'll give me some hint about what he wants. But even with that added bit of help, he's not the easiest to deal with. So, in short, Goddess speed."

Deandra whimpered dramatically. "Thanks so much."

"I'll tell you what," he said slowly, and a bit cautiously. "If you still have any energy left after your first yeti-sitting session tomorrow, we should … get dinner. My treat."

"I thought I owed *you* dinner."

"Ah, yes, the vending machine buffet."

"I prefer smorgasbord."

He laughed. "Well, I assume you'll be wiped out, so I'll take one for the team tomorrow and choose the place. I wouldn't want you to overexert yourself with vending machine research. All you'll have to do is show up. Or I could come pick you up?"

She decided it was very cute that he sounded as nervous as she'd felt when she'd first texted him. "Sounds good. The vending machine research is tedious. I have a map tacked to the wall. There are lines of red string—it's very elaborate. We can figure out transportation tomorrow. You may just have to scrape me off the sidewalk outside the Basnets' house."

"Lucky for you, I have a very large spatula."

Given the massive net she'd seen one of the vet techs wield a couple of months ago, she wondered if that statement was literal.

She said, "Thanks for the … chat. Uhh, talk. It was nice talking to you. I'll see you tomorrow?" Shaking her head, she wondered why her mouth and brain were only *sometimes* in communication with each other.

"Definitely. Good luck with Kiwi."

She groaned. "Thanks."

"'Night, Dee."

"'Night, Cruz."

She hurriedly pulled the phone from her face, slammed a finger onto the end-call button, and tossed her phone to the other side of the couch again. She pressed a throw pillow to her face and screamed into it, kicking her feet.

Havoc woke with a snort and scrambled upright. He slipped in his own puddle of drool, though, and crashed chin-first to the floor. Righting himself just as quickly, he made a menacing woofing noise, turning this way and that, pupils dilated, as he searched for the intruder that had caused her to scream—albeit softly.

She laughed. "Havoc! It's okay. I'm fine, I'm fine. Sorry I woke you."

Turning back toward her, he plopped onto his haunches. Faint tendrils of white smoke wafted from his nostrils, and his eyelids didn't blink in sync. He yawned, his blue-black tongue on full display. Then he slid back to his stomach, limbs splayed. Lights out.

She ordered a pizza, got resituated on the couch under her blanket, and finally started up the latest episode of *Faet of the Heart*, unable to keep the small smile off her face.

CHAPTER NINE

Deandra walked into Oleander Basnet's neighborhood with Havoc in tow at eight thirty the next morning, per Oleander's request, for their first visit. After today, Deandra's start time would be nine o'clock. Though the area was a mere ten-minute walk from Wendy's apartment, it was immediately clear this neighborhood was inhabited by the more well-off residents of Axia. The homes were twice the size of most of the more cottage-like houses she'd seen in the town so far. These houses all had long walkways that led to their front doors, flanked by well-tended grass, and many boasted elaborate gardens that were likely maintained by someone other than the homeowners.

Ivy climbed along the front of Oleander's navy-blue two-story home, though the vines had been neatly trimmed back from the white shutters of the multi-paned windows that sat to either side of the shiny black front door. The Basnets' yard was minimally landscaped, with only a row of small hedges lining the walkway. They'd been shaped into balls; Deandra imagined they were a long row of gophers who had poked their heads out of the ground simultaneously to give the newbie a good once-over. They'd just be monster-sized green gophers in this case, which was honestly a possibility in Axia.

She shook the image loose as she stepped onto the spongy black welcome mat. Now that she was closer to the house, it was evident that everything about it was larger than average. The top of the doorjamb was a good four feet above her head, the mailbox affixed to the wall was nearly the size of her torso, and the button on the doorbell camera was the diameter of a golf ball, rather than a quarter. A weatherworn ceramic frog even larger than Havoc sat on the porch like a silent sentry. After pressing the doorbell, she angled an anxious smile down at Havoc, who stood dutifully by her feet.

Something crashed from inside the house, followed by a bellowing yell from someone who Deandra assumed was Oleander's husband. He sounded like a ticked-off lion.

The door was wrenched open without warning, and Deandra shrank back. The absolutely massive creature crowding the doorway briefly made her consider hauling tail back to Wendy's apartment and never looking back. Her heart thundered in her chest as she remembered Cruz's story about Fredrick the shifter mauling a man who had come to his door when he was ill and in a bad mood. This creature looked furious.

While the creature had the same long, silky fur as Oleander, his was more of a slate gray, compared to his wife's mostly white coat. Or maybe his fur was a soft blue? She decided on blue-gray. He was dressed in a long-sleeved shirt and overalls, instantly making her think he must work in construction. The sheer size of his clothes pulled up a memory of Large & Wide, the chain of franchised stores owned by Callie's late uncle. The creature's work boots were impossibly large. If he decided to kick her in the stomach, he'd probably launch her into next week.

"Who are you?" he bellowed.

"I … I um … I'm your new pet sitter? *Babysitter*, I mean! I'm Deandra Hendricks. I met with your wife yesterday. She told me she needed me to start today to look after Kiwi?" Her voice had gotten smaller and squeakier with each word.

The giant creature's shoulders immediately slumped, and he clapped a furry hand on his equally furry forehead. "Goddess. I'm so sorry. I completely forgot about that. Please, come in …"

He stepped aside to clear a path for Deandra. She glanced down at Havoc, who had pressed himself flat to the welcome mat, tail tucked between his legs. He looked even more scared than he had at the door to the bowling alley.

The yeti must have noticed the effect he was having on Havoc because he was suddenly squatting in the foyer instead of looming. He reached a massive hand into one of the pockets of his overalls and produced a strip of bacon jerky.

"Hi there, pup," the yeti said, gentling his voice by a mile. "I didn't mean to frighten you. Would you like a treat? Kiwi likes these a lot, too." He glanced at Deandra. "I get famished on the job, so I keep my pockets full of dried meats."

She nodded absently. Sure, of course. Everyone kept loose meat in their pockets.

Havoc, who hadn't tried bacon in any form yet as far as Deandra knew, army-crawled toward the offered snack. He gently eased it out of the yeti's fingers, then hastily backed up to sit by Deandra's feet again as he gobbled down the treat. A moment after Havoc swallowed it, he swung his wide eyes up to her, as if asking, "How is this the first time I'm tasting this miracle food?"

He then launched himself at the yeti, licking his furry face and wiggling like an electrified snake. The yeti man was knocked onto his backside, but he was issuing a deep, rumbling laugh, so

Deandra figured all was well. She let go of Havoc's leash and stepped into the house, closing the door behind her.

"Havoc, leave him alone," Deandra said, laughing.

When the dragon came bounding back over to her, several pieces of bacon jerky sticking out of his mouth, she figured his enthusiastic greeting had been more about discovering the treasures in the yeti's pockets than saying hello to a new best friend.

The yeti climbed to his enormous feet and wiped at his face with his hands. He patted his pockets a moment later, put his hands on his hips, and stared down at the dragon—who was licking his lips. "You cleaned me out!"

Havoc chirped happily.

The man laughed. Addressing Deandra, he held out a hand. "Sorry again about the less-than-friendly greeting. It's been a hectic morning. I'm Cenzio. What's your name again?"

Deandra shook his hand, which engulfed hers. "Dee."

"Dee," he said, nodding. "All right. Well, let's go find Ohlie and Kiwi, eh? She was trying to get him to eat breakfast when you rang the bell." He strode ahead of her down a long, wide hallway.

She scooped up the loop of Havoc's leash, and she and her dragon trailed after the yeti. Deandra marveled at how the house must have been designed with elephantine fae residents in mind. Hallways were wider, ceilings and doorframes were taller, and furniture was bigger. Even though Deandra had gaped at Oleander's seven-foot-frame, Cenzio was much closer to eight feet. He walked comfortably in his home, with his massive shoulders back and his head held high; he'd no doubt be ducking constantly in Wendy's little apartment. Deandra felt a bit like a doll come to life in this house.

It wasn't until they stepped into the kitchen that Deandra also noted it was exceedingly chilly inside. The adrenaline of her initial meeting with Cenzio had fled her system, and now she was fighting to keep her teeth from chattering. She glanced down at her arms to find the fine hairs standing on end and her skin dotted with goose bumps.

Oleander was indeed in the kitchen with Kiwi. The room was wide enough that a center island would have been a great addition for extra counter space, but Deandra supposed the yetis preferred having more room to move around in.

Oleander stood before a high chair that was so tall that Deandra probably would need a stool to reach it comfortably. Since Kiwi was no bigger than a human toddler, he looked especially small in the tall chair. Deandra figured the height was for the parents' benefit, so they didn't have to hover over the kid while trying to get him to eat.

Oleander held a small bowl in one hand, and the other held a plastic spoon that looked impossibly tiny in her grip. Deandra wasn't sure what she was trying to feed Kiwi, but the copious amount of splattered blueberries on the plastic sheet below the high chair suggested the baby yeti was not in the mood for fruit.

Kiwi spotted Havoc and began thrashing around in his chair. The kid was strapped in tight, though, and no amount of squirming freed him from the seat belt–like bands making an X across his chest. When Kiwi realized he wasn't getting out, he threw his head back and shrieked as if the world as he knew it were coming to an end.

Oleander turned around then and smiled tiredly down at Deandra. The fur on Oleander's face prevented her from having visible bags under her eyes, but the whites were streaked red as if she hadn't slept at all. "I'm so glad you're here!" she said loudly, to be heard over her wailing son.

Deandra had a brief flash of worry that when Oleander and Cenzio left the house today they weren't going to come back, leaving Deandra to care for the little menace indefinitely.

Cenzio said, "Hon, why don't you get Dee situated, and I'll hose the kid off."

Oleander nodded, then gestured for Deandra to head back the way they'd come. Oleander gave Cenzio's arm a light tug on her way out of the kitchen; he angled his face toward her so she could kiss him on the cheek.

It was nice to see that the two of them were still doing okay in their marriage despite how worn out they both were. Deandra was also glad to see that Oleander's exhaustion wasn't being exacerbated by a husband shirking his duties. They were in this together.

That means they'll definitely come back to the kid later, right?

Oleander took Deandra and Havoc on a tour of the house, including Kiwi's favorite hiding places, which didn't bode well. A list of Kiwi's favorite shows and movies lay on the coffee table in the living room, as well as an absurd number of instructions on how to get the TV and sound system turned on. There were four remotes.

Kiwi's bedroom was upstairs and had been designed with a jungle theme. The wallpaper had a forest-green background and was decorated with wide leaves and giant colorful flowers. A few animal faces—monkeys, jaguars, parrots, and toucans—peeked out from behind the foliage. The longer Deandra looked at the walls, however, the more she was sure it wasn't wallpaper at all.

Oleander must have sensed where Deandra's focus was aimed because she said, "It took Cenzio almost six months to paint the walls. He sketched it all out by hand first, then was in here for hours every day adding to the mural. He's a housepainter by trade, so he likes opportunities to flex his creative muscles wherever he can."

"It's beautiful," Deandra said, turning in a slow circle.

Kiwi's crib looked like a standard mundane crib, complete with a mobile featuring more jungle animals spinning lazily over the small bed. What was different, though, were the runes etched along the length of every blond-wood leg and spoke.

"What are the runes for?" Deandra asked, gesturing to Kiwi's crib, hoping the question made her sound at least mildly knowledgeable about all this magical stuff. The only reason Deandra knew what runes were was because of Havoc's collar and the glamour spell written onto the white leather.

"Oh ..." Oleander said, sounding a touch embarrassed. "We're doing everything we can think of to keep that boy in his crib at night. He still wants to sleep in bed with us, and we're trying to wean him off. Cenzio partially rolled onto him one night, and Kiwi bit his father in the back, which finally convinced us we needed different arrangements." She shook her head. "It's safer for him in here, but he resists. This is his fourth crib in six months. He, uh … he chewed his way out of the others. These runes seem to be the winning combination so far."

Fifteen hundred a week was *definitely* hazard pay.

She shivered.

"Oh, Goddess above," Oleander said, taking several steps toward Deandra and looking down at her in concern. She grabbed one of Deandra's arms and lifted it, shaking her head. "I forgot to tell you that we keep the thermostat low. We prefer it cold, given all the fur. But fifty degrees is probably too cold for you! You can adjust the temperature to whatever is comfortable while you're here. One second."

Oleander darted out of the room with surprising speed. When a distant hum quieted—a sound Deandra hadn't been aware of until it was absent—she figured Oleander had given her AC permission to take a break. Their electric bill was probably astronomical year-round.

Once she returned, Oleander pointed out Kiwi's favorite toys, the best stories to read to him to get him to nod off, and the industrial freezer in the corner full of frozen fruit and dry-ice chips. Gloves and tongs for Deandra's safety rested atop the long white appliance that Deandra had originally mistaken for a toy chest.

"There are also premade bottles for him in the fridge if the dry ice doesn't calm him down around nap time. Just don't drink them yourself," she said, laughing good-naturedly. Deandra tried to laugh back even though she was beyond overwhelmed at the moment. "They're a special combination of breast milk and antifreeze."

Deandra tried to maintain her level of forced mirth because she knew that hadn't been a joke. There were *actual* bottles of antifreeze in this gigantic furry woman's fridge that she prepared specifically for her baby—because her baby was a freaking *yeti*.

How on *earth* had she gotten herself into this?

The next stop on the tour was back in the foyer, where Oleander pointed out a series of items hanging from hooks on the wall: a baby carrier, the straps of which were also lined with runes; a harness and leash, not unlike the one Deandra used for Havoc; and a set of keys.

Plucking the keys off the hook, Oleander handed them to Deandra. "House key, backyard gate key, and a spare for the station wagon in the garage. It's set up with a car seat. We got it primed and ready to go for a mundane-sized sitter once Kiwi was kicked out of daycare for the last time." With an air of regret, she added, "There aren't any caregivers in Axia who are also elephantine fae."

Deandra recalled what Cruz had said about Oleander's usual attitude when she brought Kiwi to him for a checkup. Currently, Deandra couldn't quite tell if Oleander was offended or embarrassed by her predicament. Did she blame her own and her husband's parenting skills for needing to make so many accommodations for a "mundane sitter" after Kiwi had been repeatedly kicked out of daycare? Or did she blame the care system in Axia for not having more resources for people like her and her family?

Oleander cleared her throat and returned her focus to the wall hooks. She pointed to the harness and leash. "We're not toilet training him yet; he goes in the yard. When you need to go into the backyard, it's best to keep him in the harness. There are anti-jumping runes stitched into it. Without the runes, he'd scale the fence faster than you can move. The barbed wire along the top of the fence will stop him, but it's much less stressful if he can't scale the walls at all, you know?"

Deandra nodded. *Sure. Yes, of course. None of this is insane. Not at all.*

Cruz was definitely going to need to bring that industrial-sized spatula later.

Next, Oleander pointed to the baby carrier. "I believe I mentioned that, if he's really rowdy, you can tell him 'Let's go for walkies,' and he'll practically put the baby carrier on himself. Give him a snack, strap him in there, and walk until your legs give out. Works even better than driving him around in the car. There are runes stitched into that, too. Anti-tampering runes. They keep him from escaping."

Oh boy.

The final stop was back in the kitchen, which was devoid of the male Basnets. A faint shrieking peal of laughter sounded from somewhere beyond the kitchen.

"Cenzio is literally hosing him off in the backyard," Oleander said, as she walked to the fridge.

Deandra noted that the smashed blueberries still littered the plastic sheeting, so she discreetly let Havoc's leash go. He understood her intention, and he trotted over to hoover up the mess.

From the door of the refrigerator, Oleander pulled a sheet of paper free that had been held in place by a fridge magnet advertising a local plumber. "This is the same food list I emailed you, but I left one here for convenience. Cenzio will feed him lunch around three, so really all you need to worry about is snacks. There's a long list of the things he likes. Yetis aren't really built for large meals the way mundanes are. We graze all day long, so he's free to have as many snacks as he wants."

Oleander gave Deandra a rundown of the contents of the pantry—which was the size of a walk-in closet—including the location of the box of plastic sheeting to place under his high chair and a doomsday prepper amount of paper towels.

"Well," Oleander said, clapping her hands once and beaming at Deandra. "Any questions?"

So, *so* many.

"I think I've got it," Deandra said. "I'll text you if anything comes up."

Oleander's eyes welled with tears, and she quickly closed the gap between Deandra and herself. She took Deandra's hands into hers. "You don't know how much this means to me. Harmony is truly Goddess-sent for recommending you. I feel really good about this. The weight off my shoulders is … just … thank you."

Aha! So this was all the foul-mouthed gnome's fault. The size difference between the two women was probably a sight to behold.

Deandra smiled as brightly at Oleander as she could manage. "I'm happy to help."

The next several minutes were a flurry of activity as the Basnet parents got ready to leave. A very damp Kiwi and a blueberry-glutted Havoc were road-racing around the living room under Deandra's careful supervision.

Oleander left first, calling out a goodbye to her son that went completely ignored because Kiwi was too busy rolling in endless somersaults after Havoc, like a miniature multicolored snowball.

After calling out his own goodbye and promising to relieve Deandra at two o'clock, Cenzio left, too.

Deandra let out a calming breath. She could do this.

With terrifying speed, Kiwi darted around the back of the enormous sectional couch and out of sight. Before she could take a step in his direction, he'd already scaled his way to the top. He scanned the room for Havoc and found him hiding—ineffectively —behind a potted plant beside the TV stand. Deandra had no idea what the little fuzzball was planning; Havoc was clear on the other side of the room. When Kiwi bent his little legs, preparing to spring, she only managed two steps forward, a word of protest on her lips, before he launched off the back of the couch, limbs splayed wide like a flying squirrel. He soared an impressive ten feet, hit the carpeted floor with a belly-flopping *splat* that made Deandra wince, and then was on his feet again, waddling toward Havoc, screeching all the while.

Deandra could just exploit her dragon's boundless energy and wear them both out every day, right?

A minute later, however, Kiwi suddenly stilled in his romp with Havoc. He cocked his head as if listening for something, his rounded pink ears turning independently of each other like antennae searching for a better signal. He pushed himself onto two legs and tottered across the living room past Deandra, where she stood sentry in the open doorway between the living room and foyer, and toward the front door. "Mama?" he asked, his small voice a bit raspy as he stared at the door. "Papa?"

"They went to work, buddy," Deandra said, keeping her post in the doorway.

Kiwi turned toward her on unsteady legs and peered up at her. Havoc plopped into a seated position by her feet. Not even the sight of the dragon snapped Kiwi out of the staring contest he waged with Deandra.

"Kiwi ..." Deandra said slowly when the baby yeti hadn't moved an inch in several long seconds. "You want to play with Havoc some more?"

Havoc peeped.

No reaction.

"Are you hungry?" she tried.

Kiwi's face screwed up, and his bottom lip quivered dangerously.

Uh-oh.

"Hey, buddy. It's okay. Your dad will be back by—"

Kiwi, like a piece of plywood, tipped over backward onto the floor, let out an agonized noise, then burst into loud, noisy tears. He kicked and flailed and beat his little fists on the ground. Every time she tried to talk to him, he only wailed louder.

Deandra gusted a sigh.

It was going to be a *very* long day.

CHAPTER TEN

Kiwi sobbed on the floor in front of the door for a solid half hour before he ran out of tears. Deandra had spent that time sitting on the bottom step of the staircase so she had a perfect view of the wailing yeti, the front door, and the doorway into the living room. She'd opted to just let him cry himself out, as anything she'd tried to comfort him with in the first five minutes of the meltdown had only made him cry harder.

Havoc had tried cheering Kiwi up, too. The dragon dropped into play stance, he nuzzled the yeti's side with his muzzle, licked Kiwi's face, and even put on a very impressive dressage horse routine. Kiwi had been unmoved by any of it.

When Havoc had licked the bottom of the yeti's foot ten minutes into the tantrum, Deandra thought Havoc had snapped the baby back into himself, because his crying had finally stopped. The yeti sat bolt upright, stared at Havoc as if he'd just witnessed Havoc backhand his mother with the spade of his tail, and then used his entire body to scream bloody murder in Havoc's face. Havoc, startled by the outburst, had hopped backward a full three feet, then blown a gout of fire at the yeti.

Deandra's soul had left her body at the thought that Havoc had just roasted a toddler to death.

However, the yeti seemed to be blessed with the same lightning-quick, fear-induced instincts as the dragon, because half a breath later, the yeti's mouth hinged open, and out came a fire hose of icy water. A thick cloud of steam rose in the air as the two elemental blasts hit each other.

Havoc, soaking wet, had gone bucking and thrashing down the hallway back toward the kitchen. His wet feet meant he had a hard time finding purchase, and Deandra flinched every time she heard her dragon slam into something.

Kiwi, crisis averted, had flopped onto his back on the sopping-wet tile and resumed his tantrum with renewed vigor. When she'd tried to scoop him off the floor so she could go check on the destruction her dragon had wrought, the yeti tried to bite her with all the ferocity of a feral gerbil.

So she'd parked herself on the bottom step and waited the yeti out. Havoc had returned eventually, looking miserable. He'd curled up in a ball by her feet, keeping a watchful eye on the yeti.

Deandra had just hit level 37 on the recently downloaded

Lollipop Jumble when the crying abruptly stopped. She and Havoc both hazarded a glance at the yeti.

Kiwi was sitting now, little fist rubbing against an eye as if he'd just woken from a nap. Perhaps he went into a kind of fugue state when he lost his marbles during a tantrum.

His gaze flicked between Deandra and Havoc. After running a pink fist under his pink nose, he asked, "What do?"

Deandra cocked her head. "What?"

He pointed a little finger toward her phone. "What do?"

"Oh, what am I doing?"

He bobbed his head.

She turned her phone around where there was still a looping display of exploding confetti congratulating her on clearing her level. "It's a game. Want to see?"

Bobbing his head again, he got to his feet and ambled over, stopping when he was a few inches away from Havoc, who currently barred the path between the ground floor and the first step. Havoc issued a low growl. Deandra had never heard him growl before.

Kiwi stumbled back a step, his face screwed up. With the pink ring of fur around each eye, he looked like an irate panda. "Doggie not nice."

Deandra placed a hand on Havoc's side. "It's okay, boy."

Havoc tipped his head back to look at her.

"I need you to promise no more fire, okay?"

The dragon's muzzle bunched up as if to say, *"You're going to take* his *side?"*

"I know you didn't use your fire on purpose, but if you'd hit him with it, he could have been hurt badly."

Havoc's unchanged expression suggested he didn't see a problem with her proposed scenario.

"If Kiwi gets hurt, then his parents will be very upset with me. You'll end up back with Ranger Vicks—"

Havoc growl-yipped.

Startled, Kiwi fell onto his furry backside. Thankfully, it wasn't punctuated by another blast of cold water. He scrambled back to his feet.

"—and I'll probably go to people jail. We'll never see each other again. You don't want that, do you?"

In one fluid motion, Havoc had launched himself at her. He wrapped his forelegs around her neck and vigorously licked the side of her head. She laughed and pushed him far enough away that she could look him in the eye. His back legs were on the floor while his front paws were on either of her knees.

"No fire, okay?"

Havoc peeped.

She glanced around the dragon at the yeti, who had a finger up his nose. "No spitting water either, okay?"

Kiwi thought about it, then nodded. "I see game?"

Havoc dropped back to all fours on the floor, but inched out of the way so Kiwi had an unobstructed path to Deandra.

"If you apologize to Havoc, you can see the game," Deandra said.

Kiwi yanked his finger out of his nose and took a few cautious steps toward Havoc. The dragon lowered his head. Kiwi patted it —albeit where he *thought* Havoc's head was—and said, "Good doggie."

Eh. Close enough.

Havoc licked Kiwi's face, which earned the dragon a happy giggle.

"All right, climb on up here," Deandra said, intending to make Kiwi approach her rather than the other way around. It gave Deandra a bit of an upper hand because she was the one calling the shots, but it also gave Kiwi some agency. If he made the conscious decision to approach her, it would hopefully cut down on the potential biting.

Kiwi wasn't terribly graceful, so it took him a few tries to get situated in her lap. With her arms bracketing him, she held her phone in front of them with both hands, her forearms resting on her legs. She started up Lollipop Jumble, turned on the music she'd muted until now, and started on level 38. The game was too complicated for Kiwi, so he merely watched her play, clapping when she successfully matched three or more lollipops of the same color. She occasionally set off lollipop fireworks that made colors cascade across the screen. He liked those best.

After she'd cleared two more levels, Kiwi abruptly wiggled out of her lap, climbed down the step butt-first, and then peered up at her. "Boring."

She laughed. "Noted. You hungry? You didn't eat much of your breakfast."

"Chewy ohs!" he cheered, then raced down the hallway toward the kitchen, his footfalls like little drumbeats, shrieking in delight.

It took some work, but Deandra figured out that "chewy ohs" weren't his favorite cereal brand, but papaya gummy rings. He ate ten of them before he went racing into the living room. Havoc trotted after him, acquiring a papaya gummy of his own.

The next three hours were like that—each activity only keeping Kiwi's interest for twenty minutes, if that, before he went tearing off through the house looking for his next entertainment fix. Deandra was grateful there were no more epic tantrums, nor blasts of fire or ice water, but she now understood why the daycare facilities had kicked the kid out. He was constantly on the move, wanted to eat every half hour, got bored very easily, and any little frustration was almost sure to make him weepy. A well-timed lick of the face from Havoc, or Deandra coming up with a distraction on the fly, was usually enough to stave off a meltdown, but she had to be *on* at all times. Kiwi needed one-on-one attention that a daycare catering to several kids at once probably couldn't provide.

He finally started to run out of steam a little after noon, which was good timing since Deandra also needed to check on Barnaby.

There was one thing Deandra needed to do before the trio set out for their next adventure. When Kiwi was playing quietly in his room with blocks and she noted his eyes were a bit droopy, she waved Havoc over to her sentry post in the doorway. Havoc's role in the block-building game was to help Kiwi knock the tower to the floor in as chaotic a fashion as possible, but the dragon got a very stern, "No, doggie!" if Havoc tried to participate too soon.

Havoc met her at the door.

Squatting low, Deandra whispered, "Stay right here, and don't let him out of your sight, okay? Block him in here if you need to. I need to use the restroom. I can't hold it anymore. I'll be five minutes, tops."

Havoc peeped in acknowledgment, but very softly.

She was going to have to spend a considerable chunk of her earnings on buying Havoc as much cheese as he could stomach as payment for being her assistant.

Deandra tiptoed into the bathroom, eased the door shut, and took a moment to bask in both the quiet and the lack of baby yeti. She'd just finished using the facilities and was washing her hands when a crash sounded from beyond the door. It didn't sound like a block-tower crash, either.

She wrenched the door open and darted for the stairs first, sure she'd find either the yeti or the dragon at the base of them, having taken a tumble. She'd be lying if she said thoughts of Lydia hadn't flitted through her mind. How could Deandra have thought that leaving the yeti with only another baby for supervision for even five minutes was a good idea? Had the baby gotten annoyed that Havoc was blocking his path, so he'd somehow water-blasted the dragon out a window?

No bodies lay at the bottom of the stairs, so she ran two doors down the hallway and skidded to a stop outside Kiwi's bedroom door. The block tower was still standing, the windows were intact, but the room was otherwise empty. She frantically checked the remaining rooms upstairs.

No baby yeti.

No baby dragon.

"Havoc! Kiwi!" she called as she ran down the stairs double-time.

She half expected to find the front door blasted off its hinges, but it still stood resolutely where she'd last seen it. She would have asked it where the baby monsters went, but if the door answered back, Cruz would need more than a large spatula to scrape her off the ground.

Hitting the first floor, she grabbed hold of the knob at the end of the banister to help whip her around the corner and down the hallway toward the kitchen. Her steps faltered minutely when another crash echoed from ahead.

When she came to yet another skidding stop, her eyes doubled in diameter. Every cabinet in the kitchen was open, a trash can had been knocked over, and Kiwi was on *top* of the refrigerator. A very familiar-looking pink spade stuck out of the overturned trash can.

"Havoc!"

Thud.

Havoc wiggled out of the trash can butt first. His cheeks bulged, like an overindulgent chipmunk. He had the good grace to look ashamed as he sat in his dejected Eeyore pose.

"What on *earth* are you eating?" Deandra asked.

Havoc spit out a mouthful of what looked like coffee grounds.

Rolling her eyes, she spun around to face her newest charge who ... was no longer on top of the refrigerator.

She spun in a frantic circle. A faint scratching sounded behind her. Stepping over the mess Havoc had left on the floor, she peeked into the pantry. The door stood wide open. "Kiwi?"

No answer.

Creeping farther into the pantry, she reached up to grab the pull cord that hung from the ceiling. "Reaching up" entailed jumping to snag hold of the cord. It took three tries.

As light flooded the pantry, she scanned the shelves. Scrambling sounded to her right, and she turned just as Kiwi, arms splayed, leaped off the top shelf, seemingly aiming for her face. She stumbled back a step and managed to grab the furry snowball before he hit the floor. He cheered, tiny fists in the air, proud of her for catching him. He seemed content after that to let her balance him on her hip.

Coffee grounds clung to the top of his head.

Hork!

Deandra whirled around just as Havoc vomited up yet more coffee grounds in a brownish watery mess. She started to worry that the coffee had made him sick, and that he would need a trip to the vet, when he vomited again. Two action figures landed in the puddle. A pair of magic-wielding characters, presumably from a kid's hub-made show, now looked like they were mud wrestling.

Havoc stared up at her, tongue lolling out the side of his mouth and looking quite pleased with himself.

"You were supposed to watch him!" Deandra admonished. "How did you two make this much of a mess in five minutes?"

"Want plum," was all Kiwi had to say for himself.

"What if we go on a walk and you eat your plum on the way?"

Kiwi's little face puckered. Oleander had said the promise of a walk would amp the kid up. But then Deandra remembered Oleander's unfortunate phrasing.

Sighing, Deandra reworded the question. "Do you want to go for walkies?"

Kiwi came unglued, bucking and kicking in her grasp. Thankfully, the digits of his toes weren't tipped with claws. "Walkies, walkies, walkies," he chanted as he lost his ever-loving mind.

"Chill, kid! I'm going to drop you, and then we'll have to go to the doctor instead of walkies."

Kiwi instantly went deadweight in her arms, hanging over her forearm like a sack of flour. With her hands hooked under his armpits, she turned him to face her. He still hung there limply as if his bones were made of rubber. "No like doctor," he said gravely.

"Okay. I'm going to put you down, and then we'll put on your walkies clothes, okay?"

"'Kay!"

The second his feet touched the floor, he was off like a shot. Havoc issued a chirp-bark and went tearing off after him, slipped in his pile of coffee grounds, righted himself, and kept moving. Deandra sighed deeply. When Kiwi went down for his nap, she might join him. Though she probably needed the remaining time —and all the paper towels—to clean up the house. After grabbing a plum from the fridge, she ventured toward the foyer.

She found Kiwi below the hooks that held his baby carrier. He hopped continuously on the balls of his feet. Havoc joined him in the bouncing for no discernible reason.

Kiwi was surprisingly cooperative about getting into the contraption. After getting him strapped in, she hooked the baby yeti to her torso like a backward backpack.

The yeti kicked his feet in delight. "Walkies, walkies, walkies!"

She fished the plum out of her pocket and handed it to him.

He grabbed it in his little fist and kicked his feet even harder. The baby carrier somehow minimized the kid's thrashing. "Plum, plum, plum!"

After grabbing her purse, hooking Havoc's leash to his harness, and making sure she had the Basnets' house keys, she set off for Angela's house. Deandra hadn't let herself think too much about how badly Barnaby was likely to lose his marbles over the arrival of visitors.

Once she'd gotten permission from Angela to bring Kiwi and Havoc with her, Deandra had pushed the rest of the process out of her mind until just now. What if the poor little guy fainted? Clearly, Havoc and Kiwi were a terrible influence on each other— what if they corrupted Barnaby?

A long, snorting inhale made Deandra come up short. She glanced down at Kiwi strapped to her chest and goggled down at the miracle that was a dozing yeti. He still had the plum clutched in his fist; he hadn't even taken a bite before he knocked out.

Maybe Barnaby would be less likely to suffer heart failure if Kiwi wasn't conscious during the visit.

AS A GIFT FROM THE UNIVERSE, BARNABY WAS INSTANTLY ENAMORED of Havoc who, notably, was on his best behavior now that Kiwi was fast asleep. The two didn't romp, the way Havoc did with the yeti, but walked side by side amicably, which was saying a lot for Barnaby.

During the ten-minute walk to Angela's house and the thirty-minute walk with Barnaby and Havoc, the yeti never awoke. The constant buzz of his snore and the occasional violent twitch of one of his hanging feet were the only indications that the little guy was still breathing.

Instead of heading east on Coterie Road toward Wheeler Avenue and taking the same path to the Basnets' house that she used to get to Angela's, Deandra decided to go west instead. She hadn't been in that direction yet, and the slightly longer walk back might keep Kiwi asleep for even longer. Her only worry was that her dragon's energy was starting to flag, too. She couldn't carry him back *and* keep the yeti strapped to her chest.

As she neared the corner of Coterie and Eddy Way, she realized that, if she went left, Eddy would deposit her at Heather's Elixirs after only a block. As much as she would love to see Wendy, Deandra knew she had to get back to the Basnet house soon, not only for Havoc's sake, but for the sake of Oleander's house. Deandra whimpered at the memory of all the thrown-up coffee grounds she still needed to wipe up.

Sighing, she trudged ahead, chanting, "Turn right, turn right, turn right" in her head.

But when she reached the apartment complex on the corner, she stopped altogether. The Pointe on Coterie was a pair of three-story buildings that housed apartments—or maybe townhomes.

Condos? There was nothing particularly noteworthy about the beige walls, black accents, or wrought-iron balconies.

Nothing except the yellow caution tape that marked the door of downstairs unit 3 with an X.

"You a podcaster, too?"

Deandra jumped slightly at the sound of the voice, scanning the area around her for the source. An even larger complex stood on the other side of the road to Deandra's left. She scanned the few windows she could see from this angle.

The creak of rusty hinges drew her attention the other way, back toward The Pointe on Coterie. An elderly woman in a pink bathrobe came shuffling out of a downstairs unit next to unit 3. Deandra guessed she was at least eighty. The woman flapped a hand in Deandra's general direction as she moved down the walkway that led to her front door, then across the sidewalk toward Deandra. A swatch of grass and a walkway were all that separated Deandra from the caution tape.

"Are you a podcaster?" the woman repeated as she stopped a few feet away.

She stood with her hands on her hips as she stared up at Deandra. At first glance, Deandra would peg her as mundane, but she knew not to make assumptions in Axia. This seemingly fragile woman could have aging magic, just like Deandra's own grandparents.

"No, ma'am," Deandra said, turning to face the woman instead of the door.

Havoc cautiously inched forward to sniff the toes of the woman's grubby slippers. She either didn't notice or didn't care. The dragon only inspected her for a few moments before returning to Deandra's side.

"Pah!" the woman said. "I was right next door to a crime, and no one wants to interview me on their podcast! I'd be a great guest."

Deandra had been sure the woman had come out to chase Deandra off for snooping. Suddenly remembering something

Mavis had said back at Gorgon's Alley. *"The old lady next door to Lydia kept trying to say she heard a commotion around midnight the night before."* Deandra eyed the door the woman had hustled out of. She'd emerged from unit 5. She also remembered Mavis had said the woman had bad eyesight and was a busybody.

"Did Lydia Monroe live in unit 3?" Deandra asked.

"Aha! You've heard about it," the woman said, clucking her tongue. "Granted, it's not like murders happen often here, so it was bound to make the rounds eventually. They certainly don't happen next door to me often!"

"Murder?" Deandra asked, feigning ignorance. "I thought Lydia accidentally fell down the stairs."

"This is why I need to be on a podcast! I have the whole scoop. Well, maybe not the *whole* scoop, but I should be considered a key witness."

"Did you talk to the police already?" Deandra asked.

"Oh, sure. I talked to the werecats, and the mundane police, and that tiny, mean friend of Lydia's, too."

"Mavis?"

"I think that's her name. Skinny little thing. Needs more meat on her bones. I told her as much, and she yelled at me to mind my own business. Then in the same breath asks me to tell her what I heard and saw. I told her I'd already talked to the police, and I wasn't going to talk to the likes of her. But she *needs* to talk to me, because she keeps saying her friend kicked the can on Monday afternoon. She doesn't even know the right day! But meanies don't get juicy gossip. She called me an 'old bat'! The nerve. Couldn't be sure if that was a dig at my age or my animal, but it was disrespectful either way."

"Your animal?" Deandra asked.

Poof!

The woman had literally turned into a bat the size of a dirt bike. The tuft of fur on top of its head was the same color as the woman's bathrobe. Deandra shrieked so loudly it woke up Kiwi, who started snarling and gnashing at the air. He squeezed the plum in his hand so hard, the fruit exploded. He tossed the ruined fruit to the ground, threw his head back so hard it thudded against Deandra's chest, and he wailed as if everyone he loved had just perished simultaneously.

The woman snapped back to her human form. "What's with all the racket!" Her eyes widened to the size of dinner plates at the sight of Kiwi. Had she not seen him until now? With surprising agility, she darted forward, grabbed one of the ties of her bathrobe, and tickled the bottom of Kiwi's foot with it.

He stopped crying abruptly and leveled an intense stare at the woman. Deandra had every intention of swinging her body one hundred eighty degrees, considering what had happened the last time someone had violated one of Kiwi's feet, but before either Kiwi or Deandra could react, the woman had produced an apple from her pocket and held it out to him. The apple was a shade Deandra had never seen before—some color between red and purple.

Kiwi squeaked and took it happily, the fruit so large that he had to hold it in two hands. He took an enthusiastic bite. Havoc, from the sound of it, was inhaling the pulped plum off the sidewalk.

Deandra sagged as adrenaline once again ebbed. As much as she wanted to go out with Cruz later, she wasn't sure she'd be able to stay awake past two thirty at this rate. No wonder Oleander and Cenzio were so tired.

"That's a maroon maiden," the woman said. "Best apple money can buy. I keep them handy for all occasions. There aren't too many things in this life that can't be solved with a maroon maiden."

Deandra genuinely had no idea how to react to any of this. "Murder probably couldn't be solved by a maroon maiden," she said without thinking. She was so tired, her brain filter was on the fritz.

The woman cackled. "I like you!" She held out a wrinkled

hand with perfectly manicured nails—lacquered in pink, of course. "I'm Ursula."

Deandra shook it. "Dee."

Ursula planted her hands on her hips. "You new to town or something? I haven't seen you around here before."

"I've only been living in Axia for a few weeks. I just started caring for Baby Basnet here today, so I'm getting to know the neighborhood," Deandra said.

Ursula hinged forward to get a better look at Kiwi. She squinted hard, even though she was only a few inches from him. "His markings threw me off at first. I thought he was a jilan, but now I'm thinking yeti?"

"That's right," Deandra said.

Ursula stood straight as a board, her expression shuttering a bit as she shoved her hands into the pockets of her robe. "I see."

Deandra's brows smashed together. "Something wrong?"

"I told everything to the police," Ursula said, almost like an apology. "I called it in on Sunday night—or I guess technically Monday morning. Told them I heard shouting and a loud thud. Told them something wasn't right and that they should come see what happened. I told them …" She took a few steps back, gaze focused solely on Kiwi now. "I told them I saw a ginormous white creature outside the house that night. It was moving pretty quick, too. Hard to mistake seeing a creature that big, you know?"

Mavis hadn't mentioned anything about Ursula seeing a possible suspect fleeing Lydia's place. But maybe that was because Mavis had called Ursula an "old bat" by then, and Ursula had kept her intel to herself.

"So Lydia really *didn't* die on Monday afternoon?" Deandra asked, watching the slowly retreating woman.

Ursula shook her head. "I tried telling the police what I saw, but they don't listen to me. I heard a commotion really late on Sunday. I was playing my game—one of them mystery detective games where you gotta creep around places and find clues—and I got up around midnight to use the john. Or was that when I topped off my drink? Mighta been the time I made a peanut butter and maroon maiden sandwich. Either way, that's when I heard it. I remember looking at the clock by my bed right when I heard the thud because it was so loud. The numbers are huge and bright red on account of my eyes not being so good sometimes. It was 12:24 a.m. It's been burned into my head. If I close my eyes, I can still hear that Goddess-awful crash and see those blazing numbers. I called the cops right away and told them they had to come check things out."

"Did they?" Deandra asked, wondering why the death witch would have told Mavis that Lydia's death had been around noon on Monday, rather than midnight on Sunday. A twelve-hour difference was huge. Wendy and Keith, though neither of them was an expert by any stretch, had thought four hours was too soon for a body to be "ice cold." If Lydia had actually been deceased for upward of *fourteen* hours by the time Mavis found her, that changed things considerably.

But what would explain the discrepancy? Deandra only saw three possibilities: the death witch was wrong, the death witch had given Mavis an incorrect time of death on purpose, or Ursula was misremembering. Ursula's eyesight seemed to be as faulty as Mavis had suggested; maybe Ursula had read the time wrong when she'd gotten up to use "the john" or top off her drink or make a sandwich. After all, Kiwi had been literally strapped to Deandra's chest the entire time, and yet Ursula hadn't seemed to notice him until he was screaming his little head off. She still hadn't seemed to notice Havoc at all, and most everyone reacted to the sight of a dire wolf.

And yet, was it that easy to misinterpret the sight of a yeti hauling tail down the sidewalk?

"The werecats said they'd send someone out," Ursula said, redirecting Deandra's attention. The woman was still slowly inching backward. "But they tell me that a lot. They get annoyed with me for doing their job for them. They need to patrol the area more—that's what I always tell them. All kinds of mayhem happens in that apartment complex down the road. I call the cats several times a week. Crime in this town would be down by half if they took me seriously."

"Maybe you should start your *own* podcast," Deandra offered, hoping to lighten the mood a bit.

Was Ursula eyeing little Kiwi—who was still munching happily on the maroon maiden—because she honestly thought one of his parents had killed Lydia?

"Maybe I will," Ursula said, finally tearing her wide-eyed gaze away from the yeti and returning it to Deandra's face. "Be careful, young lady. I don't think the Basnets are who you think they are."

With that, Ursula scurried back to unit 5 and slammed the door behind her.

Unnerved, Deandra studied the yellow X of crime-scene tape one more time before she tugged at Havoc's leash and headed back toward the Basnets' house.

As she walked, it wasn't Ursula's parting words that repeated in Deandra's head on a loop, but something Oleander herself had told Deandra.

"I didn't sleep at all Sunday night, tossing and turning because I was worried sick I'd made another mistake—made a choice that benefited me and not Kiwi," she'd said. *"I, of course, didn't want Lydia out of the picture this way."*

Had Oleander been unable to sleep on Sunday night—the same night Ursula claimed to see a large creature fitting the yeti's description—because she'd gone to Lydia's house against her better judgment? Had the yeti not been plagued by the weight of making a potentially bad hiring choice, but by an even worse decision made in the middle of the night?

It wasn't lost on Deandra that the walk from Lydia's apartment to Oleander's front door took all of five minutes. The distance could be eaten up even faster with legs as long as the yeti's and if one weren't weighed down by a dragon dragging his feet.

After putting Kiwi in his crib and instructing Havoc to keep him company on the floor—both of them were out cold before Deandra reached the doorway of the bedroom—Deandra set about tidying the house.

As she scrubbed, swept, and wiped down surfaces, she couldn't shake the nagging thought that she only had this job because her new employer had murdered the previous candidate.

CHAPTER ELEVEN

"Should I be concerned?"

Deandra opened her eyes to find Wendy staring down at her, hands on her knees. Deandra lay flat on her back on the living room floor in her classic starfish pose. Havoc was curled up next to her, his head on one of her arms. He'd been drooling excessively again, but she couldn't be bothered to do anything about it. The tip of one of his wings dug into her side, and she felt the sporadic flick of his tail's spade whacking her softly in the shin every once in a while as he dreamed, but she couldn't be bothered with any of that either.

"Can I turn this spot into my bedroom?" Deandra asked. "You can rent out my room. Just tell any newbies to step over my body."

"Rough day?"

"I don't think it was as bad as being turned into a rabbit—"

Wendy's eye twitched.

"—but it's gotta be a close second," Deandra said. "I have so much to tell you, but I don't think I'm long for this world."

Wendy had gotten in late last night, well after Deandra had gone to bed, and then Deandra had left that morning before Wendy had gotten up. She could have texted Wendy about everything, but it was too much to type—plus talking in person was better anyway. Except today. Talking today in any form was the worst.

"I guess I'll just eat these cinnamon bun scones on my own, then," Wendy said.

Deandra propped herself up on an elbow. Havoc snorted awake.

"Cinnamon bun, you say?" Deandra asked.

Wendy had already walked away.

When Deandra heard the crinkle of a paper bag, she decided to get up. For Wendy's sake, of course. If Deandra stayed sprawled on the floor, Wendy might eat *all* the scones and make herself sick. She was doing this for the health of her cousin, Deandra told her aching body.

Deandra was halfway to the dining room when she realized Havoc wasn't trotting alongside her. She glanced over her shoulder just as the dragon flopped onto his side. He arched his back, stretching out all four limbs, before going limp again. He groaned like a grumpy bear, then closed his eyes. It spoke to how worn out he was that he couldn't even muster up the energy for a snack. It was also a relief that whatever amount of coffee grounds he might have consumed hadn't hopped him up on caffeine.

After positioning herself in her usual place at the dining room table across from Wendy, Deandra picked up the scone already waiting for her on a small plate. However, she froze with the pastry only an inch from her mouth. She slowly lowered the cinnamon-dusted, icing-drizzled treat.

"This isn't laced with a truth tincture or something that'll force me to blab all my secrets, is it?" Deandra asked.

Wendy cocked a brow. "Are there truths that need blabbing?" Then she narrowed her eyes. "You *did* use the last of my shampoo, didn't you?"

"It wasn't on purpose! We both have green bottles in there. It won't happen again. Mostly because I don't love the green apple scent."

"To be honest, I don't really love it either, but Nathan does. So now I'll be buying it in bulk."

Deandra laughed. "How was dinner?"

"Axian Delights is amazing, but it's way too expensive," Wendy said. "There was a big hubbub because a Collective sorcerer from Kensey was there last night. *Annnd* our waitress said Claudia Williamson from *Faet of the Heart* was there last week."

Deandra choked on a bite of her scone, having forgotten that she'd been worried Wendy had truth-poisoned her. "Whoa! I figured I'd left celebrity sightings behind in LA. Claudia's incredible in season one so far."

"Oh, you sweet summer child," Wendy tsked. "You have twelve seasons to go. You're not ready for what's coming. After the last season finale, I'm surprised Claudia risked going out in public after what her character did to—"

Deandra dropped her scone on her plate so she could clap her hands over her ears. "No spoilers!"

Wendy mimicked locking up her lips, so Deandra slowly unshielded her ears. "Anyway, Nathan's eyes bugged out of his head when he saw the bill. He wouldn't let me pay half, but you'd better believe he got boodled later."

Deandra's face screwed up. "TMI much? Did you two boodle *here*? When there are *children* present?"

Havoc, as if on cue, issued a loud snore from the living room.

"*What?*" Wendy asked with a snort. "Oh! Oh my Goddess. No. Boodle is a money-transfer app! I think it comes from 'the whole kit and caboodle.' But now my brain will go straight to the gutter every time I hear it, so thanks for that."

"You're welcome!" Deandra said cheerfully, then took another generous bite of her scone.

Wendy gestured at her. "These aren't from Extra Sensory Pastry, by the way, so there's no truth tincture in it—also how dare you accuse me of slipping something into your food?" She didn't look remotely offended, so Deandra kept chewing. "Besides, Sebastian and Isabel only add extras that are tailor-made to the purchaser for exactly that reason. They don't want people to buy something meant for the buyer and then have the person turn around and give the pastries or beverages to someone else who might not take kindly to magical tampering."

That was good to know.

"Wait," Deandra said. "Is truth tincture really a thing? I was kidding!"

With complete seriousness, Wendy said, "From what I've heard, the Collective as a whole has truth serum on hand that they use on criminals who commit serious crimes. But I don't think even run-of-the-mill murder is enough to get you truth-serumed. You gotta be involved in some real shady stuff for that to happen. Once you're at the point of getting the truth juice, you're probably either going to get exiled from the hub system entirely, or you're going to wind up shipped off to the prison hub in Antarctica."

Out of all of that, Deandra was somehow most hung up on the phrase "run-of-the-mill murder." Axia was like a different universe sometimes.

"Enough about criminals and me boodling Nathan," Wendy said. "Tell me about the yeti."

As Deandra recounted her afternoon with Kiwi and Havoc,

she had to pause on occasion to allow Wendy the time needed to laugh uproariously at Deandra's pain. She sobered up, though, when Deandra got to the part about Ursula, the elderly, farsighted bat shifter.

"Do you have any idea how many yetis are in Axia?" Deandra asked.

"Oh yes, let me pull up my personal copy of the census records ..."

"Your sarcasm is not appreciated," Deandra said.

"We both know that's a lie." Wendy stared off into space as she thought. "Is census data public? I feel like I should know this ..."

When Wendy grabbed her phone off the table to do some light research, Deandra remembered she was supposed to go out with Cruz tonight. What if he'd texted her details and she hadn't answered him, and now he thought she was second-guessing the date? Or even worse, ghosting him. She wasn't even sure where her phone *was*. She'd more or less stumbled inside after climbing the four million—fifteen, max—stairs up to Wendy's apartment and then collapsed in a heap.

She pushed away from the table to hunt it down.

It turned out that she'd left her phone in the bathroom—*inside* the medicine cabinet, for reasons that were a mystery even to herself. The screen told her it was just after five o'clock. It also told her that, between two o'clock and now, she'd missed eight texts and one call from Wendy, a call from her grandma, two texts from her mom, and two texts from Cruz.

She pulled up Cruz's first.

2:15

Hi. Did you survive?

3:45

The spatula is ready when you are

Standing in the bathroom doorway, she quickly typed out a reply.

CRUZ

DEANDRA

Hi! Sorry! I came home, promptly lost track of my phone, then collapsed on the floor. I would have napped, but I was too busy questioning my life decisions

CRUZ

Ha! Did you ever figure out who recommended you to the Basnets?

DEANDRA

Oh! Yes. Harmony. She's a gnome with a cat named Marshall

CRUZ

Doesn't ring any bells, but I'd be happy to help you rough her up for having the audacity to sing your praises

DEANDRA

How sweet! Also, I'm not sure if "roughing up" residents is the right brand message for a veterinarian

CRUZ

I'm off the clock in half an hour and I have a pair of brass knuckles in my glove box

She snorted.

CRUZ

You still up for dinner? Wasn't sure if lying on the floor in a fit of existential dread was restful enough that you'd have the energy to leave the house

DEANDRA

I'm still up for dinner. Last night I was feeling a little guilty about the idea of leaving Havoc trapped in the apartment for a few hours, but Kiwi wore him out so thoroughly, he didn't even get up for a pastry

CRUZ

I normally would chastise someone quite extensively for feeding their pets pastries, but "dire wolves" are known for their iron stomachs

DEANDRA

He was bested by coffee grounds today

CRUZ

I have many questions, but most importantly, how's 6:30 for a pick-up time?

DEANDRA

Perfect

After texting him Wendy's address, then feeling foolish because he already had it, Deandra jogged down the hallway. "DEFCON 6!" she said as she came to a stuttering stop by the dining room table.

Wendy looked up sharply from her phone. "Aren't there only five levels? I think level 1 is the worst one."

"DEFCON 1!" Deandra corrected. "I have a date in T-minus 90 minutes."

Wendy shot to her feet, phone abandoned. "Where are you going?"

"I don't know. He just said 'dinner,' that he was choosing the place, and he's picking me up," Deandra said.

"Ooh, he's taking charge but also being super vague. I like it."

"He doesn't strike me as an Axian Delights kind of guy," Deandra said. "But that's not based on actual information."

"You are equally unhelpful," Wendy said. "Go take a shower because you smell vaguely of garbage and disinfectant. I'll have outfits ready when you're done."

This had been their routine in high school, too, whenever either of them had a date. Wendy had always been better at wardrobe, while Deandra had been on makeup duty. Deandra scurried for the bathroom.

Though it took them an inordinate amount of time to decide

between a soft pink knee-length sundress or skirt/blouse combo, Deandra was ready to go with enough time to spare that she and Wendy were able to take a sleepy Havoc on a quick jaunt around the neighborhood. As she walked, she felt confident in her choice of black skirt with built-in shorts, a flowy mint-green blouse, and ballet flats. If walking was part of this date, she'd still be comfortable.

She could have asked Cruz where they were going to help dispel some of her preparation jitters, but where was the fun in that?

When Cruz texted that he'd just pulled into the parking lot, Wendy and Havoc were curled up on the couch together. Deandra grabbed her things, gave Havoc a kiss on the head, and thanked Wendy for, well, being Wendy.

"Remember, if you two come back for a nightcap, a white sock on the doorknob means—"

"Goodbye!" Deandra called, cutting Wendy off with a slam of the door.

She found Cruz wandering down the walkway that ran between her block of apartments and the parking lot. He squinted down at his phone, then up at the building, muttering to himself as he tried to find the building in question.

"Good evening, Dr. Caddel!" she called out, though for some reason she'd slipped into a voice reminiscent of a 1940s radio announcer.

Maybe it wasn't too late for her to run back inside. She was deeply concerned that the majority of her companionship being oddball mythical animals was making her even weirder than usual.

Cruz looked up sharply from three doors down, the setting sun in his eyes. When he lifted a hand to shield them and finally spotted her, the slightly shy smile he offered her made her stomach flutter.

It was honestly nice to know that the butterflies taking up resi-dence in her belly had just been dormant all this time and that they hadn't been reduced to desiccated husks. She'd cared for her ex, Mark, of course, but hindsight over these past several months had made it clear she hadn't been *excited* about Mark in longer than she'd cared to admit.

She waited while Cruz closed the gap. He was in a pair of dark-wash jeans and a nice button-up shirt, suggesting he was taking her somewhere classier than a fast-food joint but not as fancy as Axian Delights—for which she was grateful. She, too, would feel inclined to boodle Cruz after dinner if the bill was excessive, and the current state of her bank account probably wouldn't allow it.

"I'm uhh … back this way," he said, hooking a thumb over his shoulder. "Sorry. I get turned around in this place every time. Would it kill them to choose a color other than gray?"

They headed for his car.

"I think confusing layouts and a muted color scheme are requirements for apartment complexes."

Slowly walking alongside her, he said, "I lived in a complex for about four years that made so little sense, food delivery drivers started requiring residents to meet them at the rental office. Everyone got lost. There was a running joke that there were portals scattered around the place that opened at random, sucked people in, then deposited them in another spot in the complex."

"Your own personal Glitch, huh?"

He smiled down at her. "Did some research on hubs, did you?"

They reached his car—an older model slate-gray Subaru—and he hustled over to open the passenger-side door for her.

"Before you get too excited about how chivalrous I am …" He gave the door a very hard yank, and it creaked on its hinges. "The door sticks."

She climbed in, noting that the back seat was covered in a beige, tarp-like hammock. There were four loops—two on each side of the rectangular piece of fabric—and each loop ringed a headrest. The light dusting of dark fur in the hammock suggested the back seat was designated for a dog—or possibly something more exotic.

The interior of the car was overall a bit worn, but tidy.

Cruz slid into the driver's seat. *His* door was quiet as a whisper.

"What happened to the door?" she asked as she strapped herself in. "Are you really terrible at parking? Do you bump into dumpsters and trees a lot? It's okay. You can tell me."

He turned in his seat to eye her curiously. "Should I be concerned about *your* parking if you think *bumping into trees* isn't highly alarming?"

"I believe curbs are more of a suggestion of where not to drive, more so than a hard rule, you know?"

His gaze roved her face. "You're very strange."

"And yet, you still asked me out."

"That I did."

They stared at each other for a beat. Her face flushed. He coughed awkwardly and looked away.

Once he'd started up the car and pulled onto the road, he said, "To answer your door question, I got T-boned about six months ago. I'd gotten a little restless and decided to take a trip out into the mundane world for the weekend. The car accident happened as I was backing out of a spot at a restaurant. A teenage boy who was texting didn't see me, and *crunch*.

"Insurance claims get really complicated, it turns out, when it's a hub-registered car that gets in an accident with a mundane one. The damage to my car wasn't *that* bad, all things considered, and the kid was adamant that his parents were going to ground him until he was ninety. The bumper on his car fell clean off. I got the kid's info, but once I realized how much of a hassle filing the claim would be, I decided not to. Instead, I watched a *lot* of videos on DIY car repair and was able to make enough adjustments that I could get the door to close again. Good enough for me."

"How resourceful."

"Eh," he said, coming to a stop at a red light. "I'm not sure if it's resourcefulness or an unhealthy emotional attachment to this car." He cleared his throat. "Uhh ... so *have* you been doing research on hubs?"

Ah, yes, her comment about the Glitch. She *wanted* to ask about his emotional attachment to the vehicle, but she resisted. "I was having a hard time falling asleep after I talked to you last night. Not because ... not because *of* you or anything." Heat crawled up her neck. "I was nervous about my first day with Kiwi. I've been trying to get through the booklet I got from the Welcome Center on my first day here. Now I know that the Glitch is an event that happened in the early 1900s where portals opened all over the world—some for only a few minutes, and some for a full two days. Lots of fae or magic-touched ended up in this realm by accident, since the portals opened and closed at random. And then, forty-eight hours later, the portals all closed for good and magical people got permanently stuck in this realm."

"That's the gist of it," he said, smiling over at her before resuming the drive toward locations unknown.

"Is it rude of me to ask if you're considered fae or magic-touched?" she asked, still unsure what the etiquette was. People like Callie openly announced their abilities, and shifters like Ursula and Allegra burst into their animal forms on a whim, but Deandra had to guess that others kept their powers to themselves.

"Not rude, no," he said. "Besides, the defining line gets blurrier every generation as bloodlines get diluted."

"Oh! Like how draken who are descendants of dragon shifters are now people who have heightened senses but can no longer shift since so many of them mated with the magic-less native humans in this realm?"

"Exactly," Cruz said, nodding. "The terms are largely interchangeable, but not everyone who is magic-touched is also fae, as some magic-touched people existed in this realm prior to the Glitch. Vampires, werewolves—Goddess rest their souls—nature witches, psychics, and mediums were already here. The Glitch introduced new magic to this realm. Native magic-touched commingled with newly arrived fae, which caused mutations and new species. Usually, the more undiluted a bloodline, the more likely it is that the being would prefer *fae* as their label. Most everyone else is okay with *magic-touched*, which is my answer for myself. There's literal magic in my blood, which is genetic, and that's where my zoolinguist ability derives from."

"I find you much more informative than my welcome booklet," Deandra said. "And yet the booklet comes with glossy pictures, so I'm at a fifty-fifty split on which I prefer."

"*Ouch*," he said, laughing. "I'm only *as* interesting as a book you got for free?"

"If you start holding up pictures when you share your font of knowledge with me, you might fare better," she said. "By the way, I have more hot goss to tell you."

"I can't say I like 'hot goss,' but I'm deeply intrigued anyway."

A moment later, he flicked on his turn signal and eased into the left turn lane behind a trio of idling cars at a red light. Deandra eyed the nearby shopping center. The only name on the cement directory board standing vigil on the corner that suggested a restaurant was the Drake Inn Cafe.

As Cruz followed the three cars through the intersection and into the parking lot, Deandra eyed the sea of cars. Everyone who emerged from their vehicle headed in the same direction.

"This is one of my favorite places, but I haven't been here in a while," Cruz said as he eased into a parking spot on the far end of the lot, near a small mechanic shop that was closed for the evening. "This is one of the more popular spots in town. Lots of out-of-towners come here—Kensey and Pinebough residents mostly. There's a telepad a block away. It's popular because it's both good *and* affordable, rather than swanky like Axian Delights."

Deandra liked the sound of this place already. She waited for Cruz to get out and forcibly yank the passenger-side door open. After she got out, she leaned her hip against the side of the trunk as she watched him struggle to get the door shut again. He had to lift up on the door and close it quickly; otherwise, it wouldn't latch.

Task finally done, he slowly turned around. Even in the dim lighting of the parking lot, she could tell his cheeks were a little rosy. "I didn't realize how much of a pain a malfunctioning door was until this evening, by the way. The DIY videos forgot to mention that part."

She laughed, then pointed over the car's hood. "Too bad they're closed." The sign, however, said the mechanic shop specialized in vehicles that ran on "fae essence," so maybe that place couldn't have helped him anyway. She had no idea what "fae essence" was, but it made her think of the movie *Soylent Green*, so she redirected her attention to Cruz. "And don't sweat it. I had a car in high school that was so old, the horn went off every time I reversed. It was … very loud. Once I was backing out of a spot in a grocery store just as an elderly man was putting a large bottle of vodka. My car horn blared, scared the bejesus out of him, and he dropped the bottle. It shattered in spectacular glory. My windows were up, and I could *still* smell the fumes. Did I stop, apologize to the man, and replace his upsettingly large bottle of cheap booze? I did not. I fled the scene because I was mortified. The horn finally lost its mind that day, too, and blared the entire way home."

Cruz tucked his lips between his teeth in an effort not to laugh. "If anything, I'd say you gave that man a wake-up call. Maybe you scared him into realizing he had a drinking problem."

Deandra had seen the man again two weeks later, his cart loaded down with more bottles. She'd hidden behind a chip display until he was gone, lest out of spite he ran into her ankles with his cart. "Sure," she said. "Let's go with that."

Laughing, he gestured toward the Drake Inn Cafe. The cafe, which was a quaint word for a building so large, looked from the outside more like an industrial greenhouse than a place for diners. She'd actually seen the looming shape of its second floor from the street but had discounted it as the location of the cafe simply due to its size. The outside of the restaurant bustled with activity—a line of people waited in a queue for a table, and clusters of friends chatted and laughed in the parking lot, as if they weren't yet ready to call it a night.

Cruz led the way to the freestanding kiosk before the front doors that was being manned by one of the largest individuals Deandra had ever seen—not counting Cenzio. This man was at least six and a half feet tall, and his shoulders were two to three times the width of a human's. He was built like a refrigerator. Adding to his overwhelming aura of otherness wasn't so much the fact that he was as bald as a cue ball, but rather that he had neither eyebrows nor eyelashes.

She stopped dead in her tracks a few feet away from the kiosk where Cruz was chatting with the giant man.

It took Cruz a moment to realize she wasn't beside him and glance over his shoulder. She only broke her wide-eyed stare at the massive man when Cruz closed the distance and blocked her view.

Brows arched, he asked, "You all right?"

Deandra swallowed, then hunkered down a little so she was fully shielded by Cruz. "Is that a draken?"

Understanding loosened the worry lines on his forehead. "I thought your welcome booklet came with pictures," he said, keeping his voice low but failing at hiding his amusement.

"I haven't read the entire draken section yet," she whisper-hissed back. She knew her eyes were wide, but she couldn't get them to return to normal size. "You can't make fun of me! Not only am I a mundane transplant, but I've just had the longest day of my life."

"You're right. I'm sorry," he said, doing his best to look contrite. "Want me to introduce you? He's a good guy. We went to high school together."

She nodded tightly.

He turned so he was standing beside her and held out his crooked arm. Shooting a leery glance at the behemoth of a man behind the tiny kiosk, she looped her arm around Cruz's. Even so, he had to tug at her to get her legs to work.

"Flint, this is Deandra," Cruz said when they reached the draken. "She just moved here last month."

Flint's dark eyes roamed Deandra's face, his own face expressionless. He was like a boulder with eyes. She took an involuntary step backward, but Cruz held fast to her arm.

All of a sudden, a bright smile spread across Flint's face, revealing perfectly straight white teeth. He leaned forward on the kiosk, which protested with a creak, his bulky arms crossed on the top. He wore a short-sleeved black shirt that was stretched to its limit; it was a wonder the stitching in his sleeves didn't burst under the strain of biceps that were as thick as tree trunks. He flicked his gaze to Cruz.

"Wasted no time snatching up the fresh meat, eh, Caddel?" Flint asked good-naturedly. When his attention slid back to Deandra, he cupped his large hand around his mouth and stage-whispered, "If this guy is acting like a lady-killer, don't believe it. Find me later, and I'll show you his freshman picture."

"Don't you dare, Flint," Cruz said, jabbing a finger at his friend. "Not everyone was blessed in high school with chompers as perfect as yours."

"They *are* rather impressive chompers," Deandra managed.

Flint smiled even wider. It was such a goofy expression on what should have been a terrifying face, the smile was contagious. "*There* she is," he said, nodding. "This your first hub *ever*?"

"Yep. I was living in Los Angeles before this."

Flint's laugh was deep and booming. "Axia is truly stranger than Hollyweird?"

"By a mile," Deandra said.

"Well, if I ever decide to visit your old stomping grounds, maybe you can give me a tour."

Deandra honestly couldn't decide if this giant man would fit in in Los Angeles or if people would run away screaming. Maybe he'd make it as an actor—he'd get typecast in an instant, though.

"You done flirting with my date?" Cruz asked, shaking his head in mock sadness. "It's like high school all over again."

"If a lady had to pick between you or me, I was the easy choice." Flint winced dramatically at Deandra. "Seriously, you need to see that freshman picture. It wasn't quite a headgear situation, but *woof*."

"Did you find our reservation or not, you big lug?" Cruz asked.

"Yeah, yeah," Flint said, standing up straight to consult the seating chart on the kiosk's top. "I got you in a booth by the window." He plucked a walkie-talkie off his belt and hit a button on the side. "Rose, got a reservation for your section. Caddel for two." Once he got a reply, he nodded at them. "It'll just be a few minutes. Sorry, Caddel. I gotta get back to work. Hang out in the lobby, and Rose will come get you. Good seeing you, man. Been a while. Should have figured the only thing to get you out of your house was a pretty lady."

Cruz unhanded Deandra so he and Flint could do the one-handed bro hug thing. Though when half of the pair was the size of Flint, Deandra briefly worried the clap of Flint's baseball mitt of a hand on Cruz's back would snap his spine.

Flint broke away from Cruz and took a step toward Deandra, hand out. "It was lovely to meet you, Deandra."

"You too," she said. "Sorry for the gawking earlier."

He waved a dismissive hand. "I'm used to leaving the ladies speechless." He winked, then craned his neck to catch the attention of the next set of people in line and waved them over.

Cruz led Deandra into the small lobby, where a few others waited in plush leather booths. The place was so boisterous, it was like walking into a wall of sound.

Even the inside of the restaurant looked like an industrial greenhouse. While the glass walls of the building's exterior had been tinted so black they could have been mistaken for dark wood siding, the roof was made of crystal-clear glass. The corner of a small second-floor loft area formed an awning over a section of tables to the far left of the lobby, but overall, most of what Deandra had assumed would be a second floor was only open air. The restaurant probably felt wholly different in the light of day.

Directly across from the lobby was an oval-shaped open bar ringed with occupied stools. At least five draken were fast at work in the center of the bar, several of them crafting elaborate neon-colored drinks. Waiters and waitresses—all draken—bustled to and fro in the thoroughfare between the lobby and the bar, carrying heaping trays of food and drinks to the tables and booths on either side of the bar.

Music played from somewhere—not so loud that it drowned out the din, but enough to constantly linger on the fringes, like sweet-smelling smoke wafting through the air. It was instrumental music, but not like anything Deandra had ever heard. She wondered if it was a recording being piped in through hidden speakers or if there was a live band playing fae instruments somewhere beyond her vantage point. The melody was somehow both haunting and upbeat.

There had been a restaurant as lively as this a mere walk from the LA apartment where she'd lived with Mark. It was one of those places that felt alive, like it was creating its own energy and atmosphere. Deandra had only gotten Mark to go there once. He'd hated it, and never wanted to go back—the music, the ambiance, the bustle, the food … he'd complained about all of it.

Deandra, however, had loved it. Every day, Deandra had to walk past the restaurant on her way home, hearing the laughter and music pouring out into the sidewalk but never going in. She still didn't know when the transition between being her own person and being Mark's Girlfriend had happened, but she felt relieved now that she could see pieces of her old self reemerging as she slowly figured out who she was again.

She turned to Cruz, who was a short distance away, hands in his pockets. "Thank you."

He cocked his head. "For what?"

She shrugged. "Helping make me feel welcome here."

With a small, curious smile, he said, "Thank you for not running away when Flint started being … Flint."

"Oh, don't worry. I'll be running toward Flint before the night is over."

Cruz's brows smashed together.

"I need to see this headgear. You know how I feel about pictures."

"I wonder if I can sneak away from the table when you aren't looking, steal Flint's phone, and chuck it into the river …"

"Is there a river in Axia?" Deandra asked.

"There is not. I already see there might be a flaw in my plan."

"Caddel, party of two?" came a voice from behind her.

Deandra found a woman as massive as Flint standing at the mouth of the lobby casting a curious look around the assembled group. Although she too had no eyelashes or eyebrows, she sported a brown-haired wig that was pulled into a high ponytail.

"That's us," Cruz said, hand in the air.

Rose smiled warmly. "Sorry for the wait. Follow me."

Cruz gestured for Deandra to go first, so she hustled after Rose, whose long strides ate up distance with surprising speed. Deandra glanced this way and that as she took in the sheer variety of diners in the cafe—draken, faun, gnomes, humans, and people with skin in every shade. She even spotted a pair of yetis along a far wall—their fur more of a blue-gray color, like Cenzio's—answering her question about whether the Basnets were the only yetis in town.

But then she remembered Cruz had said the nearby telepad brought in visitors from other hubs.

Rose stopped at a booth a few tables shy of the staircase that led to the loft area. Though the windows beside the booth were black as pitch from the outside, Deandra could easily see into the parking lot beyond. "I'll grab you some waters, and then I'll be back to take your order."

After they were seated across from each other, Rose handed them each a hard-backed menu that she'd had wedged under her arm. Then she was off again, weaving around tables and chairs with a graceful ease despite her size.

Deandra sagged a little in her seat as tiredness suddenly weighed her down again, and she relaxed into the plush seat. Though she held the menu in both hands, she kept gazing around the greenhouse-turned-cafe instead. A few stars winked in the darkening sky above. She eventually felt eyes on her and dropped her gaze to Cruz. He was smiling at her.

"What?" she asked, cheeks heating.

"I've lived here for most of my life, so I guess I take it for granted," he said. "It's fun to watch the novelty play out for you."

"Part of the problem is that I turned into a bit of a hermit for a while, so pretty much everything outside my shell is thrilling now."

"Hold that thought," he said. "I have a million questions to ask you, and I also need my gossip—"

"Hot goss," she corrected.

"Never." He screwed up his face as if he smelled something foul. "I'm going to run to the restroom, but the interrogation will start when I get back."

"Okay," she said. "That'll give me time to panic over the menu —and the fact that I don't have the first clue about draken food."

"Literally everything is good, so you can't go wrong," he said as he slid out of the booth. "Be right back."

Deandra had been perusing the menu for all of a minute before she felt someone standing at the foot of the table. She figured Rose had returned with the promised glasses of water, but when Deandra swung her gaze upward, she only found open air. When she lowered her eyes, she found a familiar, much more petite person standing there—a familiar person who was scowling at Deandra as if she were the cause of all that was wrong in the world.

"I don't know who the heck you are, but I'm going to get to the bottom of it, Deandra Hendricks—if that's even your name."

"Uh, hi, Mavis ..."

CHAPTER TWELVE

Mavis's scowl deepened. "You're certainly making the rounds in Axia, aren't you? First you weasel your way into an industry you're not qualified for, then you steal a lucrative job from *my* boss, who has been nothing but kind to you, and now you've snagged the attention of the town's most eligible bachelor? You're probably just trying to butter him up to give you more industry connections. Does *he* know you're just using him for his client list?"

"Who? Cruz?" Deandra asked, honestly baffled by all of this.

"Don't play dumb," Mavis snapped. "Ursula said you were creeping around Lydia's house today. What were you doing there? How did you even find out where she lived?"

Deandra could understand that Mavis was starting to unravel at the seams in the wake of her best friend's death, but latching on to Deandra as a suspect was turning the grieving woman into something like a cartoon villain. If Mavis was trying her hand at the amateur sleuth thing, she was doing a terrible job. "Are you sure *you* weren't creeping around, and Ursula told you to scram, or she'd call the police?"

The hot flush that crept up Mavis's neck was all the answer Deandra needed.

Putting down the menu and folding her arms on top of it, Deandra asked, "What do you want, Mavis? I genuinely don't know what you're expecting. Obviously, something about me bothers you on principle. I can't change your mind about whatever your preconceived notions are. So what is it you want to know?"

In a fluid motion, Mavis slid into the booth next to Deandra. Startled, Deandra scooted back until her backside hit the tinted window.

Mavis, with a bent leg propped on the bench seat, stared intensely at Deandra. If there had been utensils on the table, Deandra might have worried Mavis was going to try to stab her with a fork. Then again, Deandra didn't know what, if any, abilities this tiny woman had. Mavis might have something magical up her sleeve that was much more dangerous than cutlery.

"All I can find about you is that you're a mundane from Los Angeles," Mavis said in a rush. "Hardly any social media, but there's random stuff dating back at least six years. And not only random stuff, *boring* stuff. But maybe you're a con woman who's good at the game. You used to work at a place called Urbean Edge. I also found an old address for you in Colorado. Maybe your parents' house?"

Deandra's jaw clenched. "You're *spying* on me? I barely know you! I knew Lydia even less. And what the heck are you doing researching my parents?"

Mavis quickly lifted her hands, palms up, as if Deandra was the one acting unreasonably here. "Is it true, then?"

"Is *what* true?"

"That you're just a mundane?"

"*Yes.*"

Mavis's shoulders slumped. "You're not like a siren or something?"

Deandra wasn't sure if she was more confused by the question itself or the dejected tone Mavis had asked it in. "*What* is going on, Mavis?"

Mavis dramatically sat correctly on the booth seat, planted her elbows onto the table, and cradled her head in her hands. "I thought I was on the right track."

"You thought a person who just moved to town officially a few weeks ago murdered someone she barely knew?" Deandra asked, incredulous. "You know that sounds bonkers, right?"

Mavis whirled toward her, and Deandra shrank back once more. "Someone was stalking Lydia."

Deandra's brows shot up. "Did she have any idea who?"

Mavis frantically shook her head, her eyes a bit wild. "She said she thought someone was trying to get into her townhouse for months. You enter her place on the ground floor, and there's one bedroom down there, but the rest of her unit is upstairs. The window screens on her upstairs windows kept disappearing, but the hinges weren't loose or anything. The clasps holding the screen in place would still be there, but the whole screen would be gone. There's nothing on the backside of the building—no built-in ladders or balconies or anything. There are hedges that line the wall on the lower level, but it's still a good eight feet between the top of the hedges and the bottom of her windows.

"She set up a camera on her dining room table to face them. She'd be out for the day and would get a notification on her phone that her camera went offline. Then, when she got home, her window would be open a crack when she'd obviously left it closed and latched before she left."

Deandra worried at the inside of her cheek. "Did she have any enemies?"

Mavis laughed bitterly. "I loved the girl like a sister, but she wasn't always the easiest person to deal with."

It unnerved Deandra how obvious it was that Mavis needed help. *Professional* help, probably. Her under-eye bags were dark, her cuticles had been chewed down to the quick on most of her fingers, and her brown hair that Deandra, upon first meeting the woman, had thought was so shiny it was reminiscent of a flowing waterfall now looked greasy and lank.

"Are you here alone?" Deandra asked, trying to channel Sarah's matronly tone. If only Deandra had the power to ease people's anxieties with comforting scents.

Deandra cast a look around the busy restaurant, not sure what she was looking for. Someone who looked like Mavis, maybe. What she *did* see was Cruz loitering diagonally across from the table, near the other staircase that led to the loft. He lifted a hand in greeting to acknowledge that he'd seen her. He rested a shoulder against a pole, crossed his arms, and then tipped his head to the side as if gesturing to Mavis from afar. She got the impression he was waiting until her chat with Mavis was over.

"I came here to talk to *you*," Mavis said, redirecting Deandra's focus.

"You followed me here?" When the young woman didn't reply and just glared at the table's surface, Deandra sighed deeply. She had a vague idea of what might have happened today. "Were you staking out Lydia's house earlier when you happened to see me walk by? You saw me talking to Ursula, and then when I was gone, you tried to get Ursula to tell you what she and I talked about?"

The fact that the conversation, especially from a distance, probably looked as if a friendly chat had turned into Ursula being scared of Deandra probably hadn't helped. It also suggested that Mavis hadn't *heard* the conversation, so she didn't know the potential connection Lydia's case had with the Basnets.

The side of the young woman's thumb moved toward her mouth, but she'd run out of cuticles to chew on, so she jammed her hands under her armpits instead. "The werecats aren't doing anything. Someone was harassing Lydia for weeks, no one helped her, and now she's dead."

Deandra's interactions with Axian law enforcement had been limited, but from what she'd seen, they were thorough and efficient. *Too* thorough, in Ranger Vicks's case. Deandra had a sneaking suspicion that if the werecats hadn't helped Lydia track down her stalker, there was probably a reason for it.

"Did she report the harassment?" Deandra asked, then braced herself to get snapped at again.

"No," Mavis said, her voice shaking. "I told her over and over again that she should. She kept saying she'd figure it out on her own. She yelled at me anytime I suggested she report it. She kept saying she didn't want the police involved because it would just scare the stalker off before she could catch them."

"You'd think scaring the stalker would be the *ideal* scenario," Deandra said.

"That's what I said." Mavis sniffed. "I should have gone behind her back and reported it. I ... I called the police for an update about an hour ago, and the werecat assigned to the case was asking me if Lydia had any enemies who could easily scale her wall or who could fly because ... because her window—that same one where the screen kept disappearing—was broken. They think they broke the glass enough to access the latch. There was glass on the floor inside, under the window. They think whoever it was got in through there."

"They hadn't mentioned the broken window to you before this?"

Mavis sharply shook her head. It made Deandra think of the discrepancies in the reported time of death. The death witch had told Mavis one time, while Ursula claimed Lydia's attack had happened up to twelve hours earlier. Were the werecats holding back some information and tweaking other details in hopes of catching one of their suspects in a lie? Deandra didn't need to be a connoisseur of true crime to know the number-one suspect in murders was often the person closest to the victim. If it was true that Lydia didn't have many close friends, Mavis was probably near the top of that suspect list—especially since she was the one who'd found the body.

As if reading her thoughts, Mavis said, "The day I found her, I didn't even think of the whole stalker thing. I didn't mention it at all. I never went upstairs that day because the cops said I would contaminate the crime scene more than I already had. They said I moved the body too much when I was checking for vital signs, but it's not totally my fault. Opening the door pushed her body farther into the foyer. Honestly, I was so in shock, I could hardly form sentences.

"But now I can't stop thinking that if I'd ... if I'd reported the stalking *for* her, she might have been so mad at me that she wouldn't have spoken to me again, but at least she'd still be alive."

Then, all at once, Mavis burst into tears and flung herself at Deandra, burying her face in Deandra's side and hugging her around the middle like a little kid. Deandra awkwardly wrapped an arm around the sobbing woman, offering tight-lipped smiles to nearby patrons who kept glancing over in concern. In her periphery, Cruz speed-walked from his post to snag Rose. The two exchanged a few words, Rose glanced over at Deandra a few times, and then the draken nodded and scurried off. Cruz returned to his post.

When Mavis's tears began to subside, Deandra cleared her throat. "Can I ask how me possibly being a siren would have fit into this?"

Just as Mavis sat back, Rose cruised by with all the grace of a figure skater, depositing both a stack of napkins and three glasses of water on the table before flitting away again. She and Cruz exchanged thumbs-ups. Deandra reached over and grabbed a napkin, handing it to Mavis. She noisily blew her nose.

Deandra inched a water glass closer.

"Before I got the news about the broken window," Mavis said, "I was trying to figure out the stalker angle. It had to be someone with magic who threw her down the stairs, or at least someone with a lot of strength. And it had to be someone with magic or wings who was tampering with the window. The happy-hour group are the people who knew Lydia best, so I've been trying to eliminate them one by one."

"And, what, you thought I was some criminal mastermind from another hub who used my siren abilities to charm my way into the pet-sitter group so I could get closer to Lydia?"

Mavis's mouth bunched up.

"Did I have a motive in this scenario?" Deandra asked.

"I was still working on that part. Lydia was from Pinebough. I'm from Kensey. Neither one of us has family or anything here; we moved here to start over. I don't know that much about what Lydia was running from, so I thought you could be tied to her old life. And maybe you were the one doing the stalking. Mundanes don't usually integrate as fast as you have."

"You don't think she would have told you if someone from her old life was suddenly in Axia and harassing her? She told you about the stalker …"

Mavis tossed her hands up. "I don't know, okay? The guilt is making me sick. I haven't slept in two days. I swear I'm starting to hallucinate. I can't eat."

"Mavis …" Deandra said, frowning. "You have to take care of yourself, or you won't be any good to yourself *or* Lydia."

Her bottom lip wobbled dangerously. "She didn't have anyone she could rely on. I was it. And I let her down. I can't let her down again and let her stalker … her *murderer* … get away with this."

"Even if it doesn't seem like it, I'm sure the werecats are doing everything they can," Deandra said. "They just can't share every detail with you, or it could jeopardize the case. You have to trust that they know what they're doing. It's only been three days."

Deandra regretted the words the moment they were out of her mouth. But it wasn't the word "only" that Mavis took offense to.

"*Three* days?" Mavis asked, head cocked. "She died Monday. Today is Wednesday. That's only *two* days."

Deandra didn't like Mavis's tone. Mavis wasn't correcting Deandra because she thought Deandra had slipped up. She was seeking clarification, wondering—*desperately hoping*—Deandra had pertinent, insider information.

"You're right. Two days," Deandra said.

Mavis leaned forward a fraction, studying Deandra's face. "You're not secretly a shifter, are you?"

"No," Deandra said slowly. "Don't magical people have to, like, register or something?" She thought of Ranger Vicks and how adamant he'd been that Havoc have a registration number that could then be checked against the larger, hub-system-wide Parks Management database. Did such a database also exist for fae and magic-touched?

Mavis looked mildly disgusted. "You really *don't* know how hubs work, do you? Of course there's not a registry. No one has to disclose who they are. It gets recorded in some cases—like fingerprints do in the mundane world—because abilities are often a topic in hiring conversations. But there's not a public record of everyone's lineage or anything. The census board would have that information, but those details aren't made public until thirty-five years after the census was originally taken. I think in the mundane world it takes twice as long for details to be available."

Brow cocked, Deandra asked, "Did you learn all that while prying into the lives of the happy-hour group?"

Mavis gave the back of her head a frantic scratch. "Maybe."

"Who have you ruled out—*other* than me? Because, no, I'm not a shifter, either."

"Honestly, most everyone is off the list except Tansy. She and Lydia hated each other, Tansy has a bird who could reach that window, and Tansy is a nature witch. I don't know that last one for sure, but I'm almost positive. She could probably open the window with a wind spell and/or use electricity to short-circuit the camera. I don't know if ravens can manipulate locks, but they're really smart birds. Maybe Rufus tapped at the window until it broke, got inside, unlocked the front door to give Tansy access, and then lay in wait for the perfect time to confront Lydia. A powerful wind spell could be enough to do the damage to the wall and Lydia's body."

Mavis sounded more resolved and lucid now, which was better than sobbing, but Deandra didn't think this broken woman should be investigating a murder while she was in this state of mind—or at all.

"When the werecat told you about the broken window, did you finally tell them about the stalker?" Deandra asked.

Mavis sharply shook her head. "I'm too scared. What if they arrest me for withholding evidence?"

Deandra didn't think that was how things worked—in the mundane world *or* the hub system—but pointing that out wouldn't help. "I'll tell you what, I'll go with you to talk to them—"

The young woman sat up straighter. "Really?"

"On one condition."

Mavis deflated.

"You *have* to get some sleep. And take a shower."

"That sounds like two conditions," Mavis muttered.

"Take it or leave it."

Mavis huffed. "Fine."

The two women exchanged numbers. Mavis downed a glass of water in one go, and then she slid out of the booth and walked away without another word. When Deandra was sure the younger woman was gone, she slouched in the booth seat. She wasn't sure how much more she could take today.

Cruz was across from her in a matter of seconds. "What on earth was *that* about?"

Whimpering, Deandra dropped her folded arms on the table

and leaned forward, the edge of the table pressing into her rib cage. "Is this the worst date of your life?"

He mirrored her posture. "Are you kidding? One time a girl vomited in my lap. In a movie theater. During the opening credits."

Deandra bit her bottom lip, trying not to laugh. "What was the movie?"

"*That's* your question?"

"Okay. Revised question: Did you stay for the movie, or did you bail?"

"I got cleaned up the best I could. We switched seats and planned to stay. She kept apologizing, and I kept saying it was fine and that we should try to just make the most of it. She agreed. Then she abruptly left halfway through because she'd discreetly texted her ex during the movie to come pick her up."

"*No.*"

"*Yes,*" he said. "And it was one of those flashback movies where you get to watch an older movie on the big screen. *Ghostbusters.*"

"A classic."

There was a long beat of silence.

"You're dying for the hot goss, aren't you?" she asked.

"You have no idea. But I'm also starving because all I've had is a granola bar today."

Deandra clapped her hands over her face. "I'm sorry! I shouldn't have talked to her for so long." She peeked at him through her fingers. "Is this in the running for the *second* worst date?"

He reached across the table to gently pull her hands away from her face. One of his thumbs caressed the heel of her palm. "Not even in the top *twenty* worst dates. I promise. Food first ..." Clearly in pain, he added, "And hot goss after?"

Grinning, she said, "Deal."

CHAPTER THIRTEEN

P er Cruz's suggestion, Deandra ordered something called a tinka fish bowl while he selected a wherian beef platter. Deandra was picky about her seafood, but one bite of her meal made her point her fork at him.

"Holy crap," she said.

"I told you."

His platter came with three sauces, a variety of colorful seared vegetables, and a stack of a bread-like side that looked like a cross between pita bread and Ethiopian injera. Deandra watched as Cruz used his hands to line the bread with meat, vegetables, and a drizzle of sauce before folding the flat bread in half and taking a healthy bite. Currently, her only regret about dinner was that she and Cruz didn't know each other well enough yet for her to start mooching off his plate. Some people hated sharing food, so she didn't want to overstep in that regard either.

Rose stopped by the table. "How's everything?"

Deandra covered her mouth, as she'd just taken a bite, and waiters had impeccable timing. "It's amazing."

Beaming, Rose said, "Happy to hear it."

"Rose, could I get a side plate? My date has been eyeing my food with an intensity that suggests she's going to steal it all if I don't share soon."

"Sure thing," she said with a laugh. "I'll grab water refills, too."

When she'd left, Deandra said, "Was I *that* obvious?"

"You're practically drooling."

She discreetly wiped at her chin with the back of her hand, finding it dry. Jabbing her fork toward the pile of vegetables, she asked, "Do you know what they all are?"

Many bore colors she'd never seen in vegetables before, but she was far from a jet-setting foodie, so for all she knew, the vegetables were from this realm. Given how draken-focused the place was, though, she guessed the vegetables were at least partially fae in origin.

"I don't know what most of them are, no. The blue ones are potato-like. The green ones sort of taste like carrots. The yellow ones remind me of sweet peppers," he said, pointing to each one. "I think the vegetables are a lot like magic-touched people at this point—some part fae, some part mundane, and now they've mutated into something that you can't find naturally in either realm."

It made her think of Tor Meller and the unique vegetables that his earth magic had allowed him to create for the restaurant he'd run with his wife—until Rae Corly had magically sabotaged them, anyway. Deandra wondered if magic was at play with the food here the way it had been at Elements of Flavor.

After Rose dropped off the extra plates and napkins and

refilled their waters, she placed a dessert menu at the end of the table and then was off again.

As Cruz divvied up a helping of his platter onto an extra plate, he said, "Now that I'm no longer under threat of passing out from low blood sugar, please tell me who that lady was and why she was sobbing in your lap."

Deandra took a long preparatory sip of water before she began. "That was Mavis—Lydia's best friend. And the first piece of hot goss we need to discuss has to do with *you*."

The blue potato he was shifting from his plate to hers rolled off his fork and hit the table with a muted splat.

"*Me?*"

"According to Mavis, you're the most eligible bachelor in town."

He stared at her for a long moment. When she didn't elaborate further, he jutted his head toward her a fraction. "Wait, are you serious? What is this, a Hallmark movie? Why would my marital status be of interest to anyone?" He sat up straight and held out his hands as if warding off a crowd. "Ladies, please!" he said loudly enough that Deandra ducked her head, covering an embarrassed laugh behind her hands. "Hands off, all right? This is just embarrassing. You'll need to take a number like everyone else."

Deandra glanced around, only finding a gnome woman glaring their way. She lifted a finger to her lips and shushed them, which was extra humorous since the restaurant hadn't been quiet to start with.

When Deandra returned her focus to Cruz, he looked quite pleased with himself for making her laugh.

In a normal volume, and resuming his preparation of her plate of food, he said, "Axia is a small town, so it's not unheard of that far more people than you'd like know your business, but as you can see from the crowd in this place alone—we get a lot of tourists, too. I can't imagine why anyone would be paying that much attention to *me*."

Deandra shrugged. "Maybe it's the whole doctor thing? Fancy job equals money equals prestige."

"I guess so," he said, then handed her a plate piled with food.

Deandra made grabby hands. Though her tinka fish was delicious, she was desperate to try the wherian beef. Mimicking what she'd seen Cruz do, she wrapped the meat and vegetables into a fajita-like configuration and took a tentative bite.

She chewed, paused, and then looked at Cruz with wide eyes.

He nodded sagely. "I know."

If she was supposed to be a dainty eater on a first date, the memo had clearly gotten lost in the mail. By the time she resurfaced from her food-induced blackout, the wherian beef wrap was gone, and a drizzle of the decadent sauce was inching across the length of her palm. With a knowing smile, Cruz quietly handed her a napkin.

She wiped her hands slowly. Dabbed at her mouth. Coughed awkwardly. "You didn't see that."

"See what?"

"Good answer," she said. "Now! As for the whole eligible bachelor thing … any chance you've got a connection to Mavis, one of her friends, or someone in her family? Have you left such a trail of broken hearts, lady-killer, that you've lost track?"

He rolled his eyes good-naturedly. "I didn't get a great look at her, but she wasn't familiar."

Deandra considered that. "I guess that tracks. She said she's a transplant from Kensey and moved here to start over. I don't know how long she's lived here."

"I studied zoolinguistics at a university in Pinebough—that's in Oregon. I lived there for seven years; I interned at a Pinebough emergency animal clinic for three years after I graduated. Other than that, I've been in Axia."

"*Lydia* was originally from Pinebough," Deandra said, eyeing him curiously. "If she really *was* a zoolinguist and not a fraud, maybe you went to school with her?"

"Let's find out," he said and picked up his cell that had been lying on the table. "There's a list of graduating students posted every year—it essentially doubles as a job board. Need someone who's a literal certified horse whisperer? Check the Pinebough Zoolinguistics graduate list. What's her last name again?"

"Monroe."

She waited semi-impatiently as he typed and swiped at his phone. She'd polished off the last of her tinka fish bowl by the time he glanced up.

"No Lydia Monroe listed during any of the four years I was there," he said. "Do you know if Monroe is a married name? Maiden name?"

"I have no idea. Mavis mentioned that Lydia moved to Axia because she was running from something in her past. An ex-husband is just as likely as anything else, I guess."

Cruz swiped and tapped at his screen a few more times. "Here," he said and placed his phone on the table in front of her. "The list is filtered for the four years I was at the university. Each listing has a picture. See if you recognize her. Lydia could be a middle name, for all we know."

Shrugging, Deandra picked up his phone and swiped through the list. She'd feared going through four years of pictures would take half a lifetime, but class sizes weren't that large, all things considered.

She'd just passed into the final year when she paused. "Wait. Wait, this is her. I mean, it *looks* exactly like her, but it's a different name. Alison Griffiths. She's also blond in this picture, and the Lydia I met was a brunette."

Glancing up, some part of her feared his face would be drained of color as he realized Deandra had just discovered the name of the fiancée he'd left at the altar back in Pinebough. Though if he'd recognized her picture and still handed his phone over, it would either mean he had an iron-clad poker face or was a sociopath. But his expression merely looked thoughtful.

Remembering something Harmony had told her about Lydia,

she asked, "Is it common for magic-touched to have multiple abilities? Being a zoolinguist and a fire elemental, for example?"

Cruz shrugged. "I'm sure it's possible, but it's not common as far as I know."

"Most people are scared to confront Lydia though since she's supposedly a fire elemental," Harmony had said.

Deandra wondered if Lydia had made up the fire elemental thing to further distance herself from this apparent other life she'd had in Pinebough. She also might have just been a compulsive liar.

Deandra clicked on Alison's picture, finding a brief description.

Alison Griffiths graduated in the first quarter of her fourth year with a specialization in zoological empathy. Her readings are strong to excellent with all mundane animals on our standard testing list *(see fig. 8f)*, strong with sentient mythical animals on our standard list *(subject to availability; see fig. 12r)*, mid-level to weak with sapient mythical animals on our standard list *(subject to availability; see fig. 12b)*, and null on all shifters on our standard list *(see fig. 8a)*. Griffiths graduated with top marks, but it should be noted that she did so with a demerit.

"What does it mean to graduate with a demerit?" Deandra asked, glancing up.

That was enough to make Cruz go a little pale.

"A demerit means you've violated the 'do no harm' code of conduct," he said. "There's two sides to every power. This is a super oversimplified example, but say you can wield fire—you can both create fire *and* snuff it out."

"Arsonist versus firefighter," Deandra said.

Cruz nodded. "Exactly. Doctors of all stripes are in the profession to *save* life, to enhance it, to ease suffering. I communicate with animals to help find the best care for them—it's for *their* benefit. But the flip side is that I could technically plant thoughts, feelings, and images into their heads. I could manipulate them into actions they wouldn't otherwise take to benefit *me*.

"If Alison, or Lydia, or whatever her name was graduated with a demerit, it means she violated the law numerous times. The only way to fail out of the school entirely is if a student's violation of the law results in the death of an animal or shifter. A demerit upon graduation also suggests no one at the school could fully prove anything Lydia did manipulation-wise had been done with malicious intent." He held out a hand. "Can I read her bio?"

Deandra handed the phone back over, recalling Tansy's story about Lydia's supposed manipulation of Rufus. Tansy's move to the top of Deandra's own suspect list was sullied a bit by the fact that Mavis, with all her off-the-wall theories, had pegged Tansy as her number-one culprit, too—but even a broken clock was right twice a day.

"She looks more and more familiar the longer I look at the picture," Cruz said, his forehead bunched. "And even though graduating with a demerit is rare, it wasn't unheard of. There was a guy—Bryce—who graduated at the end of the program with me who also had a demerit. There was a hot-headed lion shifter who was the professor for shifter studies who worked closely with the zoolingual department. Bryce and the professor hated each other. Bryce's zoolingual abilities had a heavy specialization with shifters. Bryce pulled one stunt too many over the years trying to get under the professor's skin, and it bit Bryce in the butt by the final exam."

"The professor was one of the shifters grading the exam?" Deandra guessed.

"Yep. No one knows what happened during that last test but those two. Bryce swore the professor didn't grade him fairly; the professor recommended failing Bryce on the shifter portion. The rest of the grading staff had given him high marks, so the idea that Bryce failed in his specialty was unlikely. But the staff then had to decide whether they were going to tank Bryce's grade to save face with a long-established professor or tick off the hot-headed lion and find another shifter to conduct the exam. Instead, on Bryce's certificate, it says he has a medium to high proficiency in shifter communication when it should be that he has excellent proficiency. *And* he got a demerit." Cruz shrugged. "If Lydia/Alison's infractions were numerous but minor in scale, it might not have been enough to make it to the rumor mill, as small as the school was. Especially if she graduated in her first quarter. It would have been old news by fourth quarter for sure; Bryce's scenario was the talk of the school."

"Would getting a demerit hurt Bryce's chances of getting hired?" Deandra asked.

Cruz's head tipped side to side. "Yes and no. If he was, say, going to start a private practice, the only thing required on the pertinent paperwork is a license number. He's fully licensed, regardless of his path to get there. If someone needs an expert and is looking at the graduate list, however, seeing the demerit notice could make Bryce get passed over."

"Any idea what happened to him after he graduated?" Deandra asked.

"He's a lead director at a mythical zoo in Maine," Cruz said. "If you'd decided you wanted to rehome Havoc, he would have been the first person I'd call."

The "would have been" let her know he *hadn't* called Bryce. She wondered how tempted Cruz had been to let his old school-mate know about the discovery of a thought-to-be-extinct dragon —how tempted he might *still* be.

"Flint out there?" Cruz said, gesturing beyond Deandra's shoulder and toward the cafe's entrance. "He's a good guy through and through. I'd trust that guy with my life. He's loyal and honest to a fault. Bryce? He's extremely good at what he does, and he cares deeply about animals and their well-being, but he also thinks like a businessman. He's not the kind of guy I could casually mention Havoc to. He'd see dollar signs and wouldn't let up until he cracked both of us. I have zero doubt that Havoc would be treated like royalty at Bryce's zoo, but one phone call would seal Havoc's fate. I'd never make that call until you were one thousand percent sure it was what you wanted."

Her eyes inexplicably welled with tears, and she wasn't even sure why.

"Speaking of which ..." Cruz said, "I almost forgot. I got you something." He grabbed his wallet off the table, which had been stacked under his phone all during dinner. He flipped open the leather billfold and pulled out a piece of folded paper. Hesitating for only a moment, his face reddening a little, he handed it over

It was a rectangular piece of white paper that had been folded once down the middle. She shot him a curious look before unfolding it. Her first thought was that it reminded her of a temporary driver's license—which she had recent experience with, seeing as her purse had gone up in flames in Wendy's car the night Rae Corly had tried to torch the car while Deandra and Wendy were still in it.

Magical Fauna Registration Form

Owner's Name: DEANDRA HENDRICKS
Owner's Address:
Fauna's Name: HAVOC
Date of Birth/Estimated Age: 8 MONTHS
Species: FIRE-ALIGNED DIRE WOLF
Advising Veterinarian: DR. CRUZ CADDEL
Zoolingual License# (if applicable): L8641-67292
Veterinarian Signature: *Cruz Caddel*
Owner's Signature:
Date:

"Ranger Vicks is going is going to try to track you down eventually," Cruz said, sounding a touch self-conscious—possibly because Deandra had done nothing but stare at the paper for several long seconds. "I figured we'd get ahead of it as soon as possible and get Havoc in the system. The age was just a guess, obviously. You can add a date if you'd like. A 'gotcha day' rather than a birthday. Just let me know, and I'll update it in the system. If that's—"

"Thank you," she said, cutting off his increasingly nervous rambling. "Are you sure you're comfortable doing this, though? What if, you know, the secret gets out? Could you get in trouble for *falsifying a record*?" She'd blocked her face with the paper and whispered the last three words.

"The collar will buy us some wiggle room if somehow his cover is blown," he said.

She briefly glanced down at the paper, chewing her bottom lip. "Could you end up with worse than a demerit if someone found out?"

"Unlikely, but it's a possibility. It's a risk I'm willing to take, though. It's a temporary solution to the problem, anyway. As he ages—especially if there's a significant growth spurt coming—we'll have to figure out something else. But that's a ways off."

"Thank you," she said again. "I really do appreciate this."

"You're welcome," he said, shoulders seeming to lose some of their tension now that she'd decided *not* to tear the paper up or berate him for overstepping—or whatever it was that he'd been worried about. "I'll text you the address later of where you can mail it in. They'll send you the official registration tag after it's processed."

"Once I get it, Havoc and I should strut into the Parks Management building so I can wave the paperwork in that guy's face," Deandra said. "Though I might end up in jail if Ranger Vicks says something annoying and I'm forced to punch him in the throat."

"Eh," Cruz said, waving a dismissive hand. "Do what you gotta do. I'll bail you out."

She knew her smile was downright goofy as she stared at him, so she was grateful when Rose showed up again to collect their plates, forcing Deandra to look elsewhere. Cruz insisted they try the chocolate lava cake for dessert.

When Rose left again, Cruz asked, "What else did you and Mavis talk about?"

Deandra told him about Lydia's supposed stalker and that Mavis believed this unknown entity was the killer. She explained that Mavis had theorized that Deandra must be a siren or shifter who had followed Lydia to Axia to exact revenge in retaliation for some infraction that occurred in Pinebough. "The police told her today that they believe Lydia's killer's point of entrance was a second-story window—which still matches up with the theory that whoever it was has magic or magic-enhanced strength. It's just too bad that the best witness to what might have happened doesn't have the most reliable eyes. I never would have guessed before today that Mavis's insult of 'old bat' had been literal."

"Uhh …" Cruz said. "You've lost me."

Right. She hadn't even gotten into the heart of her day—six hours with Kiwi the energetic yeti and Havoc, and the walk that had led Deandra to Lydia's door.

As they shared the newly arrived lava cake, Cruz was clearly fighting hard not to laugh at Deandra's hectic day while the pall of Lydia's demise hung over them like a dark cloud. Deandra recounted the events that preceded Mavis showing up and spilling her guts because she felt so guilty about not forcing Lydia to report her stalker to the police that the young woman now couldn't sleep or eat.

"Whew," Cruz said when Deandra finally finished catching him up on everything. "No wonder you collapsed as soon as you got home."

Deandra, mouth parched from the chocolate and too much talking, downed a glass of water. "Who's *your* top suspect?"

"One sec …" he said and grabbed his phone. He typed and swiped at the screen for a minute or two before he handed the phone to her once more. The Pinebough Zoolinguistics graduate list was on the screen again, and this time there were only three names listed. But Deandra didn't need to scroll past the first one.

"Tansy Buckley," Deandra read out loud. "How did you know?"

He shook his head. "I didn't. But I figured 'Tansy' is a unique name, and if she's bonded that closely with a raven, that's either her familiar, or she's got a zoolingual background."

The photograph of Tansy was a good thirty years old, but it was unmistakably the same woman. The only thing that had really changed about her appearance was that her face bore more wrinkles and her black hair was streaked heavily with gray—and was also home to a bird.

Deandra clicked on the picture.

Tansy Buckley graduated in the first quarter of her second year with a specialization in zoological empathy and thought-share. Her readings are excellent with mundane avians on our standard testing list *(see fig. 8c)*, strong with sentient avians on our standard list *(see fig. 12e)*, null with all sapient mythical animals on our standard list *(see fig. 12b)*, and null on all shifters on our standard list *(see fig. 8a)*. Buckley graduated with adequate to top marks.

"What's thought-share?" she asked as she handed the phone back so he could peruse Tansy's bio as well. "Does that mean animals share thoughts with her, or the other way around?"

"Both," he said. "Thought-share is almost exclusively pictures. Instead of telling Rufus to come to her, she could send him an image of him landing on her outstretched arm. Instead of him trying to get her attention to let her know he's hungry, he could send her an image of a grub."

"Or of him opening a window or unlocking a door," Deandra mused.

"Theoretically," Cruz said. "Do you know anything about Tansy's history? Maybe it was *Tansy* who followed Lydia here from Pinebough."

"I got the impression that Tansy's been in Axia for a while—longer than Lydia. But Tansy definitely hated her. Seems like their animosity toward each other started well before the incident with Rufus in Mythic Pet Kitchen. I figured Tansy was just fiercely loyal to Sarah and that Tansy despised Lydia because Lydia had poached Sarah's clients. But maybe the feud ran deeper than that. There's at least a twenty-five-year age difference, though; it doesn't seem like it could be a school connection."

The chime for Deandra's business email sounded.

"Oh, sorry. Let me check this really quick," she said, plucking her own phone off the table for the first time that night.

She had a text from Wendy that was just a picture of her and Havoc curled up on the couch. Havoc, as a dire wolf, was on his back with his back feet draped over an armrest and his front paws flopped over his chest.

There was also a series of texts from an unknown number.

7:43 — UNKNOWN

Hi, Deandra. This is Cenzio.

8:15— UNKNOWN

When you get a chance, please respond. I have a request about Kiwi's care

8:37— UNKNOWN

This is a bit of an emergency

8:42— UNKNOWN

Please check your email ASAP

He must have just sent the email. She wasn't sure how she hadn't heard the texts come in. Then again, the cafe was only *slightly* less boisterous now than it had been when they'd arrived.

"Everything okay?" Cruz asked.

"I'm not sure," she said, swiping out of her texts and pulling up her email. The email in question was only two short paragraphs long, but Deandra's mouth went dry again all the same.

"*Dee*," Cruz said. "What is it? What's wrong?"

She swallowed hard and glanced up. "It's Oleander. She's been detained. She's being accused of murdering Lydia."

CHAPTER FOURTEEN

Deandra reread the email for what felt like the millionth
time.

Hi, Deandra. This is Cenzio. Oleander was detained this evening for
being a person of interest. They somehow think my wife is guilty of
murder because someone placed her at the scene on Sunday night.
The police found a few strands of white fur near Lydia Monroe's body
and on the staircase. They're detaining her until they can get an
analysis of the fur. Can you look after Kiwi until 5pm tomorrow? We'll
pay you extra for your time, of course. He really likes you and
knowing he's cared for will help lessen my anxiety by a mile; I have to
meet with our lawyer tomorrow afternoon.

Please let me know as soon as possible. We are desperate.

She handed her phone to Cruz so he could read it for himself. Her mind was spinning. She figured the "someone" who'd placed Oleander at the scene of the crime was Ursula. Seeing Kiwi earlier in the day likely had spooked Ursula badly enough that she'd called shortly after she'd fled Deandra's company.

"Jeez," Cruz said, handing her phone back. "I honestly didn't put any stock in the Oleander theory. I was thinking—"

He was cut off by Deandra's yelp of surprise when her phone started to ring.

"Sorry!" she said to Cruz. "It's Cenzio."

"Go ahead and answer it. Maybe outside where it's quieter? I'll take care of the bill," he said. "No arguments. You'll bruise my fragile ego."

She laughed, thanked him, grabbed her purse, and slid out of the booth. As she hotfooted it to the front door, she hit accept on the call just before it went to voicemail. "Cenzio? Hi, sorry. I've been at dinner."

Cenzio gusted a sigh so loud that Deandra almost dropped the phone. "I apologize for interrupting your dinner. I just don't—"

"It's okay. I just read the email. When the heck did this all happen?" she asked, hurrying through the small lobby and pushing her way outside.

Flint was still manning the kiosk, and he startled when she hustled past him. "Aw, man! Dee! Did Caddel do something awful? Need me to beat him up?"

Several people were waiting in line—though the queue was much shorter than it had been two hours ago—and they eyed her curiously as she scuttled away. All she could do was furiously shake her head at Flint, wave awkwardly, and hurry into the heart of the parking lot where it was quieter.

"Sounds like you've got a lot going on over there. I'm sorry. I shouldn't have—"

Heaving out a breath and resting her back against a lamppost, she said, "No, it's okay. Honest. What happened?"

"Werecats confronted her at her office," Cenzio said in a rush. He clearly needed to talk to someone. "She was in the middle of a meeting with a new client, and they just barged in. They told her they have evidence of her presence at Lydia Monroe's home the night she died."

"Wait, sorry. You said Lydia died on Sunday? I've heard both Sunday evening and Monday afternoon," Deandra said.

"The werecats are adamant that it was Sunday night and that someone saw Oleander leaving Lydia's place around midnight."

This had almost assuredly been Ursula's doing.

"The werecats told Ohlie that she'd be detained until they could do further analysis on the sample they found. Thing is, they detained her in Kensey, and she's currently in a Kensian jail cell. People of interest are too much of a flight risk when there's something as accessible as the telepad system in place, so they're holding her. It can take up to seventy-two hours to get results, according to Ohlie. She's well versed in the way the system works.

"I'm meeting with the lawyer because Ohlie believes we have a shot at getting the detainment reduced to house arrest—which she thinks is a possibility since we have a young child at home. But even if the system works in our favor, I'll need as much time as possible tomorrow to get to Kensey to negotiate this. I got approved for a half day at work. The lawyer couldn't meet me until after two anyway, so I might as well get some hours in, you know?" He'd been talking a mile a minute until this point, but his voice broke on the last word. "I'm ... I'm really scared for her. She knows how things like this work. I don't. I've never even had a parking ticket, and now my wife is being detained in a jail cell in another state because they think she *murdered* someone?"

"Hey, hey," Deandra said, trying her best to sound comforting despite feeling completely out of her depth. "Take a few deep breaths, okay? I'm more than happy to help you with Kiwi tomorrow. Even if it runs later than five. I'll stay there as long as you need me to."

Cenzio had clearly started crying, but it was silent except for a few sniffles and great shuddering gasps. She wished she could hug the big guy. "Thank you," he finally choked out. "I don't know how to explain any of this to him. He keeps asking where his mama is, and I don't have the words *or* thought-pictures to tell him."

"Do you have any family that might be able to stay with you at night or over the weekend? Just to help out a bit with Kiwi?"

"Ohlie's parents are in Alaska," Cenzio said. "They're … not my biggest fans. They'd find a way to blame this on me. Looping them in to this is a last resort. Both of my parents have passed. And, frankly, none of our friends can handle Kiwi that well. Not many can. Which is why I was blowing up your phone—you were our first choice. When Kiwi woke from his nap after I got home, he was chatting both verbally and in thought-pictures for nearly an hour—telling me all the fun things you three did together."

Deandra sighed internally. She guessed she was pleased Kiwi liked her so much, but she was already preemptively exhausted at the idea of spending the *entire* day with him tomorrow. "I'm happy to help. I'm just sorry I can't do more for you."

There were a few more choked gasps from Cenzio. "This is more than enough. You have no idea."

A sudden idea struck her. "I don't know if this is a stupid thing to even mention—I'm sure the police already went over it. But can't you just supply them with Oleander's alibi? If she was in bed at midnight, you can vouch that she was home at the time of the murder."

Cenzio was quiet for a long moment. "That's just it … I *can't* vouch for her."

Her heart rate doubled. *"What?* What do you mean?"

"There has to be an explanation," he said, and Deandra wondered if he was trying to convince her or himself.

"An explanation for what, Cenzio?" she asked slowly, already deeply worried she wouldn't like his answer.

"During her one allowed phone call to me, she didn't confirm or deny any of the accusations. Yet she asked three separate times, in three different ways, about the nanny cam we have positioned in the stuffed frog toy in Kiwi's bedroom. Thing is, we don't *have* a nanny cam. When it comes to cameras, all we have is a baby monitor that we use at night, especially since Kiwi kept chewing through his crib, and a doorbell camera. The way she'd say certain things on that call was off *just* enough that I knew she was trying to tell me something without possibly incriminating herself since the call was being recorded. I realized after we hung up that there's a ceramic frog on the porch under the doorbell camera," he said. "So I checked the footage."

"*And?*" Deandra asked, practically vibrating with curiosity.

It took Cenzio a moment to speak. "This won't change your mind, will it? You'll still help me with Kiwi?"

Deandra braced herself. "This won't change my mind."

"Oleander left the house on Sunday night around eleven thirty. I was already asleep by then. I turn into a pumpkin by ten most nights and sleep like a log. She stays up late reading. Helps her unwind. She was back by five after midnight. I have no idea where the heck my wife was for a full half hour on the very same night someone who lives walking distance from us was found murdered."

"What do you think Oleander wanted you to see on the footage? Was that her way of letting you know she was, in fact, out of the house, and she wanted you to know without saying so directly?" Deandra asked. What she *didn't* ask was if Cenzio thought his wife had indirectly confessed to the crime—wanting her husband to find out from her before someone else broke the news to him.

Or did Oleander hope that when Cenzio found the incriminating evidence he'd destroy it?

"I really don't know." Cenzio gusted another long sigh, but he swallowed it when a bloodcurdling screech sounded in the background. "Uhh ... I should probably see what *that's* about. I'll see you at nine? Thank you again, Dee. From the bottom of our hearts."

"See you at nine," she confirmed.

The call abruptly ended, cutting off the sound of an almighty crash.

Heaven help her.

WHEN DEANDRA POCKETED HER PHONE AND FINALLY TOOK STOCK OF her surroundings, she found Cruz and Flint in deep conversation in front of the restaurant. Hopefully, Flint knew by now that Deandra hadn't fled the cafe like her tail was on fire because of anything Cruz had done. The two men glanced over at her periodically, though, suggesting she was at least one of the topics of conversation.

Still reeling from what Cenzio had told her, Deandra started the trek back across the parking lot. She was halfway to them when Cruz noticed her approach. She could tell, even though she was too far away to hear their conversation, that Cruz was cutting the chat short in light of her being off the phone. She halted in her tracks. After another quick bro hug, Cruz ate up the distance between himself and Deandra. She craned her neck to offer a wave to Flint, who waved back with more enthusiasm than necessary, probably to make her laugh. He succeeded.

Cruz stood before her, scanning her face. "You okay? You look like you're going to pass out on me."

"I'm so tired," she said with a whimper.

"Let's get you home, then." He only hesitated for a moment, then slipped an arm around her shoulders and guided her back in the direction of his car. She leaned into him a bit as they walked.

After he wrenched his passenger-side door open for her, she climbed in, and he got it latched again. Deandra felt her remaining energy go out of her like the tide. Now she was emotionally wiped out on top of physically. She kept thinking about little Kiwi being distraught about his mom being inexplicably absent and poor Cenzio being unable to explain why. She feared the call had taken her over the edge, and now bursting into tears was on the near horizon.

She could *not* break down in front of Cruz. He might have said this date didn't even rank in his top twenty worst firsts, but if she started openly weeping in his car, it might very well end up on the list. With her head resting on the headrest and her eyes closed, she tried to think happy thoughts to crowd out the ones about the Basnets.

Cruz's door closed with a quiet snick. "Can I do anything to help? The whole 'Oleander was detained under suspicion of murder' thing aside, an eight-hour shift with Kiwi tomorrow is going to be a lot for you. It would be a lot for anyone."

She rolled her head until her left temple was almost flush with the headrest, then opened her eyes. The sight of his pinched brow and bunched mouth made her eyes burn and throat constrict. "It may even be longer than eight hours." She gave him the more detailed rundown of events that she'd gotten from Cenzio. She gusted a sigh. "What if Oleander really *did* do it? Cenzio doesn't have much family. I don't know what kind of sentences people get in the hub system for crimes like this, but Oleander could get put away for a long time. As much of a menace as Kiwi is, the idea that he may never see his mom again breaks my heart."

A little sob escaped. Oh no. *Don't you dare lose it, Deandra!* she chastised herself.

Cruz reached across the center console and grasped one of her hands. Double oh no. If he was too nice to her, she'd sob like a baby for sure.

"I have back-to-back surgeries in the morning, but I should be able to take a lunch break around three," he said, his thumb caressing the back of her wrist this time. The steady feel of it eased some of the tension in her shoulders, and after a few deep breaths, the burning *I'm going to cry!* feeling in the back of her throat eased. "If you need lunch, or a break, or want to go for a walk with Kiwi and Havoc—just let me know, and I can meet you."

The overhead light in the car had gone dark. She wasn't sure how much of her face he could see; she could only make out part of his.

"I don't want you to have to—" she started.

He lightly squeezed her hand, causing her to swallow her weak protest. With a soft chuckle, he said, "In case it's not obvious, I like you, Dee. I like spending time with you. I wouldn't offer to see you or to help if I didn't want to."

Her face flushed hot. "Then a lunch-break drop-in sounds great."

"Cool," he said, giving her hand one last squeeze before slipping his hand free. He started up the car and headed out of the lot.

It was a fifteen-minute drive or so, and they sat in companionable silence for most of it. Deandra currently was just trying to stay awake. She really hoped Havoc was still bushed, too, because if she got home and he'd gotten his second wind, she really *would* cry. She did not have the energy to play tug-of-war with a bouncy dragon.

"The thing that's still a sticking point for me is that window," Cruz said out of nowhere.

"What?"

"According to Mavis, the killer got into Lydia's townhouse through that upstairs window, right? I'm assuming the windows are standard size—you were outside the building. Did the windows seem especially large? As in large enough to accommodate someone as big as Oleander?" he asked.

"They seemed normal to me, but I didn't see the *back* of the building. Maybe they're panoramic windows," Deandra said.

"Maybe," Cruz said. "But if she went through the trouble to go through the window to get into Lydia's place—assuming she did so to minimize anyone seeing her—why did she then flee out the *front* door?"

"Because she was so shocked by what she'd done, she wasn't thinking clearly? Ursula said she heard shouting prior to Lydia's fatal crash into the wall. Maybe Oleander was so sick with worry that Lydia had been using her abilities to manipulate Kiwi that she went over there to confront her, the confrontation got heated, and Oleander tossed her down the stairs."

Cruz bobbed his head. "But even in that scenario, you'd think Oleander would have gone to Lydia's *front* door for that confrontation. If she wanted to *talk* to Lydia, why sneak into her house in the middle of the night? Ursula saw a yeti-like creature on the sidewalk, but she didn't say if they were coming or going, did she? She was mixed up about why she'd gotten up while taking a break from her game—and she'd gotten up at least three times that night, right?"

That all was true.

Cruz didn't have to say it out loud for Deandra to know that he liked and respected Oleander. Did he just not want to accept that someone he knew could be capable of murder? He'd known his bear shifter client even less, and the details of that case clearly still bothered him.

Deandra didn't want to think Oleander was capable of something like murder either, but it was also suspicious as heck that she'd left the house in the middle of the night and hadn't told her husband about it. By her own admission, Oleander had been unable to sleep on Sunday evening. Was it that restlessness that had caused her to leave her house, or had her late-night—potentially deadly—confrontation with Lydia been the reason she'd developed insomnia?

Cruz pulled into a spot at Wendy's apartment complex and shut off the engine. He didn't make any immediate move to get out of the car. "What times did Cenzio mention from the doorbell camera?"

"Eleven thirty to five after midnight," Deandra said. "I just wish I knew why she dropped so many hints to Cenzio to find that footage. Was she trying to confess, or was she trying to exonerate herself? She's a lawyer. She's either been trying to puzzle out all the details of who killed Lydia—*or* she's searching for the right spin or angle to get herself off the hook."

"And what time did Ursula say she heard the thud from next door?" Cruz asked, his gaze a little distant as he stared into space, doing some puzzling of his own.

Oh!

Deandra sat up a little straighter. "Twelve twenty-four—which is well after Oleander was back home. Even if it's true that Ursula took several breaks during her gaming session, and she got mixed up about how many of them she took and when, the *reason* she took a break doesn't really matter. If twelve twenty-four a.m. is stamped in her head, there's probably a reason for it. But that would mean Oleander went to confront Lydia, left, and then someone *else*, less than twenty minutes later, snuck through that window to kill Lydia and then snuck back out."

"Couldn't they have used the window to get in, then gone out the front door?" Cruz asked. "Ursula wouldn't have had eyes on the sidewalk the whole time."

"Yes, but ..." She unfastened her seat belt so she could turn in her seat to better face him. "Okay. Wait. Let me put this together ..."

His grin was a flash of white in the dark. "Someone got their second wind."

"Shh. I'm working here," she said. "Okay, so there are a few discrepancies in the stories, both from the death witch and from Ursula. Maybe the inconsistencies are because of unreliable sources—namely guilt-stricken Mavis and memory-and-optically challenged Ursula—but maybe it's also because the werecats aren't showing all their cards. Today was the first time they mentioned the broken window to Mavis, even though it's almost guaranteed that they discovered it during their initial investigation. They told Mavis that's how they believe the killer got *in*. I don't know if it was on purpose or by design that they didn't say anything about how the killer got back *out*. But I think Mavis indirectly told me the killer left via the window."

"Oh?"

Mavis had said, "*I never went upstairs that day because the cops said I would contaminate the crime scene more than I already had. They said I moved the body too much when I was checking for vital signs, but it's not totally my fault. Opening the door pushed her body farther into the foyer.*"

"Lydia's body rolled to its final position in front of the door. It didn't block the door completely, but in order for Mavis to get into the house, she accidentally moved Lydia's body when she pushed the door open," Deandra said. "So if Oleander was *actually* seen leaving the scene of the crime, how did she get out the front door if Lydia's dead body was already in the way? Oleander is not a tiny woman; she wouldn't have been able to squeeze out if there wasn't much clearance."

Cruz sat up a little straighter. "Oooh. Good point."

"So is Oleander somehow getting framed for this, or was she just in the wrong place at the wrong time when Ursula saw her leaving Lydia's?" Deandra asked.

"The biggest problem with the theory that Oleander *isn't* the killer is that it relies on Ursula being right about the time she heard the noise," Cruz said. "If she used her cell phone, there would be a time stamp in her call log. There must be a log of calls at the station, too. And yet, the only eyewitness we know of has poor eyesight, a penchant for crying wolf, and a compromised memory.

"In my albeit limited experience with how the werecats work —they don't move on a suspect until they have pretty solid evidence. If they've determined that Ursula is too unreliable as a source, Oleander could be in real trouble. The mere fact that her fur—assuming it's hers—is at the scene of the crime *and* there's evidence on her own personal doorbell camera that she left the house in the middle of the night during the suspected time of death, is pretty damning."

Deandra deflated.

"There's still a chance the fur analysis will clear her," Cruz said. "I don't want to believe she did this, either. She's such a good advocate for other sapient beings—it would be a blow to her client list if she goes down for this." He stared at Deandra for a beat, then sighed. "I should probably free you from my car ..."

She waited as he ran around to her side to get the door open. As she climbed out, she offered him a sad smile. It only took him two tries to get the door shut, then he walked her to the staircase that led up to Wendy's apartment. "Thanks for everything—it was fun. Except for the last part."

"Finding out your new client might be a murderer is a downer, for sure," he said.

She managed a laugh.

"I'll uhh ... see you around three tomorrow? Assuming there aren't more fires than usual to put out at the office," he said.

"Sounds good."

He hesitated briefly again before opening his arms. She happily stepped into them for a hug.

After breaking the embrace, she took a few steps backward, pausing with one foot on the bottom step. "For the record, Dr. Caddel," she said, "I like you, too."

His smile was sudden and goofy. "Goodnight, Dee."

"'Night, Cruz."

CHAPTER FIFTEEN

Deandra and Havoc arrived at the Basnets' a little before nine o'clock the following morning. She noted that the doorbell camera was gone entirely. Deandra figured the werecats had a way to check devices for magical tampering, as they'd taken all the hardware outside of the art gallery as well when investigating the arson case.

When Cenzio opened the door, Deandra frowned at how red-rimmed his eyes were. She couldn't be sure if it was due to sleep deprivation or if he'd been crying. Maybe both.

"Any news?" Deandra asked as she stepped inside.

Cenzio closed the door behind him and rested his back against it. "Nothing new from Ohlie. Werecats came by shortly after I talked to you last night. They had a warrant, so I had the fun task of wrangling Kiwi while the cats prowled around looking for Goddess knows what. They downloaded footage from the doorbell camera *and* took the whole unit. They hardly said a word to me, other than asking for a fur sample. They also had a warrant for that. Kiwi was in near hysterics, as if he was worried the cats were here to take me away from him, too."

"I'm really sorry this is happening," Deandra said, bending to unhook Havoc's leash. He went trotting down the hall and then disappeared into the kitchen. "Did they say anything to you about why they think Oleander would do this?"

Cenzio shrugged helplessly. "Ohlie was on the fence about hiring Lydia, I know that much. But the last I'd heard, she was still looking for someone. I think that faun woman—what's her name? The one who runs Pawsome Pets or something? Susan?"

"Sarah," Deandra said.

"Yeah, her. She was in the running, I think. Ohlie's better at reading people—especially mundanes, uhh ... humans—than I am. No offense."

Deandra shrugged. "Mundane" didn't seem to be a derogatory term, but she supposed it could be, depending upon who wielded it.

"I left the hiring to Ohlie. I probably should have asked more questions, but we've both gotten so slammed with work in the last month or so, we've been splitting tasks. Divide and conquer, you know? If something went down between Lydia and Ohlie, she didn't mention anything to me," Cenzio said. "I'm not even sure I could have picked Lydia out of a lineup."

It sounded like Oleander had bitten off more than she could chew when she'd already been running on fumes. Deandra wished she could go back in time and tell Oleander to talk to her husband, to assure her that he would weigh in on the decision. There was little doubt in Deandra's mind that Cenzio would have vetoed Lydia as a choice if there was even a *hint* of suspicion that

Lydia had been manipulating Kiwi. But maybe Oleander had been so desperate to get this task off her plate, she'd hired Lydia against her better judgment—and then immediately regretted it. Had she called Lydia that night, and when she didn't get an answer, snuck out of her house to confront the woman in person?

Even if Oleander ended up being innocent of the murder, she had crossed a line. As terrible as Lydia was, showing up at the woman's door so late had been a step too far—and Oleander knew it. Especially if the fur found at Lydia's was a match. It wouldn't automatically mean Oleander was guilty, but she certainly hadn't done herself any favors.

It suddenly registered to Deandra that she hadn't heard a peep from Kiwi *or* Havoc. She was about to inquire as to the where-abouts of the baby yeti when Havoc came prancing into the room with Kiwi on his back. The yeti had a bottle in hand that he was drinking from, but he was simultaneously weeping quietly. There were fewer sadder sights than someone weeping while eating or drinking.

Cenzio gusted a sigh so deep it set a few flyaway hairs around Deandra's head flapping and made her ponytail tickle her neck. "He's been crying off and on since yesterday. All his thought-pictures are of his mom."

It wasn't until Kiwi and Havoc were halfway down the hallway that Kiwi finally figured out that, if Havoc was there, Deandra must be, too. He paused in sucking at the bottle, tossed it onto the floor, and very unceremoniously spilled off Havoc's back. Kiwi tottered toward Deandra, wrapped his little arms around one of her legs, then burst into raucous sobs.

Kiwi put up little fuss when Deandra reached down to grab him. She propped the sobbing yeti onto her hip. His arms were too short to circle her neck, so he merely tucked them between his belly and her side, buried his face against her shoulder, and blub-bered softly.

"I *would* say the kid is making me feel like chopped gizzards, but I know how he feels. I just don't have anyone's shoulder to cry on," Cenzio said, frowning down at his son. "Thank you, Dee. Truly. I know I already said it, but I couldn't even begin to unravel this mess with Ohlie if I also had to worry about Kiwi. The circumstances that led you to us were horrible, but I'm still glad they brought you into our lives."

"Stop," Deandra said, trying to wave a dismissive hand while holding fast to Kiwi. "You're going to make *me* cry."

Cenzio rubbed a furry fist against an eye. "I'll just, uh, finish getting ready. Kiwi *was* strapped into his high chair eating breakfast. I don't know how he got loose. I probably didn't strap him in well enough. Ohlie is always better about that. She's better at a lot of things." He frowned deeply. "Sorry. Rambling. I'll be back."

Deandra watched as Cenzio trudged up the stairs. When he was out of sight, she tried to reposition Kiwi so she could look at his face, but the more she moved, the more he tried to burrow into her armpit, like a turtle pulling into its shell—a very weepy turtle who had already left a very long string of snot along the front of her shirt.

Her arm had nearly gone numb by the time Cenzio left half an hour later. Every time Deandra tried to place Kiwi on the floor, or the couch, or in a chair, he clung to her as if he'd been slathered in superglue.

And yet, within ten minutes of Cenzio leaving, Kiwi went from sad about the absence of his mother to apoplectic over the sudden disappearance of his father. He cycled through panic, frustration, fear, and rage at Deandra, who for a good hour had become the cause of all his woes. He didn't blast her with ice water or bite her, but he *did* chuck toys at her at every opportunity. Later, while they were outside for a potty break, he chewed through the leash on his walking harness and scaled the backyard fence. The barbed wire, as Oleander had promised, *did* keep him in the yard, but wrangling the kid back into the house was like trying to grab a bitey, greased-up piglet.

The "game" that took up the better part of the following hour was involuntary hide-and-seek. Without warning, Kiwi would abandon an activity, sprint away from her with alarming speed, wedge himself into an obscure hiding place, and then scream bloody murder until she found him. He had a knack for hiding in places where she couldn't reach him, thanks mostly to the Basnets' oversized furniture. Usually, once she started moving said oversized, heavy piece of furniture or searching for a flashlight, he'd slip past her, his thundering little footfalls across hardwood or tile the only tip-off that he was on the move again.

After the third time, he started cackling maniacally once she'd located him. The laugh was so off-putting that goose bumps rose on her arms. She realized then that he'd been doing it all on purpose to maximize her stress level. Under normal circumstances, she would have ignored his antics until he grew bored, but he was so emotionally unstable, she was worried he'd hurt himself. That Cheshire grin flashing in the dark among the wires and mechanisms that made up the base of the Basnets' reclining couch, however, told her she'd been bested by the psychotic furry baby.

She stared at him, and once she was sure she had his full attention, she scrunched up her face, let out an agonized wail, and flopped onto her back. She kicked her feet and pounded her fists on the floor. Havoc almost ruined her plan when he was suddenly in her face, snuffling in her ear.

She gently shoved him away while continuing to wail and carry on, then placed a finger in front of her lips without actually quieting her faux sobs. Havoc sat on his haunches and cocked his head as if he was questioning her mental stability.

When she heard a faint creak from the vicinity of the couch, Deandra's eyes widened, and then she renewed her staged meltdown with vigor. Havoc, apparently deciding that Deandra wasn't actually in distress, flopped onto his back beside her and kicked his feet in the air as if he were doing a bicycle exercise in an aerobics class. It didn't look like he was mimicking a tantrum so much as scratching a hard-to-reach itch, but it would have to do. Deandra wailed. Havoc tried his best approximation of an answering howl. He sounded like an ambulance's broken siren.

The pitter-patter of little feet sounded beside her. She noted the steps were cautious, rather than the cadence of "you can't catch me, coppers!" that Kiwi had been employing for the past hour.

Deandra clapped her hands over her eyes when she heard his approach, so she *felt* him leaning over her face now more than she saw it. She downgraded her crying a bit, mostly because her throat needed a break.

Kiwi sniffed. "Why you cry?"

Deandra pried her fingers apart to peek at him. "Kiwi doesn't like me."

She dramatically flopped onto her side so her back faced him. She gave a great wail. Havoc was still on his back, but he was now focused on trying to use his tongue to lick the end of his muzzle despite his tongue clearly being too short.

The pitter-patter of feet sounded again as Kiwi ran around to her front side. She separated her fingers once more to find him squatting by her head, his brow scrunched. He looked like a tiny gorilla. "Kiwi like Dandra," he said, bewildered, as if *she* were the one who had completely lost her marbles.

"No. Kiwi doesn't like me."

She flipped back over but kept her hands off her face this time. She instead wedged them between her knees and stared down at the floor, looking as sad as possible.

Kiwi quickly waddled around her head to squat in front of her face again. "Dandra Kiwi's friend."

When she finally glanced up at him, his eyes were shining with the start of new tears. "When you throw things at people, it makes them think you aren't their friend. It makes me think you don't like me."

Kiwi's bottom lip trembled. "I sorry." He flopped onto his bottom and grabbed hold of one of his feet with both hands. He stared listlessly down at the floor. "Do you know where's Mama?"

Great. Now *she* had to try to figure out how to explain why his mom hadn't come home. She propped herself up on her side, head on her hand. "Have you heard of Kensey?"

"Mama work," he said, still holding fast to his foot and frowning at the floor.

"Yeah, that's where your mom works," she said. "Do you know what a telepad is?"

He perked up at that. In one fluid motion, he pushed himself to his feet and took off running.

Deandra levered herself into a seated position. Havoc snorted awake. She glanced down at him. "You fell asleep on the job?"

Havoc peeped happily.

Deandra would have scrambled after Kiwi had he left the room, but he'd only run to the other end of the living room. His butt and back legs wiggled in the air as he scrounged around in an open box of toys. After extracting what he wanted, he came tottering back with a cylindrical object in his hand. He'd been moving too fast, though, and he stumbled and dang near face-planted.

"Ouch," he said, somehow making the word three syllables. He was back up before Deandra could move. "I okay!" he called out triumphantly, then closed the distance.

Deandra sat cross-legged, curious what had prompted his behavior.

He stopped, heaving, and thrust the cylinder at her. It was roughly the size of a standard toilet paper roll. "Telpad, telpad, telpad!"

Taking the plastic tube, Deandra turned it this way and that until she found a little switch on the bottom. She flicked it on.

The solid gray plastic tube gave a hum, and then, all at once, everything but the flat rings marking either end of the tube vanished. It startled her so much, she almost dropped it. The walls of the cylinder were still there—she could feel them—but they were transparent now. Glowing blue rings of runes lined the bottom of the tube's interior. As she watched, the figure of a man seemed to walk into the tube from some spot beyond her hand. He stood in the center of the rune circle, his body started to vibrate as if it were breaking into bits of static, and then he vanished. A few seconds later, a woman appeared, and the cycle continued with her.

A little unnerved, Deandra flipped the switch back off. Almost instantly, the toy looked like an innocuous tube of plastic again.

"Makam ... Greeboy ... Nina ..." Kiwi said, as if listing things off. Deandra had no idea what any of the words were. He pointed to the device in her hand. "They go telpad."

Deandra wondered if the people featured in the toy were characters from a show.

"Right," she said. "So, your mama rode in a telepad to Kensey yesterday for work, but she couldn't finish everything. She stayed there because the work is taking her longer than she expected."

"When come back?" he asked, his big eyes hopeful.

"I don't know, buddy," she said.

His bottom lip wobbled. "Dandra friend but Mama best, best friend."

Now Deandra's lip wobbled. "Your mama thinks you're her best, best friend too. And she's trying to finish her work so she can come back to be with you and your dad. That's where your dad is today. He's trying to help her finish her work so she can come home. It just might take a few more days."

"New days happen after sleep?"

"Yeah," she said hopefully. Maybe he understood things better than she thought. "A few more sleeps, and hopefully she'll be home."

"Okay! I go sleep now so Mama come home more sooner!" Kiwi took off running for the open doorway of the living room.

It *was* almost noon, so his nap time was fast approaching. But how much of a meltdown would the kid have if he woke up and discovered that taking a nap hadn't magically brought his mom back? Had Deandra worded that all wrong? Given him false hope?

She hurried out of the living room to find him trying to crawl up the stairs. Climbing up each individual stair was like scaling Mount Everest. She scooped him off the third step and carried him to his room. He probably hadn't slept much last night, so even if he woke up mad at the world, a nap would do him some good, regardless. Once he was in his crib—with his eyes squeezed tight as if willing himself into a sleep so powerful it would knock him out until his mom was home—Deandra slid to the floor near the door, the wall at her back. Havoc curled up beside her legs, rested his head on her knee, and shut his eyes.

She really wasn't sure her sanity would hold out until five.

CHAPTER SIXTEEN

D eandra flailed awake, which was just as well because the monster that had been hurling lightning at her had almost zapped her into oblivion. Her tailbone hurt.

A sudden buzz against her thigh made her startle again. That sensation most likely had been her sleeping mind's inspiration for the lightning-wielding beast.

It took her a moment to get fully oriented back to the present. She was sitting on the floor of Kiwi's bedroom, there was a crick in her neck, Havoc had left a substantial puddle of drool on her knee, and Deandra's phone was buzzing.

Oh gosh, what time was it?

She blinked rapidly several times, flipped her phone over, and noted the time was just after two. She had a pair of text notifications; both were from Cruz. One had come in at one fifty-five, and a second at two ten.

CRUZ

> Second surgery ran long. I'm famished and need to get the heck out of here. I can meet you for lunch around 3:30 if you need that break

CRUZ

> Blink twice if you need rescuing

DEANDRA

> Hi! Lunch sounds great. I currently need a chiropractor more than a rescuer. I'm too old to sleep on the floor

CRUZ

> I, once again, have questions

DEANDRA

> I'll explain later. I need to get over to Barnaby in a few minutes, but the gang and I are up for an outing after that

CRUZ

> Text me the address and I'll pick you all up when you're done. How does sandwiches at Oracle Park sound? Could be a good place for Havoc and Kiwi to burn off some steam

Havoc was still curled up beside her. Kiwi, however, was awake and literally gnawing on the slats of his crib. He had a wild look in his eye, which probably meant he'd be wide awake when they made it to Barnaby's.

Perfect. Kiwi is awake and unglued

She texted him Angela's address and her sandwich order, then pried herself off the floor. Sleeping against the wall like a discarded rag doll was not recommended.

Havoc sprang to his feet out of a dead sleep as soon as she moved, and he set about prancing around Kiwi's crib. Flaunting his youth at her was terribly rude. The prancing only made Kiwi chew harder on the slats, desperate for his own freedom.

Deandra rested her arms on the lip of the crib's wall. "Wanna go for walkies?"

Kiwi let go of the wooden slat so he could properly bellow his approval of this plan. He grabbed hold of the bars and shook them violently as he screeched *"Walkies!"* at the top of his little lungs.

Deandra hoisted the thrashing ball of fur out of his crib and managed to hold onto him as they made their way down the stairs, but he wriggled out of her grasp when they reached the ground floor, and he slid down her leg as if it were a firefighter's pole. He went galloping down the hall and into the kitchen on all fours, Havoc close behind. Today, Kiwi wanted his fill of "nana chips" instead of the papaya "chewy ohs." After munching his way through half a bag of the dried banana crisps —with quite a few going to Havoc, too—Kiwi tottered back down the hallway.

He'd only been out of her sight for ten seconds, but by the time she made it out of the kitchen and into the hallway, he was standing a foot away from the front door. "Mama? Mama here!"

Deandra perked up at that, wondering if Oleander had somehow already worked her lawyer magic and gotten her detainment sentence commuted to house arrest. But a muted thud just outside the door made Deandra doubt Kiwi's assessment. Even on tiptoe, Deandra couldn't see out the peephole. The sound of a door rattling closed, the gentle roar of an engine, and the eventual hiss of air brakes suggested it had been a delivery driver on the doorstep and not Oleander.

Taking a few steps away from the door, Deandra braced herself. "That wasn't your mom, buddy. It'll still be a while."

Kiwi stood staring up at the door for a few more seconds before turning around to face her instead. She was grateful there weren't any toys in the immediate vicinity that he could lob at her head. His little shoulders slumped. "More sleeps?"

"Yeah. Still a few more sleeps till she comes home," Deandra said. "But we can go for walkies now. That'll be fun. You like walkies."

"Like walkies," he repeated without enthusiasm.

He stood still, like a depressed stuffed teddy bear, while Deandra got him strapped into his baby carrier. When she asked him if he wanted a snack for the road or to have a bit of his prepared lunch from the fridge, he answered with a sad, "No hungee."

After moving the delivered package inside and locking up the house, she and Havoc set off for Barnaby's. Kiwi hung listlessly on her torso, his arms and legs flopping gently with each step. Havoc kept peering up at Kiwi as they walked, clearly sensing the yeti wasn't acting himself but just as at a loss on how to help as Deandra.

The only plus to Kiwi being so dejected was that his demeanor gave Deandra hope that the Barnaby visit would go as smoothly as it had the day before.

Alas, it was not to be.

Barnaby was waiting at the gate of his hutch as usual, tapping his taloned feet in anticipation of his visitors. Deandra was only a foot from the hutch when Kiwi suddenly thrust his limbs in four directions, squeezed his fists into tight balls, and screeched, "*Chickennn!*"

Kiwi's voice had gone deep and guttural, as if possessed by a tiny demon.

Barnaby fainted.

"*Oh* my God!" Deandra yelped. "Kiwi!"

Somehow, his little voice only went deeper and creepier. "Chicken, chicken, chicken …"

Kiwi often expressed excitement by repeating a word in threes. This, however, sounded more like a ritualistic chant to be uttered in an old-growth forest. Barnaby was clearly not a chicken; he didn't even have feathers. But maybe the sight of the frilled dendrune had unlocked some dormant predatory instincts in the yeti.

Kiwi's arms were short enough, and the baby carrier was secure enough that Deandra was able to scoop the deadweight dendrune out of his cage and get him into his harness without incident. When Barnaby came to, the group was already outside, and the dendrune was lying in the grass. Deandra had taken several steps back, giving Barnaby ample distance between himself and Kiwi. Still, she held fast to Barnaby's leash, just in case he got scared again and tried to bolt.

Kiwi had gone quiet once they were outside, as he'd grown distracted by a swallowtail butterfly that was flitting about in the flowers in Angela's front garden. Movement from the lawn, however, drew the yeti's attention back to his prey. The guttural chant resumed.

Havoc trotted over to the dazed Barnaby and gently nosed his side with his muzzle. The sight of the dragon startled Barnaby, but he recovered quickly. Recognition kicking in, Barnaby shrieked happily at Havoc, and the two bounced around each other in the grass. Deandra did her best to keep the leashes from getting too tangled.

Kiwi, either overcome with blood lust or frustrated by not being included in the antics on the lawn, bellowed, "Me want chicken!"

Barnaby whipped around, clearly having forgotten about the threat his life had been under mere minutes ago. He took a few tentative steps forward. Kiwi kicked and thrashed, but even with the unhinged little guy strapped to her chest, she could barely feel it. Whoever had crafted this magically enhanced contraption had earned every penny.

Unfortunately for Kiwi, both of Barnaby's brain cells were online today and firing at full capacity. It didn't take the dendrune long to realize that, despite Kiwi's intense desire to cause Barnaby bodily harm, Kiwi was stuck. And much like Barnaby's ultimate nemesis—the world's squirrel population—that gave Barnaby a sense of confidence he otherwise lacked. He puffed out his chest, bent at the waist, and then sprang back to full height, using his entire body to issue a screech of righteous indignation at Kiwi.

Kiwi's demonic chanting increased in depth and vigor. Barnaby scratched at the ground like a bull preparing to charge.

"Both of you need to calm down!" Deandra admonished.

Neither listened.

Havoc tried his best to distract them with play stances and dressage horse prancing, but that didn't work either.

Deandra tried patting Kiwi's head, but that only enraged him, and he tried to swivel around to bite her. She yanked her hand away.

As she tried to decide whether just bringing Barnaby back inside would be the best option, Barnaby issued a terrifying hiss and opened his neck flap, shaking the vibrant red skin.

Kiwi screamed bloody murder and, in the next breath, unleashed a torrent of icy water at the dendrune. Deandra assumed the frilled lizards had been prey animals in the fae realm. What the dendrune lacked in fighting prowess and intelligence he made up for tenfold in agility. He dodged the deluge with little effort.

The water had been expelled from Kiwi's mouth with such force, there was now a substantial bald spot in Angela's lawn, and where there had once been bright green grass, there was now a muddy puddle. Two small ice cubes bobbed on the shallow surface.

The creepy, unfortunately familiar, sensation of Barnaby's little scaly arms on Deandra's leg made her look down. It also gave

Kiwi a better view of the dendrune. Before Deandra could issue a protest, the yeti screeched and unleashed another torrent of water. There was far less of it this time, and it was also lukewarm. Once again, Barnaby darted out of the way in time.

The same could not be said for Deandra's shoes.

Despite knowing the flood of warm liquid that hit her legs and feet was water, and that it had come from Kiwi's mouth and not the other end, it still felt like she'd been peed on. The only consolation was learning that Kiwi's icy-water-blast power was finite, which lowered Barnaby's chances of getting washed away in a flash flood by a considerable margin.

Frowning, she shifted her weight from foot to foot. Her socks and tennis shoes squelched. "Ughhh! Kiwi! Really?!" she whimpered.

Kiwi tipped his head back, his furry head pressing against her chest. She could only see his face from the nose up at this angle. "Dandra mad Kiwi?"

She gusted a very long sigh, trying to expel her frustration. "Not mad."

"Just … just dismapointed?" Kiwi asked, his voice quaking. "Dismapointed even more badder than mad!"

And then, once again, Kiwi burst into raucous sobs.

Deandra glanced down at Havoc, who had been sitting innocently by her feet all this time. The dog-like grin on his face suggested he found the chaos deeply entertaining. "Do you have anything to offer?"

He peeped.

Deandra yelped when she was yanked to the right. The blast of water to the grass had disturbed an ant colony, and now the cement walkway that bisected Angela's lawn was covered in a mass exodus of small black insects. Barnaby had used all his might to drag Deandra a few feet so he could gobble up as many as possible. Her left arm was yanked forward next as Havoc decided to sample the ant buffet as well.

Havoc hissed in discomfort a moment later, however. The

mouthfeel of live ants couldn't be pleasant. Havoc hopped on all fours, growled, and then snatched up a mouthful of dirt and grass. He chewed it vigorously, then spat it all back out in an attempt to expel the ants from his mouth. His tongue was the color of mud.

Barnaby apparently was unfazed by a meal that stung, and he chirped happily to himself as he licked the ant-swarmed cement.

With both leashes in one hand, Deandra absently grabbed hold of one of Kiwi's small round ears as she tried to verbally calm Havoc down. She rubbed the ear between pointer finger and thumb, marveling at its silky feel. It reminded her of the ear of one of her favorite stuffed animals growing up—a floppy-eared rabbit whose inner ears had been lined with smooth velvet. It took her a few moments to realize the yeti had stopped sadly repeating "Dandra dismapointed wiff Kiwi." His periodic sniffles said he was still awake, but at least he was no longer caterwauling.

She surveyed the water-blasted and chewed-up lawn and considered texting Angela to say walks were on the house this week. She also considered quitting pet sitting altogether.

Gusting a sigh, she started down the walkway—skirting the panicked ant colony as best she could—dragging Barnaby away from the insects. Normally, it was nearly impossible to pull him away from his version of wild game, but a squirrel chittered at him from up the street. Barnaby's eyes narrowed, and he marched forward, opening and closing his neck flap in irritation.

Apparently, as long as the dendrune wasn't flashing its frill *at* Kiwi, the yeti found the display amusing. He clapped and giggled every time the dendrune did his best to look menacing. "Funny chicken!"

Barnaby wasn't picky about the kind of attention he got, so he waved his neck frill around more than usual simply because Kiwi got a kick out of it. Deandra was just glad everyone was getting along.

She was less glad about the constant squelch as she walked. Little bubbles materialized from the mesh top of her sneakers every fifth step or so. Her toes would resemble prunes by the time she was able to take her shoes off.

As Deandra stood near the same corner where she'd first met Lydia Monroe and Harmony, she considered texting the gnome to see if she had any juicy gossip. The gnome and Oleander were friends, after all. Harmony was the reason Deandra currently had a baby yeti strapped to her chest.

Before she could decide if she wanted to add a cell phone to the mix, as her hands were already occupied by two leashes and a full poop bag, a yipping bark snagged her attention. Seconds after that, Deandra noted the distinctive sound of clomping hooves.

Turning around, she spotted Sarah strolling down the side-walk toward her with a Pomeranian in a yellow polka-dot dress trotting alongside her. It took Sarah a moment to register what she was looking at, as loaded down with creatures as Deandra was. But when all the pieces clicked into place, Sarah waved enthusias-tically. Even from several feet away, the comforting scent of pine swirled around Deandra.

"Looks like someone has their hands full," Sarah said.

Today, Sarah wore shorts and a plain black tank top. Deandra tried not to get fixated on the logistics of Sarah getting her goat legs through those small leg holes. Her short ringlet curls were pulled back from her face and neck into a chic messy bun. It made her black horns appear even longer.

The animals all greeted each other. Well, Goldie and Havoc greeted one another by sniffing unmentionables, while Barnaby ignored everyone in favor of scratching at the dirt in search of grubs.

"Hi, Kiwi," Sarah said, bending at the waist a bit to be at eye level with the yeti.

Kiwi didn't reply.

Sarah gave him a moment, her expression hopeful, but she eventually shrugged and stood to full height again. Addressing Deandra, she said, "I didn't realize you were the one who got the Basnet job."

There was no malice in her tone, and yet the statement came with a faint whiff of forest fire.

Deandra knew rumors ran rampant in Axia, but this was also only Deandra's second day caring for Kiwi. It felt like a lifetime ago that Oleander had hired her. If the news of Deandra being the Basnets' newest caretaker hadn't made the rounds yet, it was also likely Sarah didn't know Oleander was in a Kensey holding cell awaiting lab results that might put her on trial for murder. Deandra opted to keep that information to herself.

"Yeah, it all happened so fast," Deandra said. "I got an email from Oleander on the same evening as the happy hour, actually. A friend of hers recommended me."

"Hm," Sarah said noncommittally. "Must have been *some* recommendation for her to make a decision that quickly."

Deandra honestly wasn't sure if Sarah was more annoyed with her or Oleander. "I didn't realize you were walking Goldie now," she said, hoping to change the subject.

Sarah glanced down affectionately at the Pomeranian, who was cycling through a series of tricks trying to get Barnaby's attention. Havoc was on his back, chewing on the end of his own tail.

Kiwi, as energetic and reactive as he usually was, had gone totally mute. Deandra was still gently massaging one of his ears, but she didn't think that was relaxing enough to the baby yeti that he'd clam up. Oleander *had* said that, despite Kiwi developing language, he actually spoke to very few people.

"We absorbed quite a few of Lydia's clients," Sarah said.

"Any of the ones she previously poached?"

Sarah's lips thinned. "Almost all of them, yes. The circumstance that brought them back to us wasn't ideal, but I'm glad Lydia's charges, like little Goldie here, didn't see a disruption in service."

Losing their former sitter to murder seemed like a pretty big disruption.

"Well, if you somehow have too *many* clients now," Deandra

said, "feel free to send some my way. What you see currently is the entirety of my client roster."

She'd meant for the comment to sound lighthearted, partly to try to distract Sarah, who kept watching Kiwi with an unsettling intensity.

"I'd love to, but ..." Sarah said with complete seriousness, finally looking at Deandra instead of the yeti. "You'll learn in this job that things can change at the drop of a hat. We're at the complete mercy of our clients, and when their life circumstances change on a whim, so do ours."

"What happened?" Deandra asked, assuming this was a separate issue from Lydia's sudden demise.

The burnt-wood smell tickled Deandra's nose.

"We had a bit of a monopoly on the pet owner base in a thirty-unit apartment complex over on Downey Road," Sarah finally said. "A little over two months ago, the owner of the building decided he was going to turn it into a hotel. He gave everyone ninety days' notice that they had to move."

"*Ouch*," Deandra said.

"Awful for all those people who will be displaced—especially ones who have been living there for years—but on a more selfish note, we're about to lose eighteen steady clients in one fell swoop in a couple of weeks. Several of them have said they're leaving the area entirely. Some are going to have to downsize and put pet-sitting expenses on the back burner." She shook her head. "It's stressful enough when you only have to worry about your *own* source of income, but I'm responsible for the livelihood of six other sitters. It's been tough. My natural predisposition to nurture is overwhelming sometimes. I'm not saying I'm such a nice person that I'm worried sick out of altruism. I mean my very genetic makeup *forces* me to care too much. I have to find to find a solution to everyone's problems so I can personally function again."

Deandra stared at Sarah, who in turn stared at Kiwi. Had Sarah been so worried about losing her clients, and therefore putting her sitters' financial stability on the line, that her nurture magic compelled her to take drastic measures against Lydia? It was likely that Lydia had at *least* eighteen steady clients—some of whom had worked with Sarah in the past. Had Sarah's magic convinced her that those once-poached clients were supposed to be hers anyway, and it was within her rights to get them back by any means necessary, if it meant helping her employees weather the storm of a potential flood of lost clients?

It would be easy to assume Sarah couldn't be capable of hurting Lydia, solely because Sarah was so nice, so mothering, so caring. But the label "mama bear" existed for a reason. When a mama's cubs were threatened, the claws came out.

Deandra's gaze dropped to Sarah's lower half. Those hooves were no doubt strong enough to bodily kick someone down stairs. Was Sarah agile enough that she could have climbed out Lydia's second-story window and gotten to the ground without injuring herself? Wouldn't someone have noticed if a faun were hauling around a ladder in the middle of the night?

"If you ever need help with Kiwi," Sarah said, redirecting Deandra's focus, "I have a team of people who are ready for the challenge. We prepared for it for weeks. It must be tiring to be the sole person responsible for him all day."

"I'll keep that in mind, thanks," Deandra said.

Sarah's smile was strained.

Goldie issued a yip. She was flat on her belly and staring longingly at Barnaby. Her tail wagged a million miles an hour, looking like a vibrating cotton ball. Barnaby turned and scratched at the ground, inadvertently sending a spray of dirt at Goldie. She shook off the damp earth and plopped onto her haunches, tongue lolling as she gazed at the indifferent lizard in adoration.

Havoc had been sitting beside Deandra's ankle for a while now, his gaze focused up at Sarah. Perhaps he'd sensed how quiet Kiwi had grown in the woman's presence and was leery of the woman who had caused it.

"How's Mavis doing?" Deandra asked. "I figured she'd be the one walking Goldie. She was Lydia's emergency contact, right?"

Sarah's button nose wrinkled. "I had to fire Mavis. I was trying to work out some kind of bereavement leave for her so she could still have some money coming in while she grieved, but she became a liability. She's been harassing clients—asking them all kinds of nosy questions, as if she's a detective on the case. She even used a vacationing client's house keys so she could hold stakeouts in their home to better spy on Tansy across the street."

"*No!*" Deandra said, eyes wide.

Sarah nodded solemnly. "I feel for Mavis, I really do. But violating a client's property by creeping around in it at night—even if they're currently out of town—is a deal-breaker for me. I don't care what her reasons were."

"Totally understandable," Deandra said, already second-guessing her promise to Mavis that she'd escort the woman to the police station to tell them about Lydia's supposed stalker. Was Deandra just enabling reckless behavior, when what Mavis really needed was to speak to a grief counselor? "Have *you* escaped her suspicions? I had to plead my case that I wasn't a transplant from another hub who was here to seek my revenge on Lydia. Mavis accused me of being both a siren *and* a shifter."

Sarah huffed a laugh. "If being a transplant from somewhere else is a criterion for being on the suspect list, half the population of Axia would be on it. Relocating in the mundane world is much more involved and labor-intensive than it is in the hub system. There are even telepads built for vehicles. Need to get a moving truck across the country? Two or three telepad jumps will get you there. A cross-country trip can be completed in a few hours if the lines for the telepads aren't too long."

Deandra could see how near-instant travel could drastically change how firmly planted some people's roots were. Moving away from family would feel like less of a big decision if telepad travel meant you could pop across state lines in a blink. Her welcome booklet had informed her that the farther the distance between telepads, the greater the risk of something going horribly awry during teleportation. She wondered if teleporting from the United States to Europe was possible, or if the traveler was sure to end up in pieces and scattered across the ocean. She shuddered at the thought.

"Are you originally from Axia?" Deandra asked.

"I am!" Sarah said, smiling. "Of my team of six sitters, Fialova and I are the only native Axians."

If Mavis was right that the killer had been among the pet sitters at the happy hour, Sarah might be one of the best sources for information, especially since she employed half a dozen of them. Not to mention that Sarah was on Deandra's personal suspect list as well, even if Tansy was currently at the top of it. Kiwi would think Deandra was a superhero if she figured out that his mom wasn't the killer, but rather a fellow pet sitter. "What about Keith and Tansy?"

"They aren't from here either—but like a lot of older folks, they wanted to retire here. Tansy is from Pinebough, and Keith is from Luma. Tansy's family owns a zombie cactus farm, and she did delivery runs for a long time. It's a very sensitive plant that needs specific conditions to even survive transit. She's got to have an earth witch lineage somewhere in her family tree; she's very in tune with nature."

Mavis also suspected Tansy was a nature witch, which, according to the welcome booklet, was a "native earthen realm witch," meaning Tansy's magical lineage had existed in this realm prior to the Glitch. It would make Tansy magic-touched rather than fae.

"Anyway, I ran into her one day in the Zombie Cactus, and we got to chatting. My nurture magic went off the charts around her; I could tell she was at a crossroads as far as careers went. I told her about pet sitting, and that was that! It was like a light went off in her head. She knew Axia pretty well from her years of delivering here. Within a month of our conversation, she'd quit the farm and moved here, and a week later she met Rufus."

It was obvious that Sarah took great pride in having played a role in Tansy finding a new path. It might also explain Tansy's fierce loyalty to the faun: Tansy's conversation with Sarah had changed her life.

"So you don't share Mavis's theory that Tansy's the one who attacked Lydia?" Deandra asked cautiously, curious both about the answer and Sarah's reaction to the question. As much as Deandra liked Sarah, the faun had just as much of a motive as Oleander, even if Tansy's temper and penchant for making empty threats spoke to a more violent personality than that of the faun or yeti. Deandra supposed Wendy's early suspicions about Sarah had burrowed into the back of her mind.

"I don't know what's going on in that noggin of yours," Sarah said, sounding lighthearted enough that Deandra didn't think she was being offensive. "But as eccentric as Tansy can seem, she's not violent. Prone to outbursts and making idle threats, sure, but she's sweet as a lamb underneath the rough exterior. There was no love lost between her and Lydia, but she would never have hurt her."

Deandra remained unconvinced. "Did any members of the group know each other prior to moving here? It seems like Fialova and Keith are pretty close." She left out the part about knowing that Tansy and Lydia had both attended the same zoolinguistics school, though decades apart. Keith could have trained there too, for all she knew.

"Not that I know of," Sarah said. "Tansy's been here for over a decade. Keith only settled in Axia in the last year or so. He bounced around a few hubs doing odd jobs after his wife passed. It was a brutal thing—she was killed during a mugging in Luma. There was a trial and everything. He said that, after that experience, he lost his way until he saw a job flyer on a community board in a Kensian cafe. It was one of mine. Fialova was already working for me by then. The two of them met first and clicked right away. We joke that they were father and daughter in a past life.

"Anyway, even though Keith answered the job ad, I could tell from his questions that he didn't want a boss so much as advice on how to start his own business. So I gave him the gist and told him he was more than welcome to shadow me on some of my gigs here to get a feel for the job. He did just that, and he, just like Tansy, was living here within a month of our initial conversation and was running his own little operation. They say my nurture magic should be called pied-piper magic instead—it's as if it lures wayward souls to me."

Deandra wondered if Sarah's financial worries about her company wouldn't be as pronounced if the faun weren't so open to helping others start—and maintain—their own businesses.

She then remembered part of a conversation from the happy hour.

Sarah had said, "*Some of my employees are full time, some part time, and I still pass on business to other sitters all the time.*"

And under his breath, Keith had muttered, "*For better or worse.*"

Perhaps Keith thought Sarah's magic was getting in the way of making proper business decisions, too.

"*Now,*" Sarah said in a very motherly tone—the kind of motherly tone that made you sit up a little straighter because you knew you were in trouble for something. "All that information soothed you. Why? Are you playing detective, too? Am *I* on your list of suspects?"

Sarah still didn't sound cross, but Deandra couldn't shake the feeling that some nebulous authority figure was disappointed with her.

Kiwi was right: Someone being "dismapointed" was so much worse than anger.

But a little voice in the back of Deandra's head questioned where this cloying feeling came from. Deandra not wanting Sarah to be offended at her mild suspicion of her innocence in Lydia's death was one thing. But Deandra needing to swallow down the tightness in her throat—a sure sign she was going to cry—because she was terrified of upsetting Sarah was a different matter entirely.

The sudden enveloping scents of pine, pancakes, sizzling bacon, and the decadent sweetness of fresh maple syrup were so comforting, it almost brought Deandra to her knees.

"What suspicions do you harbor?" Sarah asked in a smooth, even tone. It was the kind of relaxing voice perfect for podcasts used to promote sleep.

Deandra felt a bit sluggish. Even her lids seemed heavy. It was like being under a warm blanket on a blustery day—perfect cozy nap conditions.

"What can I tell you that will assuage your concerns?" Sarah asked.

This ethereal being before Deandra couldn't be capable of murder. She was too good. Too pure. Too innocent.

Cool water misted across Deandra's arms and legs. Sarah shrieked. Goldie and Havoc both barked—well, Havoc tried to, anyway.

Deandra's mind suddenly cleared, and she found herself staring at Sarah, who was drenched from the neck down. Goldie hadn't been hit head-on by the deluge, but she was damp. She gave herself a full-body shake, knocking water loose from her fur *and* her polka-dot dress.

Barnaby, unfazed, slowly stalked a nearby snail.

Sarah propped her fists on her hips. "Now, Kiwi, why on—"

Kiwi jabbed a tiny finger at the faun. "You no hurt Dandra!"

Sarah jerked back slightly in surprise—whether from Kiwi actually speaking to her or from the accusation, Deandra wasn't sure. Probably both. "I wasn't hurting her. I—"

"You make head pictures go ..." Kiwi said, then waved his fists frantically while making sounds like television static. "You same as Lidya. I don't like. Dandra no do that. Dandra friend."

Huh. So Lydia *had* manipulated Kiwi, just as she'd done with Rufus.

Sarah took two clomping steps backward. Goldie hopped back on all fours. "I apologize to you both. I ... I didn't intend ..." She worried at her bottom lip. "My magic detected that information would soothe you, Deandra. I sensed that you had questions about me as well. It seems my ability overstepped its bounds. Again."

"You really can't control it?" Deandra asked, unnerved.

"I can, but when I'm stressed, it almost takes on a mind of its own and starts trying to nurture and soothe *me*," Sarah said, her gaze a little distant. "If I let it take the reins, so to speak, it's like I —Sarah—take a back seat, and the magic goes on autopilot, making the decisions that are most beneficial for me but not always in the best interests of others. It's like a built-in self-care mechanism—but sinister, almost."

"Sinister?" Deandra asked.

Havoc woofed low in his throat. He and Kiwi had both gone eerily still again, watching the faun closely.

"I remember once in high school, in my senior year, I was supremely stressed about a group project that would determine my final GPA," Sarah said. "I *needed* an A. My group wasn't taking the project seriously enough for my liking. Messages often went unanswered. My teacher ignored my requests for a new group assignment or to let me do the project on my own. At the height of my stress, I lost two days. I just ... blacked out. When I came to, my project was done, none of my groupmates would speak to me—two seemed downright terrified, honestly—but I got that A. I still don't know what happened."

Deandra didn't know how to reply to any of that. "If you're feeling that stressed out again, maybe you need a little vacation. I'm sure your employees could hold down the fort for a few days. If your magic is starting to man the helm, it's probably best to take a breather."

Sarah plucked at the front of her damp shirt, which clung to her torso. "Perhaps you're right. I'm ... sorry again for overstepping. And I apologize, especially to you, Kiwi. I shouldn't have frightened you so much that you had to expel your limited magical stores to stop me."

Kiwi didn't reply.

Deandra's menagerie watched as Sarah and Goldie skirted around them, then headed through the crosswalk and around a bush-lined corner—the same path Lydia had taken the first, and last, time Deandra had talked to her.

As Deandra turned and faced the path back to Angela's house, she spotted a few strands of fur dotting the sidewalk—probably knocked loose by Kiwi's blast of water. It wasn't lost on Deandra that, though Sarah's fur looked gray while on her body, when lying loose in individual strands, it appeared just as white as Oleander's.

CHAPTER SEVENTEEN

By the time Cruz pulled up outside Angela's house, Deandra's shoes were mostly dry, but she felt like a disheveled mess. Meeting him at the curb, she pulled open a back door and got Havoc into the back seat before Cruz had a chance to emerge from the car. She waited patiently by the passenger-side door so Cruz could pry it open for her, deciding to keep Kiwi strapped into the baby carrier in lieu of a car seat.

The smile she offered Cruz, who was still in scrubs, was apparently not an expression mirrored by the yeti. Cruz's own smile slipped off his face as his gaze settled on Kiwi.

Hands in his knees, he bent at the waist to be at eye level with the yeti. "Hey, Kiwi. What's the matter—"

"*Noooo!*" Kiwi shrieked, then bucked wildly. "Kiwi be good! Kiwi sorry! Kiwi no like doctor!"

Deandra mentally thunked herself in the forehead. She'd completely forgotten that Kiwi had both a human pediatrician and a vet who managed his care. She grabbed hold of one of his ears and tried to massage it to calm him down, but he was flailing so much, she was worried she'd tear the thing off.

"Kiwi!" she called over his loud protests. "Kiwi, it's okay."

Kiwi did not believe it was okay.

Deandra shot Cruz an apologetic look, dropped her arms to her sides, and, for the second time that day, threw a tantrum of her own. Though her tears were fake, there was something cathartic about releasing pent-up energy with a few good screams.

She half expected Cruz to hop into his car and speed away from her. Instead, he tossed his head back to wail at the sky, too. A muted howl sounded from inside the car. She pictured Havoc with his head thrown back, trying his best to mimic the wolf everyone thought he was.

It took what felt like hours, but in one of the quiet moments between her faux sobs, she heard a sniffly, "Dandra no like doctor, too?"

She mimicked rubbing her fists against her dry eyes, though Kiwi couldn't see the whole of her face at this angle. Cruz stopped carrying on as well, but he pulled a tissue from his pocket to dab at his eyes and nose to help keep up appearances.

"I like the doctor," Deandra said, offering Cruz a dramatic smile and wink over the top of Kiwi's head. Cruz fought valiantly to keep his features in line with mock sadness. "I'm sad because you don't like my friend. He came to have lunch with us."

Kiwi sniffed.

"Can I show you?" Cruz asked, gaze focused solely on Kiwi.

From below her chin, she saw Kiwi tentatively nod.

A second later, Kiwi shrieked, but it was a happy sound this time. "Apples, apples, apples!"

Cruz glanced up at her. "Baby yetis are always hungry, so I got him a couple of bags of maroon maiden apple slices off the kid's menu. Then I remembered Havoc and got a couple more."

Deandra stared at him for a few long moments.

"You're very nice," she said in wonderingly, in a tone akin to having spotted a unicorn.

Oh, goodness. Were unicorns a thing here?

"Don't worry," he said. "I have plenty of flaws. This is just me on my best behavior. Give it a few months, and then you'll be like, 'Oh, so *that's* why Axia's most eligible bachelor is still single ...'"

"I don't know what it says about me that I'm even more intrigued now," Deandra said. "I must find all the skeletons in your closet."

"Aha!" he said, holding a clenched fist aloft. "My plan, she is working!" He paused dramatically. "Also, it's cute you think they'd all fit in something as small as a closet. You beautiful, naive fool."

Deandra blushed.

"This *boring*," Kiwi said, dejected. His limbs hung loosely, and his head was pitched forward, his chin likely resting on the front of his baby carrier. "Want apples."

Cruz chuckled. He got the passenger-side door open on the first try. As he ran around to the driver's side, Deandra tried to figure out the best way to strap herself and Kiwi in so as to minimize the chances of them flying through the windshield should they manage to get in a collision during the short five-minute drive to the park.

A loud snuffling sounded from the back. Deandra turned in

her seat enough to spot Havoc with his muzzle against the thick fabric hammock that covered the back seats. He seemed to be fixated on an area in the middle of a backrest.

"The sandwiches are in the trunk," Cruz said as he pulled out onto Angela's road. "I learned from Max that wax paper, masking tape, and plastic bags can be torn through in roughly twenty seconds. I figured Havoc could do it even faster."

"And Max is …?" Deandra asked.

"Oh! Right. Maxine, my black lab."

"Plain ol' mundane dog?" Deandra asked.

"Yep. She is the best girl on the planet."

Havoc growled in indignation, despite being neither a girl *nor* a dog.

"When do I get to meet this Maxine?" Deandra asked.

"Whoa, whoa, whoa, hotshot," Cruz said, shooting her a wildly over-the-top look of pure incredulity. "It is *way* too soon for you to meet the family. Maxine is a *ruthless* judge of character. I'm not sure you're ready."

Deandra laughed, raising her hands in placation. "She sounds terrifying."

"She's an absolute monster. Tore the head off Mr. Hippo last night, and left his fluffy entrails all over the rug," Cruz said. "Not even I—a trained surgeon, mind you—could save him. She just stood beside the corpse … grinning."

Deandra placed a hand over her heart. "RIP, Mr. Hippo."

"I would say he'll be missed, but Maxine never feels remorse for the destruction she causes."

"Want *apples*," Kiwi said mournfully.

"You can have apples when we get to the park," Deandra said.

"Apples, apples, apples!"

Once at Oracle Park, Cruz got Havoc out of the back seat and the sandwiches out of the trunk, then they found a bench near the pond. It was the very same bench she'd sat on three days ago with Oleander.

After getting Kiwi out of his baby carrier, she set him on the ground. Her torso and shoulders were damp with sweat from carrying the yeti around for so long. Cruz hadn't blanched at her slovenly state, but that was probably just because he was a nice guy.

Deandra handed Kiwi apple slice after apple slice until he was glutted, while Cruz did the same with Havoc. When the two monster babies ran off to play in the grass, Deandra groaned in defeat and slouched on the bench.

Cruz mimicked her. "How irresponsible would it be if we both took a cat nap?"

"Every time I use the restroom, even when it's at the speed of a pit crew, the two of them get into trouble," Deandra said. "Today I had to put them both in the bathtub just so I could keep an eye on them. Kiwi got bored after ten seconds, scaled the shower curtain, and pulled it loose from the rod. It scared Havoc so badly, he managed to knock several bottles of industrial-sized shampoo off a rack. I thought the Basnets' air conditioning bill would be astronomical, but can you imagine how much shampoo and conditioner they go through?"

"Do you think they air-dry or use a hair dryer?" Cruz asked.

She glanced over at him. "I appreciate that you ask the important questions. Has to be a hair dryer. Oleander's fur is so sleek, though. I wonder if she uses a flat iron. I have wash days for *my* hair, but maybe they have wash *months* because bathing is a whole-day affair."

"Maybe they have to wait until Kiwi goes to bed so they can brush out each other's backs," Cruz mused, staring at the pond where several colorful ducks were idly paddling around.

"How'd your surgeries go today?" she asked, remembering that he'd said one had run long. Hopefully that didn't mean there had been complications.

"First one was a knee replacement for a faun," Cruz said. "Pretty standard procedure. That one was fine. The second one was for a werecat who needed a kidney transplant. Shifters need to be in their animal form for surgery. The traumatic nature of surgery usually triggers an innate defense response. There are some real horror stories in the literature from the early days post-Glitch of shifters going from human to animal in the middle of surgery without warning."

"Eesh," Deandra said. "Did the kidney not take or something?" she asked, hoping she sounded like she had a clue what she was talking about—which she did not.

"The organ transfer part went fine," he said, a distant look in his eye. "I just don't love operating on shifters. They have a tendency to not stay fully unconscious long enough. Their magic eats away at whatever sedatives we try, and they come to faster than non-shifters. Their mind comes online first, and since I can hear them telepathically when they're in their animal form, it can be very disorienting to have my hands in the open cavity of someone who then starts talking in my head out of nowhere. It's a surefire way to accidentally nick an artery."

Deandra almost didn't want to ask. "And ... *did* you nick an artery?"

He gusted a sigh. "Thankfully, no, but it was close. I was zoned in, concentrating hard, and all of a sudden I heard, 'How's it going, doc?' I almost passed out."

She coughed, trying to cover up a laugh. "Aren't they warned not to get chatty when you're armed with scalpels?"

"Oh, they are. Repeatedly. But she sounded doped-up, so I don't think she was fully aware of what she'd done," Cruz said. "One of the final units at the university was on conducting dissections while shifters periodically break your concentration mentally. They usually did it in the loudest and most chaotic way possible. Need nerves of steel to operate on shifters. It's just been a while since one startled me that badly. I keep thinking about what would have happened if I'd flinched harder."

"But she's okay, right? You kept your cool, and now she's got a new kidney."

He nodded. "Yep. She's okay. She desperately needed that kidney, too."

She scooted over a fraction so she could bump her shoulder with his. "You did good, then. I won't say it'll never happen again, because it might. But you'll be more conscious next time. You'll prepare better." She paused. "You know what this reminds me of? My mom said she played this game called Operation where you had to pull plastic pieces out of a guy's body with tweezers. If you touched the side of the piece's cavity with the tweezers, there was a loud buzzer. There was a timer, and if you didn't get all the pieces out in time, the body popped up and tossed the pieces everywhere. Doing surgery on a shifter sounds like that game—only worse. Maybe you need to rent a shifter so you can do mock surgeries and they can scream in your head."

"I've honestly thought about it."

"Is there something like Craigslist on Forage? 'Wanted: Shifter to berate me mentally while I perform surgery on Mr. Hippo. No weirdos.'"

Cruz barked a laugh that seemed to surprise even him. "An excellent suggestion."

They finally each picked up their sandwiches and ate in companionable silence while the dragon and yeti continued to roughhouse on the pond's shore.

After wolfing down her sandwich, Deandra wiped her fingers and mouth with a napkin, then briefly glanced over at Cruz. "Thank you. You had a super stressful day, and you still went out of your way to get us lunch."

He stared at her for a beat, then quickly looked away, as if embarrassed. He'd been finished eating for a few minutes already. "I, uh, have a tendency on long days to get snacks from the convenience store down the street from the clinic and then eat in my car. Or I go home and hang out with Max for a bit and eat a peanut butter sandwich. Sometimes I skip the sandwich and just take a stress nap. So the offer to meet you for lunch was a pretty selfish one on my part. I knew today could be hard, and I figured getting out of the office to talk to another person and be outside would be a better choice." He paused, gazed over at her, and looked away again. "Plus, I ... just wanted to see you."

Her cheeks heated. "Well, regardless of how selfish it was, I still appreciate it. And I wanted to see you, too, so that was a bonus. Seventy-thirty split with the sandwich in the lead, though."

He gasped in mock offense.

After a moment, he said, "Unfortunately, I have to get back to the office soon. Got any sleuthing updates to give me a quick fix?"

She laughed. "Hmm, let's see ..." She filled him in on what Sarah had told her about absorbing Lydia's old clients, how Deandra had gotten confirmation from Kiwi that Lydia had used her zoolinguist power to manipulate him into acting as if he liked her against his will, and that Sarah's power had started manipulating Deandra before Kiwi had intervened.

Cruz sat in contemplative silence. "Is Sarah at the top of your list now? Nurture magic gone haywire to the point she blacked out, so to speak, and got rid of Lydia because her absence would mean Sarah's company would hardly feel the sting of losing several clients if they were replaced by Lydia's?"

Deandra shrugged helplessly. "I don't know. The way her magic changed the way I thought and felt was ... really creepy. Even *she* said her magic has a sinister side. But as much as I don't want that fur analysis to come back as belonging to a yeti, I don't want it to belong to a faun, either."

"There haven't been any reports of black feathers found at the crime scene, right?" Cruz asked. "Tansy's *my* top suspect, but Tansy doesn't have white fur, and neither does her raven accomplice."

"Daaaaandra!"

She glanced away from Cruz to scan the area for Kiwi. The little yeti was trudging forward on two legs, but he was currently doing a spot-on impression of a parched man trudging through the desert in search of life-saving water.

"Dandra," Kiwi said, distressed. "Dandra. Kiwi no walk."

He plopped onto his backside.

"I guess that's our cue," she said.

She helped Cruz gather up their trash and stuffed it into a bag. He grabbed Havoc's leash and ventured over to the dragon, who looked just as tuckered out as the yeti. Havoc flopped onto his stomach when he realized Cruz was coming to rescue him. By the time Deandra got Kiwi strapped into his baby carrier and the contraption strapped to her chest, the yeti was out cold. She turned around to find Cruz walking toward her with the dragon cradled in his arms.

He stopped in front of her. Havoc's eyes were closed, and he cracked one open to look at her. She propped her fists on her hips. Havoc tightly closed his eyes.

She glanced up at Cruz. "I hope you know he's faking."

Cruz glanced down at the dragon. "Is this true?"

A moment later, Cruz shot her a wide-eyed look.

"What?" she asked.

"He sent me a thought-picture," Cruz said. "It was of him walking to his bed in Wendy's living room and curling up on it. I don't really know what he's trying to tell me, but it's pretty cool he showed me anything at all."

Deandra wrinkled her nose. "I'm kinda jealous."

"I'm pretty sure he's got a strictly self-serving agenda," Cruz said as they started walking toward his car. "I can't decide if I'm offended or not that his first attempt at communication was to convince me he was too tired to walk."

"He tried it with me, too. I had to bribe him with cheese."

It was a little after four by the time Cruz dropped Deandra and company off outside the Basnets' house. Kiwi was still asleep when Cruz opened the passenger-side door with a loud creak. She stood on the sidewalk with a baby yeti strapped to her chest and a sleepy dragon sitting by her feet.

Cruz stood before her, hands shoved in the pockets of his scrubs. "Need anything?"

"Nah, I'm good. Hopefully these two will sleep until five—

assuming Cenzio gets back by then," she said. "Do *you* need anything?"

He started to say something, thought better of it, and then shook his head. "Also good." The bags under his eyes were dark, and his shoulders were rounded. She couldn't tell if he was sad or just dog-tired. Maybe both. He offered her a small smile before saying, "Let me know if you get any hot goss from Cenzio upon his arrival."

Managing an answering smile of her own, she said, "Will do."

With a sigh, he turned away, climbed into his car, and drove off.

She was starting to worry about him. Flint had said, "*Good seeing you, man. Been a while. Should have figured the only thing to get you out of your house was a pretty lady.*"

Cruz, by his own admission, took his lunch breaks in his car—if he took them at all.

Said car had been hit and damaged six months ago. And yet, after he'd needed to yank the door open for her several times on their date, he'd said, "*I didn't realize how much of a pain a malfunctioning door was until this evening, by the way. The DIY videos forgot to mention that part.*"

Had he not had passengers for six months? It certainly implied he hadn't been on any dates.

She'd wondered quite a few times—especially after Mavis's "most eligible" claim, and even Flint's use of the terms "lady-killer" and "fresh meat"—if perhaps Cruz had a commitment problem. He'd warned her that a mere closet wasn't enough to house his plethora of skeletons. She'd even worried at some point that he'd left some jilted fiancée at the altar—or a string of ex-girlfriends or a wife back in Pinebough.

But perhaps it wasn't a person he was married to, but his job. The potential parade of exes might not be the result of his being a commitment-phobe, but rather a workaholic.

She was still pondering this as she got Kiwi settled into his crib and convinced Havoc to take a nap on the floor nearby. As she straightened up the house and wiped down surfaces, she contemplated how she could help Cruz take more time for himself.

All her brilliant ideas for how to save the guy from himself flew out of her head, though, when she heard the sound of the front door to the Basnets' house open. She scurried into the front hallway from the kitchen. Standing in the foyer were Cenzio—*and* Oleander.

"You're back!" Deandra said and hurried into the foyer. "This is good, right?" Head tipped back, she scanned their faces.

"Hi, Dee," Oleander said tiredly.

Deandra's gaze shifted to the woman's feet. There wasn't a boxy black device strapped there, but rather a jade-colored band around each ankle that looked like too-tight anklets tamping down her white fur. An undulating wave of bluish energy danced between the two bands.

Cenzio, who'd just closed and locked the door behind them, said, "It's good as far as her being home, yes. We got the detainment commuted to house arrest. But ..." He cast a wary look at his wife.

"It's okay," Oleander said, wringing her hands and staring at the floor. Deandra hadn't known the yeti long, but she'd never seen the woman look so ... defeated. So unsure of herself. "You can tell her."

Cenzio worried at the corner of his bottom lip as he stared down at his wife. He slipped an arm around her shoulders, and she leaned into him. Addressing Deandra, he said, "Preliminary test results have come back. The fur at the crime scene is yeti."

Deandra swayed a bit on her feet.

"Our lawyer was able to get a request approved for a second lab to run tests as well. There was an inconclusive result mixed in there," Cenzio said. "It was a lot of scientific stuff I didn't really get. But even if the second test comes back as yeti in origin, we decided we're going to fight this. We'll go to trial if we have to."

Oleander finally glanced up then, and the hopelessness in her expression made Deandra's stomach bottom out. "Since I'm home for at least tomorrow, you can have the day off. We'll still pay you, of course. You've been the one bright spot in all this. I want ... I want to have as much time as possible with my boy, in case I end up getting arrested. I'm not sure what we'll do in that case, but I do hope you'll consider still helping us with Kiwi as we navigate this."

"Of course," Deandra said without thinking. The devastation pouring off them both made her throat tighten. "Whatever you need."

Oleander swayed, in relief, Deandra thought, and Cenzio tightened his hold on her shoulders. Staring Deandra dead in the eye, she said, "I didn't do this. I know I made some really questionable choices, but I didn't kill her. I swear it."

"I believe you," Deandra said, though she wasn't sure if she actually did. She *wanted* to believe it. *Desperately* wanted to.

Yet on her walk home with her sleepy dragon trudging alongside her, she couldn't help fear that Oleander's admission of making "questionable choices" was the woman's attempt at convincing Deandra, Cenzio, *and* herself that she wasn't as guilty as the evidence suggested.

CHAPTER EIGHTEEN

The last time Deandra had stood outside Axia's police station, she hadn't gone in. She'd escorted Callie as far as the door. Today, she stood just beyond the shiny glass doors while she waited for Mavis to arrive.

Deandra had texted Mavis yesterday, though she'd been dreading contacting the woman. Mavis needed to be processing her grief, not sleuthing.

DEANDRA

> I have most of Friday off. What's your availability to stop by the police station?

MAVIS

> Totally free. Sarah fired me. Which has been kind
> of a blessing, honestly, because I've made a lot
> of progress. If you want to swing by my place
> early to talk strategy, we can go over what I've
> figured out so far.

The picture that Mavis had sent next had been alarming. It had been an honest-to-goodness murder board. Deandra had opted not to drop by Mavis's to talk strategy *or* to see the disturbingly detailed display in person.

She only had to wait for a few minutes before she spotted Mavis walking up the sidewalk that stretched in front of the police station and the coffee shop next door. True to her word, Mavis had showered; her brown hair had its luster back and undulated around her shoulders in a shiny sheet. She'd donned a pair of black slacks and a white blouse covered in a smattering of black polka dots. Though the shirt was heavily wrinkled, suggesting Mavis had pulled it out of the bottom of a hamper, the strap of the messenger bag across her chest helped smooth out the fabric a bit. The bags under her eyes were still dark.

"Hi," Mavis said as she stopped in front of Deandra. She gave her wrinkled blouse a few ineffective straightening tugs. "Thanks again for this. Especially since I haven't been super nice to you."

"What, accusing a stranger of murder isn't nice?" Deandra asked.

Mavis laughed awkwardly, clearly unsure if Deandra was serious or not. "Sorry about that."

Deandra waved the comment away. "I do have a last-minute condition to add before we go in there."

Mavis folded her arms tightly over her chest, and her face screwed into an expression somewhere between suspicion and apprehension. "What's that?"

"That you have the police help you find a grief counselor."

Mavis's frown deepened. "I'll be fine once we figure out who killed Lydia."

"No, you won't," Deandra said. "You're distracted by the mystery right now. Once that's solved, then you'll *really* start to miss your friend. You're going to need someone to help you through that."

Mavis's chin wobbled. "And if I say no?"

"Then I go home. I have the day off, a weekend looming, and a dozen seasons of *Faet of the Heart* to watch."

Deandra eventually won the staring contest, and Mavis looked away first.

"Yeah, all right," Mavis said.

Gesturing toward the door, Deandra said, "After you."

The lobby of the police station was sleeker and more modern than the cottage-like exterior would have suggested. Two sets of four plush chairs—one set upholstered in red and the other in navy blue—faced each other, with an oval wooden coffee table positioned in the space in the middle. A series of shiny-covered magazines fanned out across the table's surface. All the chairs were currently unoccupied.

The brown tile floor stretched toward closed black double doors on either side of the lobby. Above the rightmost pair of doors, individual silver letters affixed to the beige wall spelled out HUMAN DEPARTMENT. Above the left pair of doors read WERECAT DIVISION.

Directly across from the entrance was a solid slate-gray wall that was broken only by a single window, reminding Deandra a bit of the DMV. The sign above the window read RECORDS AND RECEPTION. The woman behind the glass glanced up and started, clearly having missed Deandra and Mavis's arrival. She slid a panel aside, then waved the pair over.

Her skin was a mint-green color, and a curved dark-blue horn —no longer than Deandra's pinky finger—sprouted from either temple. Her black hair was streaked lightly with gray and had been plaited; the braid hung over one shoulder. The woman had a lithe frame and bright light-brown eyes, and her angular face wore a wealth of laugh lines. Deandra had no idea what species

Fialova was, but she suspected she and this woman had similar lineages, even if their skin colors differed drastically.

"Sorry I didn't notice you two sooner," the woman said as Deandra and Mavis approached the window. Her voice was high and light. "Been a slow day. What can I help you with?"

When Mavis just stood there, eyes wide, Deandra said, "We were hoping to speak to one of the werecats assigned to the Lydia Monroe case."

The woman clucked her tongue. "Nasty business, that." She leaned heavily to the right, partially vanishing from view as she rummaged around on a desk Deandra couldn't see. When the woman sat upright again, she had a clipboard in hand that was topped with a sheet of paper. She clicked open a pen. "Do you have a personal connection to the victim?"

Deandra opted to keep her mouth shut this time. Mavis said nothing, just lightly wrung her hands. Unsure of what to do, Deandra placed a hand on Mavis's shoulder. The slight woman yelped.

"She is—she *was*—my best friend, she … she …" Mavis started to hyperventilate.

"Ooh, dear," the green-skinned woman said, then abruptly disappeared from view.

Within seconds of Deandra ushering Mavis into one of the chairs in the lobby, a pair of officers had joined them. Deandra backed up as the officers crouched in front of Mavis. Deandra assumed they were werecats, based only on their preternatural grace. They were both gorgeous, muscled men whose uniform sleeves seemed to be barely keeping their biceps contained. Mavis stopped hyperventilating once they were both fussing over her. The young woman issued a couple of nervous giggles and played with her hair more than necessary, so Deandra figured Mavis had mostly recovered from her near panic attack.

Deandra stayed well out of the way while the men asked Mavis a series of questions, first about her medical history and then about the reason for her visit. The green-skinned receptionist was back behind her window; she didn't seem at all concerned about Mavis now that the officers had taken over. Once the cats had deemed Mavis stable, they escorted Deandra and Mavis through the doors on the Werecat Division side of the lobby.

Some part of Deandra had hoped that the werecats' half of the building would be full of gigantic cat trees, fluffy beds instead of desks, and balls of yarn the size of beach balls.

Alas, it was a relatively normal-looking station—based solely on what she'd seen in movies and on television. A dozen or so desks filled most of the open-plan space. While the lobby had been almost eerily quiet, this area was abuzz with activity. Nearly every desk was occupied; officers worked behind computer monitors or diligently filled out paperwork. Phones rang, officers took statements, and people who Deandra assumed were assistants flitted about completing errands.

Holding cells took up the far wall. Even from a distance, Deandra could tell the cells had magical properties. The thick metal bars were etched with glowing runes, as if they'd been decorated with neon-blue paint. Only one of the four cells she could see from her vantage point was occupied. A massive brown bear paced around inside the enclosure, occasionally growling its displeasure. Every few seconds, the bear would shift into a human man—who was both naked as a jaybird *and* drunk as a skunk. The frequency with which he shifted from man to bear suggested his intoxication was affecting his ability to control his power. Perhaps this area was the equivalent of a drunk tank, and the criminals who had committed worse offenses were kept somewhere beyond the closed door positioned between the four rune-lined cells, two on either side.

The handsome werecats stopped at an unoccupied desk in the middle of the room and encouraged Mavis to sit in the chair positioned beside it, so she was sitting catty-corner to the currently empty office chair behind the desk. One of the cats wheeled over a second chair for Deandra, depositing it beside Mavis.

"You sure you're all right?" the cat drawled, placing a large hand on Mavis's slim shoulder. There was a slight southern twang to his voice.

She giggled. "Totally fine. Thank you so much."

"You bet," he said. "Officer Sutter will be with you in a moment."

Deandra and Mavis's chairs faced the holding cells, so the pair were able to easily watch the two men saunter in that direction. The drunk bear saw them coming, growled menacingly, shifted into a human and uttered obscenities, then was back in bear form again. The officers didn't pay him any mind as they disappeared through the door embedded in the wall between the cells.

"If one of *them* was a grief counselor, I'd sign up immediately," Mavis said as she glanced at Deandra once the werecats were no longer available for ogling.

"I think half the town would sign up," Deandra said, glancing around as she took in the bustle of the place. No one seemed to be paying them any mind; they were all preoccupied. The receptionist had said today was a slow day, though—what on earth did it look like in here on a busy one?

Mavis let out a squeak of alarm. Deandra glanced at her, finding her gaze fixated ahead. When Deandra followed her line of sight, she smiled.

"Well, well," Officer Sutter said, as she approached her desk and dropped a manicured hand onto her chair's headrest. Her blond hair was in its usual tight bun. "Nice to see you again, Dee. Under less than ideal circumstances once again, but at least you're not fleeing a burning car this time, hm?"

Mavis shot Deandra an incredulous look.

Deandra pretended not to notice. "I'm here more as moral support. Again."

Officer Sutter bent forward languidly and held out her hand to Mavis. "I'm Officer Sutter, and you are …?"

"Mavis!" Mavis squeaked, then shook the offered palm.

Officer Sutter glided into her chair and picked up the single sheet of paper that was lying in the middle of the desk's black leather desk pad. Unlike several of the desks belonging to Officer Sutter's neighbors, hers was meticulously organized. Loose papers were tucked into mesh shelves, file folders were stacked neatly, and various office supplies were in tidy rows, sitting in designated dishes, or hidden within drawers. The flat-screen computer monitor sat at an angle so as not to impede her view of her interviewees.

After giving the sheet a quick perusal, Officer Sutter trundled open a desk drawer and pulled out a legal pad. She flipped through a few pages and laid it on the desk before plucking a pen from a mesh cup on her desk. Slipping it between pointer and middle fingers, she then folded her arms on the desk's surface and offered the ladies a warm smile. As much as Deandra liked Officer Sutter, there was something deeply off-putting about the woman —some combination of unwavering rigidity and sincere compassion.

Deandra could have sworn she heard Mavis swallow when Officer Sutter focused her intense gaze on her.

"I hear you were close friends with Lydia Monroe, Mavis," the officer said in a friendly tone that belied her stern appearance.

"Yes, ma'am," Mavis said without Deandra needing to prompt her to speak. "I'm sure you already have your suspects and everything, but I wanted to report that Lydia ... she had a stalker."

Officer Sutter's brows hiked. "How long was she being stalked?"

"Um ..." Mavis swallowed hard, then abruptly leaned over to grab her messenger bag off the floor. She produced a black composition notebook. A quick glance at the book suggested nearly every page was crammed full of Mavis's scribblings. Plastic tabs in a rainbow of colors fanned out from the pages. Mavis turned to a page a third of the way in, marked by a green tab. "I still have the text logs in my phone, and I can show you those too, but I cataloged all the messages Lydia sent me about the stalker. It started four months ago."

"What was the nature of the stalking?" Officer Sutter asked.

Deandra merely listened as Mavis laid out the details. Aside from mentioning the constant tampering with the upstairs window, Mavis also told Sutter that Lydia had been sure she was being tracked by a mangy black-and-white canine.

Officer Sutter flicked a questioning look at Deandra then, but all she could do was shrug.

Mavis lost a little of her momentum in light of the officer's quiet skepticism, but she soldiered on. "Lydia was a zoolinguist. A low-level one, but she could still communicate with animals—especially with mundane ones. Her ability let her sense where they were, too. Almost like a natural detection system. She could *feel* the dog nearby, even if she couldn't always see it. She said there was an intelligence to it, and when it *did* show itself, there was a very clear message of 'I'm watching you.' She wasn't, uh, as good with the more magic-touched animals, so since she could never get it to come out of hiding—by using her magic, I mean—she thinks it might have been a shifter or a sapient canine."

Curious.

Officer Sutter asked, "Do you have any idea who would stalk Lydia? I get the impression you think it was someone she knew and not a stranger who was fixated on her."

"It was definitely someone who knew her," Mavis said. "They left her notes. Slipped under her front door, left under the windshield wipers on her car, taped to the *inside* of the window that kept being opened while she wasn't home."

Mavis fished around in her messenger bag again and pulled out a stack of small slips of paper from an inside pocket. She stood long enough to deposit dozens of them on Officer Sutter's desk. The type of paper used for the notes varied—white card stock, crudely cut yellow legal pad paper, red construction paper, pink sticky notes. From what Deandra could tell from her seat—even though she wanted to spring out of it and read the notes over Sutter's shoulder—there were only two messages repeated over and over.

LIES HAVE CONSEQUENCES.
SUBMIT TO A TRUTH SERUM TEST.

The handwriting was inconsistent—some notes were written in all caps, some in cursive, and others spelled out with cut-out magazine letters. Deandra wondered if the sender had been trying to disguise their handwriting or if they'd gone a little mad along the way.

A pulse of Officer Sutter's menacing werecat magic flared as she finally glanced up at Mavis. Sutter held a note in either hand, while the rest were spread out across the desk pad in a haphazard tableau. "Why didn't you alert us about this sooner?"

Mavis pulled her head toward her shoulders, making herself smaller.

"She was scared," Deandra blurted. "Lydia wanted to figure out the identity of her stalker on her own, and Mavis was honoring that, even after she passed."

Officer Sutter scowled at Deandra for a few beats, then lowered her unsettling gaze toward the desk, scanning the notes. "Perhaps a more important question is, how are you in possession of these, Mavis? If Lydia didn't want anyone to know about her stalker problem, I doubt she would have handed these off to you for safekeeping."

Deandra hazarded a glance Mavis's way, noting that a blush had crept up her neck and into her cheeks. The composition book lay in her lap, and her hands grasped her knees in a death grip.

Swallowing, Mavis said, "I found them in Lydia's townhouse yesterday."

Sutter worked her jaw. "The townhouse where there's still crime tape up and officers positioned at both the front and back of the building because it's an active crime scene and we're trying to preserve it?"

Mavis chewed on her bottom lip. "I'm gonna get in trouble for this, aren't I?"

"You broke into a crime scene, Mavis," Officer Sutter said,

incredulous. "I understand that you want to know what happened to your friend, but any DNA you left in that townhouse could jeopardize the investigation, *and* it could erroneously incriminate *you*. Depending on what happens with the case, the mere fact that you snuck in and potentially contaminated the scene could result in the very person you want arrested going free."

"I didn't contaminate anything!"

"That's not the point. No one knows what you did while you were in there. Do you know the field day a defense lawyer would have if they had this little kernel of information? They could claim that our department can't be trusted to effectively run a crime scene if we can't even keep a civilian out. *Who knows who else has contaminated the scene,* they'll say. *Or what evidence was snuck out or even planted. How can we trust anything they've reported?* If that defense lawyer makes a compelling enough argument to a jury? It's all over. Is that what you were going for?"

Mavis had begun quietly crying halfway through Officer Sutter's rant, though the woman had never raised her voice.

Kiwi's little voice echoed in Deandra's head. *"Dismapointed even more badder than mad!"*

Deandra felt terrible for Mavis—no one liked getting chewed out. But someone had to knock some sense into her. Snooping around a client's house had gotten her fired. Would creeping around an active crime scene now get her arrested?

"This is me giving you a direct order not to set *foot* in that house again until it's cleared," Officer Sutter said. "I'm going to file paperwork today that states I ordered you to stay out of that building. I hear from *anyone* that you were back in there, you're going to get slapped with a misdemeanor or possibly a felony evidence-tampering charge. You hear me?"

Mavis nodded so hard, it was a wonder her head didn't snap off and roll away.

Sutter blew out a long, steady breath. "How did you get in?"

Mavis slid her composition book onto the corner of Officer

Sutter's desk. A beat later, Deandra yelped as Mavis vanished into thin air. Sutter popped to her feet.

Squeak!

Deandra leaned over the armrest of Mavis's chair to find a tiny brown mouse sitting on the cushion. Mavis glanced up at Deandra, her tiny pink nose wiggling. The mouse's fur was as silky as Mavis's hair.

Deandra thought back to the evening of the happy hour. Wendy and Deandra had both thought it was odd that the death witch on scene had supplied Mavis with so many details. If Mavis had been eavesdropping as a mouse, though, it could explain how Mavis learned as much as she had.

Just as quickly, Mavis was back.

Sutter expelled a sigh and returned to her seat. "I suppose it's easy to get in when you're that tiny. I'm assuming that messenger bag, if you have it on you when you shift, adjusts in size?"

"Yeah," Mavis said. "Custom made from a specialty shifter shop." She swallowed hard. "This is terrible, but some part of me didn't fully believe Lydia even *had* a stalker. And then the other part of me felt so guilty I didn't force her to report the stalker that I felt like I had to make up for it. So I went looking for evidence to prove the stalker was real. She'd mentioned getting notes, but I never actually saw them. I found them in a folder that was taped to the underside of a desk." She wrung her hands. "I'm really sorry. I was just trying to help."

Sutter frowned down at the sea of notes. "I know."

Mavis cleared her throat. "Can … can I ask a question?"

"Sure. Doesn't mean I'll answer it."

Deandra tamped down a smile. Sutter had said something similar to her months ago.

"So … another reason I went over there was to see how easy it was to get in as my animal," Mavis said. "Tansy Buckley is my number one suspect. I think she used her raven, Rufus, to get in. Anyway, there was this musty smell from the staircase, like the carpet was wet. Reminded me of damp towels. If the townhouse has been locked up, it seems like that would make the musty smell worse."

"Is there a question in there somewhere?" Officer Sutter asked.

"Um. Did you know Tansy is a nature witch? People's powers and heritages aren't public knowledge, so I was thinking you might not know she can manipulate nature. I'm not even totally sure what that means, but it's like elemental magic kinda, right? She wouldn't be as powerful as a water witch or anything, but she could still have strong enough magic to blast Lydia with water. It would probably deplete her magical stores in one go, but if she was rested up, and—"

Officer Sutter held up a hand, and Mavis's increasingly fast rambling was abruptly cut short. "We did know that, thank you. Besides the fact that her nature magic isn't strong enough to classify her as anything but a kitchen witch, she also has an airtight alibi. She had a very well-documented doctor's appointment, and Rufus was getting a spa treatment at Beak-A-Boo. It was confirmed as of this morning. This, incidentally, is my next formal warning: Do not interrogate Tansy Buckley about her supposed involvement in Lydia's murder. If I need to file a request for a restraining order, I will. I'm aware of you taking up a sentry post in the house across the street to spy on Tansy. Tansy is aware of it, too." In a slightly gentler tone, she added, "I know you mean well, but even I can see you're spinning out of control, Mavis."

In a stage whisper, Deandra said, "Don't forget about my last-minute condition."

Mavis groaned. "I hoped you wouldn't remember." Addressing Officer Sutter, she said, "Dee is forcing me to ask you for recommendations for a grief counselor."

Officer Sutter angled a small smile Deandra's way. "That'll be the third piece of paperwork I file after we're done here." She eyed Mavis. "Any other suspects or trespassing I should know about?"

"No," Mavis said, gaze focused on her lap. She was deflated *and* defeated.

Deandra wanted to mention Lydia's alias to Officer Sutter in case the werecats were somehow unaware of it. But she didn't want to say anything in front of Mavis and set the woman off on another sleuthing spree that could send her into the welcome arms of a telepad. If Mavis disappeared into Pinebough in search of clues about Alison Griffiths's potentially sordid past, who knew what kind of trouble she'd get into?

"Well, if you two think of anything else, give me a call, okay?" Officer Sutter said before pulling open a drawer on her desk.

After grabbing what she needed, she stood up, prompting Deandra and Mavis to do the same. The officer handed each of them a business card.

"That's my personal cell. Please don't abuse it." When Mavis took hold of hers, Officer Sutter didn't let go. "Stay out of trouble, all right?"

Mavis bobbed her head vigorously. When Sutter let the card go, Mavis hastily scooped her composition book off the officer's desk, snatched her messenger bag off the floor, and hustled toward the exit. Deandra watched her go.

"Can I ask you a question?"

Deandra, surprised, glanced up at the officer. "Me?"

Crossing her arms, the officer studied Deandra. "You work for the Basnets now, right?"

Deandra blinked dumbly at her, wondering how she knew that. But then she remembered that Oleander had been detained for the better part of twenty-four hours. Sutter was the lead officer on the case, so it stood to reason that she'd interrogated the yeti. "For the past two days, yes."

"Has she mentioned anything to you about Lydia? She was in line for your job first, wasn't she?"

Deandra swallowed. She didn't want to say anything that could get Oleander in further trouble, but Sutter perhaps wanted to hear confirmation of Oleander's story from additional sources. So Deandra told the officer about Oleander's suspicion that Lydia had used her zoolinguistic ability to manipulate Kiwi. Deandra also told her about the interaction she'd had with Sarah that pushed Kiwi into revealing that he had, in fact, been coerced by Lydia to act against his will.

"Interesting," Officer Sutter said. "Thank you." Her gaze slid to some point behind Deandra. "I'll let you get back to your friend. She looks like she could do with a ride home." She wagged a finger, and that menacing werecat aura overtook Sutter as she added, "Don't let her be a bad influence."

"Yes, ma'am," Deandra said, without dropping into a curtsy *or* peeing her pants.

She scurried for the exit.

After dropping an exhausted Mavis off at home with the promise to check on her over the weekend, Deandra headed for Barnaby's house. It wasn't until she was walking the dendrune—just the two of them for a change—that she realized she'd forgotten to mention Alison Griffiths to Officer Sutter.

She didn't feel particularly concerned about it; the werecats were clearly on top of things. If they didn't know about Lydia's alias yet, they would soon enough. Deandra was more preoccupied by Mavis's deteriorating mental state. She hoped the young woman would be okay on her own today after both getting torn a new one by Sutter *and* having her top suspect theory debunked.

Deandra resisted the urge to text Cruz for the millionth time that day. He hadn't contacted her either, but she figured he was decompressing after his rough day yesterday. Plus, he'd said that Fridays were often chaotic at the clinic. He was probably just busy.

After Deandra pulled into a parking spot in Wendy's apartment complex, she slowly trudged toward the stairs. She had been so caught up in thoughts of Mavis that she was scared nearly out of her skin when something darted out of the bushes. She turned just as a mangy black-and-white canine ran by in her peripheral vision and disappeared behind the side of the cement structure that housed one of the complex's dumpsters.

She'd been ready to discount the incident as a human

bumbling through an animal's territory when a high-pitched yip redirected her focus toward the left. The small, mangy dog stood in the middle of the sidewalk a few hundred feet away, its head low as it surveyed her.

"She said there was an intelligence to it, and when it did *show itself, there was a very clear message of 'I'm watching you,'"* Mavis had said.

Deandra's heart thundered.

The canine wasn't very big, but for all she knew, this creature could wield lightning. After an intense staring contest, the dog yipped again, turned on its heel, and galloped out of sight.

Deandra took the stairs two at a time. Maybe she was being paranoid, but once inside, she made sure the door and all the windows were locked tight—just in case.

CHAPTER NINETEEN

When Wendy got home later that day, Deandra and Havoc were on the couch, hearts in their throats as they watched the season one finale of *Faet of the Heart*. Well, Havoc was chewing on a bone and frankly didn't seem to care one iota that Francois and Ferdinand were identical twins who had been separated at birth. Deandra was starting to get the impression her dragon didn't appreciate fine television at all.

Later that evening, Deandra and Wendy went to their grandparents' house for dinner. Deandra had finally made the decision to have them meet Havoc, warning them that he was a dire wolf puppy. Her grandparents liked dogs well enough, but a part of Deandra worried that her shrewd grandmother would somehow figure out that Havoc was a dragon in disguise. As much as Deandra adored her grandmother, the woman couldn't keep a secret to save her life—which also meant that Deandra's mother would know by the end of the evening that Deandra was the proud owner of a fire-breathing wolf.

Deandra hadn't been *avoiding* talking to her mother, so much as—okay, yes, she'd been avoiding her. Her mother hadn't been upset that Deandra decided to move to Axia, per se, but it had made her incredibly nervous. Deandra suspected that she was torn between wanting to come visit Deandra to make sure she was, in fact, okay, and warring with her own personal struggles with venturing back into a hub. Deandra still didn't know all the details of what her mother and aunts had endured in their home hub town, but clearly it was bad enough that the female siblings had been so traumatized by the hub system that they wanted nothing to do with it.

If Deandra told her mother that she was babysitting a baby yeti whose mother was under suspicion of murder, her mother might finally return to a hub, if only to drag Deandra back out of it by her ear and lock her in a basement.

Beyond all that, Deandra also worried that Kiwi had been having too much of a negative impact on Havoc and that her dragon would somehow turn into an unadulterated heathen in their house. She needn't have worried. He was on his best behavior. That was in part, she suspected, because her grandpa had slipped the dragon a few pieces of steak under the table when he thought no one was looking.

After dinner, once Wendy and Deandra had cleared the table and washed the dishes, Deandra found her grandmother standing at the sliding glass doors off the kitchen that looked out on the backyard. On the lawn, in the waning sunlight, her grandpa and

Havoc played fetch. Grandpa Morris didn't have the arm strength to throw the tennis ball for long, but he had no problem using his wind magic to lift the ball and chuck it across the yard over and over for Havoc.

Grandma January glanced up at Deandra and smiled. "He bought that tennis ball today in anticipation of your visit."

Her grandpa was the biggest softie.

"I didn't even know Havoc knew *how* to play fetch before today," Deandra said.

Wendy came up on Grandma January's other side.

"Where'd you find him, again?" her grandma asked, gaze focused outside as she watched her husband fondly. "He's such a well-behaved dog. I've only heard terrible things about dire wolves. I was more than a little nervous about having him here."

"Found him in a dumpster," Deandra said. "The vet said Havoc had a really powerful sleep agent still in his system. We still don't know if someone tried to hide him or throw him away."

Grandma January clucked her tongue. "Shameful."

"Thanks for giving him a chance, despite the nerves," Deandra said.

"Well, I trusted *you*." The nice moment evaporated like smoke as her grandmother turned to face Deandra head-on. She cocked an eyebrow. "I've been hearing rumors that you're dating a doctor? You haven't mentioned him once!"

Deandra shot a look over the top of her grandmother's head at Wendy, who shrugged helplessly, silently telling Deandra that *she* hadn't been the one to spill the beans.

"Don't look to her for help. *I'm* the one who asked you the question," Grandma January said.

"He's the vet who tended to Havoc," Deandra said, refocusing on her tiny but fierce grandmother. "We're not *dating*. We went out twice. Sort of. One formal date and one less formal."

"When do I get to meet him?"

Deandra barked a laugh before she could stop herself.

"Grandma, there is no way I'm bringing him here anytime soon. You'd scare the crap out of him."

"Oh, I will not," her grandmother said, waving a dismissive hand. "I just want to get to know the boy who makes my favorite granddaughter smile like that when he's the topic of conversation."

"I'm *right* here," Wendy said.

"Pah," Grandma January said as she turned to face Wendy now, placing a dark hand on Wendy's much lighter cheek. "You're my favorite, too."

Grinning solely because her grandma couldn't see it and Wendy could, Deandra said, "If you want to talk about boys dating your favorite granddaughters, then you should probably ask Wendy about Nathan."

Grandma January and Wendy both gasped for completely different reasons—one in shock and the other in betrayal.

Quite pleased with herself, Deandra skedaddled out of the dining room and toward a short hallway that would grant her access to an outside door. She wanted some quiet time with her grandfather and Havoc before Wendy sought her revenge.

In apology for throwing Wendy under the bus last night, Deandra had breakfast ready for her in the morning. Wendy didn't hold grudges long, and she could usually be won over with food. Even so, Deandra would be checking her shampoo bottles for any odd smells that might indicate a hair-loss enhancer had been added and double-checking that her shoes hadn't been filled with shaving cream.

Wendy stumbled out of her room, lured by the scents of French toast and coffee. She was still in her pajamas, and her messy bun looked like Rufus had nested in it last night.

Deandra had just placed a full plate in front of Wendy when the business-email chime sounded from her phone. She practically sprinted back into the kitchen to snatch the device off the counter. Maybe it was an update from Oleander!

Instead, it was an email from Sarah.

Hello, Deandra.

I hope you're doing well. I figure there's a real possibility that you'll want nothing to do with me after the other day. I do apologize again that my magic overstepped its bounds.

Anyway, I'm writing to invite you to a birthday lunch I'm throwing for Fialova at my place. She doesn't like making a big fuss over her birthday, so you don't need to bring a present or anything. If you want to bring a dessert, that's cool, but Hogarth's Hoagies is catering the little shindig, so food is covered. We usually play some board games. Nothing too wild. Things kick off at 3.

If you're interested, Wendy and Havoc are more than welcome, too.

If you'd rather keep your distance from me, I understand that as well.

I hope to see you there,
Sarah

Deandra noted the decided lack of exclamation points in this email as compared to the last. She glanced at her cousin, who had already wolfed down half of her French toast and had a dribble of syrup on her chin. "You look like a feral raccoon."

Wendy hissed at her with a mouth full of food.

Laughing, Deandra said, "Do you have plans today?"

Washing down her last bite with a swig of coffee, Wendy shook her head. "Nope. I have to work for part of the day tomorrow and might see Nathan after, but I'm free today."

"Want to go to a birthday party?"

"We talking a kid's party at Srang's Soup Shanty or like an adult party with booze?"

Deandra stared at her. "There's a kid's birthday place called a soup shanty?"

"It's run by goblins, and it's horrible," Wendy said. "Goblins make the absolute worst food you can possibly imagine. Goblins come from all over the world to hit up the Soup Shanty, though. I thought maybe Kiwi's next birthday bash could be held there, then remembered the whole 'his mom is on house arrest' thing."

Deandra sighed. She'd been trying so hard not to think about that too much. She'd had the irrational thought that if she kept it out of her mind, it would somehow protect Oleander. "The party is somewhere in between. It's probably the same crew from the happy hour. More of a board game and sandwiches kind of thing than a boozy one."

Wendy shrugged. "I'm in. I mean, it can't be any more eventful than the happy hour, right?"

Deandra propped her hands on her hips. "You know what happens when you put that stuff out into the universe."

"Pah," Wendy said, sounding like Grandma January. "Are you going to invite *Cruz*?"

"I don't know. Is that weird? Is it too soon?"

"Too soon for what?" Wendy asked. "There's no rule book for this stuff. If it feels right, ask him. If it doesn't, don't."

Deandra blew out a breath that puffed out her cheeks. "Maybe I'll just check in instead. I haven't heard from him since Thursday."

DEANDRA

Hey

She'd finished her breakfast, took Havoc for a walk, and showered, and there was still no response from Cruz.

After Deandra had checked her phone for the thousandth time, Wendy said, "Maybe he took Max hiking." There were no hiking trails in Axia.

Wendy was in the bathroom fussing with her hair while Deandra—all ready to go, save for a quick change of clothes—stood leaning against the doorjamb, lost in thought.

Cruz had seemed so worn out on Thursday when they'd parted ways, Deandra had wanted to give him the space to recover from a stressful day of surgeries. Now she wondered if she should have checked on him sooner.

Wendy abruptly turned around, startling Deandra out of her musings. "How are we feeling about Sarah being a suspect?"

Deandra honestly wasn't sure. "She seems to have more of a motive than anyone else does, in my opinion, but the evidence seems to be pointing at Oleander."

Wendy pulled her phone out of her back pocket to check the time. "We have two hours before we have to be there. I was going to suggest we go dessert shopping, but I have a better idea."

"I'm scared to ask …"

"I seriously think we need a murder board."

"We do *not* need a murder board!"

"Mavis has one …"

"She's also unraveling due to guilt that she didn't do enough to help her friend—and now her friend is *dead*." That had come out harsher than Deandra had intended. "Sorry."

"It's okay." Wendy sounded a bit cautious as she asked, "You mentioned that Officer Sutter really laid into Mavis. What happened, exactly? You got kind of snappy when I tried to get you to talk about it yesterday."

"Sorry," Deandra muttered again.

"I didn't say it to make you feel bad," Wendy said. "I just wasn't sure if you were up to talking yet. Don't get me wrong, I'm happy to binge *Faet of the Heart*. There's so much from season two I forgot."

Deandra gave her the gist of Mavis's dressing-down. "I didn't disagree with anything Sutter said. I just hope it was a reality check, and that it doesn't send Mavis further off the deep end."

There was a long beat of silence.

"What about a murder *sheet*? Just *one* sheet of paper so we can write down all the suspects and their motives?"

Deandra huffed a laugh. "Fine."

Wendy pumped a fist in the air, skirted around Deandra, then ducked into her bedroom. Shaking her head, Deandra headed for her own room to grab her laptop. The pit stop on her way to the living room gave her a chance to check on Havoc, who was passed out on his back on her bed, sleeping off his breakfast. He was in the throes of a dream—feet kicking and flicking.

Shortly after Deandra had sat at the table with her computer, Wendy flopped down across from her armed with several sheets of computer paper, a handful of pens, highlighters in five colors, and two rolls of stickers—one with smiley faces and one with frowning ones, for reasons Deandra couldn't fathom.

"Are we making a murder sheet or a murder scrapbook?" Deandra asked.

When Wendy didn't immediately reply, Deandra cocked her head in question. "For the record," Wendy said, "you might not see it, but you're unraveling a little bit, too."

Deandra shrugged off the comment. "I'm just tired."

"And you're worried about Kiwi and Oleander and Cenzio, and now Cruz, too. You're worried that Oleander is innocent and will end up arrested for something she didn't do. You're worried she's guilty and that it'll crush Kiwi and Cenzio both. You're worried it's actually Sarah who's guilty—and that it will affect not just her clients, but also the employees who rely on her for income. You're worried Cruz is working himself into the ground."

Reluctantly, Deandra said, "Yeah, maybe."

"You showered after you got home on Thursday," Wendy said slowly. "Know where I found your pile of dirty clothes? Because I can assure you they weren't put in the hamper in your room."

Deandra winced. "Where were they?"

"In the towel cabinet." Wendy cocked a brow. "Your shoes were in the kitchen sink."

"I thought I rinsed them off ..." Deandra said, a little alarmed that she didn't actually remember doing it. "Though I don't know why I used the kitchen sink and not the bathtub."

"*I* rinsed them," Wendy said. "That's why they were clean and dry and waiting for you by the door yesterday."

That was definitely alarming.

"When you get stressed, your brain glitches, and you start doing some really weird stuff." Wendy reached across the table with both arms, knocking over one of the rolls of stickers in the process. Bright-yellow smiley faces stretched across the table in a line as the roll unfurled. Palms up, she stared at Deandra expectantly. Sighing, Deandra placed her hands in her cousin's. "Talking stuff out has always been what lessens your stress. Gets your brain to unscramble. I don't know how else to help you. So much of what's happening right now is out of your control. This," she said, glancing at the pile of supplies she'd laid out on the table, "is all I've got in my arsenal right now."

Deandra's eyes welled up a little, which was yet another sign that she was stressed. "Nathan better realize you're a catch."

Wendy beamed. "I *am* pretty great."

It took Deandra a while, just sitting there thinking with her cousin holding fast to her hands, to finally say, "I don't think a murder sheet or murder scrapbook or whatever you have planned is what I need. The thing I keep thinking about is that people here had so many different labels for Lydia. Fire elemental. Animal empath. Pet medium. Grouchy. Hard to deal with. Rude. Brash. Hard worker. Reliable. Maybe some of those are true. Maybe none of them are.

"The only thing no one is talking about—not even Mavis, her supposed best friend—is that Lydia had a whole other identity in Pinebough. Who was she when she was Alison Griffiths? Why did she leave all that behind, change her name, and move here? If Mavis is right, Lydia's stalker is who killed her. And as much as the happy-hour group—and even Oleander—all had reasons to hate her, was anything Lydia did while in Axia worth killing her over? If whatever happened in Pinebough was so bad that Alison created a new identity and then didn't even tell her best friend what she'd been running from, it seems more likely that that trouble *followed* her here."

Wendy bobbed her head. "As much as I love a good murder board, I agree that Mavis sounds like a mess. How much stock do you think you can put in the stalker theory?"

"After seeing those notes? Pretty solid. And that theory feels way less terrible than the idea that Oleander killed Lydia in cold blood," Deandra said.

"Okay, let's get this murder sheet started then," Wendy said, letting Deandra's hands go. She wrote four names at the top of the paper, then immediately crossed one out, seeing as Officer Sutter had revealed Tansy had an alibi.

VICTIM: ALISON GRIFFITHS / LYDIA MONROE
SUSPECT 1: OLEANDER BASNET
SUSPECT 2: SARAH MINK
SUSPECT 3: MYSTERY STALKER
SUSPECT 4: TANSY BUCKLEY

"Mink, huh?" Deandra asked.

"I looked it up on her website a couple of days ago. I found it in roughly five seconds. I'm a *master* detective."

Deandra laughed.

Wendy said, "Okay, let's come up with some specific stuff to look up about Alison Griffiths. She was a graduate from the zoolinguist academy, for one …"

They fired ideas back and forth until Wendy had a few topics of interest.

Zoolinguistics graduate, animal psychic, animal medium, pet sitter, Pinebough resident

"Mavis was able to find my old social media accounts, the name of the cafe where I worked, and even my parents' address. Maybe we'll have similar luck with Alison," Deandra said.

Wendy fetched her own laptop, and the two settled in to snoop.

Social media accounts came up first but revealed little. Either Lydia had scrubbed most of them, had locked them behind privacy walls, or hadn't used them much to begin with. An account on the Forage-based Picayune—similar to the mundane Twitter—only had a handful of messages posted by Alison Griffiths, who was easy to weed out from the one other Alison Griffiths from Pinebough, thanks to a profile picture that gave a clear view of her face. Based on the years they'd been posted and some quick math, Deandra figured the messages were from when Alison was in high school.

A Fith of Ali: you say so much without saying anything

A Fith of Ali: i'm lonely but not lonely enough to call you

A Fith of Ali: tonight might have been the best night of my life. luv you, qualls

A Fith of Ali: this will all catch up to you soon and i'll be laughing when it blows up in your face

A Fith of Ali: cherish your time on this planet, kittens. you never know when it'll end

---

Though they were all out-of-context posts that only people in her inner circle would understand, they still reminded Deandra of her own time in high school when everything felt too big, too small, too dire, and too inconsequential all at the same time.

The last post gave her arms goose bumps—and she wished she could write back to young Alison and warn her that her time on this earth *would be* been snuffed out too soon.

Wendy reported that Ali Griffiths's Pet Services had been in operation for several years in Pinebough, and from what she could find, Alison had received good reviews.

Next, Deandra searched for "Alison Griffiths Pinebough Zoolinguistics." The website Cruz had shown her was the first listing. The next five links were for published papers in *Zoolinguist's Monthly* that included Alison Griffiths as a contributor. The papers were full of zoolinguistic jargon Deandra didn't understand. One paper was about the similarities between a zoolinguistic thought-bond with an animal and a witch's bond with their familiar. It sounded like the kind of thing Deandra would have loved to read, had it been a fictional tale, but the researchers had managed to make it all sound dry and clinical. She lost interest after a couple of paragraphs.

Wendy sucked in a breath. "Might have found something. I searched for her name plus 'pet psychic.' There was a full page of five- and four-star reviews that came up first, all of them about Alison and her ability to communicate with deceased pets. On the *second* page of results, though, halfway down the page is a six-year-old blog post titled 'Alison Griffiths is a Sham.'"

"Oh dang," Deandra said, sitting up a little straighter.

"Pull it up on your screen, and then we'll discuss," Wendy said.

As Deandra opened a new search page and typed in the title of the blog post, Wendy said, "It looks like the blog is run by a woman who owns a holistic pet company in Pinebough. From what I can tell, the woman—Emily Waters—is a certified psychic. Oh, here … in the top corner of the page, Emily lists her license number. If I click on it … oh, it takes you to a very official-looking website for the International Hub System of Psychics and Mediums. I didn't even know that was a thing."

Scrolling up a bit on Emily's blog, once Deandra had it pulled up revealed that while Emily had once been a prolific blogger, she hadn't updated it in over three years. Deandra returned to the Alison Griffiths post.

Good morning, everyone!

It's been my mission for years now to root out the shams among us. The stigma around psychics and mediums is nowhere near as bad in the hub system as it is in the mundane world, but every person who hangs their shingle under false pretenses, no matter the location, hurts us all. I try to visit a new shop every month to get a reading, and then, here on my blog, I evaluate whether the practitioner is the real deal or not. Any psychic worth her salt knows why I'm in their shop the moment I walk in. The fakes, the charlatans, the liars? They never see me coming.

Today's charlatan is Alison Griffiths, a self-proclaimed animal psychic and medium. You can check out her website here: Alison Griffiths Pet Psychic & Medium.

I brought Bella, my golden retriever, with me, as I do whenever I visit a pet psychic. It was obvious from the start that Alison was making things up as she went. Even context clues and subtle hints dropped by yours truly didn't help her. If she's going to pretend to be a psychic, the least she could do is study psychology and body language!

I could forgive all of that to some degree, but the most alarming thing about Alison's practice was the effect she had on Bella. Bella is a certified therapy dog. She doesn't spook easily. She loves everyone she meets. And yet, in this shop, she was immediately on edge. She was panting heavily, tried squeezing her too-big body under my chair, and whimpered often, despite the three of us being the only ones in the small shop.

At one point, when Bella was particularly agitated, Alison paused in relaying a message from a deceased gray parrot I'd never had—I had a parakeet when I was seven—to slip out of her chair and squat on the floor. Bella had been cowering under the table. Alison told me she was "great with dogs" and lifted the tablecloth to peer at Bella.

After several moments of silence, Bella came out from under the table, sat before Alison, and licked her face. The weird thing is, Bella was acting almost robotic. Her tail didn't wag. She hardly blinked. When we finally left the shop, it was as if Bella came out of a trance. She practically dragged me all the way to the car.

She's never acted that way before or since, and we've been in our fair share of sham psychic shops—both in the hub system and the mundane world. I don't know what Alison Griffiths is, but she's a terrible psychic and a false medium, and she possesses a disturbing ability that allows her to control animals.

I've reported her to the International Hub System of Psychics and Mediums.

Stay safe out there!
Emily

DEANDRA WISHED SHE KNEW WHY LYDIA HAD TRIED SO HARD TO BE more than what her zoolinguistic biography detailed. Why risk it, when there were people like Emily who would call her out on it— especially in the hub system, where psychic and medium abilities could actually be verified?

"What do you think?" Deandra asked.

"Honestly? I mostly want to know how and why people kept hiring her. Her bio on the academy website clearly says she graduated with a demerit ..."

"Cruz made it sound like the academy site isn't always checked when people hire zoolinguists. They're in short supply, so maybe hiring teams aren't picky. And, like you said, even though Emily's blog post is negative, it was buried on the second page of results," Deandra said. "If someone was desperate to connect with a lost pet, that first page of positive reviews might be enough to sway them. Even if Emily thought Alison was a poor imitation of a psychic, clearly not everyone had felt that way."

"I guess so …" Wendy said, still baffled.

That fact—that Alison must have been believable *enough*—was the only explanation Deandra had for what she found in her next round of searches. Because Alison Griffiths, it turned out, had, for a brief stint, been an expert witness in criminal cases.

"Oooh, holy crap," Deandra muttered.

Wendy glanced up. "What?"

"Give me a second. I just found an article …" Deandra said, scanning a long exposé on "The Murky World of Expert Witnesses." Alison wasn't the focus of the article, but she was mentioned several times. The article had been written in reaction to an infamous expert witness known as Pinebough's lead "hoof, claw, and talon analyst," who was so corrupt that nearly forty cases had to be reexamined, thanks to evidence that he had offered favorable test results to whoever was willing to pay the highest price.

Alison Griffiths was mentioned because her own expert-witness testimony in three cases had that resulted in convictions being reevaluated years later. In one such case, the convicted killer had been set free as the result of an overturned conviction. Though there was never proof that Alison had completely falsified her testimony, there had been enough doubt—in part thanks to reports submitted to the International Hub System of Psychics and Mediums—that the defense was able to secure an appeal.

Head spinning, Deandra relayed the information to Wendy.

"Whoa. Are any of our suspects connected to those cases?" Wendy asked.

"I'm not sure. I didn't get that far yet," Deandra said, then got back to reading, her heart thumping hard.

The first two cases involved breaking and entering where the homeowner had been severely injured. In one case, the only witness had been a goldfish who had watched the whole thing, and in the second one, a house cat had been hiding under the bed.

The names and circumstances in those cases didn't trigger any sparks of recognition.

The third case, however, intrigued Deandra. "Okay, listen to this …"

Wendy closed her laptop and folded her arms on top of it. "Hit me."

"In this third case, a woman was out walking her pet fox one night when a half-troll attempted to mug her. The guy was twice her size and much stronger, but the woman was a water witch and tried using her powers to fend the troll off. The fox came to the woman's aid and bit the guy several times. The man, according to the reading Alison got from the fox, was so enraged at the woman, he punched her …" Deandra swallowed. "Let's just say it was a fatal blow. The reading from the fox revealed that the woman had used ice to freeze the man's feet to the cement several times to try to slow him down so she could escape. He was so strong though, he kept breaking out of the hold as fast as she could cast the ice."

"Oh, that's awful …" Wendy said.

"The fox ran home to fetch the woman's husband and led him back to where the woman lay dead on the sidewalk. The sidewalk was still icy in places from her magic."

"Was the troll long gone by the time the husband got there?"

"Yep. He took her entire purse with him, too. No trace of it was ever found. Her credit cards weren't used. He didn't take her cell phone, though; that was still on her."

"Were there cameras or something around that area?"

"Nope. There was footage of a few guys half a mile away from the location, but no one knew who they were supposed to be looking for. The incident took place in Luma—so any number of fae or magic-touched people could have been responsible. It's one of the biggest hubs in the country. By the time a death witch got over there, the only trace left for her to detect was that the single blow to the face was what killed the woman."

"So how did they find the guy?" When Deandra's only

response was to lift an eyebrow, Wendy's mouth fell open. "No way. Are you serious? They caught the guy *because* of the reading Alison got from the fox?"

"Apparently," Deandra said. "The guy, Yavo, supposedly signed a confession letter and everything after he was found—in an entirely different hub, mind you. He also had several bites on his calves and ankles that matched the width of a fox's jaw. The *whole* case hinged on Alison's expert-witness testimony. She was a recent graduate from the Pinebough academy, and the prosecution recruited her based on her publishing credentials and two lines from her academy bio: *Her readings are strong to excellent with all mundane animals on our standard testing list,* and *strong with sentient mythical animals on our standard list.* The prosecution needed someone who could get a reading from the fox, and the strong to excellent ratings got her the call.

"It sounds like she had a legit skill, but she also had this weird compulsion to lie about the extent of that skill. Maybe she was just trying to make extra money when she was working in the psychic shop where Emily got that bad reading. Maybe Alison desperately *wanted* to be a medium and hoped, if she kept at it long enough, a power would manifest. I don't know. Either way, she'd told enough lies that they caught up with her, and it had a ripple effect across all the cases she was a witness for—whether her testimony was true or not. They either had to keep them all or throw them all out. So they threw them out, and Yavo was eventually released. It sounds like Lydia was blacklisted on the International Hub System of Psychics and Mediums database, too."

"Oh!" Wendy said. "What you just said ... *she'd told enough lies that they caught up with her.* Isn't that what one of the messages said on the notes Lydia's stalker left for her?"

"Yeah, that's right. *Lies have consequences.*"

"This all explains why she'd change her name and flee Pinebough," Wendy said slowly. "But *why*, when she was starting over here in Axia, did she *still* try to claim she was an animal medium when she clearly wasn't?"

"Who knows," Deandra said, skimming the rest of the article. "Are you telling me, in all your true-crime binges, you never ran across stories of people who were repeat offenders? People who kept making the same wild mistakes over and over?"

"Fair point," Wendy said. "Wait. You never said if this case has a connection to anyone on our suspect list."

"Umm … the woman's name was Nancy Davis," Deandra said. "Her arctic fox was named Alpine. And …"

Deandra stared at a sentence toward the end of the section about Mrs. Davis and how her killer had literally gotten away with murder, despite being convicted of the crime.

"*And what?*" Wendy asked.

Deandra glanced up. "Nancy's husband's name was Keith. Keith Davis. They were both water elementals."

Wendy's eyes grew wider and wider by degrees. "You don't mean Keith-Keith, do you? As in the nice guy who sat *next* to you at Gorgon's Alley? Oh my Goddess! He totally said his wife's name was Nancy and that she was killed during a mugging, didn't he?"

"And! Lydia claimed she was being followed by a mangy black-and-white dog. *I* saw a mangy black-and-white canine-like animal in the complex here yesterday after I got back from dropping Mavis at home. There was something really off-putting about it; it definitely felt like it was watching or … I don't know … stalking me?"

"Deandra Hendricks! How could you not mention that a creepy sapient dog creature followed you home?!"

"I wasn't even sure that's what was going on! But also, now that the word 'fox' is in my head, maybe *that's* what I saw? But aren't arctic foxes white?"

Wendy's eyes somehow got wider and she dramatically snatched her phone off the table, rather than opening her laptop again. Her tongue poked out the side of her mouth as she frantically typed. "Oh! This says arctic foxes shed their white coats for summer, and their shorter coats range from gray to brown before they start growing their white coats again in September. Look at this ..."

Goose bumps rose on Deandra's arms when Wendy turned her phone's screen toward her to reveal a picture of a white-and-black fox. It was clearly in the middle of shedding its coat—part of it black and other parts coming in in thick white chunks. It looked like a small, mangy coyote. But the creature on the screen was strikingly similar to the one Deandra had seen staring her down from the sidewalk.

In a rush, Wendy said, "White or gray fur was found at Lydia's place, right? What if the fur they found in the townhouse belonged to an arctic fox and not a yeti? They're both creatures associated with ice. Could they be close genetic cousins or something?"

Deandra wanted *her* cousin to stop talking so fast, so she could get her own thoughts in order. "I mean, maybe? But this doesn't necessarily mean that Keith, *if* he's the culprit, had Alpine with him in Lydia's townhouse. If Keith had gray fur on his clothes and a few strands came off him and were left behind at the crime scene, that could be an explanation."

"How long ago was that conviction overturned?" Wendy asked.

"Uh, let's see. It looks like the first two cases were thrown out about five years ago, and then this last one got held up in appeals for a while but was finally overturned about two years ago."

"And when did Keith move here?" Wendy asked, in a tone that suggested she already knew the answer.

"About a year ago." Deandra recalled what Sarah had told her. *"He bounced around a few hubs doing odd jobs after his wife passed,"* she'd said. *"He lost his way until he saw a job flyer on a community board in a Kensian cafe."*

Had it been some weird twist of fate that Keith had ended up in the same hub as Lydia after all these years, lured here by Sarah's pied-piper magic—or had Keith known exactly where Lydia was, and was looking for a viable reason to move to Axia?

"I just thought of something else," Wendy said. "Mavis said the staircase area smelled musty, right? As if the carpeted steps were wet? Nancy used her ice magic on the troll when she was trying to escape. Weren't both she and her husband labeled as water witches in the article?"

Deandra squinted, unsure where her cousin's thoughts were leading her. "Yeah ..."

"The death witch told Mavis that the time of death, based on the condition of the body, had to be around noon on Monday. But then Ursula claimed the attack had happened around midnight on Sunday. That's a huge difference. How could the death witch get that wrong?"

"I'm pretty sure Mavis overhead a lot of what the death witch said while Mavis was eavesdropping as a mouse. Who knows how much she actually heard and how much she tried to piece together on her own. And given that she was convinced I was a siren from another hub and was fueled by revenge or whatever?" Deandra asked, shaking her head. "I don't know how reliable her initial report was, honestly."

"That's true," Wendy said. "Remember how Mavis got snippy with me and Keith because we both thought that four hours was too soon for a body to be 'ice cold'? What if Lydia's body was *frozen* when it hit that wall? If she had recently thawed out by the time the death witch got there, the witch could have suspected that the time of death was off because the magic used to kill Lydia was messing with the witch's reading."

Deandra shuddered. "If that's true, Keith is even creepier for pretending to just be a fan of *Dateline* when he was actually the one who did the freezing."

Wendy shivered. "I totally shared mozzarella sticks with that guy."

"And we might see him again at this party," Deandra said, glancing at the time in the corner of her screen. "Oh crap, we gotta get moving if we want to be there on time. It's two thirty."

They sprang from their seats and ran to their respective rooms to finish getting ready. Deandra had planned to wear a sundress, but decided to go for shorts and a blouse instead, just in case she needed to chase down a perp. Or run from one.

Once the three of them were in the car with Wendy behind the wheel—they'd decided they didn't want to bring dessert, and potentially feed a murderer—Deandra pulled out her phone.

"Is it cool if I make a call while we drive?"

Wendy cast her a curious look before backing out of the parking spot. "Sure …"

Holding Officer Sutter's card in one hand and her phone in the other, Deandra keyed in the number. Her hands shook slightly as she pressed the phone to her ear.

The call was answered after two rings. "Officer Sutter."

"Um. Hi. This is Deandra. Uh. Dee. Dee Hendricks?"

Officer Sutter chuckled. "Hello, Dee. What can I do for you?"

"Do you know who Alison Griffiths is?"

"No. Should I?"

Deandra loosed a long breath. "Got a few minutes? I've got a story for you …"

CHAPTER TWENTY

S arah lived in a cottage that overlooked the eastern edge of Oracle Park, only a few blocks from Deandra's grandparents' house. The house looked like a building straight out of a fairy tale. A weaving path of flat stones marked the path to the front door, and a wild garden of colorful flowers rose on either side of the path, constantly being visited by hummingbirds, bees, butterflies, and pixies. The house's wood siding was painted a vibrant cerulean.

Circle-top windows sat to either side of the front door, with an additional one directly above it. The topmost window sported a flower box brimming with roses, daffodils, and tulips. The trim on the door and windows was painted a yellow as bright as a sunflower. Patches of flowers even grew on the roof.

When Sarah emerged from her front door, the sight of the faun with her curling black horns and furry goat legs made Deandra feel like she'd stepped entirely into another world. The potbellied pig from the night of the happy hour nudged itself past one of the faun's legs and out into the yard to beeline for Havoc. The animals snorted and yipped a greeting.

"This place is so beautiful," Wendy whispered as the three of them—and now the pig—walked up the path to the front door. "I'm going to be super bummed out if *she's* actually the killer—or an accomplice! It would be like finding out Santa Claus eats elf stew."

Under no circumstances was Deandra going to ask if Santa Claus was real.

"Gertrude!" Sarah called from the doorway. "Calm down, you silly pig! You act as if we never have visitors."

Gertrude snorted happily and then bounded back inside with surprising speed.

Sarah's smile was infectious. "I'm so glad you three made it!" Her smile slipped a bit as she focused solely on Deandra. "I hope your presence means you forgive me."

Deandra bobbed her head, though she feared she'd always be a little cautious around the faun now that she knew the woman's magic could affect Deandra's very thoughts.

"Hello again, Havoc. Wendy," Sarah said.

Havoc chirped a greeting, while Wendy offered a tentative, "Thanks for inviting us."

"Everyone is already here and out back," Sarah said. "You've got perfect timing—I just laid out the food order from Hogarth's."

Sarah led them through her house, the door to the backyard a straight shot from the front door. They walked through a long hallway into the kitchen. Just as the Basnets' home was designed to accommodate people of large stature, this one was designed in subtle ways for a faun. The floors were made of flat slate-gray stone. Deandra figured a goat's hooves would scuff wood floors to high heaven, and carpet would get worn down in no time. Although Sarah was slender, doorways were wider and taller to account for her horns.

The style of the kitchen was as storybook as the exterior of the house, but no light fixtures, cooking pots, or drying plants hung from the ceiling, lest they get tangled up in horns. The kitchen counter on one side of the room and a dining table on the other appeared to be made from a cross section of a tree—woodgrain and knotholes clearly visible below the shiny varnish. The color scheme heavily featured browns and greens—including appliances.

"I'm obsessed with your house," Deandra blurted.

Sarah beamed at her. "It took me years to get it to this point. I tried to make the inside feel like I was still connected to nature—even if it's a hot summer day, the windows are latched, and the air conditioning is on full blast."

Deandra laughed.

Sarah led Deandra, Wendy, and Havoc out onto the porch that sat just beyond the open sliding door of the kitchen. Deandra stared out at the modest, square-shaped backyard.

A low fence separated the outer ring of the yard from the well-tended grass that took up most of the space. Beyond the fence, a robust vegetable garden thrived. Positioned in the middle of the grass was a massive wood dining table ringed by wooden chairs with wrought-iron legs. A second table was positioned off to the left, its backdrop the low fence and the garden beyond it. An apple tree sat in one corner of the fenced-in garden, while an orange tree stood in the other. The rest of the space was taken up by tomatoes, eggplants, zucchini, snap peas, and colorful vegetables that Deandra couldn't name. She wondered if any of them had graced her sample of the wherian beef platter Cruz had shared with her.

A third table was pressed against the fence on the right. Stacks of board and card games sat on either end of the table, while a cake rested in the middle, protected from the elements—and animal guests—by a glass dome.

Several people were huddled around the table to the left, as it was loaded down with sandwiches, condiments, and cookies. Two barrel-shaped jugs—one full of ice water and the other lemonade—sweated at the end of the table.

Deandra unhooked Havoc's leash. He raced into the yard to join the other animals milling around and lounging in the grass. Deandra didn't see Alpine the fox anywhere, just as she hadn't at the happy-hour get-together at Gorgon's Alley.

Keith Davis was in attendance, though, sitting at the table beside Fialova the birthday girl. A crown of twisted vines and pink flowers sat atop Fialova's head, complementing her lavender-hued skin. Fialova laughed at something Keith said, her head thrown back.

"You can leave your purses and keys and things on the table on the porch here. We try to employ a no-phones policy as much as we can. Keeps people more present, you know?" Sarah said. "Otherwise, go ahead and help yourself to the food. There are sodas in the fridge."

With that, Sarah descended the two cement stairs onto the lawn.

Now that they were alone, Wendy leaned close to Deandra to whisper, "Do we have a plan?"

"Not really."

In response to Deandra's tale, Sutter had only said, "Interesting theory. I appreciate the information. Keep me updated." Deandra hadn't been able to tell if Officer Sutter was humoring her the way she'd humored Mavis or if the always professional werecat had merely been keeping the breadth of her thoughts to herself.

Shrugging, they deposited their purses on a table already stacked with people's belongings, then made their way down the steps and toward the sandwiches. After loading her plate and filling a glass full of lemonade, Deandra took a spot at the table across from Keith. Wendy sat beside her, across from Fialova.

The birthday girl, in addition to the flower crown, wore a white sash with PARTY ANIMAL! written in gold. Given what Sarah had said about Fialova not enjoying over-the-top parties, the sash had probably been forced over her head simply because Sarah thought it was funny.

In addition to the core group from the happy hour—including the two women whose names Deandra couldn't remember—there was a trio of lavender-skinned people who Deandra assumed were Fialova's friends or relatives. Tansy sat at the end of the table, quietly eating a sandwich and occasionally tearing off bits of bread to feed Rufus, who was perched on her shoulder instead of in her hair. Deandra didn't know Tansy well, but her being so quiet and a bit removed from the group seemed out of character.

Deandra knew Tansy had been ruled out by the werecats as a suspect, but how many interviews had that required?

Despite being concerned that the man across from her had murdered Lydia, Deandra still managed to have a good time chatting with the handsome lavender-hued young man who'd taken a seat on Deandra's other side. At first, they talked animatedly about *Faet of the Heart,* as he'd only just started the show as well, finally caving to his sister Fialova's constant harassment. Tomas told her what it was like living in Kensey, while she shared tales of Los Angeles. He worked in the gift shop of a Frederica Kensey museum—the mother of the telepad and telepost system, Deandra learned—and he was in school for museum studies and hoped to one day be a curator.

Deandra had only begun to answer Tomas's question about how she'd gotten into pet sitting when someone cut in.

"You're the one who got the Basnet job, right?"

Deandra met Keith's eye. His expression was neutral, if not a bit curious. There was nothing about the middle-aged man's appearance that screamed *"Killer!"* He wore khakis, a nice navy-blue T-shirt, and sensible shoes. He was in decent shape, but he wasn't overly fit. He was average. Normal.

"I got an email from Oleander the same night that I met all of you, actually," Deandra said.

"You didn't meet *me*," Tomas sing-songed.

"Stop flirting, Tom," Fialova said, waving a finger at him. "From what I hear, Dee is already taken."

Oh, good grief. Who was talking about her? She assumed this was Grandma January's fault somehow.

"Aw," Tomas said from beside her. "Is it serious?"

Wendy leaned forward to address Tomas. "It could be."

Deandra clapped a hand over her face, resisting the urge to check her phone yet again to see if Cruz had replied. But that would mean getting up, since she'd left her purse on the patio table along with everyone else's stuff.

The scent of pine wafted over Deandra before she heard Sarah's voice. She was seated diagonally across the table from Deandra, beside Fialova. Deandra glanced up.

"I heard Oleander was arrested?" Sarah asked cautiously, clearly unsure where she and Deandra stood when it came to conversations about the yeti family.

In her periphery, Tansy's head popped up, intrigued by Sarah's question.

"No formal arrest, the last I heard," Deandra said. "She was detained, but that got commuted to house arrest. She's home with her family now. I don't think she did it."

"Of course you don't," Keith snapped, though he tried to cover it up with a weak laugh. "She's the one signing your checks; her being guilty is going to hurt your pocketbook. But if the evidence is all pointing to her ..." He shrugged helplessly. Deandra could *almost* believe he actually felt bad about how Oleander's suspected guilt was going to negatively affect Deandra.

Her jaw clenched.

"I hope they finally nail someone for it," Tansy said, speaking for the first time since Deandra and Wendy had arrived. "*I* was one of their top suspects. They only recently backed off when they finally verified my *and* Rufus's alibis six ways from Sunday."

Fialova swiveled in her seat so she was fully turned toward the older woman. "What on earth are you talking about?"

Tansy huffed a breath. "I've been called in for questioning *four* times. The werecats got a warrant to use a zoolinguist to interrogate Rufus. The cats only stopped trailing me as of yesterday. I have an airtight alibi, and they still went overkill on questioning me. Having a healthy dislike of a person doesn't make you a murderer. Neither does leaving angry voicemails or making hostile comments online." She cut a glance toward Deandra. "Not saying I want your new client to be responsible for what happened to Lydia, but if they detained Oleander, they must have good reason."

"They questioned me, too," Keith admitted. "I barely knew Lydia, and they called me in three times. No warrants for interrogating Alpine, though."

Sarah chuckled. "Probably because she's so shy that she hardly leaves the house."

"Alpine?" Wendy asked, her tone a little off.

Though Wendy was the one who asked the question, Keith stared at Deandra while he said, "Alpine is my arctic fox."

Deandra swallowed. "Oh, how ... uh ... unique. Is she a mundane arctic fox?"

"Fae. She can conjure ice. Fae arctic foxes can regulate their body temperature in ways mundane ones can't. It allows her to live comfortably in places that don't have snow," Keith said.

"Oh my, how terribly interesting," Wendy said a bit robotically.

If interrogating murderers was going to become a habit, Deandra thought she and Wendy might benefit from taking acting classes.

Wendy, face strained as she held an awkward smile in place, asked, "Do they shed their winter coats the way mundane arctic foxes do?"

"They do," Keith said a bit cautiously, still keeping his focus on Deandra. "I heard they found white fur in Lydia's apartment that matched that of a yeti. I also heard there was an eyewitness who spotted someone fitting a yeti's description fleeing down Coterie Road after midnight. Things don't sound too good for your client."

Fialova spoke up. "Didn't Mavis say the death witch told her the time of death was around noon on Monday?"

Clearly Fialova hadn't been on the werecats' suspect list, as her only information seemed to be what Mavis had told the group nearly a week ago.

"There are conflicting stories," Deandra heard Wendy say, then she tuned out the conversation.

The problem with Deandra's current stare-down with Keith Davis was that she wasn't sure how much information about Oleander had made its way to the public yet. Maybe the time of death had become a topic of rumor, especially if Ursula kept asking random passersby if she could be a guest on their podcast —since she had the exclusive scoop on "what really happened." Even the part about seeing a yeti fleeing the scene could have come from Ursula blabbing things to anyone who would listen— anyone except for Mavis.

But the part about Oleander's fur being found at the crime scene? Mavis, with all her sleuthing, hadn't known that much. Mavis had been truly crestfallen when Officer Sutter informed her that her top suspect—Tansy—was in the clear. Oleander, it seemed, hadn't been on Mavis's list at all. As it was, Deandra only knew the cops were doing an analysis on the fur found at the crime scene because Cenzio had told her.

This all implied Keith was now testing how much *Deandra* knew.

It made sense, all things considered, for Keith to keep tabs on

Mavis. It was no secret that Mavis and Lydia were best friends. Keith may have erroneously believed that Lydia had shared the details of her past with Mavis, making Mavis the only person in town who could potentially know about Lydia's alias, the criminal case involving Keith's wife, and the subsequent release of Nancy's killer.

Had the fox seen Deandra and Mavis go into the police station together? Sarah might have believed Alpine was shy and spent all her time indoors, but Keith clearly had been utilizing the fox for spying purposes without Sarah knowing. Maybe Keith now worried that Deandra knew more than she should about Lydia and her connection to him.

Did Alpine, after following Deandra home, somehow share the location of Deandra's apartment with Keith? If she said or did the wrong thing here, would that put her and Wendy in danger if Keith felt threatened?

"Do you have any idea why Oleander would want to kill Lydia?" Keith asked now. "You know her better than any of us do. Is it unnerving to be working for someone who may have killed her previous caregiver?"

There was definitely a challenge in Keith's tone now. He was daring her to contradict him. Did he assume that, if Deandra laid out her theory, his friends and fellow colleagues would come to his defense? If she tried to accuse him, would he retaliate?

"I don't think she did it," Deandra repeated.

Keith shrugged. "I get wanting to be loyal to your employer, especially when she pays that well. But you're new here. New to the hub system altogether. You haven't learned yet that the elephantine fae are dangerous. They need their own hubs, as far as I'm concerned. Like dog parks that have a section for big dogs and small ones. No one would bat an eye at the claim that it's safer for Chihuahuas to be separated from Great Danes for safety reasons, right? I don't know why those same rules aren't applied to hubs."

A silence so uncomfortable not even Sarah's nurture magic could soothe it away descended on the group.

Fialova turned in her seat to face Keith now. "You don't mean that."

"Why wouldn't I?" Keith asked. "My wife was killed by an elephantine fae. One punch was so powerful, it killed her instantly. How is it safe to have people like my wife live in the same place as someone that strong—someone who decided on a whim that he wanted what she had and would do whatever it took to get it?"

Remembering all over again what Keith, Alpine, or both had likely done to Lydia, Deandra said, "People with magic can be just as strong. Someone my size, or an animal the size of Alpine, could use magic from afar to inflict as much or more damage with a powerful enough spell. So what's your solution? All mundanes in one place, fae and magic-touched in another, and elephantine in another still? What happened to your wife was terrible and shouldn't happen to anyone, but I'm betting most elephantine fae would never dream of doing what that mugger did. You can't punish an entire people simply because of a few bad apples."

Something pressed against Deandra's leg under the table. She leaned back on her chair and found Havoc had wedged himself between her feet. Had something happened, or had he sensed she'd grown agitated and wanted to comfort her? She wished she could share thought-pictures with him the way Cruz supposedly could. She also wished she could reiterate to Officer Sutter somehow that Keith was setting off all kinds of alarm bells in her head. Even if Deandra was sure Keith was the killer, it didn't mean Officer Sutter would agree.

Jaw tight and gaze angled toward his lap, Keith muttered something under his breath.

"What was that, Keith?" Sarah asked, punctuated with another whiff of pine and a full pancake breakfast. The faun's magic was likely working overtime to comfort this many people—several of whom likely hadn't seen this side of Keith before.

Keith swept his gaze over those in attendance, settling once more on Deandra. "I said my wife's killer was worse than a bad apple. He was guilty as sin and yet was dumped back into society. Two weeks ago, he killed again. Another mugging. Another woman who was overpowered by a fae who is too powerful to live among us. Someone else is now missing a wife, a mother, a sister, a friend. All because this ... this *elephantine monster* is roaming the streets."

Tomas cleared his throat. "That, uhh, sounds like a legal system issue, not a hub-wide one."

Deandra silently thanked Tomas for saying something, as it got Keith's murderous glare off Deandra for a moment. Havoc bumped into Deandra's knee with his muzzle. She peered under the table again and was momentarily stunned to find the strap of her purse hanging from his mouth. She took it from him, wondering how on earth he'd known she needed her bag. Had he been able to sense it down the bond?

"You're probably right. The legal system is broken, there's no doubt about that." Keith worked his jaw. "I didn't want to do this today because it's your birthday, Fia. But this conversation has solidified everything for me." He leaned forward to address Sarah. "I think I need to move on again. Axia isn't the place for me anymore. I turned into a bit of a nomad after Nancy passed, and I think the winds just shifted again. The plus side is, I'll refer all my clients to you, Sarah. It might help you some in the weeks to come."

Fialova looked supremely torn. On the one hand, she was obviously horrified by Keith's admission that he thought there should be some kind of segregation implemented within the hub system, and yet Keith was her friend. Despite the age difference, they'd formed a close friendship in the year he'd been in Axia. "How soon did you plan to leave?"

"Within the next couple of days," Keith said. "It's been a long time coming."

Would the werecats lose track of him for good if he hopped

into a telepad? What if he disappeared into the mundane world? Oleander, a lawyer familiar with criminal cases, had told Cenzio that the arresting officers had detained Oleander in Kensey, rather than bringing her back to Axia, because hub-based suspects were even more of a flight risk than ones in the mundane world because criminals had instant travel at their fingertips. It would be like a high-speed car chase, except the perp could flee across multiple states in a blink.

Deandra discreetly slipped her purse into her lap, unzipped it, and extracted her phone. There was a text from Cruz!

CRUZ

Hey. Sorry for going radio silent. I forgot I had a zoolinguistic seminar scheduled in another hub this weekend. I'll be back tomorrow. Maybe we can grab dinner

As relieved as she was to hear from him, she needed to text someone else more urgently.

DEANDRA

Keith is planning to skip town this week. It seems abrupt.

OFFICER SUTTER

Are you still attending the birthday party at Sarah Mink's residence?

DEANDRA

Yes

OFFICER SUTTER

Test results revealed that among the ten yeti hairs found at the Monroe residence, there was also one was from an arctic fox. We're obtaining a warrant to interrogate Alpine as we speak

Deandra's eyes bulged.

"Are you sending flirty texts to your beau over there, Dee?"

Deandra's head snapped up to find Sarah, and several others, watching her. "Sorry, Sarah. I know you have a no-phone policy. It's a client, is all. I'm still so new to the business, I panic if I don't reply to them right away." She offered Keith a forced smile. "If you have any clients you want to pass *my* way when you close up shop, I'd be happy to take them. If Sarah doesn't need them, of course," she hastily added.

"*Have* you already talked with your clients?" Fialova asked Keith. "I'm really bummed, K. This seems so sudden."

"I've already warned my clients that I plan to leave, yeah. I honestly considered leaving this weekend," Keith said. "But I didn't want to miss your birthday, Fia. Meeting you put me on the path I needed, and then Sarah helped me put down roots for the first time in years. I'm indebted to you both. I'll always be grateful."

Sarah smiled at him affectionately.

Keith's head cocked. "Huh. The scent of the magic just changed again. When I first met you, it was baking bread, then it switched to Nancy's perfume for a while, and now … it's the smell of the ocean."

Deandra flinched when her phone buzzed in her hand. She quickly glanced down.

OFFICER SUTTER

T-minus five minutes.

Oh, yikes on bikes, they were headed here now?

DEANDRA

He says that his wife's killer struck again. Any chance the accused is in a hub near the ocean?

OFFICER SUTTER

That's uncanny. I only found out an hour ago that Yavo's last known location is a Floridian hub

DEANDRA

My guess is that's where Keith is headed next

When Deandra had first met Keith, he'd told Deandra and Wendy that the comforting scents presented by Sarah's magic were out of Sarah's control and that the scents were unique to each person within the magic's range.

"I hadn't even met Lydia before then, only heard about her," he'd said. *"I felt bad for Mavis. She tried so hard to help Lydia that night; I think Mavis worried about her being too isolated. The confrontation, as you can imagine, didn't go well. Maybe the heightened emotions of that night are what changed the scent of Sarah's magic for me. That's the only explanation I have for why it changed from baking bread to Nancy's perfume. Maybe the magic figured if I could survive a blowout fight between Sarah, Lydia, and Mavis, I could handle anything."*

Deandra suspected that Keith had been looking for Alison Griffiths for a while. Maybe he'd found Emily Waters's blog post, too. Keith, after all, would have recognized the name Alison Griffiths, as that was the name of the expert witness during his wife's trial. Alison had changed her name, changed her hair color, and moved to a different hub. Maybe he hadn't realized until the night of that confrontation—at this very house—that the infamous Lydia Monroe he'd been hearing about and Alison Griffiths, the woman responsible for Yavo's conviction being overturned, were one and the same. Maybe he'd known well before that. The scent of Sarah's magic had changed for him that night from baking bread to Nancy's perfume. Had the scent lined up with his goal—Sarah's magic letting him know he'd found what he wanted, his wife's perfume the reminder of why he'd worked so hard to find Alison Griffiths? Whether he'd been searching for Alison/Lydia with the explicit intent to kill her was anyone's guess.

Deandra wondered now, though, if Yavo striking again had been the final straw for Keith. It was Lydia's fault Yavo was able to kill again, after all. So Keith killed Lydia, avenging his wife and this unknown woman.

Now Sarah's magic smelled like the ocean, a comforting scent to remind Keith of his new goal—tracking down Yavo, likely with the intention of killing him, too, if the justice system failed Keith once again. Maybe he planned to bide his time in Florida, start up another pet-sitting business there, and wait until the hands of fate pushed him to act once more.

"Do you hear that?" Sarah asked, head cocked. "It's faint."

Deandra hadn't been listening to the conversation, as she'd been too lost in her own thoughts, but all chatter had stopped. The animals had gone quiet, too. They'd all scurried under tables. Havoc was wedged between Deandra's feet again.

Sarah, without a word, jogged toward her house and disappeared through the open slider door into the kitchen.

"My question is …" Deandra found herself saying, suddenly *very* angry that Keith planned to leave town while Oleander was left to flounder in a legal system already predisposed to work against her kind. "Did you attack Lydia—or should I say Alison— that night *specifically* because Oleander was there, or was that just a happy accident?"

The collected guests murmured to each other, but Keith only had eyes for Deandra. His gaze dropped to the table, as if he could peer through it.

"You weren't texting your boyfriend, were you?" Keith asked.

"Nope." Deandra rolled her shoulders back, feeling more confident now that the werecats were on their way. She supposed she was a little like Barnaby in that way. "An elephantine fae was responsible for your wife's death, so another one might as well get blamed for Lydia's death. Innocent or not, elephantine fae should be punished regardless, right?"

Keith's jaw clenched and he shot to his feet, toppling his chair. "No one doubted that giant abomination was capable of it." Fialova flinched back, her eyes welling with tears. "If it wasn't Lydia she hurt, it would have been someone else."

"Oleander has a *family*," Deandra snapped. "She's got a husband and kid at home who have been absolute wrecks because of *you*."

"Nancy had a family, too!" Keith jabbed a finger at his own chest. "Janice, a widow, had ten-year-old twin boys she was raising all on her own. Now they're orphans because Alison was a fraud. Lies have consequences, and they *finally* caught up to her."

"None of that has anything to do with Oleander!"

"She might not have killed Lydia, but *hoo boy*, that fight I heard!" Keith said, hands on his hips as he paced in a tight line, like a lion trapped in a cage the width of a shoebox.

Fialova and everyone else on Keith's side of the table had stumbled out of their seats and were cowering on the other side.

Deandra finally registered what Keith said. *Lies have consequences.* Just like the notes being left for Lydia. "*You* were stalking Lydia. How did she not recognize you?"

Keith's smile was a little unsettling. "We never actually saw each other during the trial. It was in Luma, and the prosecution brought her in from Pinebough. I, uh, lost my temper in court on day one and was banned from attending. I didn't know what Alison or Lydia or whatever she called herself looked like until I started researching her after the conviction was overturned. Even if she tried to erase her old life, there was enough of a trail left online that I eventually found her. Bad reviews, blog posts, news articles. They all led me to Axia. I orchestrated a couple of chance meetings here in town with her, and it was clear she had *no idea* who I was."

Deandra wanted to smack the smug little smile off his face. "Were you creeping around outside her townhouse—probably a regular thing for you—the night Oleander showed up to confront her?"

"Guess it was lucky for me that I wasn't the only one in town who hated her. There was so much screaming and carrying on going on in the townhouse, neither of them even noticed us."

Us. Him and Alpine.

"We'd been waiting for days on end for her busybody neighbor to go to bed at a normal hour. You'd think she was a *vampire* bat with those ridiculous hours she keeps.

"That night, Oleander showed up looking like she was ready to commit murder herself. Thought she was going to do the job for me. The way she *screamed* at Lydia, though," Keith added, shaking his head in disgust. "I swear I could feel it in the soles of my feet from the other side of the building. Monstrous woman."

Wendy let loose a disbelieving laugh. "Says the man who murdered one person and was willing to let another take the fall. If anyone is a monster here, it's you. Is this really what Nancy would have wanted?"

The expression that overtook Keith's face made Deandra instinctively reach over to clamp a hand on Wendy's forearm.

Wendy, in a low, strained voice, said, "That might have been a step too far."

"You don't get to speak about her!" Keith snapped, his face going … not red, but blue.

If this had happened anywhere but Axia, Deandra would have thought he was suffering from a heart attack.

A breath later, a chill arctic wind swept over Deandra. The group collectively gasped. A dog howled. Gertrude snorted. Rufus croaked in agitation and launched skyward in Deandra's periphery. In the next breath, Keith's palms were thrust toward Deandra.

She only had a moment to think "Oooh crap!" before something slammed into her chair so hard, she toppled backward. Since she was holding on to Wendy, her cousin fell with her. They let out twin grunts of pain as air was expelled from their lungs in a whoosh.

Crash!

Deandra unhanded Wendy and shielded her own head as bits of wood peppered her arms. The party guests shrieked in fear.

Whoosh!

Deandra knew *that* sound. She quickly uncovered her face and lifted her head, giving her a clear view of Havoc's rump and tail from where he was standing *on* the table.

A chill wind enveloped her again, setting her teeth to chattering, but no sooner had she felt the cold, warmth followed as Havoc hopped forward on the table. He sprayed another gout of fire at Keith. Steam hissed like an erupting geyser. Partygoers screamed and sought cover.

Keith yowled in rage.

Worried for her dragon, Deandra none too gracefully rolled to her side, stuck as she'd been on her back with the chair underneath her. Wendy cursed and flailed around as she too tried to roll off the chair.

From behind her, Wendy whisper-hissed, "What the heck do you think you're doing?"

Deandra ignored her, getting onto hands and knees before crawling under the table. Two others were under the table as well, holding onto a leg for dear life. The whole table shook violently. Glasses were knocked onto their sides, sending water and lemonade cascading over the table's edge and into the grass. A plate with a half-eaten sandwich plopped off the table with a splat as Havoc blasted Keith with fire again. From Deandra's vantage point, she could see Keith from the knees down as he darted this way and that in his battle with Havoc. Keith's khakis were somehow both soaked *and* dotted with smoking burn holes.

Though Keith staggered around, he was also laughing. "You think you have more magical stores than me, you pathetic mutt? That last one wasn't any stronger than a candle flame! One more attempt, and your mundane human is as good as dead. Back down like a good little dog so I can get out of here and won't be forced to kill you."

Havoc, somewhere above Deandra, issued a growl, but even Deandra could tell her dragon was running on fumes.

"Suit yourself," Keith said. "Dire wolves are no better than elephantine fae anyway."

Goose bumps prickled Deandra's skin as Keith geared up for another blast.

Oh no.

Deandra, heart in her throat, charged forward awkwardly from underneath the table like a newborn foal. "Don't touch my dog!"

She managed to slam into Keith's knees a mere moment before he threw yet another blast of icy water at her dragon. Water shot harmlessly into the air.

She and Keith scrambled to get away from one another, slipping and sliding in the wet grass as the remnants of his last spell fell around them like sleet.

They quickly got to their feet, squaring off like tigers. Deandra probably should have thought this through more, seeing as she was very human, and Keith was not. The man was clearly exhausted, though, and it was that fact that was probably the only thing keeping her alive. But she couldn't let him escape before the cats got here, nor could she let him hurt Havoc. Keith's back was to the apple tree, with Deandra in front of him. The man was heaving hard, as if he'd just run two back-to-back marathons. He was soaked through, and his short brown hair was plastered to his face.

He might have thought Lydia and Oleander were monstrous, but the look in his eyes scared the crap out of her.

Just when she thought he was going to lunge for her, he cocked his head as if he heard something. His eyes widened, and then all at once he barreled right past her. Deandra figured he was heading for the low fence that ringed the yard so he could scale it and flee via a side gate.

He only made it a few feet before a croaking cry sounded and a black bird dive-bombed Keith's head. Keith shrieked and swatted at the air as the bird mercilessly dove for him. A squeal came next, and a potbellied pig darted into Keith's path at just the right time so that the water witch went rump over teakettle and slammed back-first onto the lawn.

The open doorway of Sarah's back door was suddenly full of quickly moving shapes. A moment later, three werecats in human form were on the edge of the porch, taking in the chaos of Sarah's backyard.

Sarah herself hovered near her back door, wringing her hands. The faun was a nurturer by nature, and currently everyone in attendance—except maybe the werecats—needed nurturing of some kind. At what point did the needs of everyone short-circuit Sarah's magic entirely, leaving her unable to do anything but fret?

"What in all the realms happened here?" Officer Sutter asked, cautiously inching down the steps as she scanned everyone's terrified faces. "We had to run clear across town, otherwise we would have gotten here sooner. Is anyone hurt?"

More than half a dozen pointer fingers were all jabbed in the same direction.

Officer Sutter glanced down and to her left, where Keith lay sprawled on the grass, the fight in him depleted. Not to mention that an all-black German shepherd lay on his legs, a potbellied pig sat on his stomach, and a raven was perched on Keith's forehead with its beak pointed dangerously close to one of the water witch's eyes.

"Oh dear," Sutter said, with an edge of what Deandra suspected was amusement.

By the time the trio of werecats got the animals off Keith and him to his feet, Tansy had marched over to get in her supposed friend's face. Rufus was perched in Tansy's hair.

Officer Sutter pulled out a pair of handcuffs that were etched with glowing runes. The runes reminded Deandra of the ones she'd seen on the bars of the holding cells at the station. She assumed they were magic-suppressing cuffs.

Keith offered no resistance as his arms were pulled behind him and the cuffs were locked into place. Deandra idly wondered if there was anything like Miranda Rights in the hub system.

"It was *you*?" Tansy asked Keith, incredulous.

The pair of male officers were still on the porch, likely poised to jump in to help Officer Sutter should she need it. One of them started forward when Tansy began her tirade, as if intending to nudge her aside, but Officer Sutter held up a hand. The third officer hastily pulled out a notebook from a pouch on his belt and started taking notes.

Tansy, furious, was only a few inches from Keith's down-turned face. "I complained to you for *days* about the way the werecats had been treating me—uh, no offense officers—and how they'd been interrogating Rufus. You knew I was worried sick about it. And all this time, *you're* the one who killed Lydia?"

Keith said nothing.

Deandra had taken a few steps forward to better hear what was being said, but she still wanted a good distance between herself and Keith, magic-suppressing cuffs or not. She also wanted a better view of Havoc, who was sprawled out on his belly on the table. He was out cold and snoring, the magical expenditure having zapped him of energy as thoroughly as it had wiped out Keith.

For some reason, Sunshine the newt popped into Deandra's head. The newt had been unhinged, sure, but she'd been under the influence of Rae's magic. If the officer was taking notes, Deandra wanted her next question on record. "Was it Alpine who hit Lydia with the blast of water magic that killed her?" She paused, bracing herself. "Are you going to let Alpine take the fall for this, the same way you tried to with Oleander?"

Keith glanced over his shoulder at her question. "Alpine only got us in. She wasn't responsible for anything else." He met Officer Sutter's steely gaze. "Alpine was just being loyal to me."

"Recorded," Officer Sutter said, and the note-taking officer started scribbling even faster, trying to keep up. "Keith Davis, you're under arrest for the murder of Lydia Monroe, otherwise known as Alison Griffiths."

Fialova burst into tears. Sarah abruptly turned on her hooves and ran into her house.

Keith finally looked at Tansy then. It took him a long moment to finally speak. "You've been a source of light in a very dark time. I hope you'll remember our friendship more than you'll remember ... this." He scanned the yard then, almost desperately. "Fia. Fia, you were like the daughter I never had but always wanted. The Goddess put you in my path, I'm sure of it. Maybe you were set to derail my plans, I don't know. Tell Sarah I'm sorry.

She'll find a way to blame herself for this. I know you can help her through it."

"We shouldn't *need* to help her!" Fialova shouted, then dissolved into tears again. Tomas already had his arm around his sister but hugged her tighter now as she collapsed against him.

Worst. Birthday. Ever.

Officer Sutter made a hand gesture that the officers clearly understood, as the note-taking one stowed his notebook, and then both cats got Keith turned around, up the porch steps, and into the house.

Officer Sutter lingered long enough to point a finger at Deandra. "You and I *will* talk later." She scanned the collected group, gaze landing on a weepy Fialova in her Party Animal! birthday sash. "Uh, happy birthday, ma'am. Sorry for the interruption."

With that, Sutter strode after her officers and Keith, disappearing into the house. Deandra almost laughed. She supposed she and Officer Sutter lived very different lives if the officer thought this disaster of a birthday lunch had only experienced a minor "interruption."

Slowly, seven people turned toward Deandra. Before she could say anything, the soft clomp of hooves made the whole group pivot toward the house.

Sarah made her way down the steps. Her eyes were red-rimmed, and the magic wafting off her smelled like burnt paper, but it wasn't as acrid as Deandra would have expected, all things considered. "I called Mavis. She's on her way over. Maybe when she gets here, Dee, Wendy, you can tell us all what the heck just happened?"

Deandra finally took in the carnage that had befallen the yard. The low fence that had been Keith's backdrop was scorched in a few places. Luckily none of Sarah's garden had caught fire, but the table holding the food had been destroyed. Gertrude the potbellied pig currently snuffled her way through the buffet of charred hoagies, condiments, and cookies that lay in the grass in a heap. Havoc would have been helping the pig if he weren't still passed out on the table.

On the other side of the yard, behind most of the group, a good chunk of the low fence and the table holding the birthday cake were nothing but a pile of broken wood. She recalled being rained on by a shower of splinters and realized that the blast that had been meant for Deandra had hit the table instead. Deandra swallowed. If Havoc hadn't knocked her and Wendy to the ground, that firehose of icy water would have surely killed Deandra the same way it had killed Lydia—or at least horribly injured her.

A patch of zucchini had been completely flattened by the water, as if someone had rolled over the plants with a lawn mower. The cake that had been sitting safely below the glass dome was a watery mess on the grass, the glass shattered into thick shards. The board and card games were ruined.

Deandra felt like this was all her fault. "Oh, your beautiful garden, Sarah," she said, her throat tight.

Scents of Christmas morning encircled Deandra like a warm blanket. The tension in her shoulders loosened a fraction.

"Don't you dare blame yourself for any of this," Sarah said, walking toward where Deandra still stood alone near the charred fence. The faun took Deandra's hands in hers. "You figured out who actually killed Lydia and saved Oleander and her family extra hardship. And your dire wolf saved *all* of us. Plants are resilient. They'll grow back. Everything else can be mended or replaced."

Deandra squeezed her hands back. "You can't blame yourself either. Welcoming Keith into the fold doesn't mean Lydia's death is on your hands."

Sarah nodded tightly.

Wendy said, "I was going to ask if we could have cake before we started talking about murder again, but I guess that's out of the question. Sorry, Fia. This probably isn't the birthday you envisioned."

Fialova spluttered a watery laugh. "Eh, I've had worse. I can't think of any at the moment, but I'm sure there was at least one. As long as no one sings 'Happy Birthday,' then I'll be okay."

Sarah managed a small smile for her friend. "Wish granted, party animal."

CHAPTER TWENTY-ONE

O n Sunday evening, Deandra met Cruz at *her* location of choice this time. She'd honestly considered forcing him to endure a vending machine smorgasbord, but after hearing that he frequented them for lunch more than he should, she decided against it.

Instead, she waited for him outside the Haunted Noodle. She wanted a happier memory associated with the place, since the last time she was here, she and Wendy had needed to scurry away prematurely, having realized that their dinner companion Rae—and her fire newt—were killers.

Deandra waved as she spotted him round the corner at the end of the street. She'd chosen to meet him here, rather than having him pick her up, in part because, when she'd suggested the place, he'd commented that he was within walking distance since he was at the office catching up on some paperwork.

On a Sunday.

They exchanged a quick hug when he reached her, then ducked inside. A waitress led them to a table near the Wall of Flame. Deandra was just about to take her seat when a picture on the wall caught her eye.

She pointed at a photograph on the bottom row of a miserable-looking draken who stood beside the smiling chef. The draken's eyes were red, and his nose looked a little puffy. "Is that Flint?"

Cruz swiveled in his chair to glance over his shoulder. He chuckled. "Yep, that's him. If I remember correctly, he tried the challenge four times before he finally succeeded."

Deandra slid into her chair. "Have *you* tried it?"

Cruz got a distant look in his eye. "Once," he said ominously. "That challenge is a gift that keeps on giving for days afterward—and they aren't presents you want."

With a shiver, Deandra said, "I'll pass, thank you very much."

"Wise woman."

They perused their menus in silence for a few minutes, but it was mostly for show on Deandra's part. She was trying to get up the courage to tell Cruz—someone she didn't know *that* well—that she was worried about him. Being too isolated had negatively affected Mavis and Lydia, though in very different ways. She didn't want isolation to impact Cruz.

When he placed his menu on the table, his choice seemingly made, she asked, "How was the seminar?"

"Decent," he said. "It was in the hub in Maine. The seminar was sponsored by the zoo there."

"The one where your friend is the director?"

"Yeah. But don't worry, I didn't mention Havoc," he said, hands up. "I didn't see Bryce, anyway. He funds a lot of educational opportunities but rarely attends himself. Research on mythicals is pretty limited, so zoos are sometimes the best sources for information for vets like me. The better informed I am, the better I can help my patients."

It was hard to chastise Cruz for being a workaholic when he was doing it for a good reason. She just didn't want him to burn out. He'd be no good to his patients if he was too wrecked to function.

She was about to broach the subject when their waiter showed up to take their orders. Once the waiter had vacated the table again, collected menus under his arm, Cruz folded his arms on the table.

"If you don't tell me how you 'cracked the case,' I'm going to implode," he said.

She laughed.

The message she'd sent in reply to his check-in text from all of half an hour ago had been purposely vague.

CRUZ

> I got back into town an hour or so ago but need to wrap up a few things at the office. The first person to come up with a spell that completes paperwork for you will make a mint. You still up for dinner?

DEANDRA

> I have cracked the case. If you want the hot goss, meet me at the Haunted Noodle

He'd replied almost instantly.

CRUZ

> Be there in twenty.

She caught him up on everything he'd missed since she'd last seen him on Thursday afternoon at the park. "Officer

Sutter refuses to admit that I was integral to solving the case, but—"

"An insult of the highest order."

Deandra grinned. "I think that's mostly because Keith was already one of *their* top suspects. Apparently, every time they interviewed him his story changed. I guess he's been acting really strange, too, but of course Sutter won't give me details because it's—and I quote—none of my business."

"How dare she do her job properly," Cruz said in mock disgust.

"I know," Deandra said, shaking her head. "But! She did admit that it likely would have been a few days before they'd tracked down who in town owned or could shift into an arctic fox, and Keith might have been long gone by then."

"I'd like to think I was pretty integral, too, since it was my connection to Pinebough that brought the name Alison Griffiths into your life in the first place."

"You're right, you're right. I'll include that in my letter to the mayor about why we should both get keys to the hub," Deandra said.

Cruz flashed her a goofy, affectionate smile. "An excellent idea."

Their food arrived, and they both greedily tucked in. Deandra had learned from the last time she was here that, on the spice-meter, she needed to treat this place the way she treated Thai food: always go a step lower than she thought she could handle.

After a few minutes, Cruz asked, "How did Mavis take the news?"

"Better than I expected, honestly," Deandra said. "I'm also glad she was there *after* Keith had been hauled away. She probably would have attacked him otherwise, and there was already too much magic flying around. In this case—especially since Fialova and Sarah were in tears—it let Mavis just be sad. She's spent so much time this past week being angry. There's even a slight chance Sarah will let Mavis have her job back on a probationary basis. Sarah agrees with me, though, that Mavis needs to get into counseling first."

"Glad she agreed to go," Cruz said.

"Me too. I'm guessing Officer Sutter is going to make it her personal mission to make sure Mavis is attending. She wants reassurance that she's not going to have to arrest Mavis for trespassing."

"Understandable," he said. "How's the pod leader doing?"

"He's fine. I had to carry him to the car, then up the stairs to the apartment, *and* place him on his bed. He didn't even stir," Deandra said. "Not until two a.m. anyway, and then he started bouncing up and down on the bed like a jumping bean because he was apparently starving. He's been asleep ever since. Good to know expelling that much magical energy leaves him drained for at least a day afterward."

Cruz stared at her for a beat. "And how are *you* doing?"

Deandra shrugged. "Okay, I think. Super relieved it wasn't Oleander *or* Sarah. Oleander and I talked for a long time yesterday. She admitted that the night she hired Lydia, she couldn't shake the feeling that Lydia had manipulated Kiwi into acting as if he liked her so that Oleander would hire her. She called and texted Lydia, leaving her messages stating that she needed to talk to her right away. Lydia didn't answer, so Oleander went over there. Banged on Lydia's door until she answered. Lydia let her into the front foyer, and even though Lydia never admitted to manipulating Kiwi, they agreed Lydia wasn't a good fit."

Cruz's brow furrowed. "Really? Lydia doesn't sound like the kind of person who would cave that easily. Didn't Keith say he heard a shouting match that night?"

"That's what I said. Oleander finally admitted that she threatened to go after Lydia in a legal capacity if she ever came near her son again. She chased Lydia partway up the stairs, where she fell. Oleander said she hovered over her—which was probably how her fur ended up in several places in the stairwell. *That* was when Lydia agreed, probably both out of fear of getting flattened like a pancake and also the fear of what someone like Oleander—a lawyer familiar with criminal law—might find if she started digging into Lydia's past. She said the fear in Lydia's eyes was what had kept her up all night. She knew she'd crossed a line. She didn't know what Lydia might do in retaliation, once she thought about the incident in the morning. Oleander also started wondering if she'd read the whole thing wrong and that she'd scared the crap out of Lydia for no reason."

Cruz winced. "And then, less than twenty-four hours later, Lydia was dead."

"She said she'd partly resigned herself to going down for this, as if she was being punished by the Goddess for snapping under the pressure. She said if that single strand of arctic fox fur hadn't been found, she might have ended up behind bars based on a purely circumstantial case," Deandra said. "I kept thinking about that case *you* were a witness on, with the bear shifter, and how his size probably sealed his fate with that jury. And the way Keith talked about elephantine fae. Things could have gone very badly for Oleander."

Cruz nodded solemnly.

"There *was* one little bit of information Sutter gave me without me needing to harass it out of her," Deandra said. "One of the notes that Keith left for Lydia said 'Submit to a truth serum test.' Apparently, Keith told Sutter that he wouldn't have *needed* to kill Lydia if she'd gotten one. I guess he assumed that if Lydia confessed all her lies to the Collective, they'd arrest her and toss her into the Antarctic hub. Not even Lydia seemed to have a reason for her compulsive lying. Since she refused to take his suggestion, he killed her."

"Dang," Cruz said. "Any idea what *exactly* happened to Lydia?"

"Nothing official, since Sutter said that wasn't any of my business either. But Oleander's guess, based on what questions they asked her about the nature of her water power, is that Keith blasted her with water so cold that it nearly froze her body just before the impact with the wall. Keith said Alpine only helped Keith get into the building, and Sutter seems to believe he was telling the truth about that and not that he was covering for the fox."

"I'd put money on it being Keith who delivered the killing blow," Cruz said. "I haven't interacted with any fae arctic foxes myself, but I've researched them quite a bit. They can freeze any surface their paws touch. If Alpine put her paws on the glass of the window, she could theoretically freeze it until it shattered.

"They can also make what amount to short-lived stairs of ice and use them to reach higher ground. It's reported that it can give the impression they're flying or running through the air. The ice would be strong enough to support Keith, as long as he stepped lightly and quickly.

"The stairs are a defense mechanism, since they're not very aggressive animals. Scrappy, yes, but small and bite-sized to a lot of the animals in the realm—especially in the snowier regions. A fae arctic fox's primary food source in the fae world is eggs from a particularly vicious mountain-dwelling lizard. The foxes' magic evolved to allow them to travel up the mountains quickly, while also providing a way to *escape* quickly. Climbing the mountains on foot ate up too many resources."

Deandra stared blankly at him.

"Remember when I said I had a borderline obsession with mythical animals?" Cruz said, color rising in his cheeks. "I wasn't exaggerating. I am not popular at parties."

She cracked up. "Kiwi has the power to shoot icy water from his mouth. Have you seen that? It's a pretty strong blast, even though his energy pool is small. If someone as big as Oleander has the same ability, only with ten times the volume and power?" Deandra shook her head. "It's no wonder Oleander was looked at so closely. Everything really *was* pointing to her. Keith was betting on her taking the fall for him, or at least was okay with her providing a good distraction so that he could quietly slip out of Axia."

"For the record, even if Officer Sutter isn't impressed, I am," Cruz said.

She bowed in her seat. "Oleander said they're keeping her on house arrest for a couple more days just to be thorough. They're waiting on a few more test results. She's confident they'll drop all charges, though. Which means I get a few more days off before I'm back on Kiwi duty."

"Good news all around."

They finished eating and ordered dessert. Deandra wasn't usually a dessert girl, but she had a feeling Cruz had a bit of a sweet tooth.

When the waiter brought the bill, Deandra hurriedly snatched it off the table. "My turn. Say nothing. I can actually afford it right now, so let me have this."

He laughed, hands up. "Fine, fine." His mirth didn't last long, though. "While we're here, I … uhh … wanted to talk to you about something."

She stilled. "That doesn't sound promising."

He folded his arms on the table, looked at her, looked away. "So … I, um, I like you …"

"It sounds like a 'but' is coming," Deandra said.

"I know I work a lot. My job means a lot to me. Perhaps too much at times. And it's gotten in the way of relationships— platonic *and* romantic. I'm trying to be better about it. You make me *want* to be better about it."

She chewed on her bottom lip, not wanting to interrupt him when he already sounded uncomfortable.

"I guess I'm just apologizing in advance," he said. "In addition to my usual workload, I do things like the seminar this weekend. Since I'm one of the few zoolinguists in the country with a full-slate certification, I also do consulting work, *and* I'm on call for certain shifter-related surgeries. Sometimes I need to be gone for weeks at a time when I get called to other hubs. There aren't many small hub towns like Axia, but most of them don't have proper access to good care like they do in bigger cities.

"To apply for the Pinebough Zoolinguistic Academy, you have to have a pretty substantial number of shadow hours at clinics. I had to venture out of Axia for that. The longer the telepad ride, the more it costs. Just getting my required hours was expensive and time-consuming—and that's not even bringing the cost of tuition into the conversation. I know not every student has parents like I did who could support them. It made me realize that Axia needed better zoolinguistic care—it's a big part of the reason why I stayed here rather than relocating to a larger hub. I wanted prospective students from nearby hubs to come *here* for their hours. I wanted to open doors for kids who might not otherwise pursue the discipline, simply because they couldn't afford to or didn't have access."

Deandra blew out a breath that puffed out her cheeks. "I was totally gearing up to give you a lecture about work-life balance, and now I'm glad I didn't because I'd feel like a jerk."

Normally, he would have at least cracked a smile at that, but he merely shook his head. "You wouldn't have been a jerk. It's something I need to hear. Something I *have* heard. A lot. I just wanted to warn you about what you're getting into if you want to keep seeing me."

"I want to keep seeing you," she said without hesitation.

He smiled, but it was a little sad, as if he didn't quite believe her.

"We'll just take it one step at a time," Deandra said. "No pressure, okay?"

He nodded. "Okay."

They chatted easily after that until the waitstaff kicked them out. Apparently the Haunted Noodle only stayed open until seven on Sundays. It was a small-town thing that Deandra was still getting used to as a transplant from Los Angeles.

As they lingered on the sidewalk, Deandra asked, "Need me to drop you off anywhere?"

"I'm only a couple of blocks from the office."

Deandra pursed her lips.

Cruz put his hand up in a show of innocence. "I left my car at the office, and I need it so I can pick up Maxine from my parents' place. I promise not to do any paperwork until tomorrow."

She narrowed her eyes. "If I drive by that office in the next ten minutes and the lights are on, you're going to be in *serious* trouble."

He laughed and pulled her into a quick hug. When he let go, he said, "It's a good thing you have a light schedule for the next couple of days. You might get a phone call."

"Vague, much?"

"It's my first official referral," he said. "The pet's name is Starshadow."

It took Deandra a moment to remember when she'd last heard that name. "Wait, the pegasus with a penchant for flowers?"

"That's the one," he said and started walking away backward. "You may never speak to me after this referral, though."

"*What?*" Deandra asked. "What does that mean? Cruz? Cruz!"

He grinned, turned around, and kept walking. "Enjoy the rest of your Sunday, Dee!"

Huffing a laugh, she headed for her car, wondering what in the world Axia had in store for her next.

Join Deandra and Havoc (and Starshadow!) on their next adventure in A Mythical Case of Theft! You can also join Melissa's mailing list to be notified about upcoming releases.

ALSO BY MELISSA ERIN JACKSON

A Mythical Case of Theft

If you want find out what happens when Dee meets Starshadow the pegasus, you can preorder the book at https://melissajackson-books.com/a-mythical-case-of-arson/a-mythical-case-of-theft

While waiting for the next book in the Mythical Pet Sitting Mystery series, you can check out the Witch of Edgehill series. There are five books—and the series is complete! (They're all in audio, too!)

Every town has its secrets, but no one has a secret like hers.

Amber Blackwood, lifelong resident of Edgehill, Oregon, has earned a reputation for being a semi-reclusive odd duck. Her store, The Quirky Whisker, is full of curiosities, from extremely potent sleepy teas and ever-burning candles to kids' toys that seem to run endlessly without the aid of batteries. The people of Edgehill think of the Quirky Whisker as an integral part of their feline-obsessed town, but most give Amber herself a wide berth. Amber prefers it that way; it keeps her secret safe. But that secret is thrown into jeopardy when Amber's friend Melanie is found dead, a vial of headache tonic from Amber's store clutched in her hand.

Edgehill's newest police chief has had it out for Amber since he arrived three years before. He can't possibly know she's a witch, but his suspicions about her odd store and even odder behavior have shot her to the top of his suspect list. When the Edgehill rumor mill finds out Melanie was poisoned, it's not only the police chief who looks at Amber differently. Determined to both find justice for her friend and to clear her own name, Amber must use her unique gifts to help track down Melanie's real killer. A quest that threatens much more than her secret …

Get it right meow at https://melissajacksonbooks.com/witch-of-edgehill-mysteries/pawsitively-poisonous

ACKNOWLEDGMENTS

Silly little me decided publishing two books in one month was a good idea. I thank my little beta reading team who is always up for reading my books even when I say, "*Sooo* I was scrambling to finish too close to the deadline again and I kinda sorta need feedback in a week." Instead of telling me to kick rocks, they always seem up for the challenge. Bless them all. Thank you, Mom, Margarita, Kayla, Emilie, and John for putting up with me.

Thank you, Molly Burton, as always for these covers! The image of Kiwi on the cover was all her creation, y'all. It was so fun waiting to get new covers from her because I gave her very basic ideas and then let her creativity dictate which new fun creature ended up on each subsequent cover.

Thank you, Justin Cohen and Cyndi Sandusky, for the editing and proofreading. Both of you put up with my ridiculous deadlines, too! Saints!

Thanks to the ARC team: Meg, Annie, Lesli, LJ, Jeanne, Lizz, Lola, Penny, Marie, Jo, Nadine, Alison, and Angel. You're all great and I appreciate you taking the time to read and review my books.

Thank you to Sarah Waites who updated the original super cute map of Axia and added new locations relevant to this book in particular.

Thank you to the gang over at Etheric Tales for the drawings of Havoc and Kiwi.

And, finally, thank you to Sam for the support, the brainstorming ideas, and for making me get the heck out of the house when I start to lose my marbles. You're great and stuff and junk.

See you all back in Axia soon!

ABOUT THE AUTHOR

Melissa has had a love of stories for as long as she can remember, but only started penning her own during her freshman year of college. She majored in Wildlife, Fish, and Conservation Biology at UC Davis. Yet, while she was neck-deep in organic chemistry and physics, she kept finding herself writing stories in the back of the classroom about fairies and trolls and magic. She finished her degree, but it never captured her heart the way writing did.

Now she owns her own dog walking business (that's sort of wildlife related, right?) by day ... and afternoon and night ... and writes whenever she gets a spare moment. She alternates mostly between fantasy and mystery (often with a paranormal twist). All her books have some element of "other" to them ... witches, ghosts, UFOs. There's no better way to escape the real world than getting lost in a fictional one.

She lives in Northern California with her very patient boyfriend and way too many pets.

You can find out more about her upcoming books and join her newsletter at: https://melissajacksonbooks.com

Milton Keynes UK
Ingram Content Group UK Ltd.
UKHW030853111124
451035UK00001B/106

9 781956 335231